ARMAGEDDON

A NOVEL  OF UKRAINE

#1 *NEW YORK TIMES* BESTSELLING AUTHOR

MIKE EVANS

A NOVEL OF UKRAINE

ARMAGEDDON

TimeWorthy
BOOKS

P.O. Box 30000, Phoenix, AZ 85046

Armageddon
(A Novel of Ukraine)

Copyright 2023 by Time Worthy Books
P. O. Box 30000
Phoenix, AZ 85046

Hardcover:	978-1-62961-096-2
Paperback:	978-1-62961-097-9
eBook:	978-1-62961-181-5

I dedicate this book to

the millions of innocent Ukrainian refugees...

who have suffered greatly since the war began. My son Michael has gone to the frontlines to my knowledge more than any American minister, bringing food, medicine, generators, warm clothes, blankets, and over 13 million pounds of food despite landmines and military threats.

When my wife Carolyn asked me to tell him not to go because he has four young children and could be killed, he showed me a Scripture he had circled in his Bible. After he had prayed about going, he read the Scripture that said, "I shall not die, but live, and declare the works of the Lord" (Psalm 118:17).

Our ministry continues bringing food to the frontlines to homeless, hungry Ukrainian refugees and also taking Ukrainian Holocaust survivors to Israel. One woman named Sheila who we helped move to Israel said, "I was born in the war and thought I would die in a war. But I put my faith in God and you came from me."

CAST OF CHARACTERS

UKRAINE

Taras Irvanets	A student at the University of Kyiv
Mila Korot	Taras' girlfriend
Myroslav Reznikov	Official in Zelensky's administration. Came over from the television production company
Taras' platoon members:	Oleg
	Melovin
	Vitas
	Sergey
	Roman Sharpar
	Oleh
	Sergeant Lomachenko

ISRAEL

Yehuda Eichler	Israeli Prime Minister
Yossi Oron	Mossad director
Mohsen Durak	Kurd living in Iran. Rug merchant. Operative for Mossad
Berkin Shoresh	Kurd who served as Durak's contact with Mossad

RUSSIA

Nikolai Patrushev	Secretary of the Russian Security Council
Sergei Naryshkin	Director of the Russian Foreign Intelligence Service
Sergei Shoigu	Minister of Defense
Valery Gerasimov	Army Chief of Staff
Nikolay Vorobyov	Deputy Director, Directorate S: Illegal Intelligence

UNITED STATES

Martin Jackson	President
Bruce Ford	Secretary of Defense
Clinton Kase	Secretary of State
Janice Miller	Undersecretary for Central Asia at the US State Department
Robert Donovan	CIA director
Jim Marsh	CIA Deputy Director for Clandestine Services
Sarah Foster	President's Chief of Staff
George Halstead	General and Chairman of the Joint Chiefs
Albert Newman	Director of the National Security Agency

IRAN

Ali Akbar Bizhani	Iranian President
Mehdi Kalhor	Director, Iranian Organization of Defensive Innovation
Majid Roshan	Director of Iran's nuclear program
Shiraz Parsi	Roshan's assistant
The Almumin	A radical cell led by Mehdi Kalhor
Bijan Abbadi	A member of *The Almumin*
Jalal Pirzad	Mehdi Kalhor's cousin and one of *The Almumin*

CHINA

Wei Xing	Chinese premier and Paramount Leader
Dong Jingwei	Head of China's Ministry of State Security
Zhao Guofeng	Initially, a member of Chinese government. Replaces Wei Xing as premier

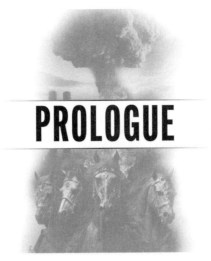

PROLOGUE

(ONE YEAR EARLIER)

ennadiy Fomichev stood on the corner outside a quaint café waiting for the car to arrive. He'd spent a long day at the office where he worked in the Office of the Presidency of Ukraine, a permanent administrative body established by the constitution to advise the president. Not like working for the president, really. More like working in a government bureau five blocks removed from the president. There was a huge difference between working for the president and working for the *office* of the president. One was the seat of power, where life moved at an incredibly fast pace. The other was the seat of a mind-numbingly irrelevant existence, pushing paper in a government office.

The current president, Volodymyr Zelensky, had been elected to office on a wave of popular support built off his career in entertainment—a short career that began as a comedian, then morphed into a politician after starring in a television show where he played an unlikely candidate who won a presidential election after a video of his rant appeared on social media. Comedian-actor-influencer-president—an unlikely path to power in the West, but absurd in a former Soviet republic like Ukraine, where politicians were hand-picked by oligarchs and the standing government was steeped in corruption so deeply it was an expected way of life. Moreover, Zelensky was Jewish. Ukraine had never had a Jewish president before and had a history of anti-Semitism that made it ripe for pogroms of the monarch era and mass murder under Nazi rule.

Fomichev had been an early volunteer for Zelensky's campaign. He was young and enthusiastic. A true believer. Arrived early at the office every day, and stayed late every night, doing whatever he was assigned to do and doing it with enthusiasm. But he was not an insider. All the insiders had come to the campaign from the television show's production company.

"Not to worry," Fomichev told himself. It would all work out once they realized how diligent he was at fulfilling his job. But that day of realization never came.

At first, Fomichev was only disappointed, but the longer he waited, and the more he saw others who were less capable than he assigned to better positions, his disappointment became frustration. Rather quickly, that frustration turned to bitterness. That's when Fomichev met Yuriy Poroshenko.

Poroshenko owned an online retailer that dealt in everything from books and clothes to toys and housewares. He also had ties to the Ukrainian mob and saw himself as a political player. Part of a loosely organized oligarch cabal that had grown from dabbling in local elections to determining the fate of candidates for national office. Poroshenko took Fomichev under his wing, supplemented his income, stroked his ego, and made him feel like he belonged.

After the election, an administrator for Zelensky's transition team offered Fomichev a position with the National Energy and Utilities Regulatory Commission. It was a pointless job with no real duties. Fomichev was insulted and complained about it in a meeting with Poroshenko. A few days later, Fomichev was offered the position in the Office of the Presidency of Ukraine, an equally meaningless job but one with a much better title and an office in the official government office complex.

Before long, Fomichev was gladly providing Poroshenko with inside information on things like oil exploration leases, anticipated approval of drugs, new products in the patent approval process, and the like. With Fomichev as his source, Poroshenko became the man to see for government deals.

Everything was looking up for Fomichev and Poroshenko until Zelensky's administration refused to accept closer ties with Russia and turned instead toward an alliance with the European Union, NATO, and the US. Putin had installed the previous Ukrainian administration to prevent just such an arrangement. He regarded Ukraine's decision to align with the West as an act of rebellion. Not long after that, Russian tanks appeared on Ukraine's border to the north, adjoining Belarus, and at the eastern border, where Ukraine abutted Russia proper.

Within weeks, Russian troops controlled the eastern half of Ukraine and were on the verge of sacking Kyiv. Then European countries imposed economic sanctions against Russia, seized property belonging to Russian oligarchs, and began sending military aid to Ukraine. The Russian advance stalled, and that's when Fomichev became a Russian informant.

✦ ✦ ✦

Fomichev had been waiting outside the café about ten minutes when a well-worn black Mercedes came to a stop at the curb. He recognized Poroshenko's driver and got in the backseat. Minutes later, they turned from the street into a warehouse, and the car came to a stop. A roll-up door closed behind them as Fomichev came from the car and made his way to an office in the back where Poroshenko was waiting.

"Is he making the trip?"

"Yes," Fomichev replied. "He wants to begin here, in Ukraine, to visit the soldiers in the field."

Poroshenko looked surprised. "To see our soldiers on the battlefield?"

"Yes."

"Does he have a death wish?"

"He thinks it will build credibility with the West," Fomichev said.

"Television," Poroshenko scoffed. "He still thinks he's on TV."

"American politicians are always visiting the 'troops in the field.'"

"This isn't America."

"That's who he's trying to appeal to," Fomichev said. "American citizens think of it as an act of bravery and comradery with the soldier. A politician standing next to a tank, surrounded by soldiers. It makes a good image."

"It makes for good TV," Poroshenko scoffed.

Fomichev shrugged. "Zelensky insists it must be done this way."

"To impress Americans?"

"To impress American voters as a way of impressing the US Congress." A playful smile turned up the corners of Fomichev's mouth. "According to him, voters actually mean something over there."

"And all of this to get American help with Zelensky's war against Putin?"

"Yes."

"So, it starts with the soldiers here," Poroshenko said. "Then what?"

"Then he will go to Europe to meet with NATO and EU leaders to solidify their support."

"And does he have a timeline for this?"

"Only for the tour of Ukraine troops."

"We must see that he never gets out of the country." Poroshenko's face was hard as stone. "Clearly, he has not learned his lesson yet."

CHAPTER ONE

Taras Irvanets, a student at the University of Kyiv, sat in the back of a Ukrainian army transport truck with a group of fellow university students and an undermanned platoon of regular Ukrainian soldiers. Until a few months ago, Taras and his classmates had been preoccupied with classes and talking politics in their favorite coffee shop. Then reports of a pending Russian invasion brought a call for civilian volunteers and they were swept up in a frenzy of patriotism, skipping class to get rudimentary training with basic infantry weapons.

When the Russians finally invaded, they entered the country from the north through Belarus and from the east through Rostov Oblast into Donetsk. The Belarusian government was friendly with Moscow and allowed the Russian army to stage troops, equipment, and armaments along its border with Ukraine. In the east, Donetsk, though technically part of Ukraine, had long been home to ardent Russian separatists and welcomed Russian troops with open arms. It, too, became a staging ground for troops, equipment, and supplies.

A week after the Russians crossed the border, artillery shells fell on government facilities on the outskirts of Kyiv, the Ukrainian capital. Within days of those first strikes, the shells began landing on apartment buildings near the center of the city. Taras watched them through the window of the apartment where he lived with his mother and sister. One of the shells hit the apartment next door. Another struck a building across the courtyard.

Rather than wait for the Russians to arrive at the door, Taras and his friends grabbed their gear and headed out to find the Ukrainian army unit with which they'd been training as student volunteers.

The platoon, part of the 112th Territorial Defense Brigade, had been assigned to Kyiv to defend the city. It was staffed with older veterans, most of whom had seen serious combat in the past but now had permanent civilian occupations and only trained once or twice a month. Their call to active duty had come as no surprise, but being undermanned, they had not expected to see action without a few months of full-time preparation. The appearance of Russian forces on the border dashed all hopes of a convenient, smooth mobilization.

Already comprised of older veterans, the 112th was expected to attract older volunteers to supplement their lack of personnel. Instead, it had received an influx of university students inspired by patriotic fervor. They were young and untrained but courageous and motivated. For training purposes, the 112th divided the new volunteers among its existing platoons in the hope that the older soldiers would instruct the newer ones. There wasn't enough time to give them the training they might otherwise have received. Units were forced to train on the move, receiving instruction as they fought.

Taras and his friends found officers from the 112th Brigade at a hotel on Vitryani Hory Street. They and officers from several other brigades had taken the building as an operational headquarters for coordination of the city's northern defense. Someone from the 112th directed Taras and his friends to a location farther north, where fighting was underway. A supply truck took them part of the way, then they walked the rest.

Their platoon was dug in on the west side of the Dnipro River, across from the Kyiv Hydroelectric Plant. Other platoons from the brigade were arrayed in a thinly manned perimeter along the northern end of the city. Russian units that had advanced on the city were massed farther out, the strongest at Fora, which lay to the west and east, on the opposite side of the river near the village of Khotianivka.

The pungent odor of smokeless powder—the propellant in artillery shells—hung in the air, and every few minutes, the rapid Pop! Pop! Pop! from thousands of infantry rifles pierced the silence between blasts from artillery rounds. No one seemed to pay much attention to the small arms fire until the bullets dinged off a truck or tank parked nearby. Then everyone ducked and shouted at each other, calling for the location where the gunfire came from. Once the enemy's position was determined, they stepped out from wherever they'd been hiding and let loose a barrage of return fire.

All that afternoon, there were periods of extreme chaos, with everyone shouting and yelling, followed by rapid bursts of gunfire. Atop all of that came the Boom! Boom! Boom! of artillery firing from both sides, then the earth-shaking explosion of shells as they detonated all around. Some exploding close behind, some close in front, some far away.

Taras was startled at how near the Russian army had advanced toward Kyiv. Last summer, he and his friends had camped at a spot not far from where he now lay sprawled behind the tire of a troop transport. As bullets struck the vehicle and whizzed overhead, he thought he was going to die, right there, that very afternoon.

While he lay on the ground wondering what to do next, Taras' mind drifted to thoughts of home, his mother and sister, and then his girlfriend, Mila Korot. An image of her appeared in his mind and he remembered her smile, the smell of her hair, the softness of her lips pressed against his. They had made plans for the future—a wonderful future full of laughter, success, and children—and then the Russians arrived, and everything seemed to evaporate before their eyes.

Remembering her filled him with sadness, and he wondered how his father had felt going off to war the last time the Russians came. A husband with a wife and two children. It had seemed gallant back then. Taras was just a boy when he stood at the door, watching his father leave to join his friends in the army. He could see him now, walking with them, laughing as if they hadn't a care in the world. Then, at the last moment, as they were about to turn the corner and disappear from view, his father turned back, caught Tara's eye, and waved to him.

Taras had been so proud that day and even though his father returned in a coffin, it had not diminished his sense of pride in his father's service. But now, with the gunfire zipping by and artillery shells exploding, being a soldier was more real than Taras had ever imagined, and he wondered how his father did it.

Tears filled Taras' eyes at the thought of all that and, in a moment of inspiration, he rolled on his side to see around the truck tire and captured an image of the battle with his cell phone. If he couldn't be with Mila, at least he could share an image of it with her. He checked the image on the screen and didn't like the way it looked, so he took another. "Oh, she'll love this," he said, laughing to himself. Then he sent the image to Mila in a text.

Five minutes later, a rocket whistled overhead. It clipped the top of the truck Taras had been hiding behind and struck the remnants of a disabled tank that sat a few feet away. The sound of it startled him and he felt suddenly vulnerable. His eyes darted from side to side as he looked around for somewhere else to hide.

The remnants of the building stood twenty yards away. All but the rear wall had been blown away, but there was a pile of bricks and concrete on the end nearest his position. It looked better than where he was by the truck, so Taras grabbed his gear and ran toward it. Before he was halfway to it, he heard a second rocket approaching. He dove for cover behind a pile of rubble and watched as the missile struck the truck where he'd been before. Pieces of it flew through the air. The ground shook. A fireball rose into the sky.

Taras picked himself up and continued to the far corner of what once had been the back wall of a building. He crouched there, hands shaking, body trembling, thinking that very instant might be his last. Once again, he thought of Mila. Hoping to send her a final message, just in case, opened his cell phone, turned the camera to face himself, and recorded a brief video. "I don't know if I'll be alive when you see this, but I want you to know I love you and if I get out of this alive, will you marry me?" Without watching to make sure it recorded correctly, he pressed a button with his thumb and sent the clip.

Almost immediately, Taras heard the sound of incoming rockets, this time more than the single one that hit before. He curled into a ball with his knees drawn up against his chest, his arms and hands over his head. Moments later, rockets exploded all around him, hitting what was left of the truck where he'd been before, the rubble pile, and the wall of the building only a few feet away. Debris and dirt rained down as the explosions continued in rapid sequence as if the rockets were coming from everywhere all at once. So many rockets he began to wonder if they would ever stop.

At last, the barrage ended and as the dust settled, Taras glanced to the right, looking beneath his arm which was still over his head, and saw a soldier's torso, the arms and legs missing. The head dangled to one side, but Taras recognized him from the truck. One of the older guys who didn't like associating with freshly recruited college students.

A quick inventory of his arms and legs told Taras they were still attached. He was relieved to know he was alive and unharmed. Then he heard the screams and cries of the wounded. Awful, blood-curdling screams of men in serious pain, afraid they were going to die. Taras listened intently to see if any of the voices were those of his friends from school, but he was interrupted by a tap on his shoulder. He looked up to see Sergeant Lomachenko standing over him.

Lomachenko was older than Taras, and far more capable as a soldier, but not the age of the veterans in the platoon. He had joined as a teenager in 2014 and stayed in for a career when everyone else moved on. Taras liked him.

"Fall back," Lomachenko said. "We're reforming near the river." When Taras hesitated, Lomachenko slapped his helmet. "That's an order, kid. Get out of here and join the others." Taras scrambled to his feet and ran toward the river.

✦ ✦ ✦

When Taras reached the river, he found most of the platoon was already there. Oleg, Melovin, Vitali, and Sergey, friends of his from the university who had joined the platoon with him, were there, too. He was relieved to see they were unharmed and reached for his cell phone to take a picture, thinking the image would look great with them in the foreground and the river in the background. But before he could capture the image, he heard Lomachenko shout. "Irvanets, what are you doing?!" His voice was loud and angry.

An instant later, Lomachenko reached over Taras' shoulder and snatched the phone from his hand. "Have you been sending messages with this?" Lomachenko gestured with the phone as he spoke.

"Only a few," Taras replied.

Lomachenko flipped off the back cover of the phone to reveal the battery, then jerked it free from the compartment, ripping the wire connection with it.

"Hey!" Taras protested. "You ruined my phone."

"And you're about to get us all killed," Lomachenko replied. Without missing a beat, he took one step forward and threw the battery toward the river, followed quickly by the rest of the phone.

As the phone splashed into the water, Lomachenko turned back to Taras. "The Russians track cell phone use," he explained. "Every time you turn that thing on, your phone number pops up on a screen somewhere. They know it's a Ukrainian number. They might even know it's *your* number. They already know we're fighting here, and they know that any Ukrainian standing here by this river can't be a tourist on vacation. That's how they knew where to send those missiles that killed three of our men."

Taras was devastated. "I didn't think—"

"That's right," Lomachenko snapped. "You didn't think."

"But I—"

"You were told repeatedly to turn off your phone, remove the battery, and leave it behind. Now, three people are dead because you didn't think the rules applied to you." Lomachenko turned to the platoon. "Anyone else got a cell phone?" he shouted.

Two men raised their hands. Lomachenko threw their phones in the river, too.

✦ ✦ ✦

Late in the afternoon, units from Taras' brigade cleared the road on the west side of the river, then crossed a bridge near the power plant and began opening a way to the east. Taras' platoon went with them. Despite the prospect of mortal combat, he was glad to get off the ground and try again to act like a soldier.

While Taras' platoon crossed the bridge at the power plant, other Ukrainian units came up the east side of the river and together they engaged the Russians who were at Khotianivka. They cleared the village with scant opposition until they reached a house on the outskirts of the village. Suddenly, two Russians appeared around the end of the house. When they saw the Ukrainians, they opened fire. Pop, pop, pop. Taras' heart skipped a beat as bullets zipped by. Everyone dove for cover, but two rounds struck Vitali, a friend from school who'd been standing a few feet to Taras' right. Taras moved close to him and tried to think of something to say. Finally, he knelt at Vitali's side, held his hand, and watched as the light went out of his eyes. It was the first time Taras had ever been that close to death, and he realized how narrowly he'd escaped the moment.

Another burst of gunfire jerked Taras' mind back to the present and he crawled to the left, finding cover behind a damaged farm tractor. Then one of the Ukrainian regulars closer to the house was hit by gunfire. He collapsed to the ground with a gaping wound to his thigh. Blood pulsed from it, thick and red, and oozed down the soldier's leg. Taras didn't know his name. There hadn't been time for that, yet. Another of the regulars rushed to him and applied a tourniquet.

To the left, more Russians appeared at a hedgerow. More gunfire. The wounded man shouted, "It's a trap! It's a trap!" Still more gunfire. Some of the Ukrainian soldiers moved to the left to confront them. Taras was scared. He didn't want to move from the safety of his position to follow them, but he didn't want to be left behind. Then the boom, boom, boom of a fifty-caliber machine gun thudded against Taras' chest. It seemed to come from the far side of the house. He peeked out for a look but saw nothing. The fifty-caliber fired again. Taras was startled by the sound of it and jumped at the noise. Dust flew in the air around him as bullets from the gun ripped the ground.

The men from the platoon who'd gone toward the gunfire continued to advance, pressing the fight to the Russians with a withering phalanx of bullets and hand grenades. Taras couldn't see them, but he knew the sound of their weapons and followed their path by ear as they moved down the side of the house and around to the back.

In the midst of that, one of the regular Ukraine soldiers tapped Taras on the shoulder and motioned for him to follow. Taras pushed himself up from the ground and saw that others had come to join them, many of them Taras' friends. They crouched low and followed the soldier toward the farmhouse. When they were close to the house, the soldier pointed to Taras and several others, then gestured to the right. Taras and his group moved in that direction. The Ukrainian soldier took the others and went to the left.

When Taras came to the corner of the house, he paused to let everyone catch up, then carefully inched forward and leaned around the edge to find a T-72 Russian tank parked in an area between the house and the road. A fuel truck was alongside the tank with a hose running to the T-72. Someone was holding a metal nozzle into the T-72's refueling port. Taras realized this was why the Russian soldiers had been there, protecting the equipment while the tank was shut down for refueling.

Melovin, one of the men from Taras' group, raised his rifle as if to shoot. Taras thought to stop him and even turned to do so, but before he could stop him, Melovin pulled the trigger. The shot glanced off the steel deck of the tank near the fuel port. Sparks flew, igniting fumes from the opening where the hose had been inserted. Instantly, a column of flame roared out of the filler neck. The soldier holding the hose was engulfed in flames. He screamed in agony and fell backward. The refueling hose slipped from his grasp and came loose. Fuel gushed from the hose and ran onto the ground beneath the tank and then over to the fuel truck. Flames already roaring from the tank grew even higher, ran down to the ground, and over to the truck. The truck blew up, destroying the rear wall of the house and engulfing the entire structure.

Taras, who'd withdrawn a short distance from the corner of the house, heard the sound of the explosion, felt the building shake, and the heat of the flames, but by then he and the others were far enough away to avoid serious injury. Melovin, the man with the rifle who'd fired the shot, was not so fortunate. He'd been standing at the corner when he fired the shot and remained there, staring at the flames as the sequence of events unfolded. After the fire dissipated, Taras found his charred remains in a clump of bushes fifty yards away.

Although everyone was saddened by the loss of a friend, they were elated at the success they'd had so soon after joining the fight.

Already they had destroyed a tank and a fuel truck. But their joy wasn't for long.

As they were recounting their victory, a Russian truck appeared with soldiers riding in the back. They opened fire and two men from Taras' platoon were instantly killed. Taras and the others scrambled for cover, but one of the older soldiers calmly lifted a grenade launcher to his shoulder and fired a grenade at the truck. It struck the engine compartment and destroyed it, setting the truck on fire. Russian soldiers bailed out the back.

Ukraine regulars stepped forward, rifles to their shoulders. Taras thought they intended to take the Russians prisoner and he wondered what they would do with them. Instead of seizing them, the regulars opened fire. The result was a bloody slaughter. Body parts flew through the haze of a red mist that filled the air. Several of the soldiers were ripped apart beyond recognition. Taras stood transfixed, staring in disbelief. It seemed to last for hours but it was over in a matter of seconds. All of the Russians were dead.

The regulars took it in stride and when it was done, they lowered their weapons, slung them over their shoulders, and turned away without comment. No laughing. No sneering. No cursing. Strictly business. Taras felt his stomach turn. He tried to stave off the sick feeling, to think of something else, something beautiful and peaceful, but the effort was futile. At last, he could hold it in no longer. He rushed behind a tree and vomited.

✦ ✦ ✦

The day had been stressful, even for the most hardened men of Taras' platoon who seemed to take the day in stride. Blowing up a tank, gunning down Russian prisoners—they took it without showing emotion, but Taras could tell it had sapped their energy. Most would have preferred to camp for the night right there, within sight of the tank's remains and the ruins of the destroyed house—Taras wanted to—but Sergeant Lomachenko said no. So, they moved on and eventually came to an abandoned house near Novi Petrivtsi.

By then, nightfall was near, and the temperature had begun to drop. As many of the men as possible crammed into the house, finding space on a bed or a chair, or the floor. A small fireplace stood along the wall of the kitchen and one of the soldiers started a fire. Taras found a place in the corner of the room and propped himself against the wall. His bed at home would have been more comfortable but after what he'd seen and heard that day, stretching out on the floor seemed too vulnerable. Better to sleep sitting upright, with his rifle across his lap. Just in case.

Sometime in the night, Taras was awakened by the rustling of someone outside the house. His heart raced at the sound of it, and he felt along the rifle for the trigger, his thumb poised to flip off the safety. All the while, his eyes darted from window to window. Searching. Checking. But seeing nothing. After a moment he heard the voice of a soldier who'd been standing watch. Then the voice of someone else. Unfamiliar. Not one of the soldiers. It sounded like the voice of a woman. No, a girl.

The door of the house opened and the one who'd been standing guard came inside bringing with him a young girl, not more than fourteen or fifteen. Taras could see her frightened look from the glow of the soldier's flashlight. The soldier called for Sergeant

Lomachenko, who'd been sleeping in another room. Someone went to get him and, in a few moments, Lomachenko appeared, demanding to know the trouble.

"This girl says she is from Bucha."

Lomachenko frowned. "Bucha? That's a long way from here. What's she doing over here?"

"She says soldiers from Chechnya occupied their town."

Lomachenko scowled. "Paramilitary dogs."

"Her father told her to run away and not come back until the Chechens were gone. She got lost and now she's here."

Lomachenko shook his head in disgust. "The Chechens came all the way to Bucha." Reports had circulated for weeks of paramilitary groups being sent to Ukraine by the Russians with instructions to inflict as much misery as possible. Few realized how close they came to Kyiv.

"They went from street to street," the girl said, "gathering the adults, most of whom they took to the edge of town and shot. Then they came for the young, boys and girls. They raped them and some they killed for sport. When they came near our street, my father told me to run away and not look back."

"And this was in Bucha?"

"Yes."

The girl was shivering and one of the men gave her a blanket which she draped over her shoulders. Another stoked the fire and added some wood. She sat near it and stared blankly at the flames. One of the men gave her an MRE from his backpack. Taras wondered where he'd gotten it and watched as the girl rapidly ate it.

Lomachenko stood on Taras' side of the room, talking with one of the regulars—an athletic man with short hair whom Taras took for a seasoned veteran. "What do we do with her?" the soldier asked.

"I don't know," Lomachenko replied. "But we can't send her back until we know Bucha has been cleared. She'll have to come with us while we figure out what to do."

Taras was disturbed by the mention of Chechens in Bucha. Chechens were wild men. Hardly men at all—more like animals. In their country, they raped the women of ethnic minorities. And the men too, committing all manner of atrocities. Now to hear that they were in Bucha, a town that adjoined Kyiv? If the Russian paramilitary made it that far, they had come much closer to the capital than Taras had realized. Right up to the city limit. A chill ran down his spine at the thought of it and once again the war felt more real. More necessary. More urgent.

Just then, the distant sound of artillery fire came from somewhere north of their position. Taras heard the cannon booming and out the window, he saw the reflection of artillery shells exploding against the night sky. It sounded like the rumble of thunder and the flashes looked like lightning from a summer storm, but it was the dead of winter, and the air was painfully cold. Taras leaned against the wall, pulled his coat tighter around him, and closed his eyes. He was exhausted and afraid, but despite the noise of the artillery and the fear, he soon fell asleep.

✦ ✦ ✦

The next morning, Sergeant Lomachenko was nowhere to be found. The older men organized themselves for the day without being told what to do. Taras and Sergey, one of his friends from the university, scrounged through the house for something to eat but didn't find much. A few of the regular soldiers had MREs but most of them had nothing, either.

Thirty minutes later, a Ukraine army truck arrived. It was loaded with MREs, and the truck's crew began passing them out. Taras was surprised to learn that the men on the truck were making deliveries to all the units in the region. In the brief training he'd received no one mentioned how the troops were supplied with meals, or anything else. Everyone gathered around the rear of the truck and took as many meals as they could cram into their backpacks. Taras and the friends who had joined with him did also, even jettisoning articles of extra clothing to make room for them. Lomachenko still hadn't joined them, but no one seemed worried about his absence.

The girl who'd fled Bucha took a meal also and sat to one side eating it alone. One of the men got half a dozen more for her from the truck and brought them to where she was. Someone else brought a canvas pouch for her to put them in. No one knew what would happen to her next, or whether she would be with them long enough to eat another meal, but at least she would have something to eat for a while.

When the men were done eating, Lomachenko still hadn't joined them. So, everyone sat around, waiting for whatever was next but no one seemed to know. Twenty minutes later, Lomachenko appeared, and shortly after that, a truck arrived. It was empty in back, but two men sat in the cab. They were on their way to Kyiv and the driver seemed to know to stop. Lomachenko sent the girl with them with instructions to deliver her to the authorities at brigade headquarters. An investigation had been opened into the atrocities at Bucha. The things she'd talked about the night before had been going on for some time, and even worse. A mass grave had been found in a field near the edge of town. It held more than two hundred bodies. Another had been reported near it but had not yet been excavated.

At the news of it, Taras and those seated with him speculated there were likely more Chechens than had yet been found. He watched her leave and wondered what would become of her. Would she grow up to marry and raise a family? Would the memory of what happened to her stay with her for the remainder of her life? Would she be scarred forever? All of it seemed likely and he wondered why things had turned out that way. Certainly, she had done nothing to the Chechens. Perhaps didn't even know where Chechnya was located. Or that the Russians used Chechen paramilitary like attack dogs.

A door to the cab opened and a soldier stepped out to help her inside. When she was seated and they were all in the cab with the door closed, the driver put the truck in gear and began driving away. Taras realized he didn't even know her name. No one else did, either.

As the truck departed with the girl, a second one arrived for Taras and his platoon. Everyone climbed aboard and they started north, toward the sound of the artillery fire that continued since the night before. The bed of the truck had seemed huge when it first arrived but with everyone aboard, men were sitting shoulder to shoulder all the way around, and some on the floor in the middle. The truck was designed for hauling heavy loads and had stiff springs, which made for a stiff, bumpy ride. Thankfully, they stopped several times for bathroom breaks, and once when they met a truck like the one carrying MREs only this one carried ammunition. Everyone took as much as they could manage.

At one of the stops Leo Sharpar, a student from the university who had joined the unit the same day as Taras and the others, failed to return to the truck when it was time to go. Taras knew he should report him missing but kept quiet, thinking he might not want to be found. Sharpar was like that, secretive and quiet. Sure enough, as the truck started forward, Taras saw him hiding in the bushes and as the truck rounded a curve, Sharpar started down the road in the direction of home.

For a moment, Taras wished he'd dared to join Sharpar, but just as quickly he dispelled the thought. Serving his country was an honor. Already they had driven the Russians from the edge of the city, destroyed several pieces of equipment, and rescued a girl from the Chechen paramilitary. He smiled with pride. Not bad for two days of work. And much more rewarding than sitting in the coffee shop engaging in endless political debate.

✦ ✦ ✦

The longer they traveled, the louder the sound of the Russian artillery became. By the sound of it, Taras thought the shells were detonating about a quarter of a mile away. That meant the artillery pieces that fired them were, at most, thirty miles away. By then, it was mid-afternoon, and he wondered if they would engage the artillery or wait until the next day.

In a little while, Lomachenko got in back with the men and they learned that the artillery was stationed about twenty miles north, perched atop a low hill. A Ukrainian unit farther to the west that had been moving north in coordination with Taras' platoon had located it with a drone.

"Our job is to take it out," Lomachenko said. "We'll divide into three groups. Some in the center, the other two flanking the canon on either side of their position. We'll advance quickly, so pay attention. Make sure you shoot Russians, not each other."

An hour later, the truck came to a stop along the side of the road at a point opposite the Russian artillery position. Lomachenko, still riding in the back, sent two men to make sure they were in the correct place. While they were gone, the platoon climbed down from the truck and inspected their weapons, making sure they were fully loaded and in proper order.

A few minutes later the scouts returned with news that they were in the right place. Lomachenko gave some quick instructions, then everyone followed him from the road, through the bushes to a stand of trees. From there they could see the artillery piece on a low rise about thirty yards away. Everyone had expected the site to be heavily protected but apparently, the Russians were confident they were in a secure location. Only a few soldiers guarded the perimeter.

The Russians had chosen a good spot. An open field between the hilltop and the trees where Taras' platoon stood exposed their position fully, making it a tempting target, but also meant anyone approaching on foot would be fully exposed, too. With only the few soldiers that were visible on the hill, the Russians could easily rip apart an advancing enemy unit.

Crouched in the stand of trees, Taras found the moment rather peaceful. A gentle breeze blew against his cheeks and the bright sunshine made it seem like a good day for a picnic. But all too soon one of the Russian soldiers spotted them and fired his rifle in their direction. Several rounds hit the trees, then another struck one of the Ukrainian regulars, an older guy from Boryspil. Taras was standing nearby when the bullet hit him in the top of his head. He didn't cry out or flail in pain, but simply let go of his rifle and fell forward landing with his face against the ground.

More gunfire followed and everyone took cover. Some on the ground, others behind the trees. Taras returned fire, shooting indiscriminately at first but constantly. As they had discussed in the truck, the platoon divided into two parts. Some scurried to the right and others to the left. Taras and four friends remained in the center, firing as fast as they could, hoping the rest of the platoon made it to safety. And hoping some of their shots found a target in the body of a Russian.

Most of the men on the left found safety in a low depression that was deep enough to prevent the Russians from seeing them. Those on the right took refuge behind a fallen tree partway up the hill.

Taras was still in the center with Oleg, Vitali, and Sergey. The rush of the first moments had passed and he steadied his nerves. No longer shooting his rifle haphazardly, he aimed carefully and fired in a deliberate, methodical manner. Some of his shots went awry, hitting first the ground, then the side window of a truck parked quite far from where the Russians had placed their cannon. Taras took a deep breath and forced his muscles to relax deeper. When a Russian raised up to fire again, Taras trained the sights of the rifle on the man's chest and pulled the trigger. The Russian fell back, clutching his ribs in pain. The sight of it was awful but Taras felt the satisfaction of being a soldier.

After exchanging several volleys in that manner—the Russians firing, then the men in the center returning fire when they showed their faces again—Taras remembered the grenade launcher. He called out to the others to see if they had it and Vitali took it from his shoulder. "Send off a round," Taras called. A moment later Vitali fired the launcher and a grenade fell to the right of the cannon. An explosion followed, then they heard the screams of wounded men.

The remainder of the platoon, having come from the security of their cover, were moving up the hill on either side of the artillery, flanking the Russian position. When the grenade exploded, they rushed forward firing as they came. Taras glanced up to see they were methodically working their way through the Russians, killing every soldier they encountered.

At last, the fighting died down. Lomachenko called from up the way and Taras stepped out from where he'd been hiding. The others with him did, too, and they ran up the hill to join everyone else standing near the artillery piece. Someone counted the wounded and dead, including the man who'd been hit when they first arrived, and called on a radio for a truck to collect the bodies.

No one wanted to go near the bodies, but Taras felt obligated to remain with them, especially the older guy from Boryspil. As he stood there, looking down at him, he noticed a web belt around the man's waist with four grenades hanging from it. He slipped the grenades free and hooked them onto his own belt. Oleg claimed his sidearm. Someone else took his rifle and the extra clips that were in the utility pocket of his shirt.

By then, the truck had arrived for the bodies. Taras and the others helped load the dead into the back. When that was done, they all hurried to join the regulars who were breaking down the artillery piece and preparing it for transportation. It was Russian, but it was a nice piece and it fired standard artillery shells. No one wanted to destroy it.

CHAPTER TWO

Late in the evening, Jim Marsh sat at his desk in the study of his home in Salona Village, a residential neighborhood of McLean, Virginia, not far from the CIA headquarters campus. As he did most evenings, he read through a stack of sensitive but unclassified reports he had brought home from the office. Leftovers from a busy day.

Across the room from Marsh were four television screens mounted to the wall above a row of bookcases that filled the space between the door on the right and the corner of the room to the left. Each screen was tuned to multiple live news feeds from the world's major news outlets, giving him instant access to the latest newscasts from around the globe. He listened while he skimmed through the collection of reports and memos that were stacked on the desk.

As the CIA's Deputy Director for Clandestine Services, Marsh was privy to details regarding all covert operations currently being planned or conducted by CIA personnel. He was also aware of the hundreds of non-sanctioned operations being handled through clandestine operatives in the field. Operatives with no official connection to the agency, receiving no official support, with no official existence. Organizationally, Marsh was the choke point for all of it. The one person who, quite literally, knew where all the bodies were buried. Which meant that he knew as much about the agency's conduct—authorized and unauthorized—as anyone could know.

In addition to the many official communications channels at his disposal, a laptop sitting on his desk gave Marsh access to multiple anonymous email accounts that he used to maintain private communications with a select group of field agents. Handpicked, they were the best of the best, working on critical projects regarding the most vital areas of interest to the country.

To keep Marsh's activity safe and secure from prying eyes, his study had been designed and equipped with the latest in physical and digital security, converting it from a typical home study into a SCIF—a Sensitive Compartmented Information Facility—capable of safely and securely handling the government's most sensitive information, digital or print.

When the Russian army invaded Ukraine, the CIA had several ongoing operations in the region. Rather than recalling them, Marsh expanded their assignments. Most were dedicated to gathering intelligence to assess the potential for US involvement, anticipating a US role in supplying material and expertise to the Ukrainian army. In the weeks following the initial invasion, Marsh had commissioned a series of updates to existing models that were expected to determine just how far the US might be able to go in that effort. Data for those models came from the operatives that remained in Ukraine after the Russians entered the country.

Leading up to the invasion, analysts from the Department of Defense thought Russian forces could easily take control of Ukraine, but Marsh had seen satellite photos of Russian forces and he had read reports from operatives on the ground. Russian mechanized units were equipped with tanks and armored vehicles that appeared to be older and less robust than Russia's newest models. "It's like they're cleaning out the warehouses and the junkyards," one CIA expert had said. "And they're filling their combat units with guys from prison and with paramilitary units they've recruited from the worst regions of Russia. Guys like that tend to be brutal, but they aren't good enough soldiers to win with second-rate equipment."

It seemed like a recipe for a long engagement at best, or total disaster at worst. And it was happening in an area that bordered a major portion of NATO's member countries. Precisely the kind of situation planners and commanders had dreaded since the end of World War II and one that made the potential for global war far too real. It didn't take an analyst from the CIA or the Pentagon to imagine a regional conflict that pitted Russia against Central Europe, with its support from NATO and the US, attracting participation from China, Arab countries from the Middle East, and anyone who thought they had a score to settle with the West. It was the kind of scenario that kept Marsh up late many nights trying to anticipate everyone's next move.

Just before midnight, Marsh received a text that read, "Check your email." The text was from a six-digit account that wasn't included on his contacts list.

Instinctively, Marsh glanced at the laptop and saw an email had arrived with a subject line that read, "All of you are going to die." He hovered the cursor over it to reveal the sender's address. It wasn't one from his contacts list, either.

The laptop and Marsh's cell phone operated over secure, encrypted networks. Operatives in the field had access to only the email account and phone number that pertained to their assignment. How did anyone else get access to the phone number? Were they in the system already? Had the laptop been corrupted?

Marsh's first impulse was to open the email and find out the sender's name but as he reached for the mouse, he hesitated. If the message was corrupted, opening it might release malware into the system or unleash a virus with software that could give someone else control of the laptop. He had been assured that programs installed on both devices could prevent that from happening, but he had always been suspicious about whether that was true. Better to notify someone in the technical sector and let them examine the message. They had people who did that kind of thing every day.

✦ ✦ ✦

When he finished reading the memos he'd brought home from the office, Marsh returned them to his leather satchel, closed the screen on the laptop, and went upstairs to the bedroom he shared with his wife. He had expected to find her already fast asleep, but instead, the lamp on her nightstand was on and she was lying in bed reading a book. He dressed for bed and got in beside her.

"Is the world still safe?" she asked.

"The world is never safe," he replied.

She laid the book aside. "If you came with me to church regularly you would know, nothing anyone can do will ever destroy the world."

"Are you sure about that?"

"I am positive," she said. "God has the final say. And even when this world ends, another awaits."

"*Revelation*."

"Ahh," she said playfully. "You *do* remember some of what you've read."

"It's difficult to do my job and find time for church."

"I know," she said.

"And don't say I could have gone to work for your father instead of the government," Marsh added. "He struggled with balancing his schedule, too."

She rolled on her side to face him and draped an arm across his chest. "I appreciate everything you do for us and for the country. Your job has given us a great life." She snuggled closer and placed her lips against this ear. "But you need to forget about all of that for a few minutes." She massaged the lobe of his ear with her lips, then worked her way down to his neck as she pushed his sleeping shorts off his hips.

✦ ✦ ✦

The next morning Marsh awakened early and when he had showered and dressed, he went downstairs to the kitchen for a cup of coffee. While he waited for it to brew, he stood at the kitchen sink and stared out the window. Outside, the sky still was dark. Traffic on the highway a few miles away sounded light, as if the day hadn't started yet for most people. A quiet moment for the truck driver sipping his first cup of the morning, the factory worker munching on a breakfast sandwich with the radio tuned to a news talk show as he drove to work. They all shared the same start to their day. A commonality that united them, even though the day that awaited each of them would take them to different places with different priorities and different issues. The coffeemaker finished brewing the coffee. Marsh poured a cup and returned to his place at the sink while he waited for the toaster to finish.

The sound of the traffic faded into the background as Marsh's mind moved away from the moment with the traffic to the issues from the office that awaited his attention. The Russian army fighting its way across Ukraine with nervous NATO members not far away. Russian allies around the world deciding how much to help, or not. All the weapons that had been manufactured for war—pistols, rifles, missiles, rockets, mortars, grenades, airplanes, bombs. And the unthinkable nuclear option. Russia had it. Russian allies like China and North Korea had it. What would happen if a war between Russia and Ukraine came to a stalemate? What if Russia faced retreat or the use of nuclear weapons? What would Putin do then?

Before the Russians invaded Ukraine, Putin talked about it, signaling the action long before the tanks started rolling across the border. Marsh read the reports, listened to the speeches, and carefully examined the CIA's analysis of it. When would he start talking about using nuclear weapons? Would anyone take him seriously? And what would they do in response?

Of all the countries in the world that possessed a nuclear arsenal, Russia had the largest. The greatest number of nuclear devices of any kind or size, from the very small to the very large. Nuclear weapons that could fit in a child's backpack. Those that required a truck for delivery. And some that needed only a syringe.

They had used them, too. Not that anyone seemed to notice. A spy in London who was about to tell all—poisoned with an injection of polonium that brought instant death. An operative flying in a commercial airliner to meet a French reporter—killed when a micro explosion in the cargo hold obliterated the aircraft. A yacht carrying a Greek businessman and his family to a villa on the Black Sea for a meeting with a Russian candidate who was challenging Putin for the presidency. They all disappeared with no trace of the poisonous substance or explosive that brought their demise. Nothing to suggest a cause, a device, or a means.

Just then, the toaster dinged. He took the bread from it and laid it on a plate, then buttered it while it was hot and ate it as he sipped his coffee. As he chewed and swallowed, he tried to slow his mind and think of something else—the stars still visible in the early-morning sky, the smooth taste of the coffee after he added cream and sugar. A memory of drinking coffee with his father in the morning before he left for work—his with just enough coffee to turn the cream and sugar a light tan color. But it was no use. His mind refused to go there and returned to the day that awaited him and a vision of the future that plagued him.

News reports treated the emerging conflict between Russia and Ukraine like it was just another European pushing match. A bully throwing his weight around. Two countries revisiting old grudges. Political leaders jockeying for continental influence. But to Marsh, it was much more than that. He grew up in a devoutly Christian family and although his professional career had taken him far beyond the views of life and morality he had learned back then, he still remembered the stories he had heard in church. Especially the part about the end of time.

Marsh had read apocalyptic literature as a teenager and although his life had moved beyond the rhythms of conservative Christianity, the apocalyptic paradigm still resonated deep in his soul. Beasts and cauldrons, famine and judgment, had morphed into countries and organizations, religious zealots and rightwing radicals, nuclear arms, and armed drones. As if the ancient stories were being retold in life, only now in an era when a political leader could easily bring them to pass.

✦ ✦ ✦

When Marsh arrived at CIA headquarters the next morning, he went straight to Technical Services and showed the message to Agnes Marshall, a technical supervisor with whom he'd worked in the past.

"I received an email last night on my laptop," he said.

"The one you have at home?"

"Yes."

"Did you open it?" Marshall asked.

"Yes."

"Did you read it?"

"It appeared on the screen."

"Did you access it with any other device?"

"No."

"Your phone?"

Marsh hesitated. "No. Not actually."

"What, then?"

"I had a text on my phone telling me to check my email."

"You opened the text?"

"Yes."

"Where's the phone?"

"In my pocket."

"And the laptop?"

"I left it at home."

Agnes took a lead-lined evidence bag from a drawer and held it open. "Drop your phone in here," she said, gesturing with the bag.

"My phone?"

"Put it in the bag."

Marsh was reluctant. He used the phone almost every minute of the day. The thought of being without it was unsettling. "I can't get—"

"Put it in the bag," she insisted. "We'll give you a replacement."

"Now?"

"Yes," she said. "You'll have it before you head back to your office."

Marsh dropped the phone in the bag and Agnes sealed it closed.

"We'll need to examine your computer, too," she said.

"Do you want me to bring it in?"

"No," she said. "We can access it from here."

With a few clicks of the keys on her keyboard, Agnes accessed the laptop that was still sitting on the desk in Marsh's study at home. The directory for it appeared on the screen. While Marsh watched, she downloaded the entire contents of the hard drive to a protected directory and forwarded it to a technician. "We'll let you know what we find," she said.

✦ ✦ ✦

Shortly after lunch, Marsh received a message from Agnes asking him to come to her office. "The text message that came to your phone was sent from a non-traceable number."

"Is that the end of it?" he asked.

"Ha!" she laughed. "Surely you know we're better than that."

"That's why I came to you. Can you work around the number issue?"

"The short answer is yes, but finding details about the messages sent to that number may take a while," she admitted. "But details about the mysterious email you received proved much easier."

"Okay."

"The email you received on the laptop was sent over a Virtual Private Network using an account that was accessed through the internet from a hotspot that had been created with a laptop that was connected to a—"

Marsh waved his hands in frustration. "Slow down and give it to me one step at a time."

Agnes started over. "Someone used a laptop to log onto a Wi-Fi network that took them to the internet."

"Okay."

"Then they went to a VPN provider and logged into an account. Probably thought it would hide their identity. And it *could have* except for one thing. The internet service provider for the Wi-Fi was connected to the internet through an LCI account."

"LCI." Marsh's eyes opened wide. "They used our internet service provider?"

Agnes nodded. "All it took was a simple email to LCI and there you have it." She pointed to details showing on her monitor screen. "The device that sent you the email was in an apartment in Dubai."

"Was the phone that sent the text in the apartment, too?"

"I can't tell you that yet," she said. "The technicians are still working with the phone. It might take a while for them to dig deep enough to tell us where the phone was located when the user told you to check your email. But whoever sent you the email did it from a device that was connected to the internet through a router that was in a Dubai apartment. I'll forward you the street address."

"How difficult was this to find?"

"Not very in this instance," Agnes said. "It might have been impossible if they hadn't used LCI for their internet connection."

Marsh was suspicious. "This is almost too good to be true."

"Sometimes it works out that way."

Marsh shook his head. "Never trust a coincidence."

"So, what do think happened?"

"I think whoever sent that text wanted us to find out where

it came from, and they led us right to the place they wanted us to look."

"Maybe," Agnes replied. "But they would have to had to know the access code to log onto the Wi-Fi. Did they have someone on the inside, or did they hack into a preexisting LCI account?"

Agnes shook her head. "I asked that question, too. LCI says the router in the apartment wasn't connected to their service until the day the email message was sent."

"Find out how they paid for that account."

Agnes smiled. "Waiting for a response already."

"Is the apartment where the router was located one of ours?"

"It's not on anyone's list," Agnes said.

"Did the sender of that email get into our system?"

"The technicians say they didn't even try."

"Have they looked?"

"They checked whatever they normally check and said it was clear."

"Can they find out exactly how far into our system this person has been?"

"It'll take a while," she said. "And you'll have to approve the expense."

"Find out," Marsh replied. "We'll cover the budget."

✦ ✦ ✦

When Marsh reached his desk, he contacted the CIA's Special Operations Group and requested a team be sent to the apartment in Dubai. The request was little more than a formality. It was approved immediately. Shortly before midnight, Dubai time, the team entered the apartment. A body camera captured their movements and transmitted them to an operations center at CIA headquarters. Marsh, Agnes, and an analyst from her office watched the images as they appeared on a large screen at the end of the room.

The apartment had two bedrooms, both of them sparsely furnished with only a bed, a dresser, and two chairs. A search showed the drawers of both dressers were empty. The closets were empty, too, as were the cabinets in the bathrooms.

In the kitchen, however, they found a laptop on the counter. A power cord connected it to an outlet in the backsplash. The lid was open, but the screen was dark.

Someone pressed a button, and the screen came alive with a video clip showing the central business district in Boston. The top half of the John Hancock Tower, the tallest building in the city, was visible in the background. As those at the operations center watched, the building on the screen morphed into an image of the North Tower of the World Trade Center in New York City as it collapsed on 9-11.

An expletive was heard from someone watching in the apartment. "We need to get out of here," the team commander said. "Get the laptop."

Someone closed the screen and disconnected the power cord. Another stuffed the laptop into a backpack. Everyone turned to leave but before they were out of the room, one of them glanced over his shoulder and he stopped. A worried look furrowed his brow. "What's the matter?" he said to the person behind him. The body camera turned in the direction he was looking and showed a member of the group standing motionless near the kitchen counter. He pointed towards the floor. "The tile moved."

"What tile?" the team commander asked.

"The one I'm standing on."

"You're sure?"

"Yeah. I'm standing on a pressure trigger."

"Okay," the commander said. "Just stand right there and don't move." He glanced at the others. "Anyone else feel any movement from the tile?" They all shook their heads.

"Anyone hear anything?" Again, everyone shook their head.

"Okay," the commander said. "Get out of the apartment."

"Where do we go?" someone asked.

"Anywhere. Just get out of here."

There was the sound of footsteps shuffling toward the door, then the man with the body camera turned to show the man standing on the trigger. "Just relax," the commander said. "I'm gonna squat down here beside you and have a look. Don't move."

"Am I gonna die?"

"Everyone dies. It's just a matter of when."

There was an image of a foot on the screen. Then one of the men who'd already started toward the door shouted, "We've got trouble."

The body camera turned in his direction and the image on the screen in the operations center showed the entire team standing motionless at the door.

"What is it?"

"There's a motion detector," someone replied.

The body camera pointed to a sensor in the corner of the room.

A red light at the top blinked. Once. Twice. Then there was a click and a charge beneath the floor exploded. Debris filled the air, followed by thick smoke that rapidly dissipated to reveal the kitchen cabinets were on fire.

CHAPTER THREE

Six thousand miles away, Majid Roshan came from his apartment on the campus of a uranium enrichment facility in Natanz, Iran. Roshan, a nuclear scientist by training, was the director of Iran's nuclear program. He oversaw the enrichment of fissile material at the site as well as the research and development of a bomb that the enriched material might equip.

The morning was bright and clear with a gentle breeze that made the walk across campus pleasant. Far down beneath the lawn where Roshan walked lay an enormous underground labyrinth of tunnels and rooms. Modern, clean, well-lit, some of the spaces contained offices and research facilities but most of them held only one thing—centrifuges. Acres and acres of them. Large, sophisticated industrial machines standing taller than a man's head, meticulously arranged an equal distance apart in neat, tidy rows. Humming all day and all night. Slowly transforming natural uranium from a substance that arrived much the same as it was when mined from the ground, into a form pure enough for use in a well-ordered nuclear weapon.

Normally, Roshan would have been underground with the machines checking the gauges, reading the meters, and calculating the results from the previous twenty-four hours. But that morning he was scheduled to attend a meeting in the conference room on the third floor of the main building across the site from his apartment. He was glad to go. The meeting would last several hours and the room in which it was to be held had many windows that let in lots of sunlight. Most days, he only saw a few minutes of morning sun before taking the elevator from his apartment building into an underground tunnel system that led to the area where he worked. Attending the meeting that day gave him time to stroll across the campus, enjoy the beauty of the plants and trees that lined the way, gaze out from the hilltop at the valley below, and soak up the bright sunlight.

The meeting that day was attended by Mehdi Kalhor, director of the Organization of Defensive Innovation, an agency of the Iranian Ministry of Defense that funded Roshan's many projects. Kalhor was accompanied by members of his staff and the heads of the various departments that reported to him. Representatives from other Iranian nuclear research and enrichment facilities were present as well.

Kalhor and his entourage were there to inquire about progress in the enrichment program and about advances toward the ultimate goal of making a workable nuclear bomb. Normally, meetings of this type were perfunctory. Nothing more than a check to make sure all was well and proceeding apace. The notice from Kalhor's office and the daily follow-up messages had made this one seem different. Everyone arrived on edge.

The meeting began with concise questions from Kalhor about where the program stood regarding the previously determined timeline. Roshan responded with vague and illusive answers that made him appear aloof, even condescending. Enrichment and development of a warhead were Roshan's favorite programs. He didn't trust Kalhor to deal effectively with them.

As the exchange continued, those who'd come from other research facilities sided with Roshan and attempted to buttress his positions. The process was complex. Progress was steady but at a deliberate pace. One couldn't rush these things. Haste would only compound their mistakes. Perhaps lead to a catastrophe. Those who came with Kalhor were impatient and showed little restraint in expressing their differences of opinion. The meeting quickly became tense.

"Stop avoiding the questions," an attendee from Tehran finally snapped. "We need to know when we will have a bomb we can actually use."

"As we have been saying," Roshan replied. "The process is not instantaneous. It takes time."

"Not this much time," someone else noted. "We want a bomb that works, while there's still time to use it."

Roshan glared at them. "You were not like this before. Why the sudden hurry?"

"Events are moving forward. We don't want to be left behind."

"Events?" Roshan looked perplexed. "What events?"

Kalhor spoke up. "We are worried about shifts in Israeli politics," he said calmly.

"What kind of shifts?"

"They recently had an election. Their new prime minister is decidedly more conservative than the previous one. I know you don't care for politics but we in Tehran must. This new leader formed a government by appealing to some of Israel's most conservative parties."

"And you think they will come for us?"

"They've bombed our reactors before," someone offered.

Kalhor raised his hand gesturing for silence. "Tehran has assessed the situation," he said, "and they have decided we must respond in ways that make sure the Israelis are aware of the risks they face. One of those responses is by increasing the pace of our uranium project. The entire project. Not just the pace of enrichment."

The tone of Kalhor's voice and the look in his eye turned Roshan's suspicion in a different direction. "They think I am deliberately delaying development?" If they had only wanted to increase the pace, someone would have come to him directly. That they raised the topic through Kalhor seemed to indicate they were dissatisfied with him. Personally.

"No." Roshan shook his head. "No one is—"

"They are questioning my loyalty?"

"No one is questioning your loyalty," Kalhor assured. "They know you are a true scientist, conducting yourself and your program in an exemplary manner. All for the glory of Allah. But they also know that you assess things according to scientific priorities. Tehran has a different perspective. To them, Israel is our enemy, and their government has become even more conservative than those of the past. They see it as a threat."

"And they think having a nuclear weapon will give them an advantage."

Kalhor smiled. "It would at least keep things even."

Roshan took a deep breath and slowly let it out. His shoulders settled and he seemed to relax a little. "Gentlemen," he began, in a professorial tone. "Popular discussion makes it seem that producing an atomic device is simple, easy, and straightforward. I can assure you; it is none of those things. The basic *theory* is rather simple to describe, but the application of it is quite complex. There are a thousand variables in each step of the process. Each of those variables can dramatically influence the effectiveness of the outcome."

"Such as?"

"Merely the shape of the device into which one places the various components of a nuclear bomb can determine the efficiency of the reaction and the amount of energy it releases. Determining the shape of the cask that holds the bomb will take months."

Sighs of frustration were heard from Kalhor's side of the room. "This is what we've been talking about," someone said. "We need to produce a bomb quickly. Not conduct more tests."

Another added, "We aren't concerned with how efficient it is. We just need it to detonate."

"Speed is the most important part to us."

Roshan held his temper. "You will get only one opportunity to use such a weapon," he cautioned. "It would behoove you to make it the biggest, most effective detonation obtainable."

Kalhor spoke once more. "Don't we have enough uranium now?"

Roshan shook his head in frustration. "This is what makes dealing with non-scientists so difficult. Having enough uranium is only a small part of the problem and the least challenging. We are not far from achieving the goal of having sufficient uranium for a bomb, but as I have said many times, that is only one part of the issue we face."

"What is the second part?"

"We have to design and create a fixture to hold two sub-critical masses of uranium. Once we have that in place, we will need a detonator capable of smashing the masses of uranium together quickly enough to create a chain reaction. And once we have all of that, we will need a way to deliver the device to the target."

"We settled on a delivery method last time," someone replied. "A missile is the only way. If we use aircraft, Israel will shoot them down before they leave our airspace. Using them is out of the question, especially now."

Roshan frowned. "Especially now? What does that mean?"

Kalhor spoke up. "We have not been successful in convincing the Russians to provide an air defense for our facilities."

Part of Iran's grand atomic strategy had included the presence of Russian fighters patrolling the airspace over Iran as a deterrent to an attack from the Israelis. A shield, of sorts, based on the notion that Israel might be bold enough to bomb an Iranian reactor, but they would steer clear of Iranian airspace if it meant a direct encounter with the Russian air force. But that appeared to no longer be possible.

"Are the Russians also refusing to help with miniaturization?"

"Not refusing," Kalhor said. "Just not immediately forthcoming."

Roshan grimaced. "In that case, we must reconsider the delivery method."

"Why?"

"Fitting a nuclear device atop a missile requires miniaturization technology we don't have. We were counting on the Russians to supply it."

Kalhor seemed unmoved. "Where could we find that kind of expertise?"

"America," Roshan suggested, "if you could get the right person to defect." Everyone chuckled. "Or Russia," he added quickly. "Aside from that, the Chinese and the North Koreans know how to do it."

Kalhor seemed confident. "We will find the help you need. Would a greater centrifuge capacity help?"

"It might reduce the purification time," Roshan replied, "but as I said, enrichment is the least of our issues."

After listening to the discussion, Roshan was more frustrated than before. The ease with which the bureaucrats discussed technical issues they knew nothing about, the absurdity that nuclear weapons offered an ultimate solution to Iran's age-old problems—it was as if they lived in a different world, in an alternative reality. He wanted to tell them the device they coveted was incapable of solving the country's issues. That it would, in fact, exacerbate the trouble with Israel and not only with Israel but with all of their Arab neighbors, but he kept quiet. They would only see him as an arrogant, self-absorbed scientist. So, he avoided the political issues—he hated politics anyway—and confined his remarks to the complexity of the technical process and their lack of understanding.

"Making a nuclear bomb is a complex, complicated, and lengthy process," Roshan repeated. "America's first nuclear bomb was a uranium bomb, much like the one we're attempting to build. The US bomb was enormous by today's standards. Ten feet long and over two feet wide. Their second bomb was even bigger. Both of them were too large to fit onto any of our existing missiles. It took them five years and numerous test explosions to do it.

"We don't have five years."

"And we can't test," another added.

Roshan's eyes widened. "This is what I mean. You are asking me to do the impossible in a ridiculously short time and produce a desired result on nothing more than a guess."

"These are the restrictions given to us by the Supreme Leader," Kalhor responded. "Increase the pace of enrichment. We will find help for the issues we encounter as we come to them along the way."

Roshan was flabbergasted. "It's not a —"

Kalhor raised his hand to cut him off. "All will become clear as we progress."

Roshan slumped in his chair. He hated it when they talked to him that way. As if they knew better than he and all the other scientists in the world what could and couldn't be done.

✦ ✦ ✦

When the meeting ended, Roshan came from the conference room and took an elevator to the underground corridor that lay beneath the building. A few minutes later, he arrived at the enrichment facility. Shiraz Parsi, his assistant, was waiting for him. Roshan was still upset over the things he'd learned at the meeting and muttered to himself as he entered the centrifuge compartment. Parsi heard him and noted the troubled expression on his face. "What's the matter?" he asked.

"They want us to create a bomb," Roshan replied. "Without testing."

Parsi frowned. "Didn't our plan always include testing?"

"Yes, but now they say we can't."

"That doesn't make sense, does it?"

"It is insanity," Roshan said. "And not only can't we test, but they also want us to create it in a way that can fit atop a missile."

Parsi frowned. "They want us to build a bomb, using miniaturization technology we don't have, and test it with their first use in combat?"

"Apparently."

"And where would that first use occur?"

"They didn't say, but I'm certain it will be in Israel."

Parsi shook his head in disbelief. "They expect us to create such a device and test it by dropping it on Israel?"

"That about sums it up."

"If we do that, and the device doesn't work, the Israelis will know we were the ones who did it."

Roshan nodded in agreement. "The Americans will know it, too," he said. "And then all the world will rain down bombs on our heads."

"Nuclear bombs," Parsi added.

"Yes. I suspect you are correct."

"If we use it and it doesn't work, they will bomb us. And if we use it and it *does* work, they will bomb us."

"Right."

"So, either way, whether our device is a success or a failure, if we use it, we will cease to exist."

Roshan looked at him grimly. "Now you understand why I mutter to myself so often."

"And they think this is a good plan?"

"They think it's an ingenious plan." Roshan noticed Parsi's distress and patted him on the shoulder. "Cheer up," he said. "We are a long way from achieving all of that. There is still plenty of time for Allah to enlighten them."

✦ ✦ ✦

Later in the day, Parsi left the enrichment facility and rode a shuttle bus to the nearby city of Kashan where he had an apartment. Kashan was a city of about 300,000 people. It had shops and restaurants and everything he needed to live comfortably, but the thing he liked most was the fact that it lay outside the confines of the enrichment facility. No security guards, no access checks, and far fewer security cameras.

The apartment where he lived was small but comfortable and it had a balcony near the kitchen. When he arrived, he put on water for tea, then stepped out to the balcony. A flowerpot with a plant inside sat to the left. Parsi moved the pot to the opposite side and watered the plant, then returned to the kitchen. Rather than making tea, as he had intended, he switched off the stove and walked down the street to a café two blocks away. Parsi took a seat at a table in the back and ordered a cup of tea.

While Parsi sipped tea, Mohsen Durak, a Kurdish operative for Mossad living in Iran, entered the café. He ordered a cup of coffee and took it to a table outside. When he'd finished his coffee, he left the café and walked to a park one block away where he took a seat on a bench. Parsi found him there and they talked.

"There was a meeting today," Parsi began.

"Who was there?"

"Mehdi Kalhor, several of his department heads, and most of the directors of the nuclear program."

"Kalhor? Head of Defensive Innovation?"

"Yes."

"What was the meeting about?"

"We are to increase our efforts to build a bomb," Parisi explained.

"How long will that take?"

"Longer than they think."

"Realistically, how long?"

"The uranium can be ready in about two months," Parisi said. "Shorter if we get additional centrifuges. But that isn't our biggest problem."

"You still don't have a device ready to create a detonation, do you?"

Parisi avoided a direct answer. "That is not insurmountable. The real issue is having a means of delivery."

"What do they want to use?"

"A missile."

"Iran has several that could work."

"And work beautifully," Parisi agreed.

"Then what's the issue?"

"Technology. In order to deliver a bomb by missile we will need help with miniaturization."

"I thought you said before that they already had plans for that."

"Plans and techniques for miniaturizing a nuclear device are well known and easily understood," Parisi said. "But doing it is a huge task."

"They think you can do that?"

"They say they can get us the help we need."

"How?"

"That part is not clear."

"We need to know who will provide the help."

"I understand."

"And we need to know the equipment these supposed benefactors will supply."

"I understand," Parsi said. "But I do not know if I can discover that information without raising suspicions."

"Do your best."

While they talked, Durak noticed two men watching them from across the way. One was seated on a park bench, the other stood casually by a tree. Durak thought they were from PAVA, the Iranian Intelligence and Public Security Police, but he kept quiet and did not say anything to Parsi about them. Durak had spent too much time cultivating him as a source and didn't want to scare him away.

As their conversation continued, Durak took a flash drive from his pocket. "I want you to insert this into the USB port of a computer in your department."

"Which computer?"

"Any computer."

Parsi took the device from him and held it in his grasp. "What about my sister? You promised me you would get her out of here."

"We're working on it, but I need you to insert this into a computer."

Parsi put the flash drive in his pocket and looked over at Durak. "I will do as you asked, but you must remember my sister if you want me to work for you."

"I'll take care of your sister," Durak said. "Just put that flash drive in a USB port in your department."

From the outside, the flash drive looked like any other commercially available model, but inside, it contained a self-loading program that allowed it to operate within the system much like a user, setting up its own user account, scanning files throughout the host system and, on command, it could transmit the content of those files to any designated device located elsewhere. With a proper connection, it could link itself to an Israeli satellite and relay all of that information to Mossad headquarters in Tel Aviv, allowing analysts real-time access to all of Iran's enrichment and research programs.

Parsi, of course, knew none of that. Still, he was worried. "If I put it in the machine I normally use, they will know I was the one who put it there, and then they will shoot me. Right then."

Durak said, "Insert it into any computer, anywhere in the building. That's all you have to do."

They talked a short while longer, then Parsi stood and walked away from the bench. One of the PAVA agents followed him across the park. Durak waited a moment, watching them from a distance, then he left the park, too. The second PAVA Agent followed him. Durak noticed he was being followed and took a circuitous route up the street, then turned left, cut over at the corner to the cross street, then entered a store and exited through a side door, and doubled back.

As Durak rounded the next corner, he saw the second PAVA agent still behind him. Halfway up the block, he led the agent into an alley, took a stiletto knife from his pocket, and killed the agent with it. An oversized garbage bin stood nearby. Durak stuffed his body into it, wiped the blade on the agent's trousers, and calmly walked away.

Two blocks from the alley, Durak took a parallel street over to where he was certain Parsi would be walking. At first, he didn't see him, but when he reached the next corner, he caught sight of Parisi with the PAVA agent trailing behind. Durak hurried to a parallel street, then up to the next corner where he met Parsi coming towards him. He dodged Parsi and caught the PAVA agent unaware. Before the agent could react, Durak slid the stiletto knife from his pocket and shoved it between the agent's ribs, driving it to his heart. The agent fell forward against Durak, then collapsed to the curb by the street. By the time he hit the pavement, Durak was out of sight around the next corner.

CHAPTER FOUR

F our days after their meeting in the park, Durak passed by Parsi's apartment and glanced up at it from the street but saw no signal on the balcony. He passed by again the next day and still the flowerpot on the balcony had not been moved. Normally, given the nature of their latest meeting, Parsi would have alerted him for a follow-up meeting. In this instance, to let him know the flash drive had been inserted in one of the facility's computers. But Parsi had failed to give him a signal and that worried Durak. He could have asked about the flash drive's status from his Mossad contacts, but they had frowned on inquiries of that sort in the past. "Direct contact with us from Iran is too risky," they had said.

When Durak checked the balcony again later in the week, there still was no signal so he broke protocol, went inside the building, and knocked on Parsi's door. The force of his knuckle against the door caused it to move away from the jamb an inch or two. When he pushed against it firmly, the door swung all the way open and Durak saw the apartment had been ransacked—furniture turned over, drawers open, contents strewn about—as if someone were searching for something.

Without moving from his position at the doorway, Durak glanced to the left and checked the kitchen, then let his eyes move slowly to the right, scanning across the room to the opposite side, checking to make sure no one else was there. That's when he saw Parsi's body sitting upright in a chair between the sofa and the balcony door. Durak stepped forward and went as far as the sofa where he had a closer view.

Parsi was slumped forward with his head resting against his chest. Duct tape wound around his waist held him in place. The corner of a hand towel was stuffed in his mouth. Parsi moved to the end of the sofa, intending to remove the towel, then he noticed a dried pool of blood on the floor near Parsi's feet and a gaping slit across Parsi's throat. The gash was straight, neat, and except for the fact that it was gapped open, seemed to disappear beneath the fleshy creases of his neck.

"PAVA," Durak whispered. "Only an expert would have done work like that." But was it about the information he supplied about the program? How would they have known? How would they have—And then he remembered the men in the park that day when he met with Parsi. Only two were visible, but now he was certain they were not alone. "I should have been more careful," he whispered to himself.

An acrid odor filled the room. The smell of death and stale

blood. A wave of nausea swept over him, followed by a sense of deep sadness. Parsi had been recruited as an operative but turning him had taken longer than most. Over the course of their many meetings, they had become friends. Parsi was a capable scientist. Not deeply experienced, but a good man. A kind man. And he deeply loved his sister, Nazanin, and wanted a better—

Nazanin. Fear struck Durak in the pit of his stomach at the thought of her. If PAVA had found Parsi, they could surely find her. Durak had found her first before he contacted Parsi, and he had worked tirelessly to befriend her and cajole her into helping him meet her brother. He'd made countless promises to her. To get her out of the country. Set her up with a new life. A new future doing whatever she liked. Wherever she wanted. She introduced him to her brother and helped him convince her brother to work with him, to understand Iran's nuclear development program. It was urgent. Lives were at stake. Not just Iranian lives, but the lives of people throughout the world. A nuclear Iran, he argued, would set off a political chain reaction perhaps as devastating as any bomb. The world needed to know what Iran was really doing—to avoid a misunderstanding, if nothing else. To avoid a misapprehension of Iran's intentions. Most of the things he had said were lies—he had no authority to offer her anything except gratitude—but she didn't know that and the lies he had told her worked. After months of talking to her, Nazanin had agreed to introduce him to Parsi.

In the months that followed, Durak and Parsi met many times. Sometimes just the two of them. Sometimes with Nazanin joining them. On each occasion, they had followed an elaborate ruse, hoping to conceal their meetings from the prying eyes of neighborhood informants and from PAVA. But PAVA was thorough and didn't rely solely on human observations or informants to learn what a target was up to. They vetted everyone multiple times, then re-vetted them just to make sure, until they ran the vetting process to ground with no one else to talk to. Searched their homes, including those of co-workers and neighbors. Reviewed bank records, without or without permission, and eavesdropped on phone lines and internet accounts. No doubt, with Parsi working at an enrichment facility, they had gone deep into the lives of his family members, friends, acquaintances, and customers at the coffee shop he frequented. Everyone, everything, everywhere. They would certainly have known about Nazanin and her associations. He could only imagine what they might do to her if they suspected she'd been helping him.

✦ ✦ ✦

Durak took one more glance around Parsi's apartment, then turned toward the door intending to locate Nazanin and make sure she was safe. But as he started toward the door to leave, he heard footsteps coming up the stairs. Durak moved quickly to the kitchen, took a knife from an open drawer, then darted to a spot behind the front door.

By then, the sound of footsteps had stopped. Someone was outside in the corridor. Probably right in front of the door. He gripped the handle of the knife with his right hand and positioned his left foot forward to block the door when it opened. A moment later, he heard the hinge squeak and saw the door move ever so slightly but Durak's foot kept it from moving freely. The assailant realized something was blocking the door, so he pushed harder. When the door still didn't open, he shoved against it with his shoulder. Durak shoved back, leaning against the door with all his weight.

Both men pushed against each other, moving the door back and forth between them, one trying to get inside the apartment, the other trying to prevent him. Then Durak heard a pistol cock and in the next moment, a face appeared in the narrow space between the end of the door and the frame.

Instantly, Durak plunged the knife into the left eye of his assailant and stepped toward him to shove it deeper. Before he could do that, the man screamed in agony and fired the pistol. The noise was deafening, and Durak jumped at the sound of it, but the gun was in the assailant's right hand. The bullet went through the door a foot to Durak's left, missing him completely.

Durak let go of the door, and it came open wider. He leaned through the gap, withdrew the knife from the man's left eye, and plunged it into the other. The man howled in pain, let the gun slip from his grasp, and slid to the floor with both hands over his face. Blood streamed down the man's arms and dripped from his elbows.

A door opened across the corridor, but Durak ignored it. With deliberate but unhurried effort, he picked up the pistol, placed the muzzle against the man's head, and pulled the trigger. Brains and blood splattered against the doorframe and down the wall of the apartment. As the assailant's body slumped to one side, Durak shoved the pistol into the waistband of his trousers, wiped his hands on the man's shirt, and walked calmly to the stairs.

✦ ✦ ✦

A few minutes later, Durak arrived at Nazanin's apartment on the far side of the city. She answered the door on the first knock and appeared surprised to see him. She smiled at first, but her eyes darkened quickly when she noticed the look on his face. "What has happened?" she asked.

"You have to go," Durak urged. "Now." He pushed past her and entered the apartment.

"Why?" Nazanin asked as she closed the door behind him. "What is it? What has happened? Is it my brother? Is he okay? Where is my brother?"

"You can't worry about Parsi," he replied. "You have to leave. Get your things."

She moved away from him. "They have him, don't they? PAVA." When he failed to respond, she continued. "Does PAVA have him?" Durak glanced away and her eyes narrowed with anger. "I knew this would happen." She jabbed his chest with her index finger. "I knew it." Tears filled her eyes.

Nazanin was a beautiful woman and Durak had been attracted to her from the beginning, but he knew they could never be together. He was a Kurdish Christian, she was an Iranian Muslim, but right then, seeing eyes brimming with tears, he was tempted to forget their differences, tell her the truth, and take her in his arms. Already he imagined how it might feel to hold her close, pressing her body against his and holding her there until the despair evaporated. But he wasn't merely a Kurd or a Christian. He was an operative for Mossad and he had a duty to complete the assignment he'd been given. If he answered her questions, she would react to the news of her brother's death with crying and wailing that would alert the neighbors and delay them further. They didn't have time for that.

Instead of telling her what happened, he said, "We'll talk about it in the car after we are on the way."

"That's all you ever do," she said. "Talk. Talk. Talk. I want to know now." And she stamped her foot for emphasis.

Durak took her by the shoulders and turned her toward the bedroom. "Please," he urged. "Get your things. We must go. Now." Nazanin shrugged free of his grasp and folded her arms across her body, glaring at him in a defiant post.

"Go," he said, his voice louder and sterner than before and he pointed toward the room. "Get your things. We must leave immediately."

Nazanin continued to glare at him as if debating with herself about what to do. Finally, she gave a heavy sigh and put on a hijab. When it was in place, she snatched her jacket from a hanger in the closet and followed him out the door.

From the apartment, Durak and Nazanin drove toward Qom. She was seated in the back, her face covered except for her eyes, her body slumped low in the seat. When they were outside the city she asked, "Where are you taking me?"

"To a safe house in Qom," he replied.

"Nothing is safe in Qom," she grumbled.

"You'll be safe there."

"Why am I in danger?" She glanced at him through the rearview mirror. "Who is after me?"

He avoided a direct answer. "I promised your brother I would get you out. I'm doing my best to make that happen."

"What has happened to my brother?" she asked insistently. "Is he dead?" Again, Durak avoided an immediate answer. "Is my brother dead?" she demanded.

"Yes," Durak said finally.

"Who was it? Who killed him?"

"Do you have to ask?"

"Was it PAVA?"

"Yes." He spoke in a resolute tone. "It was PAVA."

In the mirror Durak saw her turn to look out the window, one hand covering her mouth. Her chin quivered and the muffled sound of her sobbing filled him with sadness.

They reached Qom later that afternoon and a few days after that, Nazanin was settled in a Mossad safehouse. But she was right about the nature of the location—anonymity was nearly impossible to maintain there. Still, it was the best he could do for her. Someone else would arrive in a few days and begin the process of getting her out of the country. As long as she stayed inside, she would be safe. He hoped.

✦ ✦ ✦

After changing cars in Qom, Durak started west. The following day, he slipped across the border into the Kurdistan Region of Iraq. By the end of the week, he reached Irbil, the Kurdish region's capital. On Monday, he met with Berkin Shoresh, a native Kurd who served as Durak's contact with Mossad.

When they were seated in an interview room, Durak asked,

"Did Nazanin get out?"

"We are working on that," Shoresh replied.

"Is there a problem?"

"No. But these things take time."

"Has she left Iran?"

"I do not think so. Not yet."

"Has she left Qom?"

"Yes."

Durak was encouraged. At least she was in the exit process. "Where is she?"

Shoresh looked away. "Better if you don't know too much."

"Are you certain she got out of Qom?"

"Positive," Shoresh replied.

Durak was uncomfortable with Shoresh's responses, but he was reluctant to press the matter further. He had done all he could do for Nazanin. Far more than some of his colleagues might have done under similar circumstances. He had no choice but to trust that others would follow through on the promises he'd made to her.

For the next two hours, Durak recounted the details of Iran's nuclear program that he had learned from Parsi. Iran's enrichment program was developing quickly. Faster than it was before sanctions had been imposed. Sometime within the next two months, they would have enough enriched uranium to build a nuclear bomb. "But even when they have accomplished that," he added, "their program will not pose an immediate threat to anyone."

"And why do you think that?"

"They need help developing a delivery device that is small enough to fit on one of their existing missiles."

"They remain committed to that method of delivery?"

"Yes," Durak said. "According to Parsi, they are convinced that using a missile is the best way."

"Their missiles do not have unlimited range."

"They only care about reaching one target."

"Israel."

Durak nodded. "Tel Aviv, to be exact."

"Not Jerusalem?"

"No," Durak answered. "They don't want to damage the holy sites."

"And where do they think they can obtain help making their device small enough for a missile?" Shoresh asked.

"Ideally, they would like for it to come from the Russians," Durak said. "Most of their missiles were designed with Russian assistance. They think Russian engineers would be able to work out the payload issues without any difficulty."

"Were you able to obtain any records on their efforts?"

Durak shrugged. "I have some documents, but I wasn't able to bring them with me."

"Physical documents?"

"Yes, but I had to leave in a hurry and wasn't able to go back for them."

Shoresh raised an eyebrow. "We heard about your trouble. It was dangerous breaking protocol like that. Going inside Parsi's apartment. And then the girl's apartment. You should have gone back for the documents instead."

Durak didn't want to argue about it. "Was I seen?" he asked.

"Not as far as we can tell."

Durak changed subjects. "Was Parsi able to insert the flash drive into his computer?"

Shoresh's eyes brightened. "Yes. He was."

"Did we get anything useful from it?"

"Oh, yes." Shoresh sounded pleased and looked pleased. "The flash drive has been very helpful."

"I suppose it has been discovered by now."

Shoresh shook his head. "Not yet."

Durak's eyes opened wide. "It's still working?"

Shoresh smiled. "Quite well," he said. "Better than expected."

"When they gave it to me, they said they could use it to infiltrate the entire system. Not just at the facility in Natanz, but throughout all of the agency's system."

Shoresh nodded with satisfaction. "It is amazing what one can accomplish these days, with the right technology."

CHAPTER FIVE

When Mehdi Kalhor left the meeting in Natanz, he decided to change his previous plans and visit Iran's other uranium enrichment sites. The meeting in Natanz was meant to obviate just such a facilities tour but after hearing the discussion at the meeting, he thought it best to check the work at the other sites, too. Visiting each of those locations took an extra week to complete and when he returned to Tehran he paid a visit to Mostafa Qorbani, Iran's Minister of Defense and Kalhor's immediate supervisor. They met in Qorbani's office.

"I understand you found everything in order with the enrichment program," Qorbani said. Kalhor hated it when news of his trips arrived back at the office ahead of him.

"The program appears to be making progress," Kalhor said.

Qorbani noticed the tentative nature of the response. "What's the rest of the story?"

"They're holding a steady pace with the work," Kalhor said, "but it's not the pace we had hoped for."

"Is there a reason for that?" Qorbani asked.

"Several."

"Such as?"

Roshan is a scientist," Kalhor replied. "He comes to the task with the methodical care of his profession."

"And what else is slowing them down?"

"Everyone knows the goal of the program is to create a nuclear device small enough to fit atop a missile. We don't have the technology for doing that right now and I think they all know it. Developing that technology ourselves will be a long-term project."

"Which is why they aren't rushing to process the material we have on hand?"

"Yes." Kalhor nodded. "And their processing equipment needs physical upgrades and software updates, too."

"Sanctions have made that difficult."

"Even without the upgrades," Kalhor said, "Roshan can produce the necessary uranium for one bomb, but everyone in the program, including Roshan, knows we can't create a device small enough to fit atop one of our existing rockets."

"That was supposed to be Parviz Attaran's job," Qorbani noted.

"Which is why Mossad assassinated him."

"Can Roshan find a way to do it?"

"Eventually, I am sure, but not within the proposed time limit."

"Did you learn anything else at the meeting?"

"One thing," Kalhor said with a sigh.

"What was that?"

"Roshan insists we have to test before we use whatever device he designs."

Qorbani frowned. "What kind of test?"

"He wants to detonate a device."

Qorbani shook his head. "Impossible. He already knows that is out of the question. We have discussed it many times before. If we detonate a nuclear device the US will know it immediately. The first test will come when we drop one of our bombs on Tel Aviv. That has always been the plan."

"That has been the plan," Kalhor acknowledged. "But should we not face the reality of the situation?"

Qorbani looked perturbed. "What are you suggesting? The plan has always been to use a missile as the means of delivery."

"We could achieve the same goal with ships," Kalhor said.

"We discussed that before, too," Qorbani replied. "I took it to the council, and they did not approve."

"But that was before Parviz Attaran was murdered. With him dead, the miniaturization issue is impossible to address in the time that we have. Placing a bomb in a cargo container would not require miniaturization."

"Will Roshan have enough material to create multiple nuclear devices?"

"Probably not, but that was all we were ever going to have. And if we sailed it into the harbor at Tel Aviv, we wouldn't need more than one."

"Just a bare bomb in a cargo box?"

"Yes."

"Wouldn't it be vulnerable to detection?" Qorbani asked.

"Not if we lined the container with lead."

"That would increase the weight of the container significantly."

"Not necessarily," Kalhor said. "Newer types of radiation shielding are available now that are much lighter than in the old days. And even if it were heavy, a shielded cargo container carrying only a single bomb wouldn't weigh more than the typical fully loaded container."

"Interesting," Qorbani mused.

"If we did it this way, we could send other ships with other devices to other locations."

"What would we do for those other locations?"

"The same thing as with Tel Aviv but using cargo containers with biological weapons and dirty bombs. One ship with the right material could land on the West Coast of the United States and release contaminants that would drift all the way across their entire country. Same with devices using conventional explosives wrapped with nuclear material. Fallout from the explosion would spread across the entire country."

"But would doing all of it by ships be enough?" Qorbani asked. "The council wanted a dramatic statement. Would a ship with a conventional bomb in it achieve that goal?"

"The attacks of 9-11 seriously disrupted the US economy," Kalhor said. "Some say it was teetering on the brink of economic collapse. And the pandemic of 2020 set off years of inflation, economic disruption, and unrest. The 9-11 attacks used only jet fuel. The pandemic involved a single pathogen. Imagine if a legitimate nuclear device destroyed Tel Aviv, and bombs released pathogens and radioactive waste over key US cities. Boston, New York, Los

Angeles. All at more or less the same time. The Americans would be caught completely by surprise. Panic and fear would paralyze them. Their thin veneer of invincibility would be shattered."

Qorbani seemed to like the idea and as their meeting came to an end, he authorized Kalhor to begin work on the logistical issues of using the containers. "But for now, only as an alternative," he cautioned. "And only for planning purposes. We must not relent in our quest for a nuclear device. That is our top priority."

✦ ✦ ✦

Kalhor left the meeting with Qorbani more convinced than ever that Western corruption had wrapped its tentacles around the Iranian government's leadership. Qorbani and the council—the Guardian Council—were committed to developing a nuclear bomb, but their goal was to dazzle the world with it as a demonstration of their brilliance, not to use it as a means of destroying the infidels of the West to bring glory to Allah. Kalhor was committed to attacking the West, but only as a way of plunging the world into apocalyptic chaos to prepare for the Mahdi's arrival and he didn't care how they achieved it, only that the end came and brought the Mahdi with it.

For the past two years, Kalhor had been meeting in secret with a group of men who shared his views. Gradually, carefully, he cultivated their beliefs and slowly transformed them from mere believers to true believers. He organized them as a cell of *The Almumin* under the teachings of Jamal Kazameyni, a reclusive Muslim cleric who believed that the official institutions of the Iranian Revolution had lost their way.

By contrast to the popular version of Islam predominant in Iran, *The Almumin* were faithful to the Quran and its teachings, but their faithfulness was informed by the deeper lessons of 9-11—that simple was better than complex; that ordinary devices were more effective than sophisticated technology; that success came to those who were willing to die for the hope of pleasing Allah rather than those who sent others to die in their place.

Members of Kalhor's cell had been recruited carefully and were meticulously vetted. Using the resources made available by his position, he had investigated each recruit as extensively as possible. Then, when he had exhausted that effort and was confident they could be trusted, he found ways to draw them into his orbit. Coffee. Dinner. A walk in the park. Lengthy discussions about the Islamic Revolution and the need to renew the effort to cleanse Islam from Western corruption. Only then did he carefully, incrementally introduce his ideas, the core of which was a radical belief in the Mahdi—a messianic figure who would arise to cleanse the world of corruption and bring them to belief in the real Allah.

To his surprise, Kalhor found that many members of his cell were unaware of who the Mahdi was and what his mission would be. This was frustrating at first, but then he realized it provided him a great opportunity to shape their beliefs. Not to corrupt the true understanding of Islam, but to emphasize the parts that served his purposes most—devotion to Allah as expressed through radical action. Placing devotion to Allah above devotion to family, friends, or the pursuit of wealth. Risking one's life to turn the world toward true belief.

Gradually, Kalhor added more recruits and their meetings moved on to discussions of how to create circumstances conducive to the Mahdi's appearance. A nuclear explosion seemed best to some, and the US seemed the best target. But how could they attack the US from such a distance with only conventional means of delivery? How could a group of citizens obtain an explosive device capable of destroying a densely populated city? Could such a device be delivered without detection? Were their views merely a simplified version of the popular belief in nuclear weapons as the only means of assuring success? Kalhor was patient, methodically instructing them and bringing them along to his idea of destroying the West and ending its practices of injustice and corruption. Progress was slow until Kalhor met Ivan Saltanov. After that, the careful, patient approach picked up speed.

Saltanov was an Iranian who had lived most of his life in Moscow where he attended school as a child and went on to study at the Moscow Institute of Physics and Technology. While a student at the Institute, Saltanov met Ravil Kozlovsky, a part-time professor in physics. Kozlovsky came to the classroom after a career with Sredmash, an agency within the former Soviet Ministry for Atomic Energy that was responsible for developing the Soviet Union's nuclear weapons. Kozlovsky had been in charge of Russia's weapons miniaturization program and often regaled his students with stories from the 1970s and '80s about Russia's infamous suitcase bombs—nuclear devices small enough to fit inside a duffel bag— some of which had been buried at remote locations in Canada to be available for future use against targets in North America. Two of the bombs had gone missing and, after passing through several interested parties, were brought to the US where, according to the stories, they were carefully concealed. One in a mausoleum in California, the other at a similar location in New York. Kozlovsky never said what happened to them after that.

Kalhor thought the stories were Soviet fables until the war in Ukraine began and Putin started hinting about the use of nuclear weapons. Discussion of using tactical nuclear devices brought up the old stories about suitcase bombs. With the renewed interest, a friend who lived in the US took a radiation detector to the supposed crypt in New York and discovered unusually high levels of gamma rays, a clear indication that a significant quantity of uranium was present. Kalhor dispatched a team to investigate and, after a night-time raid of the crypt, discovered a casket that contained a duffel bag. Inside the duffel bag was an explosive device. An examination of the device revealed that it was, indeed, a nuclear bomb still capable of working.

Encouraged by finding the first device, Kalhor sent a second team to California where they recovered a similar device from the attic of a garage in Anaheim. Like the first device, this one was in a duffel bag but unlike the first it was unshielded. For almost half a century it had been sitting atop the joists above the space where successive owners had parked their cars. From one owner to the next, no one noticed the bag or the excessive amount of radiation it emitted.

After removing the device from the garage in Anaheim, it was wrapped in a lightweight radiation shield, then placed inside a makeshift containment box and hauled to Florida in a rental truck. The one in New York was handled much the same way. Eventually, both devices arrived at a warehouse in Apalachicola, Florida where they were placed inside a lead-lined container in a vault-like room that had been built in the corner of a building purchased under the guise of storage for a construction company.

Kalhor would have preferred to have the devices somewhere closer to the Mediterranean so he could easily transport them to Tel Aviv for detonation but having them in the US seemed more appropriate. America was really the issue, not Israel. Only the older Imams and radicals, stuck in a paradigm from the 1970s, held a grudge against Israel. The younger group, coming to power now, was convinced that the US was the real culprit with its hedonistic lifestyle infecting everyone, Muslim and Christian alike. Once it was eliminated, everyone else would fall in line. And besides, doing it that way meant Kalhor was in control, which he very much liked.

Having found two of the suitcase devices, Kalhor became convinced there were others hidden in Canada—dozens, perhaps—just as the stories had suggested. Bijan Abbadi, one of the first recruits to Kalhor's cell, was assigned to locate them.

✦ ✦ ✦

Kalhor's other idea for attacking the West involved the release of pathogens capable of creating a pandemic. After suggesting the idea, he studied it further and found that although it sounded plausible at first, actually doing it was more problematic than using the suitcase bombs. For one thing, research laboratories were the best source for obtaining quantities of viral material, but most of those laboratories had only small amounts of the deadliest viruses and those were kept under lock and key. If he could somehow obtain a significant amount of even one pathogen, he still had the problem of dispersal.

An explosion big enough to spread a pathogen over a wide area would generate more than enough heat to kill the pathogen. The most effective means of distribution was through person-to-person contact. An infected person wandering the streets of a major city could spread a disease to hundreds in a single day. Those hundreds could spread it to hundreds more the following day. Meaning that, in theory, by using dozens of infected people, a major health crisis could be instigated almost overnight. All it would take was a group of people willing to die to make it happen. The men in Kalhor's cell were just such a group, but the project was a long-term affair, and he wasn't sure they had enough time to do it.

Nevertheless, one member of the cell, Karim Nawab, expressed an interest in attempting to overcome the difficulties posed by limited pathogen access and by distribution. Kalhor agreed to assist him with whatever support he could supply, and Nawab set to work figuring out how to effectively procure and distribute deadly biological material.

CHAPTER SIX

n Ukraine, Taras Irvanets' platoon and many others continued to press the attack against the Russian troops, driving them ever northward toward the border with Belarus and westward toward the far end of the country. Their effort proved far more successful than anyone expected but it had come at a high price. Many Ukrainian soldiers, some of them younger than Taras and many with even less military experience than his, had been killed. The countryside was littered with damaged or destroyed vehicles. Everywhere, houses and farms and commercial buildings lay in ruins.

Enormous amounts of ammunition had been expended in the effort, too. So much so that many Ukraine troops were intermittently forced to use confiscated Russian weapons and ammunition, not as a supplement to their own stocks but as their primary source of weaponry. The West had hinted at help but, as yet little had arrived, and Ukraine had been forced to fight on its own. It had been a scary time for all, and a wonderfully exhilarating time for many. Improvising. Adapting. Overcoming. Living one day at a time. Driving the evil tyrants from their country.

Adaptation and perseverance hadn't been limited only to Ukrainian soldiers, either. Since the Russian invasion began, ordinary Ukrainian citizens of every age and station had been forced to adapt, first to unpredictable artillery strikes and electrical power outages, then to shortages and lack of basic essentials. Food, water, and heat were scarce. Normal life, whatever it had been, was disrupted seemingly beyond return. Roads became impassable. Schools and shops were closed. Many churches, too. Farmers had been forced to abandon their fields. Daily life became increasingly bleak. The future all but lost in uncertainty.

Those who were able fled to the western end of the country and slipped over the border into Poland. From there, they took the train to relatives and friends living in Western Europe. Thousand made that trek. Thousands more filled every available accommodation in Poland and Slovakia. Employment was difficult. Accommodations scarce. Relief agencies were stressed. At least on that end of Ukraine, and in Poland, there were no bombs or artillery strikes. No drones overhead. No roaming bands of paramilitary thugs raping the women and children and killing the men.

Ukraine's government had been forced to adapt, too. From the first day of the war, Zelensky had insisted on conducting business from the capital in Kyiv, and he had adhered to that practice, no matter how difficult it had been. Since the Russian invasion in 2014, the government had constructed an elaborate underground system of tunnels that allowed government officials to move between buildings without risking exposure on the street. Facilities had been added to the complex to accommodate core functions, allowing them to conduct business on a more or less permanent basis from reinforced concrete bunkers that were connected through the tunnel system.

President Zelensky had used the underground system to move daily from location to location, dodging Russian attacks and avoiding the constant threat of assassination. He appeared every day in public, first here, then there, in a concerted effort to keep public morale high, but he conducted official business from the secure underground bunkers located deep beneath the streets of Kyiv. Desperate to hold onto his country, he contacted everyone he knew in the West in a plea for help. It was a successful effort but one that left Zelensky feeling trapped, cloistered, cut off from the world, and not himself.

Then an advisor recalled Zelensky's life as an entertainer, before politics, and suggested he should use that experience to his advantage. "And we should reach beyond the traditional routes of communication heads of state have used in the past."

"How?"

"Social media," the advisor suggested. "We can do live broadcasts directly to individual users and say whatever we like."

Zelensky liked the idea but officials from the established permanent government thought appearances of any kind on social media were beneath the president's station as head of state. Those who came with him from the election campaign thought it was a brilliant idea and exactly the thing he should do. Zelensky agreed but insisted the public addresses should be directed primarily toward Ukrainian citizens. "Give me some talking points," he said. "And set up my office for the presentation."

"When do you want to make it?" someone asked.

"Now!" he insisted.

Zelensky's security detail raised no objection to the broadcast but did object to the use of his office as the backdrop. "You should remain in one of the underground bunkers," they said. "It's not safe for you to be up there. Especially if you want to do it on a schedule. Anything done at a regular time from a regular place would be too risky."

Despite their warning, Zelensky insisted they go forward with the broadcast, and two hours later, with little preparation, he appeared live on social media platforms reaching around the world, urging Ukrainian citizens to resist Russian troops in every location and by every means possible. "On the highways and byways. In the streets of your villages and towns, and in the fields throughout the countryside." He urged citizens of the world to join the Ukrainian effort by contributing to the many humanitarian aid campaigns that had offered support for the region.

It was a brilliant presentation with hints of Winston Churchill at the beginning of World War II. "Fight them in the fields. Fight them in the streets. Fight them wherever they appear. They will never take us."

From his first appearance, Zelensky's addresses on social media were a tremendous success and became a daily regular seen by millions of viewers worldwide. The war became a popular topic on social media sites around the world with user comments and uploads appearing almost at once in a groundswell of support.

European politicians took notice and joined the rush to social media, pressing for sanctions against Russia as a sovereign nation, and against Russian corporations, urging EU nations, of which most were members, to ban and boycott commerce with Russia. Individual nations responded with sanctions and seizures of Russian assets. Individual citizens from around the world responded, too, and donations to humanitarian aid organizations soared.

✦ ✦ ✦

In the US, President Martin Jackson met with his staff to review conditions in Ukraine, as he had every day since the Russian invasion began. The meeting was orderly but lively. Some argued it was time to publicly align with the popular effort to support Ukraine by announcing US sanctions against Russia. Others argued it was too early for overt US involvement. "This is a European conflict. We should keep it that way a while longer."

Jackson agreed with the latter. "We need to frame this as primarily a European problem," he said. "Not a conflict between the US and Russia."

Sarah Foster, the president's chief of staff, was seated beside him. "Frame it that way," she interjected. "But don't state it that way."

"Right," Jackson confirmed. "As long as this war remains in that context, Putin has to respond to it on those terms. We can keep him confined in that box. Everyone will see him as the aggressor. Anything he says about 'the West' will be viewed as nothing more than a justification for the brutality he's visiting on the citizens of Ukraine. And make no mistake about it, they have been brutally assaulting Ukrainian citizens. By some reports, Russian aggression has displaced upwards of fifteen million innocent citizens. If we get involved or make reference to our involvement in specific terms, all of that will change. We'll become the focus, and this will be framed as a Russia versus the US conflict."

"And if we stay out for now," someone added, "everything Russia does, and everything Putin says, will only magnify the perception of a threat to Europe. As if he means to take it all. That's a good context for us, in terms of how he's perceived by the world."

"He does mean to take it all," someone argued.

"That isn't certain," another countered.

"It's certain he wants to reunite the Russian Empire."

"Sitting tight, for now, gives us the added advantage of providing space for Congress to take up the cause, especially in the House. They're always running for re-election. Their constituencies are overwhelmingly in favor of helping Ukraine. The members will have to come out in favor of it, too, and that will be helpful for us when we *do* start mobilizing relief."

The discussion continued until President Jackson had heard enough. He glanced at his chief of staff with a determined look. "Okay," she said to the group. "Good comments from everyone. We're holding the line on the political front. No major commitments on Ukraine support yet, but don't say it explicitly. We're consulting with European allies and considering all options. Make sure your people stay on message. Russia is the aggressor; Ukraine only wants to remain independent. And emphasize the threat this invasion poses to Europe. Nuance images of World War II, but no specific references."

Someone from the back of the room asked, "What about the energy issue?"

"What about it?"

"Europe gets most of its oil and gas from Russia. Their invasion of Ukraine and our 'non-response response' is sure to disrupt that arrangement. What's our position on that?"

"We could open talks about it with individual EU members," someone suggested.

President Jackson nodded. "I plan to call the British." He glanced at Foster again. "You have that on the list?"

"I'll make sure it's on your call sheet." She turned to a staffer, who made a note of the call on her memo pad.

When the meeting ended, President Jackson paused long enough for a cup of coffee, then met with Bruce Ford, the Secretary of Defense, and General George Halstead, the Chairman of the Joint Chiefs. They gathered in the Oval Office, and when everyone was settled, Jackson turned to Ford. "What's our latest estimate for how long Ukraine can hold out without our direct support?"

"Two months," Secretary Ford suggested.

Jackson glanced over to Halstead. "George, what do your people say?"

"Maybe two," Halstead replied, nodding thoughtfully. "That's our official estimate, but there are a lot of variables in that number. And that's the upward bound of the estimate."

"Are you suggesting it's inaccurate?"

"No, Mr. President, but the situation on the ground is fluid, and Ukraine doesn't hold equal amounts of everything."

"More bullets, not so many rockets?"

"Yes, sir. Ammunition is cheap, and everyone has it in large quantities, but this has quickly turned into a missile and drone war. They don't have a large stockpile of drones."

"So, the numbers are soft."

Halstead nodded. "There are a number of variables that could turn this thing very quickly in the wrong direction."

"What's the biggest variable?"

"Rate of depletion on their consumables is a big one."

"How fast they use up their ammo."

"Yes, Mr. President. How fast they use up their missiles and drones."

"Are they using it faster than you expected?"

"In terms of bullets and grenades, yes, sir. We suspect that's because most of Ukraine's soldiers tend to be younger and with less experience. And they are supporting many volunteer groups."

"Paramilitary," Jackson suggested.

"Some of them are less than paramilitary," Halstead noted. "Zelensky called for everyone to take up arms. That has mobilized a large number of individuals who have organized themselves into neighborhood patrols. Some of those groups have joined the regular troops at the front. It's been popular with their students."

"Why didn't they sign up with the military?"

"Some have, but they've needed bodies in the fight. So, they've accepted most volunteers without much vetting. Even the ones who volunteered through official channels have been processed quickly.

None of them are getting the extensive training they would have received under normal circumstances."

Jackson turned to Ford. "So, we have two months to come up with a plan to help them. Where are we with that?"

"We've been assessing their needs and analyzing that against what we can offer and how quickly we can get it there."

"What does that mean?"

"Our stockpiles are not unlimited, and many of the things they would like to receive from us are not only expense but require considerable lead time to restock for our own use."

"Force readiness?"

"Yes, sir," Ford replied. "Obviously, as George mentioned, the world is awash with standard bullets. Providing large quantities of rounds for their rifles isn't a problem. But they can't win this war with just rifles and ammunition."

Halstead spoke up. "And in case there is any doubt in your mind, Mr. President, Ukraine can't win without outside support."

"Our support?"

"One way or the other," Halstead replied. "Either directly from us or indirectly through NATO. They need us. And it goes beyond arms and munitions. They need intelligence, logistics, cyber support, and battlefield management. The core of their army is well-trained and reasonably well-equipped, but they don't have the depth to hold out for long in terms of troops, material, or anything else."

"A war of attrition works against them."

"Yes, sir."

"But they're motivated, right?"

Ford answered, "Popular support from Ukraine citizens has

blossomed into a popular uprising in the country. Globally, it is turning into a movement. Their use of social media has proved to be a brilliant move. Zelensky has been inspiring. And they have been innovative in their armed resistance."

Jackson frowned. "Innovative?"

"They've been modifying civilian technology to suit their military needs, especially with the paramilitary groups. And it's beyond the typical gas bombs and IEDs we've come to expect. Some of these citizen groups are re-tasking commercial drones for military purposes."

Jackson was intrigued. "The small ones you can buy online?"

Ford nodded. "The very same ones we could buy at a big-box retailer."

"This is something we might want to consider for our own troops going forward," Halstead suggested. "Using commercial drones to provide reconnaissance might be a cheaper way than buying through a military contractor. They're light. Easy to operate. My grandson has one. We were using it in the backyard the other day."

Jackson nodded. "They're determined to win this," he noted.

"Yes," Ford said. "We've even heard reports of them modifying delivery drones to carry things like anti-tank grenades. Delivery drones are larger and more powerful. They can lift as much as five-hundred pounds."

Jackson seemed to move on. "We need to develop a plan to supply these people. They don't intend to give up. Both parties in Congress are starting to voice their support for greater US involvement."

"Yes, sir, Mr. President," Halstead replied enthusiastically. "The sooner, the better."

"Do you think they can hold out for two months?"

"Their basic supplies might last that long, but strategically speaking, they're in a vulnerable position with very little margin for error. I can't speak to the political considerations, but from the perspective of fighting a war, they are in a tenuous situation."

Jackson asked, "What would you like to do, George?"

"I think we should start moving things in their direction."

"What kind of things?"

"Missiles, drones, missile-defense systems, artillery shells."

"How would we get it to them?"

Ford spoke up. "If we're going to supply them, then I suggest we at least consider using non-military delivery companies for as much of it as possible."

Jackson seemed to agree. "Will they fly into a combat zone?"

"I'm sure they will if we pay them enough."

Halstead added, "We don't want to send an air force transport over there with our markings on it. It would be better to have a European country supply the Ukrainians while we re-supply the provider."

"For instance, Germany supplies Ukraine, we restock Germany?" Jackson asked.

"Yes, Mr. President."

Jackson thought momentarily, then said, "I still want to hold off on doing anything just a little longer. We need to give the Europeans time to act first, before we get heavily involved."

"But will they?"

"I think so," Jackson said. "I'm speaking with some of them today and I'll know more after that. I assume we have people over there in Ukraine assessing the situation."

Halstead avoided a direct response. "We could start sending supplies to them this afternoon, Mr. President."

✦ ✦ ✦

Despite President Jackson's tepid public response, European leaders showed no hesitancy in reacting to the situation. Alarmed over Russia's invasion of Ukraine and the threat to their independence, they took a much bolder public stance than their American counterparts. They adopted Zelensky's practice of providing internet audiences with daily updates on Russia's actions and stoked traditional media with reports of the latest atrocities committed by Russian troops and their associated paramilitary units.

Ukrainian soldiers and volunteers from Ukrainian paramilitary groups responded, too, uploading footage of the fighting to their pages on YouTube and other online video sites. Their posts included graphic images of people wounded and dying, of houses and buildings blown apart by indiscriminate shelling from Russian artillery, and of Russian soldiers looting the homes of Ukrainians who had fled ahead of their advance. They also included videos of civilians being dragged from their homes by Russian soldiers and members of Russian paramilitary units. Many captured in that way were loaded onto trucks bound for the interior of Russia, where most assumed they would be treated as slaves.

But by far, the most popular images were of Russian tanks and armored vehicles burning in the streets and open fields. Some set ablaze by expertly aimed military rockets, others from homemade devices used by angry citizens who braved the overwhelming odds to lob gas bombs at them or climb atop them to open the turret hatch and drop the bombs inside. Those images were viewed by millions all over the world and galvanized global support for Ukraine's struggle to expel the Russians.

Spurred on by the response, European governments called for the immediate delivery of support of every kind, including military, humanitarian, and economic. France led the way in calling for EU members to provide Ukraine with tanks, drones, and artillery shells.

Millions of private viewers responded by donating to relief agencies attempting to address the growing Ukrainian refugee crisis. Celebrities joined, too, announcing their support for the cause and asking their fans and followers to join them in donating, even if only in small amounts.

With the groundswell of support for political cover, the EU announced sweeping economic sanctions against Russia—freezing Russian assets and cutting off the purchase of Russian oil by EU nations. Russian banks and financial institutions were barred from using the SWIFT international payments system, and major multinational corporations announced plans to exit the Russian market. Russian oligarchs who owned property in foreign countries saw their property seized. Within days, financial activity between Russia and the West dropped to less than half its prewar level.

✦ ✦ ✦

With the EU following through on sanctions, President Jackson initiated the first US response to the crisis by sending a wing of F-16 aircraft to Lask Air Base, a NATO facility in Lask, Poland. Not long after that, a division of troops from the US 82nd Airborne—about ten thousand in total—arrived at Lask as well. The troop movement was announced as a deployment, giving the intended impression that it was done in direct response to the situation in Ukraine. Few news outlets noted it was part of a routinely scheduled troop rotation between NATO member countries. Nevertheless, the appearance of US action had the intended effect of boosting morale throughout the coalition.

The following month—in a deal negotiated between Poland, NATO, and Ukraine—the US transferred control of the newly arrived F-16s to Poland. With the aircraft under Polish control, Poland transferred an equal number of its MiG-29s to Ukraine. As with the US troop deployment, most news outlets reported the arrival of the F-16s as a repositioning of US military assets to bolster NATO's presence in the region. Most failed to mention the deployment was part of a transaction that included the transfer of Polish MiGs to Ukraine.

Two weeks after the exchange of aircraft, the US began sending direct military aid to Ukraine. President Jackson urged other NATO countries to do the same. Even though most member nations were already supplying Ukraine with support, the US presence cleared the way for them to increase that aid. Military hardware, ammunition, and weapons begin moving toward Ukraine from multiple sources.

While public attention was diverted by the obvious effort to resupply Ukraine's military, a US battlefield management unit arrived in Poland and set up a special command-and-control hub at Lask Air Base. Arriving amid the hustle and bustle of increased base activity, no mention of it was made in the press.

Along with supporting personnel, the battlefield group brought two E-3 AWACS aircraft. Both planes were equipped with the latest in management systems that connected their onboard computers with global satellite and radar systems. The aircraft were deployed to the NATO base at Lask but routinely patrolled along the border between Poland and Ukraine. Operating solely within Polish airspace, the airplanes' onboard system had an unimpeded view of Ukraine that extended from the Polish border in the west to the Russian border in the east. As soon as the planes were airborne, every military unit in the country came into view.

To avoid the suggestion of direct US involvement, information from the E-3s was transmitted to the management group's hub on the ground at Lask. From there, it was shared with Ukrainian personnel for relay to the field using their own hub. Though the two groups were in the same building and only a few feet apart, their systems operated independently. Access to information from the US hub allowed Ukrainian commanders to deploy their troops and equipment for maximum effectiveness on the battlefield in Ukraine. The flow of updated information produced obvious results on the ground.

✦ ✦ ✦

By August, aid and assistance from the West allowed Ukrainian forces to turn back the Russian advance. At the same time, Russian units encountered significant troop casualties and equipment losses in numbers far higher than their pre-war estimates had predicted. Higher even than Western analysts had expected.

In the western half of the country, Russian units were driven from Ukraine's interior and forced to retreat north into Belarus and west toward the border. A Ukrainian surge across the southern area of the country along the Black Sea coast drove them from Odesa. Sooner than anyone imagined, Russia's military presence was reduced to the Donbas Region, an area along Ukraine's common border with Russia that included the provinces of Donetsk and Luhansk. In the south, they were pushed back to Crimea. Repeated attempts by the Russian army to mount a counter-offensive and break out from the region were unsuccessful.

Unable to advance from its position in the east, Russia turned to the use of missiles, drones, and artillery, delivering long-range attacks on both military and civilian targets in a steady, brutally destructive pounding meant to destroy Ukraine one building at a time. Russian generals hoped that a sustained, grinding attack would not only degrade Ukraine's ability to exist but also break the will of Ukrainian citizens.

With the help of NATO support, Ukrainian military units responded in kind, delivering their version of a sustained long-range attack. Ukrainian pilots shot Russian aircraft from the sky. Drones and missiles destroyed Russian equipment one piece at a time. And Ukrainian troops eliminated Russian infantry one unit at a time.

Yet the devastating effects of the prolonged artillery-intensive engagement became obvious in Ukraine's urban centers. Damaged buildings and burned-out vehicles marred the landscape.

The intensity put a strain on Ukraine's infrastructure, too. Roads, bridges, and railways took heavy losses. It also bore heavily on the Ukrainian people. With seemingly random explosions from artillery shells and rockets appearing with no advanced warning, normal life in the eastern half of the country disappeared, subsumed by a malaise as dreary and bleak as the war-ravaged landscape. Citizens fled west, crowding into cities, towns, and villages along the Polish border.

Although Ukraine bore the brunt of the attacks, Russian forces on the ground, and even the Russian people living far from the fighting, were not unscathed. Stockpiles of artillery shells, rockets, and armored equipment that had been accumulated over the past ten years—and some of it from even longer ago than that—rapidly disappeared. Equipment returned from Russia's furtive engagement in Afghanistan and a few pieces from the Vietnam era met their final end on the fields of Ukraine. Empty warehouses and depots deep in Russia's interior made the losses all too obvious.

Russia's long-range attack brought the desired destruction, but it soon proved unsustainable as domestic manufacturing was unable to keep up with the demand for artillery shells, drones, and missiles. Shortages of those items quickly appeared at the front, hampering Russia's ability to fight. Troop losses rose, too, depleting many units well below full fighting strength. And in Russia, the steady stream of dead and wounded caused unrest at home as loved ones who'd been promised a short and painless war now learned they faced a long and bitter fight.

CHAPTER SEVEN

With the war in Ukraine at a stalemate, and with serious shortages unavoidable, Putin convened a meeting of advisors in Moscow to review the situation. The gathering was held in a secure conference room at the Russian Department of Defense's main building and was attended by senior military and government leaders. Among them were Nikolai Patrushev, Secretary of the Security Council; Sergei Naryshkin, head of the Foreign Intelligence Service; and Sergei Shoigu, Russia's Minister of Defense. Also in attendance was Valery Gerasimov, the Army Chief of Staff, and several officers overseeing operations on the ground in Ukraine.

Putin spent the first hour of that meeting railing against an increased US presence at NATO bases in Poland and the steadily increasing flow of military equipment and supplies from the West. "They are intentionally trying to provoke us," he said. "Flaunting their F-16 jets. Parading their 82nd Airborne. Reminding us of what they did to our equipment in Iraq and to our soldiers in Afghanistan."

It was a rant familiar to everyone in the room. They'd heard it many times before. America was attempting to humiliate Russia. Every Russian misstep, every failure, and every frustration, always attributed to the US. Those who were present that day could recite most of what Putin said from memory. Since the invasion of Ukraine, the rants had been more emotional and further removed from reality. The most senior of those present that day had talked about it among themselves, before the meeting, wondering when they should step in to stop Putin by force. One had gone so far as to ask, "Has it not occurred to him that if what he says about the Americans were true—that they have opposed us everywhere and caused all of our problems—they would be mightier than God?" But no one dared ask that openly.

Only Patrushev, from the Security Council, attempted to steer Putin away from one more angry diatribe and toward a productive discussion about the practical issues Russian troops faced on the ground. "It might be time to consider using our newest equipment," Patrushev suggested. "There's no point in having it if we aren't going to use it in a war like this."

"Out of the question," Putin replied tersely.

All along Putin had insisted Russia's older equipment would be adequate for the task of suppressing Ukraine. "If we hit them hard and fast," he had argued, "the war will be over before they can respond. No one will have to see our best."

Most Russian officials, certainly everyone in the room that day, understood his real opposition to using the latest equipment—he did not want to risk seeing it fail in combat against equipment from the West.

"Never mind about equipment," Putin added with a dismissive gesture. "We have plenty and even the least is far superior to anything Ukraine can deploy. It is the Americans who are the real enemy of the Russian people. They are preparing to invade our territory. Already they are assembling their troops in Poland. Their recent deployment of soldiers and planes is but the beginning. Soon thousands and thousands will follow. We must hold our best in reserve, lulling the Americans into believing that what we have shown them is all that we have. And when they cross the border into Ukraine, we will smash them to pieces."

When he paused again, Valery Gerasimov spoke up. "Mr. President, we are now very low on ammunition. Even hand grenades are in short supply. Some of our troops have been unable to engage Ukraine units because of it."

One of the generals from the front of the room spoke up. "We are severely undermanned in all branches due to the dwindling number of new troops we have sent to the field. Those soldiers we have sent have gone to the front with very little training and no experience."

An officer from the battlefield joined in. "The older stock of ammunition we have been using doesn't function well, either. In some instances, not at all."

The meeting descended into a free-for-all of criticisms and ideas. Putin seemed content to let them talk.

"Mr. President," someone said, "our men are brave Russians. They will gladly fight to the death for our country. But they cannot respond with sticks and stones when their opponents have the very best the West has to offer."

"We need more of everything," another added.

"Why are our best units still in their barracks and our best tanks still in storage?"

Putin raised his hand in a call for silence. "As I am sure you all are aware, Ukraine and its allies in the West have shown greater resolve than we anticipated. And let me assure you, I understand the situation we are in and the hardships you've had to endure. Our shortages are only temporary. We have increased our domestic production and the results will soon be evident. But we cannot commit our best units or best equipment to the effort. We are holding them in reserve."

"In reserve?"

"Against what?"

"Against uncertainty," Patrushev said with resolve.

"And in anticipation of opportunity," Sergei Naryshkin added. Everyone laughed but Naryshkin was unflinching, and the laughter quickly teetered away.

"We are settling old scores," Putin responded. "And we are fighting to win, but we must not lose sight of the broader goal."

Someone commented quickly. "We thought Ukraine was the goal."

Putin seemed not to notice. "At my installment in office as President of the Russian Republic, Patriarch Krill, head of the church in Moscow, appointed me Chief Exorcist to bring about the De-Satanification of Ukraine." Most in the room stared at the floor. "And he named me Defender of Christianity throughout the civilized world. I hold these titles, in addition to the title of president, as a sacred trust. They are inseparable. President, Defender of the Faith, Chief Exorcist. They are as one. To that end, we are redeeming the Mother Land and re-asserting Russia's rightful place among the nations of the world as a statement of the righteousness of our cause and to bring the world into compliance with the Gospel. For centuries, godless Americans have scoured the earth for its resources and used them for the satisfaction of their lust for more. Buying, buying, buying. Consuming everything, but never satisfied with anything. Wasting everything. Physical resources, the minds of youth everywhere, the bodies of the poor and ignorant. Draining the life from everyone and everything to fuel their profligate lifestyle. This war in Ukraine is only the beginning of the end for that. A first step in liberating the world from American impurity and corruption. A first step toward putting everything right again."

Gerasimov, seated to Putin's left, spoke up. "These are laudable goals, Mr. President, but in order for these goals to become reality, we have to find a way forward in Ukraine."

"What about the paramilitary units?" someone asked. "The Wagner Group and others like them are in Ukraine. We've seen them in operation. Couldn't they be put to better use?" Wagner was an elite paramilitary organization that functioned as Putin's private army.

"Not those godless brutes," someone grumbled.

"Perhaps we need godless brutes for this fight."

"Godless brutes to impose a godly order on the godless Ukrainians?" someone chided.

"Wagner members are good men," Putin snapped. "Perhaps overly zealous at times, but righteous in their efforts nonetheless."

"Perhaps," someone conceded. "But they tend not to follow orders."

"None of the paramilitary groups follows orders. They are totally disruptive."

"We can get more men without yielding to paramilitary groups. We'll snatch them off the street if we have to. But we cannot train them to our usual standards quickly enough."

"We don't need trained soldiers."

"We need bodies more than they need training."

"That is correct," Putin said. "We're not looking for tactical geniuses. They only need to point a rifle and pull the trigger. Russian bravery will do the rest."

"If that is to be our strategy, the body count will be even higher than it already is."

A Putin supporter countered, "That is a fact of war in every war. People fight. People die."

"Still, we need rifles and bullets if we're going to fight a war."

"And missiles."

"Maybe not the best missiles. But we need *something*. We are running out of even the outdated stock. We've used materiel from previous eras all the way back to Afghanistan in the 1980s."

Putin tried to wrangle them under control. "What weapons are working most effectively for us?"

"Drones, artillery shells, and rockets."

"Our aircraft are effective, but we've lost about a hundred already."

"And tanks?"

"We've lost 3,500 of those."

"Mostly the oldest of the old ones," someone noted.

"But 3,500. That's a lot of tanks to lose, of any kind."

"I've seen the reports." Putin seemed to be running out of patience. "How is that so? No one has been able to tell me. Ukrainian tanks aren't that much better than ours. Are you certain the numbers in our reports are correct?"

"Absolutely."

"Most of the losses have come from small Ukrainian units and groups using improvised weapons."

"Foot soldiers?" Putin asked.

"Yes, Mr. President."

"And from drones."

"The Americans," Putin grumbled. "This is the work of the Americans. They are supplying these weapons and telling the Ukrainians how to use them."

"Some of the drones are military drones," someone noted. "But most of them are improvised commercial drones. Off-the-shelf. Like you can buy online."

Someone from the back spoke up. "We're having trouble everywhere, Mr. President. We can't keep the trucks moving toward the front. Our domestic manufacturers are overwhelmed. The supply chain is practically nonexistent."

"What about our allies?" someone asked. "Iran can make drones. They're low-tech but effective."

"And cheap."

"They can produce small arms munitions, too."

"Their products tend to be of a lower grade. Less agile and less reliable."

"Agility and reliability won't matter as long as they can make them in large enough quantities."

"What about missiles? I hear they have a couple of good battle-field rockets."

"Iran will supply those items to us," Shoigu said, "but they will want us to help with their nuclear program in exchange."

Putin grimaced. "We should keep the nuclear question at bay, for now. We don't want to become entangled with that while our supply issues are unresolved."

"If we don't resolve our ordinance issues, none of the other shortages will matter. Lack of these items is limiting our ability to fight."

"We will find the things we need," Putin assured. His voice was strained, and he seemed on the verge of another angry outburst, but he forced himself to remain calm and continued. "Our friends will help us, once they realize this is an opportunity for them to break free of US control and flourish on their own. We only need to explain our situation to them in those terms. They will give us all that we need to win this war."

✦ ✦ ✦

When the meeting concluded and the others had left the room, Putin and Naryshkin met alone. "I want you to talk to the Chinese," Putin said. "They could supply us with all the weapons we need. Talk to them. See if they will help us."

"It would be great if they would," Naryshkin said. "That would solve our problems and we could avoid getting entangled with Iran and their Middle Eastern issues."

"Pay them a visit. As soon as possible. But keep it out of the media," Putin cautioned. "There should be no official announcements."

"Yes, sir," Naryshkin replied. "Although leaking it to the press would not be a bad thing. We could use it to pressure the US into pushing Zelensky toward an agreement. Withdrawal from the east. We stand where we are."

Putin seemed surprised. "We haven't discussed peace talks."

"No," Naryshkin acknowledged. "But won't we? We need to end the fighting so we can move on to other things."

Putin was dismissive. "If we don't win here, there will be no greater things for us to do. Americans only understand power in terms of winning. A negotiated peace would be viewed by everyone as a loss to Ukraine. I am not interested in losing."

"Nor am I. But regardless of how others see it, an incremental win is as good for us as any other victory." Naryshkin had a mischievous grin. "The east today. The middle tomorrow. By next year, we could control all of Ukraine."

Putin shook his head impatiently. "I prefer to win it all at once. Just go to them and find out if they will help us."

"Certainly," Naryshkin said. He'd learned to recognize when Putin had reached his limit. Once he'd reached that point, only bad things could come of continuing to press an issue with him.

"And make sure the news media knows nothing about it."

"As you wish."

✦ ✦ ✦

In the United States, Billy Smith brought his red pickup truck to a stop at the main entrance to Fort Gordon, a military base near Augusta, Georgia. He checked his watch and saw it was almost midnight. As a guard came from the gatehouse and started toward him, Smith lowered the driver's window and held his identification badge at the ready, awaiting the guard's inspection.

Overhead, the night sky was ablaze with stars so bright that even light pollution from the base couldn't block them from view. That moment, with the night air in his face, and the stars overhead, had become the highlight of his assignment to the night shift. A silent pause before the incessant flow of voices from the headphones he soon would strap over his ears.

Though Smith had driven through the gate many times, the guard methodically compared his image on the identification card to his face, then placed a handheld scanner over the ID badge and waited while it checked the microchip embedded in it. Neither man spoke but waited in silence until the device completed the scan and emitted a harsh beep. The guard checked the scanner's screen for the results, then waved Smith through.

About a mile beyond the gate, Smith turned onto a drive that led toward a cluster of multi-story buildings before descending into an underground parking facility. He squinted against the glare of the overhead florescent lighting that illuminated the garage's interior and slowly made his way to his assigned space.

With the truck in its place, Smith gathered his satchel from the passenger seat, made sure his cell phone was in his pocket, and switched off the engine. It was hot in the cab without the air-conditioner and almost immediately, a thin sheen of perspiration formed on his forehead. He slid from the seat, then slammed the truck door shut and walked to the shuttle that ferried employees through a system of tunnels to the underground entrances for the buildings above. Ten minutes later, he was seated at his workspace, staring at an array of computer screens.

Fluent in half a dozen languages, Smith worked as an analyst at the NSA's Georgia Cryptologic Center where he reviewed intercepted conversations. Most analysts at the Center worked with real-time conversations—phone calls between terrorist cells in Syria or Gaza, chats from unidentified callers using suspicious phone numbers, or foreign businessmen discussing their latest transaction.

Smith's work involved intercepts deemed of a less urgent nature. Gathered from sources found to be less viable, the conversations he reviewed were not in real-time. Instead, they had been recorded sometime in the past twenty-four hours and digitally scanned by the agency's computers for keyword content—phrases that might indicate a conversation about topics of importance to the agency. Any that were flagged by the system were forwarded to Smith and others in his sector who then spent their eight-hour shifts listening, sorting, and gathering additional information to decide whether the content warranted further attention.

That morning, conversations assigned to Smith came from a listening device, an older style of electronic bug from the 1990s, located in the base of a flag stand that stood in the corner of an anteroom in the Russian Department of Defense's main building. Back in the day, an enterprising CIA officer had inserted the device in the flag stand when it was kept in an office frequented by

Boris Yeltsin. When Yeltsin was in power, conversations transmitted by the device were of vital importance. With Vladimir Putin, the flag and its stand had been used only for decoration on ceremonial occasions. Between those occasions, it stood alone in the anteroom where it was out of the way and ignored. The listening device had been expected to last only a short time and was fashioned from Chinese technology to mask its origin, should it be discovered, as was expected. But Yeltsin came and went and even though the device had long since become obsolete, it continued to work. Hence, no attempt had been made to remove it. As a consequence, it continued in service, occasionally transmitting conversations from the room to an NSA computer farm in New Jersey, where the conversations were duly recorded for analysis.

As time went by, the task of sifting through those recordings became an assignment for NSA recruits fresh from their initial training course in analysis. Agents working at Fort Gordon were usually the best of those young graduates. Despite the tedious nature of the job and the less-than-essential nature of the substance, they were excited when recordings appeared on their schedule sheet. At least analyzing the content was actual intelligence work, from an actual bug, in an actual room at one of Russia's most important buildings. All of the young agents took the matter quite seriously.

Smith clicked on the file for the flagged conversation and heard voices identified by the system as those of Vladimir Putin and Sergei Naryshkin, Director of the Russian Foreign Intelligence Service. No lightweights on a fool's errand, these were top officials from the Russian government. Smith sat up straight in his chair and took notes. Something about a trip to China. The need for artillery shells and drones. Keep it out of the news media.

When the conversation ended, Smith produced a transcript of it in English along with an executive summary of the contents. When it was finished, he ran it down the hall to the office of his supervisor. The office was empty, but the lights were on and a warm coffee cup sat on the desk. He laid the report beside the cup and went back to work.

✦ ✦ ✦

At noon that day, Jim Marsh returned to his office at CIA headquarters. He closed the door, crossed the room to his desk, and took a seat. On the desk before him were three folders awaiting his attention. Two were from an agency division dealing with trouble in South America. The third was a file that had been sent over from the NSA. It had arrived by courier in mid-morning but as no one had alerted him to it he assumed it did not require his immediate attention.

Marsh opened the file and found a report from an NSA station near Augusta, Georgia. An analyst named Smith had created it. The tracking slip indicated it had been reviewed at the appropriate levels before reaching him, which meant someone along the way had read it and thought he ought to be included. He wondered why no one called him about it.

With the report in hand, Marsh leaned back in his chair and began to read, thinking he would probably fall asleep before he finished. Noon in the office was always a struggle for him. But before he reached the end of the first page, he was upright in his chair and wide awake.

The contents of the file included a transcript of Putin's meeting with his senior advisors regarding the situation in Ukraine. Putin was upset about the growing NATO and US involvement. His advisors, particularly generals who came to the meeting from the battlefield, were upset about widespread shortages experienced by troops fighting in Ukraine. Armored equipment, ammunition, missiles, and drones were in short supply. Troop numbers were below the minimum. Things were so dire the defense minister was headed to China to beg for support.

Russia's ability to wage a war of attrition in Ukraine had been discussed, examined, and analyzed at great length by agency experts. All of them were convinced that Russian analysts either were woefully ignorant of Ukraine's strength and resolve or, their estimates of how Russian troops might match up with Ukrainian forces had been produced under pressure to justify a desired political result rather than as genuine estimates of potential outcomes. Now, based on the transcript of the intercepted conversation, it appeared the Russian leadership had actually believed the prewar hype—that showing up would be their biggest challenge, that Ukrainian soldiers would surrender on sight, that Russian forces would easily overwhelm any who dared to resist, and the entire operation would take no more than a week. Two at the most.

"They're in worse shape than we thought," Marsh whispered.

After reading the report and the accompanying transcript, Marsh stepped across the hall to see Bob Donovan, the CIA director. Donovan had already seen the report and had reached the same conclusion—Russia was in a desperate situation.

"I think it would be obvious even to a casual observer that Russia cannot sustain itself under present conditions," Donovan said. "The bigger question is, why won't they commit their best weapons and their best troops to the fight?"

Marsh shrugged. "Perhaps they really do think they will face us head-to-head. Or that we mean to invade Russia and they'll need them to stop us."

"They can't possibly think that."

"Well, if it's not that, then they must have something else planned for those forces."

"I think they meant to roll over Ukraine quickly," Donovan offered. "They never thought this would become a war."

Marsh nodded. "Which is troubling in itself."

"Exactly," Donovan agreed. "They could stumble into a nuclear war before they realize what they've done. But that still leaves the question of why they haven't committed their best equipment. If their bigger plan was to roll over Ukraine quickly, what else did they have in mind?"

"Most of the countries in the area are either members of NATO or applicants for membership."

"Except Moldova," Donovan noted. "Maybe they thought they could roll into Moldova. If they could have taken Ukraine as easily as they thought, they would have been able to roll up Moldova with the kind of troops and equipment they have tried to use against Ukraine. There would have been no reason to think Moldova would be a tougher target than Ukraine."

"What do you think the Chinese will do? I mean, they're an obvious source for Russia, but will Wei Xing sell them enough to make a difference?"

"Xing would be hard-pressed to turn them down, but Russia has been the world's bully for a long time. If China steps in as their ally, Wei Xing can say goodbye to positioning China as a neutral and trustworthy US alternative."

Donovan had a playful smile. "Does it scare you?"

"What?"

"This situation with Russia at war in Europe and now maybe China, too. Two huge nuclear powers lined up against NATO. This skirmish with Ukraine is starting to sound apocalyptic, isn't it? Like some of that Sunday school literature you've read?"

Few at the agency knew about Marsh's devout childhood. Not much was said about it in the official background reports when Marsh joined the Agency, or when he was considered for the Deputy Director position. But Donovan knew how to read between the lines and raised the question when he interviewed Marsh. Rather than finesse the issue, Marsh had disclosed the details—raised as a Methodist, baptized in his uncle's Baptist church, and became an Episcopalian as an adult. He was solidly committed but deeply ambiguous. A true believer working for an agency that regularly operated far beyond the line that divided legal from illegal, authorized from unauthorized, moral from immoral. Rather than being put off by it, Donovan had been intrigued, but it was a topic they rarely discussed.

"Yes," Marsh replied. "It's quite unsettling. And this current situation is the perfect storm for it. A maniacal leader, steeped in hubris, obsessed with restoring a former empire, convinced he's the One appointed by the church, if not God himself, to rid the world of evil. All the while, completely unaware of the evil that controls him."

When Marsh read apocalyptic literature as a teenager, the focus had been on the Middle East. Writers and Christian celebrities had worked hard to fit prophetic topics into a Middle East paradigm. Catastrophic war, a third of mankind wiped out. Before World War II, no one had the capacity to do such a thing but after Hiroshima, that assurance no longer applied. Still, no country in the Middle East had a bomb, so writers contented themselves with talking about a near future when they might. They'd produced a lot of *what-if* scenarios, but not much of it touched upon reality, which left the end feeling a long way off.

Reading and studying about a coming apocalypse had been one of the things that motivated Marsh to join the CIA. It seemed to offer a way to learn, from the inside, whether such a scenario was possible and whether he could help avoid it. His experience with the Agency convinced him more than ever that such an end was not only possible but very likely. China alone had enough nuclear warheads to wipe out a third of the world's population. Russia and the US could each do it several times over. A conflict involving those three nations, with nuclear war as an option, posed a direct threat to mankind's continued existence.

Donovan no longer smiled. "Well," he said with a consoling tone, "I don't think it will come to that. Ukraine isn't worth that kind of reaction. But maybe we should have a satellite focused on key Chinese military installations, just to be safe."

"Ukraine would only be the flashpoint," Marsh responded. "The real catalyst would come from Putin. He would do anything to avoid seeing Russia humiliated and I doubt he would be thinking of any target other than the US. We have our missiles preset to Russian targets. I'm sure they have theirs targeted on us as well."

Donovan's sense of humor returned. "And right now, one of those Russian missiles is targeted at this building." He pointed. "Might come through that window at any minute." Marsh wasn't amused. Donovan laughed. "You've seen the maps?"

"Yes," Marsh replied. "And it scares the hell out of me every time I think about it."

Donovan glanced at his watch, a signal the meeting was over. "I'll get them to task a satellite on the South China Sea. You got anyone in the region who could be helpful?"

"Yes," Marsh responded.

Donovan stood. "I have to get to another meeting."

"But we haven't talked about Taiwan," Marsh noted.

"We'll keep that for another day. I don't think China will do anything about Taiwan right now."

Marsh wasn't so sure about that.

CHAPTER EIGHT

Two days later, Naryshkin left Moscow on his way to China for a meeting with Dong Jingwei, head of China's Ministry of State Security. In an attempt to obscure the real purpose of the trip, Naryshkin traveled on a jet supplied by Tyumenco, a Russian oil company. When he arrived in Beijing the airplane taxied to the far side of the airport and came to a stop inside a private hangar. A limo with darkened windows was waiting for him.

From the airport, Naryshkin rode alone to a high-rise office building in central Beijing and entered it through an underground parking garage. An elevator took him to a suite on the top floor where Jingwei was waiting. No reporters were present. No photos were taken.

After a cordial greeting over tea and light refreshments, Naryshkin got right to the point. "We are in need of China's assistance," he said.

Jingwei nodded politely. "I assume you mean with your situation in Ukraine."

"Yes," Naryshkin responded.

Jingwei had a disarmingly kind expression. "The Americans have stepped up their involvement."

"We are certain they mean to drive us out of Ukraine and out of power, either by defeating us on the battlefield or by bankrupting our country."

"They have given Ukraine enough to continue the fight, but not enough to win."

"Precisely," Naryshkin agreed. "They are using Ukraine to bleed us dry."

"And what do you need from us?"

"Our manufacturers cannot keep up with the demand for artillery shells and drones," Naryshkin said.

"These have become the hallmark weapons of our current era."

"Especially in urban warfare," Naryshkin added.

"You have used many of them against Ukrainian civilians. How have they performed against the Ukrainian army?"

Naryshkin bristled at the suggestion Russia had specifically targeted Ukrainian civilians, but he did not want a confrontation. "We were very effective with them until the Americans gave Ukraine access to their battlefield management system and supplied them with rockets for destroying them."

Jingwei nodded again. "The Americans have been your nemesis since the conclusion of World War II."

"They have been everyone's nemesis," Naryshkin countered.

"And now it is time to resolve our differences with them, once and for all."

Jingwei frowned. "I thought you were fighting the Ukrainians."

"This war has always been about more than Russia and Ukraine. It's about resolving the question of East versus West. About ending American domination of world affairs."

"And you think the war in Ukraine gives you an opportunity to do that?"

"It gives *us* the opportunity," Naryshkin said. "We can show the world that America is no longer invincible and once they see that, the American grip on the world's throat will end. And with it, American hegemony." He added that word—hegemony—because he knew it was a favorite expression of Chinese politicians. A term they used to describe the subjugation of existing cultural and social mores of one country by a dominant but morally inferior society. A process by which the target country faced not only the threat of military defeat but the replacement of its societal values with those of a country having no collective interest in the greater good.

"At last," Jingwei said, "someone understands us. After the war against Germany and Japan, the evil that always lay at the American heart rose to prominence for all to see, but the eyes of the world were blinded by the dazzling victory the Americans achieved. A victory powered by a capitalist industrial complex that prospered through the exploitation of the weak at the expense of the world's resources and its cheapest labor."

"That is what we are attempting to end," Naryshkin said. "We are hoping you will supply us with the means to do that."

"What do you need from us?"

"Artillery shells," Naryshkin replied. "And drones." He smiled, sensing they were on the verge of making a deal.

To Naryshkin's dismay, however, Jingwei did not smile in return. Instead, he rested his hands in his lap and leaned back in his chair. His eyes focused on the ceiling. "We are not opposed to your efforts against Ukraine," he responded. "Or with your interest in ending American dominance. We have similar issues of Western interference with our sovereign territory of Taiwan." He lowered his gaze and looked Naryshkin in the eye. "But we are reluctant to involve ourselves overtly in your situation."

Naryshkin felt betrayed. He had sensed an agreement was just moments away. Closing it was within his grasp and he had revealed Russia's intentions more fully than he'd ever discussed with anyone. Jingwei seemed set to give him all that he'd asked for and now, at the last moment, it all turned to dust. Naryshkin wanted to kill him. A spoon lay on the tray their coffee had been served from. The end of the handle was rounded but it was narrow enough. With one thrust, he could shove it between Jingwei's ribs and pierce his heart, ending his life instantly. Then Naryshkin remembered one word from Jingwei's response, and it struck him as odd—*overtly*. So, he kept talking.

"Why?" Naryshkin asked. "You agree with our cause. You understand our position."

"We despise the Americans," Jingwei said, "but we have a lucrative trade arrangement with them. We are using it as a means of funding our plans for the future. No one wants that arrangement disrupted."

"Your plans for the future, as in military expansion?"

Jingwei avoided a direct response. "We are working diligently to present ourselves as a neutral alternative to the US. To replace them in areas of global peace and financial stability. If we supply Russia with arms, we will be seen as choosing sides in a European conflict. No doubt our choice would be viewed as self-serving and counter to our interest in appearing neutral. All of our work to insert ourselves between the US and the world would be lost."

They talked for two hours with Naryshkin returning again and again to the topic of support for Russia's war in Ukraine. Offering to provide China with access to Russian oil, military expertise, and technical assistance in perfecting China's nuclear capability. And with each proposal, Jingwei asserted China's position that aiding the Russian cause would be detrimental to China's ultimate goals.

At last, Naryshkin could think of nothing more to say. He stood and shook hands with Jingwei, thanking him for his time, then walked from the room to the elevator and rode down to the car in the underground garage.

✦ ✦ ✦

After Naryshkin departed for the return trip to Russia, Dong Jingwei went to see Wei Xing, China's paramount leader, to report on the meeting. They met at Wei Xing's dacha in Zhongnanhai, a compound just west of the Forbidden City, the grounds of the ancient imperial palace. Wei Xing suggested a walk in the garden. As they strolled in the warm sunshine, he gestured to their surroundings. "When the world seems in chaos, I come here and walk among these lovely flowers and listen to the voices of the ancients."

"This palace has been here for a thousand years," Jingwei said. "These footpaths were here before Europe knew that we existed."

Wei Xing made an even grander gesture toward the buildings of Beijing, visible over the perimeter wall. "The city of Beijing which surrounds us is more than three thousand years old. We were a grand civilization, ruling one-third of the world at a time when the British were struggling to defend themselves against the Druids and the Romans. America, as a people, did not even exist then. The greatest buildings in England were only thatched huts and stone monuments. We already were a brilliant people with magnificent structures."

"Our forebearers were very clever," Jingwei noted, sensing the direction the conversation was headed. "The ancients knew the secret of their strength lay in avoiding foreigners. Our trouble only began when the British arrived." He sighed. "The world has changed much since then."

"Yes." Wei Xing nodded in agreement. "The ancients were confronted by the British. We have been confronted by the Americans. What they taught us has opened great opportunities for our people." Wei Xing looked over at him. "But this business between Russia and their European neighbors is a family squabble. A fight between themselves over matters that mean nothing to us. They have been fighting among themselves for centuries. If we get caught in it, we will be seen as outsiders. Interlopers. They will stop fighting each other and turn on us. If we remain aloof to their situation, they will fight each other with all their might and eventually unleash their nuclear weapons against themselves."

Jingwei frowned. "That would destroy both of them."

"Yes," Wei Xing replied. "And that is what will happen. They will obliterate each other."

"And us."

"Perhaps, but only if we are involved. If we avoid entangling ourselves in their affairs, they will cancel each other out. They will be gone. We will be the only ones left to rule the world, as we did thousands of years ago. Then we can reclaim whatever we like without interference from anyone." He paused for effect then said, "Your Russian visitor was here to ask for our help with his war against Ukraine, was he not?"

"Yes," Jingwei replied.

"Rockets and drones?"

"Artillery shells and drones," Jingwei said.

"As we expected." Wei Xing glanced over at him. "You gave the reply?"

Jingwei nodded. "But I fear it will cause us trouble. They need many things, and they know we have much to offer. They will be offended if we do not help them win."

"Yes." Wei Xing nodded. "I suppose they will. We must give them help, but without giving them anything."

"Help without help."

"Yes."

Jingwei smiled. "That would be a thin line to walk."

"Then you must make sure you do not stumble," Wei Xing said. "Give but give nothing. And make certain news of it appears in the press."

Jingwei was surprised. "You want reporters to know about it?"

"Give but give nothing. Speak but say nothing."

✦ ✦ ✦

When Naryshkin returned to Moscow he met with Putin and delivered China's response. Putin seemed to have expected it. "It is just as well," he said with a shrug. "Buying weapons from the Chinese would cause trouble for us."

Naryshkin was caught off-guard by the response and wondered if the trip and the meeting had been merely a feint all along. "I thought we wanted to buy from them."

"Their response was not unexpected," Putin replied. "Is that all Jingwei said?"

"No," Naryshkin said. He was surprised Putin was that attuned to the Chinese. "Jingwei called while I was on the plane."

"And how much are they willing to do? I suppose it involves Saudi Arabian oil."

"Yes."

Once again Naryshkin was impressed by Putin's perception. He had intended to tell Putin about the phone call, but with Jingwei already turning him down, he wasn't sure China could be trusted with an arms deal.

Putin nodded. "There's plenty of oil there," he mused. "China needs oil. And don't forget, the Chinese have their own scores to settle, especially regarding Taiwan. It is very important to them. Never lose sight of that fact."

"They want Taiwan back," Naryshkin said.

"Wei Xing mentioned it?"

"Yes. When we met in person."

"And what did Jingwei say about it when he called you on the plane?"

"They will supply artillery shells and drones, but they want our help when they take back Taiwan."

"Any indication when that might be?"

"No."

"Do they understand we are committed to a war in Ukraine from which we cannot extract ourselves quickly?"

"They don't want our army," Naryshkin responded. "They want our navy."

Putin's eyes opened wide. "Excellent move on their part. Do they think our current situation might give them an opportunity to take it back earlier rather than later?"

"Perhaps, but he did not say so."

"Regardless of when they move on Taiwan, they will use our current situation to their advantage by broadening their reach in the Middle East, making inroads into Europe, and weakening us with a long war." Putin turned to face the window and looked out over the city; his hands folded behind his back. "The Chinese have become every bit like the Americans. With one hand giving, while the other is taking away. And always with the knife in easy reach."

Naryshkin waited a moment to see if Putin would say more. When he didn't, Naryshkin stepped quietly from the room.

✦ ✦ ✦

When Naryshkin returned to his office, he was met by Alexander Nijinsky, a supervisor from the imagery analysis section. "There's something you ought to see," he said.

"What is it?"

"Come down to the operations center and I'll show you."

Naryshkin followed Nijinsky down the hall to a room filled with analysts, all seated at workstations scrolling through satellite imagery as it downloaded from the many satellites the Foreign Intelligence Service monitored.

On one of the screens was an image of an airport. Nijinsky pointed to it. "This is the NATO base at Lask, Poland." He tapped the screen, and a technician enlarged the photo. "This," Nijinsky said, "is a US E-3 AWACS surveillance plane."

"At Lask?"

"Yes."

"How long has it been there?"

"We discovered it while you were away. And that's not all." The technician switched to another image. "This is a second AWACS at the same location."

"What are they doing with them?"

"They have been patrolling along Poland's eastern border. The route they follow gives them a clear view of Ukraine."

"All of it?"

"The entire country. When they are airborne, every military unit operating in Ukraine is in full view of their equipment."

"Putin isn't going to like this."

"I don't suppose he would."

"Who's operating them? NATO?"

"It appears they are operated by American crews."

"They're sharing information directly with Ukraine?"

"No. They transmit it to a facility at Lask that is manned by NATO and American personnel, but the Ukrainians have their own operations center at the same location."

"So, is that where the Ukraine army gets its information?"

"It appears so."

"Give me a print of those images."

"Of the two planes?"

"Yes."

A technician printed the images. Naryshkin scanned them quickly, then turned toward the door. "Come on," he said.

"Where are we going?"

"We have to brief Putin. I want you there in case he asks questions I can't answer."

✦ ✦ ✦

With Naryshkin leading the way, he and Nijinsky hurried downstairs to the parking garage. A car took them the short distance to the building that housed Putin's private office. Putin was on his way out but paused to hear what Naryshkin had to say.

"We have been able to confirm that not only did the US send troops and fighters to the base at Lask, but they now have established a battlefield management hub there as well." Naryshkin gestured to Nijinsky for the photographs, then handed them to Putin.

Putin's jaw tightened and his eyes narrowed as he studied the pictures. "I knew it," he said angrily. "I knew they were already here."

"The battlefield management group is located at NATO's Joint Forces Training Center in Bydgoszcz. They are using it to obtain data regarding our troop locations and movements."

"I knew it!" Putin shouted. "I knew Ukraine could not prevail against us without help from the Americans. And more help than ammunition and drones. It has been the Americans all along, supplying and directing this war. Without their interference, we would have defeated the Ukrainians in ten days, just as our estimates suggested."

"They have a presence at the base alongside the Americans," Naryshkin said. "Information the Americans collect from their AWACS planes is fed to Ukrainians who operate from their own facility at Lask. They are using that information to direct their troops through their own management system."

"We must destroy their system at once," Putin replied.

"I don't think that would be wise," Nijinsky said.

"Why not?" Putin glared at him in anger.

"If we bomb the site in Poland," Nijinsky explained, "we would be hitting a NATO installation. All of Europe would be free to respond against us with all their might."

Putin seemed to understand a direct response against Lask was impossible, but he was desperate to take it out of use. He stared at the photograph, seemingly lost in thought but after a moment he looked over at Naryshkin. "They must have an operations center somewhere besides the NATO base in Poland. There are too many units operating in Ukraine for a single center to direct them all."

"What do you mean?" Naryshkin asked.

"They must have a center in Ukraine. Their movements have been too coordinated and too precise not to have it."

"I'm sure they do," Naryshkin said. "But we haven't been able to locate it."

"Find that site." Putin's voice was terse and demanding. "And if you can't find it, bomb everywhere that you think it *might* be."

Naryshkin smiled. "That would be a bit impractical, given our current weapons shortages."

"I don't care about practicalities!" Putin shouted. "Bomb the entire country if you have to. Just shut down that battlefield management system!"

Naryshkin was taken aback by the intensity of Putin's response and unsettled by the crazed look in his eyes, but he was not about to defy Putin's direct orders. "Yes, sir, Mr. President," he said. "We will destroy it at once."

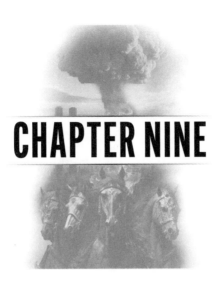

CHAPTER NINE

ack at his office, Naryshkin contacted Michael Borisov, a prominent member of the Wagner Group, Russia's most powerful paramilitary organization. The two men also were personal friends. When Naryshkin explained his situation, Borisov was all too happy to assist.

Closely associated with Putin, many in the West, especially among reporters and media celebrities, referred to the Wagner Group as Putin's private army. It had played a strategic role in most of Russia's aggressive combat action since he took office, including Russian intervention in Syria, Sudan, and Libya, as well as providing manpower for Serbian attacks against Kosovo and Russia's response against unrest in the Caucasus.

Yet, as widespread as its operations had been, the Wagner Group had remained largely unknown outside Russia until 2014.

When the Russian army invaded Ukraine that year, Wagner came with them to fight for pro-Russian separatists in the Donbas region. During that war, Wagner proved indispensable and forged deep ties with the Russian Ministry of Defense. Its members trained at Russian military facilities, received equipment from Russia's Department of Defense, and conducted military operations that were closely coordinated with the Russian army. After the 2014-2015 war, the group expanded its operations beyond former Soviet Bloc countries to include an active presence around the world, always in furtherance of Russian interests.

Always on the lookout for opportunities to expand their sphere of influence, the Wagner Group acquired and formed many different sub-groups, each with specialized skills, including expertise in internet hacking and spyware attacks. Many of Russia's pre-war cyber-attacks against the Ukrainian government and corporate websites were led by Wagner members. Their members also instigated infrastructure attacks that led to widespread internet failures among Western governments and corporations.

With Borisov's help, Naryshkin met with Roman Smolinsky, one of Wagner's field commanders, to discuss the issues they faced regarding Ukraine's use of a battlefield management platform.

"We know they're working from inside Poland," Smolinsky said. "They have teams at the Bydgoszcz Training Center and at Lask. And we are certain they are coordinating their activity through a site in Ukraine, but we haven't been able to locate it."

"We need you to find that site," Naryshkin said. "Find it and take it out."

Three weeks later, a small group that had been recruited into

Wagner from a college in London, traveled on British passports to Poland and attempted to gain access to the Training Center at Bydgoszcz. They were spotted almost immediately and confronted by security guards. An exchange of gunfire ensued and one of Wagner's operatives was killed. The other two were taken into custody.

The following week, Wagner tried a different tactic. A dozen technically proficient operatives from Moldova squatted inside an empty building half a mile away from the NATO Training Center and set up frequency scanners that they connected to digital recording equipment, then began searching the frequencies for suspicious cellular and microwave signals. A second team, posing as servicemen, tapped into telephone and internet landlines running to and from the NATO Center. Messages traveling over either route were recorded for analysis.

Shortly after that, Russian cryptographers began unlocking the encryption associated with the captured messages. Working around the clock, they succeeded in reading transmissions from Ukrainian operatives working at the NATO Center to Ukrainian forces in the field. Most of the messages provided Ukrainian troops with real-time information about Russian troop locations and movements.

A few days after the Wagner operatives gained access to the NATO system, analysts in Poland and the US detected their online activity. Rather than closing the network or blocking access to it, NATO personnel established a new network for vital information and began sending fictitious reports over the older network the Russians had breached.

✦ ✦ ✦

Despite attempts to impede Russian access to NATO communications, Russian and Wagner technicians pinpointed a central IP address that appeared to be the central online hub for Ukraine's battlefield coordination unit. That IP address was registered to the Michael Marmer Museum, a holocaust museum in Kryvyi Rih, Zelensky's hometown. When Naryshkin received news of the discovery, he scheduled a briefing for Putin.

Naryshkin explained, "The US gathers critical information from the field and hands it off to a Ukraine team at the NATO facility in Lask, Poland. The Ukraine team at Lask transmits it to their own hub in Kryvyi Rih, and from there, it is distributed to the troops. It sounds complicated but the individual transactions are completed in a matter of seconds."

"This is how they are able to use their drones so efficiently," Putin said. He was furious. "The Americans are telling them what to do. They mean to ruin us! And they are rubbing it in our faces, using Zelensky's hometown to do it."

"The initial gathering point for information is at the NATO center in Lask, Poland. There isn't much we can do about that. Poland is a NATO member. As we discussed earlier, if we strike a location on their soil, NATO and all its member nations will be compelled to enter the war against us."

"NATO or not, you must put an end to this," Putin insisted. "We must poke their eyes out and make them blind!"

"We can attack the site in Ukraine without causing an international uproar. That would take out the Ukraine side of this sharing arrangement."

"Yes," Putin said. "We need to send them a message that we are serious. Wipe that city off the map."

Naryshkin understood what Putin meant by *wipe them off the map*. He was broaching the possibility of using a nuclear weapon. He had mentioned the topic several times in their recent conversations. Naryshkin spent many sleepless nights worrying that Putin might do that on his own. If he gave the order, there would be no way of stopping a launch, and all that would follow. Europe would be an apocalyptic wasteland. Easily one-third of humanity would die.

"We can destroy their facility with conventional means," Naryshkin said. "That would send a message of Russian superiority. And it would take them by surprise. They think they are clever and that no one knows how they operate. We would show them that we do."

"Very well." Putin sighed and his tone changed. "Use as many men as it takes but destroy that facility at Kryvyi Rih. Leave no block standing on top of another."

✦ ✦ ✦

With a clear mandate from Putin, Naryshkin handed the task of destroying the Ukrainian communications center at Kryvyi Rih to Roman Smolinsky. "We'll need funding," Smolinsky said.

"What did you have in mind?"

"We'll need to send in someone to reconnoiter the site, but if it is as secure as everyone seems to think, we'll need some men with special skills."

"How so?"

"No matter how nondescript it may appear, a site like this will have redundant detection and defensive systems. We can't just walk up and knock on the door."

"You have some people in mind?"

"I do," Smolinsky said. "But let me have someone research the place, first. I'll let you know what they find."

One week later, Smolinsky dispatched a small team of Wagner operatives to recon the museum. They confirmed the hub was, indeed, located two floors beneath the main lobby of the Michael Marmer Museum. Based on plans filed with Kryvyi Rih planning authorities, access to the underground facility was obtained by means of a tunnel that emerged in the basement of a building across the street from the museum. A team member gained access to the building and confirmed the entrance—a heavy steel door similar to that of a bank vault, with a combination lock and a biometric key. It was hidden behind stacks of boxes that appeared to be placed there as storage, but which were mounted on pallets with casters that made them easy to move.

While the Wagner operative was there, two men approached. He concealed himself a short distance away and watched. As the two men came near, he removed a small digital camera from his pocket and recorded what happened.

The first of the two men rolled the boxes aside to expose the tunnel door, then the other pressed his thumb against the small screen of a biometric scanning device. After a moment, a tiny green light came on and he worked the dial on the door to a preset combination. Once it was in place, he moved the lever, and the door came open revealing a brightly lit tunnel with an immaculately clean tile floor. Ten feet inside was a guard post with a body and bag scanner manned by three heavily armed soldiers. The man who'd opened the door stepped into the tunnel while the second pushed it closed and returned the boxes to their place, hiding the door's location.

With information from the recon team, Smolinsky devised a plan to destroy the underground facility. He broke it into phases assigned to two-man teams. The first would gain and secure access to the building where the tunnel was located. The second would neutralize the door's locking system and open the door. A third team would eliminate the guards operating the checkpoint just inside the tunnel. All of that would take place within seconds and would be followed almost simultaneously by an overwhelming number of men whose task was to clear the length of the tunnel before countermeasures could be activated. They would be followed by demolition officers who would place charges designed to completely destroy the structural integrity of the underground facility.

"We have no intention of harvesting anything from this location," Smolinsky said. "We aren't gathering information. Or preserving documents. Or taking prisoners. And when we are finished, we are dropping the entire Michael Marmer Museum into its own basement, burying this intelligence facility beneath the rubble."

The plan was circulated among relevant Wagner leaders, each of whom noted necessary changes. After final review and approval, men with the necessary technical skills were identified and gathered for a briefing, after which they were sent for training to Bratsk, in eastern Russia, where an abandoned control room had been refitted to resemble the central portion of the facility at Kryvyi Rih. After two weeks of fourteen-hour training sessions, the men returned to Ukraine, ready to conduct their mission.

✦ ✦ ✦

Skip Rosen sat at his workstation at the NSA station located on the grounds of Fort Gordon, near Augusta, Georgia. scrolling through call logs from the previous day's intercepts when the computer beside him began to beep with an alert notice. A check of the notice showed the system had flagged an intercepted conversation with a voice known to the agency's database as that of Roman Smolinsky.

Details on a second screen indicated Smolinsky had initiated the call from a phone in eastern Russia. He was talking to Sergei Naryshkin who received the call at a phone in Moscow. The conversation was happening in real-time. Rosen checked to make sure the system was recording it.

When the conversation ended, Rosen notified his supervisor who requested a translation of it. At his request, the file was forwarded to Billy Smith. When Smith completed the translation, it was sent up the line to the Director of National Intelligence in Washington, DC. Analysts at the Office of National Intelligence reached the same conclusion as everyone else who had read the transcription—members of the Wagner Group were planning an action against a facility in Kryvyi Rih, Ukraine. Several hours after Rosen first noted the conversation, it was transcribed and sent to the heads of all the major agencies in the US intelligence community. A copy of it landed on Jim Marsh's desk. He reviewed it and took it immediately to Bob Donovan.

"Yes," Donovan said as Marsh entered his office. He gave a dismissive gesture. "I know about it."

"Have we told the Ukrainians?"

"They were told a few hours ago."

"And I'm just now learning of it? Why wasn't I informed before the order was given?"

"It's not a clandestine operation. It's not part of your remit."

"But the fact that Wagner found out about it means a thousand other things might be compromised."

"I'm aware of that."

"Did you go over it with the Ukrainians?"

"Yes. Yes," Donovan assured. "They were thoroughly briefed on the implications."

"But why wasn't I—"

"Listen," Donovan said sharply, cutting him off. "You can't fight all of this by yourself. You've got bona fide clandestine operations underway on every continent. We need you taking care of them and the thousand other things you're doing that I don't know about. Addressing Ukraine's underlying security issues can be handled by any of a dozen other people. They can't do what you do with those operations you're running."

"Ukraine's Foreign Intelligence Service leaks information like a sieve."

"We all know that, but we can't fix everything at once. Some of it will have to wait until the war is won."

"Or lost."

Donovan nodded. "If the war is lost, the Russians will take care of it." He looked up at Marsh. "Believe me, they know how to deal with moles and leaks."

✦ ✦ ✦

The entire operation—locating the hub, determining the layout, and breaching the entrance, took less than three weeks for Wagner to plan, prepare, and complete. Wagner operatives breached the facility's entrance and neutralized the guards. A second group followed close behind the first and made their way quickly toward the center of the underground intelligence facility. A third group of Wagner operatives followed the second and killed every Ukrainian in the facility, then hurriedly placed explosive charges in predetermined locations specifically chosen for their essential role in preserving the facility's structural integrity.

Outside, Ukrainian soldiers arrived at the building across the street and stormed the basement. Wagner members had been placed there to guard the tunnel opening, but they were quickly overwhelmed. Ukrainian soldiers rushed to the tunnel entrance, reached the entrance door, and pushed it closed, then secured the lock.

With the Wagner members trapped inside, Ukrainian soldiers detonated their own pre-arranged defensive charges that had been designed into the tunnel as a last-ditch defensive measure. The resulting explosion created a huge cavity beneath the museum, causing the building to collapse, filling the crater with tons and tons of debris from the museum building. No one from the Wagner Group escaped.

CHAPTER TEN

W hile the world had been in an uproar over Russia's invasion of Ukraine, Israel had been noticeably silent on the matter. In private, however, Israeli officials had argued loudly and forcefully about what to do. Some favored doing nothing. "It's not our fight," they argued. "Let the Europeans handle it. Let the Americans deal with it. It isn't our fight."

Others argued, "We *can't* do anything. There are almost 200,000 Jews living in Ukraine and about that many more in Russia. If we get involved in supporting Ukraine, Russia might retaliate against our people." No one needed a reminder of the pogroms that had occurred in Ukraine during the late nineteenth and early twentieth centuries. Many Jews now living in Israel had lost a relative to that era of hatred. The stories of it had been handed down to succeeding generations to make sure they never forgot. The memory of it was fresh on everyone's mind.

Others noted that Russia had obtained much of its armaments from Iran and had been asking for more. They favored an operation against Iran to interdict Russia's supply of weapons. "Iran won't give Russia the weapons for free and the money they make on the deal will only allow them to avoid the effects of current sanctions." Israel had watched helplessly while Iran exported arms to its neighbors and sold oil to China, in blatant violation of UN sanctions. A deal now to supply weapons to Russia would only mean an expansion of illegal activity.

"How is that any different from openly taking sides in the conflict?" someone asked.

"Everyone knows we have a deep and abiding distrust of the Iranians," the first one countered. "They would see an attack by us against Iran as merely taking advantage of the situation."

Older officials, some of whom served in the Israeli army in the Suez Crisis, the Six-Day War, the Yom Kippur War, and countless other wars, battles, and skirmishes that had threatened Israel's existence in the past, feared a quid pro quo arrangement between Iran and Russia. "If Iran supplies Russia with conventional weapons for the war in Ukraine, they will indeed want something in return, as has already been noted. But that *something* won't be money. It will be the final piece of Iran's nuclear weapons program. They don't have everything they need to complete a bomb. Given Russia's current supply situation, they could trade for it with conventional weapons—rockets, missiles, and artillery shells, all of which are in short supply for Russia's army."

Discussions and arguments ranged back and forth between the various perspectives, but it was little more than talk until reports began to arrive about Iran's drone development program and Russia's desire to use it as a source of supply. After reading the reports, Yehuda Eichler, the Israeli prime minister, convened a ministers meeting to discuss the latest information on the topic.

When everyone was present and seated, Eichler said, "We've recently learned of some new developments that seem to change our situation. I thought we ought to consider them together." He paused to collect his thoughts, then continued. "As you are aware, the war in Ukraine has reached a stalemate. Russian leadership assumed their army would roll over Ukraine without significant resistance, but that assumption has proved incorrect. The Ukrainians were able to hold on until help began to arrive. As the war has continued, the US and NATO have begun pouring in large amounts of military aid. Enough to keep Ukraine fighting but not enough to push Russian troops completely out of the country. That has served to prolong the war and to drain Russia's reserves of military hardware and ammunition. Their domestic factories cannot keep up with the demand. They are looking for partners who can supply the items they need. Last week, Sergei Naryshkin traveled to Beijing where he met with Dong Jingwei. Apparently, the Russians are shopping for drones and artillery shells. Yossi Oron will give you the details about their efforts to do the same with Iran."

Oron was the director of Mossad. Somewhat taller than most, he had a lean, hard appearance and his voice was raspy from chain-smoking Turkish cigarettes, but there was an intensity in his eyes and a certain rectitude in the way he carried himself. When he spoke, everyone listened.

A hush fell over the room as Oron rose from his chair. He removed a handful of images from his briefcase and began passing them around. "These images are from one of our satellites," he said gesturing to the pictures. "They were taken over Rasht a few days ago. As you know, Rasht is an Iranian city with elaborate and growing military production facilities." He held one of the images up for them to see and pointed to it. "Our analysts say the objects in this picture are molded carbon fiber parts, mostly likely for a drone. They are being unloaded from a truck at a weapons factory in Rasht." He handed it to the person sitting next to him. "Take a look at it and pass it around."

One of the older ministers spoke up. "I thought that factory in Rasht produced antitank weapons."

"It did in the past," Oron said. "But it appears the Iranians have converted it into a place for manufacturing drones. Based on the shape of those parts, we think they're now using it to make the Shahed 131 and 136."

"Loitering drones," someone noted.

"Precisely," Oron agreed. "Drones designed to remain aloft in an area for extended periods, then strike when a target appears. Iran has a record of producing Shaheds cheaply and in large quantities at other factories. Seeing them now at *this* factory suggests they have expanded their production capacity."

"And what are we to make of that?" another asked.

"Iran is home to thugs who mean to kill all of us," Oron responded, "but they are not idiots when it comes to business. If they have expanded their drone capacity, as seems obvious from the photographs, then either they intend to use them, or they intend to sell them. Our analysts think they mean to sell them to Russia."

"Are we certain of this?"

"No one is certain of anything right now," Oron said. "But as the prime minister noted, officials from the Russian Defense Ministry have been talking to others about supplying them with drones, missiles, and artillery shells. They want to make a deal with China, perhaps Bolivia, too. We think they already have made a deal with Iran."

"Bolivia?" Someone asked. "We haven't heard about Bolivia."

"We're working on the details," Oron said, deflecting the question.

"What do the Americans say about this?"

Oron shook his head. "The Americans have not seen these photos." Others in the room exchanged looks. "And if they have their own images of this new activity in Rasht, we haven't seen them."

Uri Dayan, a conservative leader, spoke up. "For as long as we have existed, Iranian leaders have vowed to eliminate us and from time to time they have attempted to follow through on those vows. That has been their sole focus since we declared our independence. That has been the point of their nuclear program. When they have enough enriched uranium, they will try to destroy us again. And whatever they are doing with Russia, it isn't about the presenting issue. It's about us."

Eichler frowned. "What are you saying, Uri? The drones are meant for us?"

"I'm saying, regardless of how it may appear, this business

between Iran and Russia and drones is all about helping Iran develop a nuclear bomb. Whatever the deal might look like to the rest of the world—drones, artillery shells, whatever—for the Iranians, it is about gaining access to the technology they need to complete their nuclear program. We can't let them continue to expand their manufacturing base. We need to hit them now, while we have the opportunity. Before the place fills up with Russian advisors."

Eichler looked perplexed. "Who said anything about Russian advisors?"

"That's how it works," Dayan said. "Wherever Russia develops one of these long-term operations, they send in advisors. And that is what Iran needs—advice. Technicians with information. If they aren't there already, they're coming. Believe me. And so, we need to hit those factories now before there are so many Russians there, we can't avoid them."

Eichler shook his head. "We've already discussed this before. If we intervene in any way, it will look like we're taking sides against Russia. There's a risk they will retaliate by taking action against Jews already living in Russia and Ukraine."

"And if we wait," Dayan rejoined, "there's an even greater risk Iran will wipe us out."

"Yes," someone agreed. "They have continued their uranium enrichment program all along and when they get enough, they'll drop it on us. We need to hit them now. We can't wait any longer. We must hit Iran now, while we have the means to do so."

Others joined in. "If the Russians need Iran's drones, they must be clearly desperate."

"No doubt, they will move to ensure the protection of the facilities where Iran produces them and that will necessitate a large Russian presence in Iran."

"And if that happens, we won't be able to attack these plants without killing Russian soldiers."

"And then we would be at war with Russia," someone added.

"And we would be on our own, too. The Americans are too preoccupied with Ukraine to come to our aid."

"The Russians are running out of everything," someone noted. "They are desperate for support and will deal with anyone they think can help them."

"And that means China."

"And Iran."

"These pictures are from a single drone factory. Have you looked at other places where Iran manufactures them? Or artillery shells?"

"We are examining all of their facilities," Dayan said. "But I think we should—"

Those in the room kept talking. "Iran can produce artillery shells in large quantities. Most of their own artillery pieces are Russian. They know how to make shells for them."

"But does Russia have the money to purchase weapons and ammunition from a third party? Aren't they running out of money?"

"They're running out of everything."

"That's why I think we should investigate what they are doing with their artillery shell production at other locations."

"Iran could trade artillery shells to the Russians in exchange for nuclear secrets. They have the capacity to enrich uranium and they have the ability to manufacture missiles, but they still don't have the technical expertise to create a nuclear warhead for them."

"Russia is so desperate for munitions, if Iran demanded technology in exchange for conventional weapons, Putin would be unable to refuse."

"Even the slightest help from Russia would drastically reduce the amount of time necessary to finish Iran's program."

"Which would place us closer and closer to our own day of reckoning."

The final comment touched on one of the deeply engrained assumptions of Israeli defense policy. A standing policy, borne from painful experience. That Israel would strike first when conflict appeared imminent, rather than wait to be attacked.

As others continued to talk, Eichler turned to Oron. "Contact whomever you talk to in Washington and make sure they are aware of what we know about the situation in Iran." He gestured to the photos making their way around the room. "Including these pictures."

✦ ✦ ✦

The next day, Oron boarded an Israeli government plane for a flight to Washington, DC. When the plane taxied to a stop and the fuselage door was open, he bounded down the steps to a car that had driven onto the tarmac. Less than an hour later, he arrived at CIA headquarters and shortly after that, he appeared at the door to Jim Marsh's office.

Marsh was surprised to see him. "Long way to travel without

making an appointment." He stood and they shook hands.

"The fewer people who know I am here, the better," Oron replied.

By protocol, the two men were not peers. Oron was an agency director. Marsh was a deputy director. Oron should have been meeting with Bob Donovan, the CIA director.

"I'm afraid Bob Donovan isn't in his office today," Marsh said. "He won't be back until later in the week. But I'm sure we can arrange to take you to where he is if you like."

Oron shook his head. "That won't be necessary. You'll do just fine."

Marsh gestured to a chair. "Have a seat."

Oron glanced around as if checking. "Don't you have a place where we can talk?"

"Certainly." Marsh pointed toward the hall. "Follow me."

They walked in silence down the hall to an interior room. One with no windows, no phones, no video screens. Only a conference table with eight chairs. They sat across from each other.

"Okay," Marsh said. "What's this about?"

"You had some trouble in Dubai recently," Oron said.

Marsh wasn't surprised that Oron knew about it, but he was curious. "What do you know about that?"

Oron removed a photograph from the inside pocket of his jacket and laid it on the table. "That's the man you're looking for," he said, pointing to the picture.

The agency had been investigating the incident but had not made that effort known outside the agency. Marsh brought picked up the photo and held it closer. "Who is he?"

"Sadeq Alizadeh."

"Never heard of him," Marsh replied, though the name sounded familiar. He studied the picture a moment longer, then returned it to the table. "What's his connection?"

"Alizadeh is a member of an Iranian organization known as *The Almumin*."

"The Faithful."

"You've heard of them?"

"No, but *almumin* is Arabic for *the ones who are faithful*."

"*The Almumin* is a secret Shia sect. Deeply committed to belief in the Mahdi."

"A Mahdi cult."

Oron nodded. "Probably more committed to the Mahdi than to Allah, but don't tell them that. They believe the Mahdi will return and put everything right but only when things are so bad that they are beyond human control."

"And they want to hurry things along."

"Yes, but *The Almumin* is not a fringe group. It has members at all levels of Iranian society. Mehdi Kalhor is one of them."

Marsh's eyes opened wider. "Mehdi Kalhor, from the Organization of Defensive Innovation?"

"The same," Oron replied.

"Why did they lure us to that apartment in Dubai?"

"That part is not yet clear to us. We think their goal is to bring the world to the brink of destruction as a way of enticing the Mahdi to return, but we haven't figured out why they wanted you to send a team to Dubai."

"Maybe to create an incident they could use to promote

anti-American sentiment. Americans on Muslim soil."

"Perhaps." Oron shrugged. "But it is more likely there is another reason."

Marsh pointed to the photograph that was still lying on the table. "Any idea where we could find Sadeq Alizadeh?"

"His last known residence was in Iran at a place called Polour. Near the base of Mount Damavand. *The Almumin* is led by Jamal Kazameyni who lives in a compound in that same area. Kazameyni has no direct contact with the outside world and relies solely on intermediaries to communicate with the group. Alizadeh is one of his primary intermediaries."

"Thank you for bringing this to our attention," Marsh said. "I'll find out what we have on them and let you know. But I'm guessing this isn't the only reason you flew over here to see us."

Oron seemed amused by Marsh's directness. "No, it's not the only reason," he said. "It appears the Russians have contacted Iran's defense ministry about supplying them with drones and artillery shells. We believe they've already struck a deal."

Marsh was concerned. "What makes you think that?"

"We have noticed changes in activity at Iran's manufacturing facilities in Rasht that suggest they have doubled their drone production capacity."

Oron opened a satchel he was carrying and removed a handful of images, then handed them to Marsh. "These are of a facility in Rasht. They were taken a few days ago. As you know, that city has many elaborate and growing factories for making arms and munitions." He pointed to an image. "Our analysts say these objects are made of molded carbon fiber. By the nature of their appearance, we think they are probably parts of a drone. They've been unloading truckloads of it at this building." He pointed to the picture again and tapped it with his index finger. "That building right there is a weapons factory."

"Any idea which drones they're using those parts for?"

"Shahed 131 and 136."

"Loitering drones," Marsh muttered.

"Our ministers aren't too worried about the drones themselves. We can take them down about as fast as they can send them. What worries our guys is the increase in production and the possibility that Iran may use this as a way of getting help from Russia with their nuclear program."

Marsh nodded. "Iran supplies Russia with drones. Russia supplies Iran with help for their nuclear program."

"Exactly," Oron said. "Iran can enrich uranium without any problems. We think they may already have enough for a bomb. But they can't build a deliverable bomb without help. Certainly, not a bomb they can use with a missile. They don't have the miniaturization technology for it."

"We're counting on that," Marsh said with a knowing look.

"I know," Oron noted. "Which is why they sent me to see you. The prime minister wants to make sure the leaders of our two countries hold similar opinions about the threat Iran poses to both of us, about the role Russia plays in that threat, and about how a deal with Iran influences all of that."

"I'm sure Director Donovan knows, and President Jackson has been briefed on the latest intelligence from the region," Marsh said. He and Donovan had discussed Russia's weapons shortages and the war's potential for expanding Russian influence into countries far from the immediate area of the fighting.

"This is a serious problem," Oron said. "Especially for us, but also for the US and every other country. Mehdi Kalhor held a meeting at Natanz a few weeks ago. Officials from all of their enrichment facilities were present, including Majid Roshan, who runs the entire enrichment program."

"Do you think changes are coming for their nuclear program?"

"We are not certain, but we've seen a lot of movement. Increased production at Rasht. Meetings at Natanz. Our ministers are getting nervous."

"Are *you* getting nervous?"

"When the ministers get nervous, I get nervous," Oron replied. "They don't want to get caught by surprise and with developments popping up all over. It seems like a situation primed for serious trouble. One misunderstanding and the whole place could go up."

Marsh pointed to the photograph. "You think you'll be the target for these drones?"

"If they use them in our region," Oron said. "We've been on their list from the beginning. But the potential influence a deal with Russia might have on their nuclear program has everyone's attention right now."

"It would certainly be much easier for them to strike Tel Aviv or Jerusalem than to hit New York or Washington," Marsh noted.

CHAPTER ELEVEN

fter talking with Oron, Marsh went to see Peter McDowell, head of the CIA's Special Operations Group. The section of the agency responsible for the team that was killed in the Dubai apartment. They met in McDowell's office.

"I'm sure I know why you're here," McDowell said with a defensive gesture. "I've been dreading this day."

Marsh had a pained expression. "I don't understand what happened."

"Have you talked to Bob Donovan about this?"

"I'm talking to you," Marsh said. His voice was forceful, but loud or angry.

"I think you should see Bob first," McDowell insisted.

"Look, I'm in charge of covert operations." Marsh was impatient. "You sent a team to an apartment in Dubai and—"

"At your request," McDowell said, pointing with his index finger.

"Yes," Marsh said. "At my request. Which is why I want to know what happened and I want to know everything about that apartment."

McDowell sighed. "The State Department—"

Marsh groaned.

"I know," McDowell said. "But we do have to work with them on occasion."

"What happened?" Marsh asked with a resolute tone.

McDowell waited a moment before speaking. "The State Department," he began, "finally got worried about Chinese expansion in the Middle East. They approached us about doing a joint operation in Dubai. They had a contact that they thought could give them inside information on China's arrangement with the UAE. I told them they should run it past you. They wanted it to be separate from our ongoing operations and insisted we didn't need you. I sent them to see Donovan."

Marsh raised an eyebrow. "And Bob approved it?"

McDowell nodded. "That's why I told you to talk to him."

"I'll get to Donovan," Marsh replied. "What about the apartment?"

"As usual, it came down to a question of budget. Someone had to cover the costs. Nobody on our side wanted to leave that much of a payment trail. So, we told State we would supply the personnel to run the operation, but the cost of the apartment had to come out of *their* budget. They acquired the apartment, and we began to use it."

"Who took care of security for the apartment?"

McDowell looked guilty. "We assumed State was. It was *their* apartment."

Marsh felt a twinge of anger. He'd seen this before. "But you don't know for certain what they did about it." It was a statement, not a question.

"Whatever they did," McDowell said, "it wasn't enough."

Marsh was livid but he did his best to keep his anger under control. "So, the special operations team that went into the apartment was killed because of a pissing match over whose budget paid would pay for it?"

McDowell shrugged. "What can I say?"

"You could start by saying you made a mistake," Marsh shouted. "Every one of those men died because you and whoever you were dealing with at State didn't know what you were doing! And instead of admitting it, you went ahead with the operation hoping it would turn out right and you'd all look like winners. But instead, it all blew up—literally—and an entire team lost their lives."

McDowell turned away and the room became uncomfortably quiet. Marsh stared at him, watching him stew in his own emotions, before saying, "Who was the contact in Dubai that State wanted to use with the Chinese?"

"I'm not sure I can tell you that."

"What not?"

"He's the State Department's asset."

Marsh leaned forward, his head over the desk, and lowered his voice. "This is the same kind of attitude that got half a dozen men killed." Then he shouted. "What is the name of the State Department asset you were using?"

"Sadeq Alizadeh," McDowell replied.

"And who was your contact at State?"

"I've told you all I'm going to tell you."

"Men died because of this."

"If you want to know more, you'll have to see Donovan."

✦ ✦ ✦

Donovan was in his office when Marsh returned. The door was ajar, so Marsh pushed it open and went inside. "We need to talk about Dubai," he said.

Donovan smiled. "Close the door and take a seat," he said. "McDowell already called. He said you'd be stopping by."

Marsh sat across from Donovan at his desk. "I thought we were working together."

Donovan frowned. "We?"

"You and I," Marsh said. "I thought we were working together. Keeping each other in the loop. Doing our best to avoid having operations stepping on each other."

Donovon's countenance darkened. "It was a one-off deal." His voice was low, but he wasn't recalcitrant.

"If I had known what they were doing—if it had been run through my office—those men would still be alive."

"These things happen sometimes."

"That's it?" Marsh raised his voice. "An entire team is wiped out and all you can say is, 'These things happen sometimes?'"

"Look, Jim. It was a simple operation. State furnished the apartment. Some of our guys were working their contacts. It wasn't supposed to be anything wet."

"Nothing wet? That's your answer? It wasn't supposed to turn out like this?"

"I know you're upset," Donovan said. "And you have every right to be, but it wasn't that kind of operation. State was looking for information. That's all. We were helping them out."

"And no one thought to vet the contact?"

"That was State's job."

"Yeah? Well, it turns out it was no one's job."

"You think the contact was the problem?"

"I think it. Mossad thinks it. Most people in the Middle East *know* he was the problem."

Donovan looked worried. "Mossad? What do they have to do with it?"

"You would know what they had to do with it if you had run this operation through me like you were supposed to."

Donovan scowled. "I don't like the tone of your voice."

"And I don't like getting cut out of an operation that clearly comes under the purview of my office."

"Who was the asset State wanted to use?" Donovan asked.

Marsh had a mocking smile. "You don't even know his name?"

"McDowell was handling that for us on this one."

"You thought McDowell was doing it. He thought State was doing it." Donovan grimaced and leaned back in his chair. Marsh kept going. "You turned over the safety of the team to people who don't know how to send a team to the shower, much less how to run an operation. And I don't hear a lot of concern about the fact that they're all dead because of it."

"So, who was the asset State was trying to use?"

Marsh didn't want to tell him, but he felt obligated to share the information. After all, he was castigating Donovan and McDowell for *not* doing that very thing. "His name is Sadeq Alizadeh."

"And who is he?"

"That's what I'm trying to find out," Marsh said. "Who was the State Department contact on this debacle?"

Donovan gave him a thin smile. "Your friend, Janice Miller." Donovan took a letter from the top drawer of his desk and handed it to Marsh. "She wants someone to brief her on Naryshkin's visit to China. You can talk about Dubai when you tell her about Naryshkin."

✦ ✦ ✦

At the State Department, Janice Miller was the Assistant Secretary for South and Central Asian Affairs. Her area of responsibility included Kazakhstan, Uzbekistan, Kyrgyzstan, Tajikistan, and Turkmenistan, a critical area for US policy in recent years.

Miller was from upstate New York and attended the University of Buffalo, where she majored in history, then received a master's degree in international affairs from Columbia. A professor with an eye for talent noticed her and brought her to the attention of State Department recruiters. She was accepted into the foreign service and, over the next several years, was assigned to the consular staff at embassies in the Caucasus region before arriving in Washington, where she worked for the South and Central Asia Bureau.

She was tall with a full figure, which she didn't mind using to her advantage. And she had a reputation for being crass, sarcastic, and opinionated. Marsh had worked with her before and found her refreshingly unlike most career government employees. They talked in Miller's office.

"Thank you for coming," Miller began. "I was wondering who they would send."

"Tell me about Dubai," Marsh said, ignoring the stated reason for his visit.

Miller looked perplexed and not at all amused. "I asked for someone to brief me about Russia and their attempts to do an arms deal with China."

"And instead, you got me," Marsh said. "Tell me about Dubai."

She glanced away. "I'm afraid I don't know what you're talking about."

"Cut the crap," Marsh said. "I've talked to McDowell. I've talked to Donovan. I know you were trying to run an operation in Dubai. So, tell me about it."

"What makes you think I was in charge?"

"Donovan and McDowell."

"I see."

"No, you don't see," Marsh snapped. "A special response team is dead. They say you were in charge. That makes them your responsibility. If you have a different story, you better get ahead of it fast. I'm not asking about the infighting over whose budget covered the cost of the project. Or the stupid decision that led to it falling apart. I want to know what you were trying to accomplish and how you came to know about Sadeq Alizadeh."

Miller looked surprised. "For an intelligence agency, people at the CIA sure do talk a lot."

"This was a covert operation. It was supposed to be under my authority. If it had been, you wouldn't have lost that team. Tell me about Dubai."

"Is that what this is about? Someone stepped on your turf?"

"It's about an operation led by people who didn't have a clue what they were doing and were too proud and too arrogant to ask for help." Marsh looked her in the eye. "Tell me about Dubai. What were you doing there?"

Miller sat up straight in her chair. "As you know, the Chinese have spent the last forty years looking for ways to flank us, undermine us, and push us aside. They tried military bluster, they tried diplomacy, and then they turned to economic development. They have projects in Africa, South America, Central America, and Central Asia. Our desk has tried to raise the red flag on it, but no one paid any attention. Companies have made huge profits selling cheap consumer goods from China. The oil market is stable. We have a more-or-less agreeable government in Iraq and our troops are out of Afghanistan."

"Mostly."

She ignored the comment. "The Chinese mean to replace us as the world's leading superpower and they're doing it with money they've earned from undermining and underselling our manufacturing base. We decided it was time someone did something about it."

"So, why not come to me?" Marsh asked. "Why not run your operation through the usual CIA channels?"

"I had things I wanted to accomplish," Miller said, defensively. "And I didn't want to go ten rounds with someone telling me at every turn I didn't know what I was doing."

"But you *didn't* know what you were doing."

"I've been in the foreign service for—"

Marsh held up a hand to wave her off. "No one is questioning your credentials as a foreign services officer."

"It sure looks like if from my perspective."

Marsh took a moment, then said, "You had an asset, Sadeq Alizadeh."

Miller nodded.

"How did you find him?"

"He found us."

"He came to State?"

"Alizadeh approached a cultural attaché at the embassy in Astana. Said he had heard we were interested in keeping an eye on the Chinese. He offered to help."

"How did he know you were interested in the Chinese?"

"I'm not sure."

"You didn't talk to him?"

"The cultural attaché did. He said Alizadeh seemed legitimate. That's when I talked to your guys."

"McDowell."

"Yes."

"Why him?"

"We were in class together at Columbia. He was someone I knew. I trusted him."

"You know me," Marsh said. "You didn't trust me?"

"I didn't trust you *because* I know you."

"What does that mean?"

"You would have pushed me aside and taken over."

"I would have insisted on being in charge," Marsh noted.

"Exactly."

"And those men would be alive today if I had been."

"That's what I'm talking about," Miller said. "You are so sure you're always right."

"I have at least as many years in covert ops as you have in the foreign service."

"Maybe so, but I—"

"So, no one else vetted Alizadeh?"

Miller shook her head. "Not as far as I know."

"Had you vetted him, you would have known he was an Iranian with—"

"We aren't idiots," Miller snarled. "We know a—"

"And," Marsh interrupted, "you would have known he was a member of *The Almumin*. A radical Muslim cell coordinated by Mehdi Kalhor." Miller knew the name. "And you would have known that they are ultimately accountable to Jamal Kazameyni, a known terrorist on the State Department's list."

The color drained from Miller's face. She turned toward the window. "We wanted to know about Dubai's relationship with China. What the interests were and why they had grown so close recently. We were looking for a point of entry that we could exploit in our favor."

"So, you went to a source with high-level contacts in Iran." Marsh meant it as an obvious indication of their lack of expertise.

Miller gave a gesture of frustration. "He convinced the people in Kazakhstan that he was part of the Dubai negotiating team."

Marsh shook his head. "No one could make this stuff up. What did you give him?"

"Alizadeh?"

"Yes."

"Access to the apartment."

"With its Wi-Fi network."

"Yes."

"Did your people use the apartment, too?"

"On occasion," Miller replied. "Why?"

"And they logged onto the internet through the apartment's Wi-Fi?"

"I'm sure they did," Miller said. "Why?"

"That's how Alizadeh knew how to contact me."

Miller was surprised. "He contacted you?"

"He sent me an email," Marsh said. "I didn't know it was him at the time, but I do now. And I wondered how he knew how to reach me."

"And you think he got that from the Wi-Fi?"

Marsh nodded. "Somewhere in the user history, maybe. Or in the devices that were connected to the server." He shook his head again. "This was a sloppy operation."

"I resent that," she snapped.

"Did your guys plant the charges in the apartment floor?"

"We didn't know anything about that."

"That's what I mean," Marsh said. "It was a sloppy operation. And it got a team of guys killed."

They sat quietly for a moment, each lost in their own thoughts, then Marsh said, "Central Asia is your area?"

"Yes."

"Why did Alizadeh come to you through the embassy in Kazakhstan?"

"Like I said, we've been attempting to monitor China's interest there."

"What is China's interest in Kazakhstan?"

"Oil," she said. "And broadening their reach in the region. They have been trying to resolve the differences between Iran and Saudi Arabia as a way of proving they really can broker a difficult international deal. Until the war in Ukraine, Russia had a robust presence in the Middle East, but the war hasn't gone the way they planned and has required more of their attention than they originally thought."

"So, there's a void in the Middle East?"

Miller nodded. "China has stepped in to fill that void. And it seems to be working," she noted. "Saudi Arabian and Chinese representatives have been meeting regularly in Riyadh and Beijing, but some of those included representatives from Iran, too. Which is why we were interested in Alizadeh. He seemed to offer a way to connect the dots."

Marsh was ready to move the conversation forward. "We think Chinese leadership sees themselves in a difficult spot with Russia and Ukraine. They need to respond positively to Russia, but they don't need to scare the rest of the world."

"Particularly us," Miller noted. "Despite all of the rhetoric lately, they do a tremendous amount of business with us. They can't tolerate economic sanctions for very long."

"Right," Marsh said, nodding.

Miller seemed dissatisfied. "But this can't be all that's going on between them. Dong Jingwei wouldn't have allowed Naryshkin to leave Beijing without getting something from the meeting."

"Any suggestions?"

"After Naryshkin made his trip to China, I reached out to representatives from Kazakhstan, Kyrgyzstan, and Tajikistan and asked to meet with them to discuss regional issues. The war in Ukraine, that kind of thing. All three declined to meet with me."

"It could have been nothing," Marsh said with a shrug. "All three of those countries are closer to Russia than they are to us. They might have wanted to avoid being seen as disloyal."

"That's what I thought," Miller said. "And then I learned about their meetings with the Chinese and the Saudis."

✦ ✦ ✦

Miller's intuition, that something more was going on in Central Asia, was not far off. Since the year before trouble began in Ukraine, negotiating teams from China had been working with strategic partners in the region in an attempt to restore full diplomatic relations between Iran and Saudi Arabia. The primary effort focused on meetings between Chinese negotiators and Saudi representatives in Riyadh, but a second set of meetings with Iranian representatives was conducted in Astana, Kazakhstan. Talks were also held on collateral issues with officials from Uzbekistan, Tajikistan, and Kirgizstan.

The official explanation portrayed these meetings as merely part of China's continuing effort to restore diplomatic relations between Saudi Arabia and Iran. Wei Xing, however, was primarily interested in the way success in improving relations between the two countries might be helpful to his goal of expanding China's influence in the world.

It also was not lost on Wei Xing that the four countries—Kazakhstan, Uzbekistan, Tajikistan, and Kirgizstan—lay between Russia and China. As the war in Ukraine developed, Wei Xing thought involvement in the region might imply that China was covering Russia's southern flank, allowing Putin to focus his attention on the war in Ukraine. That's how he intended to portray it to the World, though he knew the West would see it as an attempted land grab. Widening its own sphere of influence while Russia's attention was diverted.

Talks between Chinese and Saudi representatives had been moving forward since long before the latest rounds of negotiations began, but after years of discussion, the two sides had come to the final issue that separated them. Saudi Arabia wanted a nuclear reactor, and they were unyielding in their insistence on that point. "Iran is very near to having its own cadre of nuclear weapons," they argued. "Our urge to have a full-scale, operational nuclear program cannot be seen as unreasonable."

Wei Xing's Committee of Advisors was unconvinced. "This is a bad time to spread nuclear weapons in the Middle East."

"But we need to seal the deal between Saudi Arabia and Iran," Wei Xing argued, "and to do that, we have to satisfy the Saudis by convincing them it is safe to deal directly with Iran."

Ba Renfu spoke up. "This is a risky path, but if we are to follow it, we need to get the work finished soon. Delegates from the US have been talking to the Saudis about these very issues since the Bush administration. Rumors suggest the Saudis are listening now."

"What did the Saudis tell them?"

"The same thing they told us," Renfu said. "That they want their own nuclear program."

"And the Americans agreed to that?"

"I think they suggested they might agree to supply a civilian nuclear reactor."

"That sounds like a negotiating position. What is America's official position?"

"Many conservatives view the discussion of even a civilian reactor for Saudi Arabia as destabilizing and another step toward normalizing nuclear power in the region."

Wei Xing nodded. "That is why this is a good time for us to act. The US is preoccupied with Ukraine while attempting to contain competing interests outside the European region. That effort has stretched them much too thinly. If we agree to help the Saudis, there will be nothing the US can do about it, especially if our deal includes the restoration of relations between the two countries. All nations of the world will see it as a positive step away from another regional war. The Americans will be forced to go along."

Li Xudong glanced down the table toward Wei Xing with a playful look. "Perhaps we should handle the Saudis in the same way our Paramount Leader suggests we handle others." He paused for the others to catch up. "Perhaps we should promise the Saudis something but give them nothing."

Others in the room laughed good-naturedly. Wei Xing had used versions of that phrase in many settings, describing it as the

Dao of Chinese politics. He was intrigued by the suggestion and impressed by the reaction of those at the discussion and he laughed in response.

The next day, Wei Xing sent a message to the negotiating team in Riyadh asking them to prepare a proposal along those lines. Offer the Saudi Arabians something, that appeared to be something, but in reality, was nothing that could ever be anything.

After a week of discussion and argument among themselves, the Chinese negotiating team in Riyadh offered to give Saudi Arabia a civilian nuclear reactor. "But only if Iran develops its nuclear weapons program to the point of viability." That was enough to satisfy Saudi representatives and the two sides closed their agreement as a side deal to the effort to restore diplomatic relations with Iran.

Talks with Iranian representatives had followed a similar path, but bringing those discussions to a successful conclusion took another month. With the two sides in agreement with China about what an ultimate arrangement might contain, Iranian and Saudi Arabian representatives met face-to-farce in Kazakhstan with Chinese negotiators moderating their discussions. Those talks were troublesome but ultimately resulted in an agreement restoring diplomatic relations between the two countries.

CHAPTER TWELVE

Having found only limited success in procuring arms from other countries, Russia's effort to wage war against Ukraine remained seriously hampered by a lack of ammunition and equipment. As frustration continued to mount, Putin's rhetoric became increasingly belligerent with repeated references to a shift toward the use of stronger weapons—an implication most took to mean nuclear weapons. With each mention of the topic, US officials became more and more concerned that Putin's priorities might have shifted from a grueling conventional campaign to a campaign using nuclear weapons as a way of avoiding a humiliating defeat.

The topic came up regularly in meetings at CIA headquarters. Everyone had their estimates of likely scenarios and likely results, but no one seemed to grasp the catastrophic nature of the result such a war would bring. None except Marsh, who was deeply troubled by it.

Somewhere between college and his position with the CIA, Marsh had become a secular government employee much like every other secular government employee, but before that, before he went away to college, he had regularly attended Sunday school and church with his parents. He knew about biblical prophecies regarding the end of time. Nations lining up against each other. The disappearance of a third of earth's vegetation, a third of its sea life, a third of its freshwater, and a third of sunlight. Events surrounding the war in Ukraine seemed to be setting the table for just such a moment.

The prospect of Putin facing humiliation at the hands of a former Soviet state, in coalition with Western democracies, seemed like the perfect catalyst to put a worst-case, end-of-time scenario in motion and it could happen without anyone realizing the ultimate effect of their immediate decisions.

The same was true with China where politically myopic leadership appeared focused solely on the needs, wants, and desires of their nation alone. A perspective that made them vulnerable to blundering their way into a global nuclear confrontation without realizing what they had done until it was too late.

Putin was a prideful leader who seemed to have lost his way. The war in Ukraine had been based on horrendously weak intelligence, poor estimations, and even poorer planning. It had been executed with bad management and little strategic thought, which placed Russian troops at a decided disadvantage. When humiliation became a real possibility, Putin used his own failure as the basis for outlandish assertions that Western conspirators had worked together to deprive him of a victory. That the US had lured them into a trap for the purpose of destroying Russia. And when no one took those assertions seriously, he began flippantly tossing about the potential for the use of nuclear weapons. His recent statements on the matter seemed to indicate a downward spiral toward absurdity and seemed to Marsh like the opinions of a person who was no longer in touch with his own mind.

Events and decisions regarding China seemed equally misguided. For the past fifty years, they had made it plain to everyone that they considered Taiwan their rightful possession. With Russia and NATO draining their stocks of missiles, drones, and small arms well below amounts that could be replenished in five, ten, or even fifteen years of usual production, and with no end to the Ukrainian war in sight, the situation seemed to be a perfect storm for trouble in the Pacific.

If China moved to reclaim control of Taiwan, the US would be unable to respond with conventional weapons and would face the same choices Putin faced in Ukraine—bow to humiliation or engage in a nuclear war. And no matter what anyone said about the practicality of so-called *low-yield* nuclear weapons, there was no such thing as a non-contaminating nuclear bomb.

At night, alone in his study at home, Marsh brooded over potential scenarios, rolling them around in his mind with increasing angst. One misstep, one unguarded moment, one poorly vetted decision and those three countries—Russia, China, and the United States—could eliminate a third of the human population, a third of the vegetation, and a third of the sea life in a matter of hours, not days, just as prophecy indicated.

As if drawn to the days of his youth, Marsh found a copy of *The Bible* on the shelf in his study—the same one he had received as a gift when he graduated from high school. He took it from the shelf and began reading and re-reading the book of *Revelation*. Familiar words from the text greeted him like an old friend and he let them wash over him, like water tumbling down a rocky stream, crashing over his head, filling his mind with memories and his spirit with life.

Scenes from the pages were, indeed, unsettling—beasts, plagues, bowls of wrath—but he found the tone of the passages oddly reassuring. The end, but not the end. More an opening to a new heaven, a new earth, a new beginning. An end opening to a beginning.

Thinking of that reminded Marsh of a verse from somewhere else, but he couldn't remember quite where it came from. His laptop sat to his right, so he searched online and found what he was looking for in *The Gospel of John*. John the Baptist speaking of his younger cousin, Jesus. "He who comes after me has surpassed me because he was before me." As if John was saying, "The one born after me is ahead of me because he existed before I was born."

The quote had nothing to do with *Revelation* or the looming global crisis, but reading those words brought a smile to Marsh's face and a sense of hope to his mind. Others had faced existential crises in the past and they had found a way. A voice from a cloud. A whisper from a friend. . . That's what Marsh needed. A friend. Someone on the inside. Someone who understood the players. Someone whom the key leaders would trust.

A copy of *The Washington Post* lay on a chair to the right of the desk. It was lying face down with the part below the fold showing. On it was a photograph of Putin addressing the press corps on the steps outside The Kremlin. Marsh came from behind his desk and picked up the paper for a closer look. Several officials stood on either side of Putin and a number lined the top step behind him. One of those was Nikolay Vorobyov. Marsh's heart seemed to skip a beat.

Vorobyov was Russia's Deputy Director of Intelligence in charge of covert operations. A position like the one Marsh held at the CIA. During the 2014 Russian invasion of Ukraine, Vorobyov and Marsh regularly exchanged information between themselves in an attempt to keep US-Russia relations from getting out of hand. In the years that followed, Putin had clamped down on the flow of information, insisting that his own assistants review everything before it was disseminated beyond the Kremlin. Vorobyov, fearing reprisals from Putin and his cronies, was forced to curtail his unofficial contacts with anyone other than agency personnel.

Sitting in his study that night, staring at the photo of Vorobyov in the newspaper, Marsh wondered if he had received the answer he sought. A friend on the inside. A non-politician who knew the politicians yet wasn't enamored of them. One who understood both sides of the issues their countries faced, and the consequences injudicious decisions might produce.

Despite the fractured nature of their relationship, Marsh signaled Vorobyov that night with a request for a meeting, using a work name only they knew. Vorobyov responded immediately and a meeting was scheduled for the following month in Amsterdam, where Marsh was set to attend an unrelated meeting at The Hague.

✦ ✦ ✦

On a free day at The Hague, Marsh slipped away and drove to Amsterdam, about forty-five minutes away, where he met Vorobyov in a room at the Waldorf Astoria Amsterdam. They both were glad to see each other again, but Marsh got straight to the point. "Putin has made some troubling statements recently regarding the use of 'more powerful weapons.' Important people in Washington interpret that to mean nuclear weapons. What is he talking about?"

Vorobyov was coy. "It doesn't necessarily mean atomic weapons," he said, shaking his head. "Russia has many stronger conventional weapons. Hypersonic missiles and our version of your MOAB, among them."

Marsh pressed the issue further. "Is Putin considering the use of nuclear weapons?"

"Such weapons would leave terrible devastation."

"I know they would be terrible," Marsh said, doing nothing to hide his frustration, "but are you considering them?"

Vorobyov's shoulders sagged. "Putin has convened a study group to explore the use of *low-yield* devices."

"Nuclear devices?"

"Yes."

"And how low is a low yield?"

"The standard range," Vorobyov replied. "One to ten kilotons."

"Is he serious?"

Vorobyov shrugged. "Who can say which things he is serious

about and which ones he uses merely for effect? But the study group he convened is directed by Ravil Averin who is known to favor the use of such weapons."

Marsh's frustration boiled over. "Are they crazy?"

"You must understand, Putin and many of his top advisors see this war as part of a greater effort to reclaim the territory of the old Russian empire. They see it as a rightful reunion of the parts that were taken away from us by your country."

Marsh looked bewildered. "We didn't take anything away from you."

"Maybe others did the work for you," Vorobyov said. "But you were the instigators."

Marsh scowled. "That's ridiculous and you know it."

"Your President Reagan came to Berlin and said, 'Mr. Gorbachev, tear down this wall.' I was there. I heard him with my own ears."

"That was political rhetoric," Marsh said dismissively. "And anyway, him saying those things didn't destroy the wall or the Soviet Union."

"Ahh, but it did."

"How so?"

"When we did not tear down the wall, your President Reagan started an arms race, spending far more than was necessary for your country's defense. This was part of his plan to bankrupt our country as we tried to keep up with you. The older Mr. Bush finished that plan with your country's first invasion of Iraq."

"How did our invasion of Iraq affect the Soviet Union?"

"You put the result of that war on display for the world to see with their television sets, broadcasting how flawlessly your weapons performed. We were humiliated to see our tanks and missiles destroyed by your weapons, right there on the TV screen for everyone to see. Even our own people. It was the end of the Soviet army's supremacy."

"The Iraqi army invaded its neighbor," Marsh replied. "They asked us for help in getting them out."

"And that sideshow his son put on in a second invasion." Vorobyov shook his head in disgust. "There were never any weapons of mass destruction in Iraq. Everyone knew that. There was only your need to redeem your image after the attack on New York by Muslim terrorists you originally armed and supported. And never mind your country's subsequent intervention in Afghanistan. All of it was an embarrassment to the Russian Empire. An embarrassment your leaders planned for us all along."

Marsh was perplexed. "The Empire ended with the revolution in 1917."

"Many understood the Soviet Union as merely a newer form of the old empire. To some, Russia has always been an empire."

Marsh was perplexed by the nature of the argument. "Whatever it was," he said, finally, "it collapsed of its own weight."

Vorobyov grinned. "You are frustrated."

"Yes, I am," Marsh said even more vehemently than before. "You're blaming us for more than a hundred years of history that no one today had any part of.

"I am simply telling you how Putin sees your country," Vorobyov said. "All of your successes, he sees as attempts to embarrass Russia and Russian leaders. All of your victories are the fuel of Putin's paranoia."

"And what about his losses? How does he characterize Russian failures that occurred on *his* watch?"

"All of his failures are the result of a great American conspiracy against us and against him personally."

"And now Putin wants pay-back for all of it?"

Vorobyov nodded. "He and his advisors refer to it as 'settling all accounts.' Defeat in Ukraine is something they will never allow. If our army is about to be defeated in Ukraine, then humanity will taste defeat everywhere."

Marsh was taken aback. "You mean, Putin will use nuclear weapons to prevent defeat?"

"Yes," Vorobyov nodded. "I am afraid the fate of the world will come down to the mind of a single man. If he thinks he is about to be defeated, regardless of whether that perception is real or imagined, he will launch our nuclear weapons."

The visit with Vorobyov left Marsh more troubled than before. Putin really intended to use nuclear weapons in Ukraine. The thought of it was utterly astounding.

How could anyone be that brazen? That cavalier? That. . .stupid? He'd heard conservative pundits refer to Putin as a "demon-possessed madman," and he had dismissed it as mere hyperbole, but now, hearing the news from Vorobyov firsthand, he thought maybe they were right. Maybe Putin really was a madman. Maybe his intentions really were only evil.

✦ ✦ ✦

When Marsh returned to the US, he met with Donovan to brief him on the result of his meeting with Vorobyov. "And so, it is as we suspected," Donovan said after hearing about the visit. "Momentum is increasingly driving Putin toward nuclear war."

"That appears to be the case," Marsh replied. "The harder the Ukrainians fight, the more support we give them, the more Putin is convinced we are out to get him."

Donovan gazed to the left, toward a window that looked onto the campus surrounding the headquarters building. "This is the absurdity of the so-called nuclear option," he said softly.

Marsh couldn't quite hear. "How's that?" he asked.

"We could do all the things we can do. All the things we usually do. Infiltrate Ukraine with operatives. Train their soldiers in improvised warfare to increase the effectiveness of what they have." He turned to face Marsh. "We could maximize Ukrainian potential to its fullest extent and teach them to overcome every obstacle, but none of that can prevent a Russian leader from giving an order to launch their nuclear missiles. We have no way to force Putin to change his mind."

Marsh had thought much the same thing. "And everything we do to enhance Ukraine's conventional ability only serves to tighten the box Putin has put himself into."

"Thereby pushing him closer to the use of nuclear weapons."

"Someone needs to give him a way out."

Donovan had a skeptical expression. "I'm afraid there isn't one," he said.

"No way out, or no one to show it to him?"

"Either. All that remains is the inevitable."

"Perhaps then we should deliver it first," Marsh said.

Donovan glared at him. "Have you gone mad?"

"Not at all," Marsh replied. "I'm just saying, if worldwide devastation is inevitable, why are we waiting for Russia to go first?"

Donovan smiled. "When the fall is all that's left. . ." An allusion to a quote from *The Lion in Winter*.

Marsh nodded slowly. "I never saw that movie, but I love that quote. We could alter it a little in our case to say, 'When dying's all that's left, it matters a great deal how we do it.'"

"Fight like men of Rohan."

"Exactly."

They were silent a moment, then Donovan said, "Do you think we should continue apace? Pursuing all means of supporting Ukraine?"

"Yes, sir," Marsh said. "Our job is to gather information and forward it up the line. That's all we can do, so we should keep doing it and hope others know how to use the information properly. Though perhaps we should stop by a church on our way."

Donovan sighed. "Do you still believe in God?"

"More than ever."

"Then, if we must face an inevitable nuclear war, let us proceed to it as Americans." Donovan stood, signaling an end to their meeting, and the two shook hands. It was a surreal moment, but one that energized Marsh's determination to find a way out of their current situation. For themselves. For the country. For the world.

CHAPTER THIRTEEN

When Mehdi Kalhor told members of his *Almumin* cell about the Russian suitcase bombs that had been secretly placed in Canada, Bijan Abbadi had been caught up in the mystery and wonder of it. Suitcase nuclear bombs. Brought to North America. Concealed and waiting. All anyone had to do was locate them, take them to the US, and detonate them. He could only imagine the devastation that might result.

To aid his imagination, Abbadi located books and magazines in a Tehran library that contained images from the destruction of Hiroshima and Nagasaki. The destruction inflicted on them by nuclear bombs delivered by the US Army during World War II. The devastation seemed so complete he could hardly believe it was possible. Houses, office buildings, and industrial manufacturing sites, completely gone. Even the trees were missing and the few that remained were reduced to stark, lonely twigs, burned from the intense heat of the blast, standing alone against an equally stark background.

Although access to the internet was limited in Iran, Abbadi was able to reach online sites with before and after images of the bombings. Before the war, Hiroshima and Nagasaki were robust and vibrant cities. After the American attack, they were left desolate and barren by nuclear explosions. Abbadi projected those images onto New York, Los Angeles, and Chicago, picturing in his mind how they might appear if they were devoid of their tall buildings and complex roadways. In his mind, he imagined lower Manhattan as a barren plain. His body tingled with excitement at the image of it.

When Kalhor assigned Abbadi with the task of exploring the possibility that a cache of suitcase bombs, possibly as many as ten, might have been brought to Canada, in addition to the ones Kalhor already had found and secured, it seemed as if he'd been given the task for which he had been born. Spurred on by the possibilities of destruction and the glory for Allah that devastation might bring, he delved into the topic of suitcase bombs with religious fervor.

The library at Tehran University had copies of several reports regarding Soviet espionage in Canada, and he found a personal account of someone who had been part of that work. There also were numerous magazine and newspaper articles about Russians living in Canada during the 1970s and '80s. Abbadi read them all, making note of the people mentioned in those publications and the places where they lived. He even plotted those locations on a map, hoping that information might yield a clue as to where the mysterious suitcase bombs may have been hidden.

Despite all of Abbadi's efforts and all the tangential information he uncovered, he found nothing that told him where to begin the actual quest. A place he could go to in hopes of finding the thread that would lead him clue by clue to the cache of bombs. With no other options available to explore, Abbadi returned to Kalhor, hoping that Kalhor might mention one thing more that he had omitted in his previous accounts—a fact, an incident, a name—that might open the way for Abbadi to uncover the truth.

When they met to discuss the matter, Kalhor repeated only the information he had related before—that he had been told the suitcases existed, that their last known location was in Canada, and that they had been taken there during the Cold War.

"Ivan Saltanov told you this?"

"Yes."

"Is he still alive?"

"The last I heard, he was living in Sari, on the Caspian Sea."

Abbadi was surprised. "Sari is here, in Iran?"

"Yes," Kalhor said.

"Will you take me to him?"

"Of course," Kalhor replied, and they scheduled a date to make the trip.

✦ ✦ ✦

Saltanov was old by then, but not incompetent. Kalhor and Abbadi found him at a care home in Sari. He was seated in a wheelchair that had been parked on a patio behind the home. It faced the sea and Saltanov was turned in that direction, head slumped forward, fast asleep. He awakened when Kalhor touched him on the shoulder.

Abbadi had wondered if Saltanov would be forthcoming with information about the past, but he recognized Kalhor immediately and after they told him the reason for the visit, he seemed eager to talk about his life and work on behalf of Soviet Russia.

"It was an interesting time," Saltanov said. "Everyone was working for a cause—Americans, Soviets, Chinese—and yet there wasn't as much animosity as there is now. At least, that is how it seems now, looking back. People from back then who are still alive view those days the same way today. We knew who they were, and they knew who we were, and no one killed you just because they didn't like you."

They talked about the old days over tea, but Kalhor didn't have much time to spare. He steered the conversation to the stories about suitcase bombs as quickly as politely possible.

"I told you about three of them," Saltanov said, "but we never talked about the others."

"That's what we want to know about," Kalhor said.

"They were flown to Canada in a cargo box," Saltanov recalled. "Lead lined, to prevent detection. We called them suitcase bombs, but these were slightly larger than the ones I told you about before. I can't remember what kind of case they were supposed to be in. None of us looked at them. They were in a cargo container, and we didn't want to get too close to them. They tended to leak radiation."

"What happened to them?" Kalhor asked.

"We had paid a man at the airport in Ottawa to let the container through without inspecting it. No one inspected much back then anyway, but we wanted to be sure there weren't any problems. They had a dog sniff for drugs, but other than that, they did nothing. Once the container was cleared, a driver went to the airport with one of our trucks. They loaded it for him, and he drove it to a warehouse."

"Can you recall where the warehouse was located?"

"Not the address," Saltanov replied with a shake of his head. "It was in Ottawa, but I don't remember where exactly."

What happened after that?"

"The box was unloaded and left in the warehouse."

"That's all?"

"Yes." Saltanov nodded. "They unloaded it there and drove away."

"Did anyone ever go back for it?"

"No," Saltanov replied. "As far as I know, no one ever went back there."

"And you never heard about anyone moving it?"

"When the Soviet Union collapsed under Gorbachev, things got very chaotic, very quickly. Everyone seemed to focus on protecting their own interests. Preserving their careers. And getting on to a better position in whatever job they could find. There was a lot of uncertainty about what would happen next."

"So," Abbadi interjected, "they just walked away from ten suitcase bombs?"

"Not just the ones in Canada," Saltanov said. "But everywhere. They lost about ninety of them in total. Left them wherever they'd been cached and moved on."

Abbadi was astounded. "Ninety?"

"Yes. And almost all of them still are unaccounted for."

"Who owned the warehouse in Ottawa?" Kalhor asked, bringing the discussion back to the topic at hand.

"Bazhenov," Saltanov said. "Bazhenov Oil Company. We used oil companies for lots of things back then. They were always moving men and equipment, drilling components especially. You can hide lots of things in a five-gallon bucket of drilling mud. And if you have a pallet of them, all the more."

Kalhor seemed suspicious. "You never told me this."

Saltanov had a playful smile. "I had told you too much already. These miniaturized bombs were brought to Canada to be available as a last measure, in case something catastrophic occurred. Total nuclear war, or whatever we were calling it then. The last time I heard, the bombs were there, in the cargo container. I doubt anyone has moved them."

"Why do you say that?"

"Bazhenov Oil Company was a state-owned company," Saltanov explained. "One of the few that escaped privatization. But the company had to give up many of its assets. It's little more than a shell of what it used to be. Down to half a dozen employees in Moscow. They no longer have an office in Ottawa or conduct business in Canada, but they still own the building where those bombs are kept."

"How do you know this?"

"My brother-in-law worked for them when they were in Ottawa," Saltanov explained.

Kalhor seemed convinced Saltanov had told them what they came to learn, and he stood as if to leave. At the last moment, he paused and asked, "Whatever happened to Dr. Kozlovsky?"

Saltanov looked sad. "He was shot."

Kalhor's jaw dropped. "By whom?"

"Loyalist to the supposed democracy. Part of a post-Soviet purge. They thought he had divulged secrets. He tried to tell them otherwise, but they did not believe him."

Kalhor leaned over and gave Saltanov a hug. "I am glad you are here with us."

✦ ✦ ✦

When Abbadi returned to Tehran, he researched Bazhenov Oil Company in an attempt to confirm what Saltanov had said about it. Very little information was available on the internet about the company, but he was able to determine that Bazhenov Oil still was an existing Russian entity and that, in the past, it had operated in Canada. He also located an Ottawa address for the company but found it was an address for an office building. He needed a building at least large enough to hold a cargo container, but for that kind of information, he would have to go to Ottawa.

✦ ✦ ✦

With Kalhor's help, Abbadi obtained a tourist visa for Canada and made plans to travel to Ottawa, hoping to learn more about Bazhenov Oil Company. A few days before he was to leave Tehran, he met Kalhor for coffee.

"I have a visa and an airline ticket," Abbadi said. "But what will I do once I arrive? How will I get around? Do we know anyone there?"

"I have arranged for someone to meet you at the airport," Kalhor said. "His name is Jalal Pirzad." He handed Abbadi a card with Pirzad's contact information. "He will take you to the house where he lives. You can stay there."

"Is he safe?"

"Absolutely," Kalhor said. "Jalal teaches at Carleton College. He will be able to assist you in whatever work you do. He is one of us."

"What should I do when I locate the items?"

"Notify me," Kalhor said. "A simple message. Nothing explicit. You have a way to the airport for your flight?"

"My neighbor has agreed to drive me."

"Good. That is better than a taxi or a bus." Kalhor took a sip of coffee. "Do your best to fit in while you are in Canada. Don't call attention to yourself."

"Just visiting a friend and seeing the sites."

"Right." Kalhor handed him an envelope. "This will cover your expenses for a while. Try to make it last as long as possible."

✦ ✦ ✦

Abbadi arrived in Ottawa without incident and was met as scheduled by Pirzad, who took him to the house and helped him get settled. The following day, Abbadi went with Pirzad to Carleton College, and Pirzad introduced him to the librarian. While Pirzad went off to teach, Abbadi began searching for records regarding Bazhenov Oil Company.

An initial review of business directories yielded very little information on Bazhenov. An assistant from the library staff showed him how to access state corporate records online, where he found the names and addresses of company officers and directors. She showed him the property tax system, too, and in the listings for previous years they found Bazhenov was listed as the owner of a building in Greenboro, a neighborhood on the east side of the city.

"Does the company still own it?"

"Apparently so," she said, pointing to the entry details. Abbadi noted the address.

Late that afternoon, Pirzad came to the library to collect Abbadi, then they drove out to the edge of town to locate the building listed on Bazhenov's tax records. It was a generic commercial warehouse—steel frame with prefab metal panels for an exterior— in a business park filled with rows of similar structures.

Pirzad brought the car to a stop in front of it. "That seems to be the one," he said.

"It's big," Abbadi noted.

"Yes, it is."

"Think we could get inside?"

"It's probably locked," Pirzad replied. "And I don't want to risk a criminal charge attempting to break in."

"How can I get out here on my own?"

Pirzad gently pressed the gas pedal and the car started forward. "I'll show you the bus schedule."

"How difficult is it to obtain a car?" Abbadi asked.

"A friend has a truck. It isn't very good, and he doesn't like to use it. I spoke to him about it already. I think he will let you take it."

"You asked already?" It seemed odd to Abbadi that Pirzad had mentioned the matter to someone.

"Yes," Pirzad replied. He glanced over at Abbadi and seemed to notice the look of concern on his face. "It's okay," he assured. "He's one of us."

Abbadi wasn't sure what that meant—he's one of us—but he remembered what Kalhor had said about not causing trouble, so he let the comment pass. There really was no point in arguing over every detail. Kalhor had arranged a vehicle for him and that was enough, for now.

✦ ✦ ✦

Two days later, using the truck from Pirzad's friend, Abbadi returned to the warehouse and parked in back with the truck out of sight from the road. Two roll-up doors were located on the rear wall of the building, but they were fastened and secured from the inside. Pedestrian doors stood at either corner. The first was locked, but the second opened without difficulty and Abbadi went inside.

The building was dark and cavernous, and Abbadi's footsteps echoed with every move. He waited a moment, hoping his eyes would adjust enough to let him move about unaided, but when they did not, he used the light from his phone and made his way slowly through the space.

There wasn't much to see, just trash and dust on the floor, but in the front corner, he came to an office. It was made from plywood and appeared to have been added after the structure was completed—a building within a building. It had no windows but there was a door on one end. Abbadi grasped the knob and gave it a twist, but the door didn't budge. He had no tools, so he tried it again. Still, the door would not open.

Seeing no other option, Abbadi continued on his way through the remainder of the building, checking for evidence of a cargo box, and for something he could use to force open the office door. In the opposite corner of the building, he came to a garbage can—a steel drum filled with trash and junk. In it, he found a broken pipe wrench.

Abbadi brought the wrench back to the office door and used it to pry the doorknob loose. He would have beaten it free, but he did not want to make that much noise. After a few attempts, the doorknob fell off and the office door swung open.

In the glare of the light from his phone, he saw a square shipping container that appeared to measure about eight feet by eight feet. Small by current standards, it nevertheless appeared quite large inside the office and filled most of the space in the room. It also seemed quite large for only ten items, each being only about the size of a large duffel bag, as had been suggested in the stories he'd been told. But it was a cargo container. In Ottawa. And it was in a warehouse owned by the oil company. Exactly as Saltanov had described.

At first, Abbadi was hesitant to move any closer, being mindful of Saltanov's mention that the suitcase bombs leaked radiation, but finally, curiosity overcame his fear and he stepped to the end of the box that had a door. The handles to it were held in place by a padlock. Once again, Saltanov used the broken wrench to force it loose, then grasped the handles of the cargo box and opened the door.

Inside the container were ten duffel bags stacked atop each other in two rows along the bottom of the container. Abbadi snapped a picture with his phone, then closed the container door and backed away. Outside the office, he closed the door and used the remnants of the doorknob to wedge the door in place, then he made his way to the rear of the building and stepped outside. When he was seated in the truck, he sent a text to Kalhor that said simply, "Success."

✦ ✦ ✦

After discovering the suitcase bombs, Abbadi left them where he found them and took a few days to think about what to do next. He had expected a response from his text message to Kalhor with at least a hint of congratulation and instructions about what he should do next, but when days went by and no response came, he became increasingly concerned about the situation.

Someone might have seen him entering the building and reported it to the police. That notion bothered him initially but after reflection, it seemed unlikely. The area where the building was located wasn't a high-traffic area. But surely the company that owned it had someone—a property manager or caretaker—who checked on the building at least occasionally. They could have seen marks on the door where he forced his way inside. Then he remembered the exterior door of the warehouse was already unlocked when he found the building. But if someone went inside and wandered to the front of the building, they would see the knob for the office door was missing. And if they opened that door to see more about what might have happened to dislodge the knob, they would notice the duffel bags stacked inside. And if they unzipped one of the bags, panic would follow. But none of that happened.

In fact, a week went by after Abbadi found the bombs, and

nothing seemed untoward about it at all. No articles in the newspaper or online about suitcase bombs being discovered in Ottawa. No reports of a break-in. No police officers coming to the house to find out what he'd been up to over there. And, more important to his immediate future, no one from the embassy came around to question him.

Despite his own reassurances, Abbadi continued to worry about the bombs. One day, that they would be discovered before he could do something about them. The next that he would become ill with radiation poisoning even from the short time he was in the building. That his condition would require medical attention. That medical personnel would become suspicious and notify someone. This went on for two weeks until, finally, Pirzad forced him to talk about what was bothering him.

"I went back to the warehouse," Abbadi said.

"What did you find?"

Abbadi waited too long before responding.

Pirzad's expression turned serious. "You found what you were looking for, didn't you."

Again, Abbadi did not respond immediately. He needed to talk. He wanted to talk. He wanted to tell someone what he was doing, but could he trust Pirzad? Is that what Kalhor meant when he said Pirzad was 'one of us?' That he was someone Pirzad could work with? It must have been. A cryptic way of telling him Pirzad was part of whatever Kalhor was leading everyone into.

"Tell me," Pirzad insisted.

"Okay," Abbadi said at last. "I'll tell you, but this has to stay between us."

"Tell me."

"I did, in fact, find what I was looking for." Abbadi still was uncertain how involved Pirzad was in the things Kalhor was trying to accomplish. "Do you know what means?"

"I know it doesn't really have anything to do with that oil company you mentioned."

"How well do you know Mehdi Kalhor?"

Pirzad smiled. "He is my cousin."

Abbadi's eyes were wide with a look of amazement. "His cousin?"

"Yes. Has he told you stories about Russian suitcase bombs hidden in Canada?"

Abbadi grinned. "He told us *many* of those stories."

"And from the way you're acting, I suppose you found one of them."

"Not just one," Abbadi said. "I found ten."

Pirzad's eyes widened. "In that warehouse?"

"Yes," Abbadi said. "In duffel bags."

"And you think there are ten of them?"

Abbadi nodded. "They were stacked inside a shipping container."

"Twelve?"

"I counted them."

"What are you going to do with them?"

"Is that your garage out back?"

"It goes with the house," Pirzad replied. "Are you thinking of using it?"

"I think we should put the duffel bags in there, but I'm worried someone will detect the radiation."

"You have that many?"

"No," Abbadi said. "But that's the best place to put them. We can't leave them in that warehouse."

"Is it safe to bring them here?"

"I don't know, but I don't think we have a choice."

"Show them to me."

Abbadi shook his head. "Not until we go to get them. I don't want anyone to see us over there until we're ready to bring them out."

"But if you bring them over here, how will you keep someone from noticing? If they leak as much as the stories suggest, the whole neighborhood will get sick from them."

"I was thinking we could use Birch plywood as a shield," Abbadi replied flatly.

Pirzad looked skeptical. "Plywood?"

"Birch plywood," Abbadi corrected. "Something about its composition makes it a natural radiation barrier."

"They're probably talking about radon or something like that in a house. Not the kind of radioactive material that's in those bombs."

"Maybe. And it's probably not an absolute solution," Abbadi said, "but it might shield enough of it for us to get by. The bags wouldn't need to be here that long."

Pirzad shrugged. "It might work. I think they make a radiation shielding material by the roll for use in houses. Probably sell it at a building supply store. We could nail that over the plywood."

"Good. We can convert your garage into a suitcase bomb storage building."

Pirzad had a quizzical expression. "You think you'll need that much space?"

"I don't know," Abbadi replied. "But I think it would be easier and quicker to nail up the plywood over the entire interior, rather than building something else. Can you help me?"

"I can help you get the wood and stuff," Pirzad said. "And I can help you at night, but I have a full schedule at school."

"Good," Abbadi said. "That will be enough. We should get started on this tomorrow. My visa has a time limit."

"Someone at school can help you with that," Pirzad said. "They can help you get an extension. They do it all the time for visiting scholars. I'll check on it tomorrow."

"Great, but we still should get started on the garage tomorrow. I don't want those bags over there in that warehouse any longer than necessary."

CHAPTER FOURTEEN

H aving driven the Russian army back to the eastern end of the country, the ground war in Ukraine settled into a fight for control of smaller and smaller areas, narrowing the war to a region along the border. The big spaces in the western reaches, nearer to the Polish border, were already retaken by Ukraine forces and cleared of all resistance.

By contrast, as the Russian emphasis moved toward the eastern end, Russian supply lines shortened at regular intervals. Moreover, it was a region of Ukraine where separatists had a long history of control and an equally long history of embracing Russian priorities in opposing Ukrainian dominance. As the Ukrainian army advanced in that direction, and as Russian troops were confined to smaller and smaller spaces, the Russian military presence became increasingly denser. Consequently, fighting became more intense.

With separatist support, Russian units were dug in at Bakhmut, about two hundred miles from the Ukraine-Russia border. Using unhindered access to Russia's supply of artillery shells, though dwindling as it was, Russian artillery units bombarded Ukrainian troops with sustained barrages, using incredible amounts of conventional weaponry to provide cover for Russian ground troops slogging it out from road to road, street to street, building to building in an effort to break Ukrainian resistance.

As the fighting continued, and Ukrainian units held their ground, Russian goals narrowed from the broad idea of conquering the nation to the narrow goal of securing control of Bakhmut, albeit one building at a time. Accomplishing even that much proved a formidable task and Russian troops in the region quickly became paralyzed by the effort. All the while, their seemingly unlimited resources dwindled. Basic supplies ran low.

The Ukrainian army reached a phase of the war that should have been described as mopping up. Cleaning out the last pockets of resistance and asserting control over the broader region. However, the episodic nature of Western support meant Ukrainian forces could only fight in cycles. For a while, they had enough equipment and munitions to sustain heavy attacks. Encounters that, at times, were so intense the Russian army seemed to wither beneath them. But the intensity could not be maintained for a lack of adequate supplies and was soon followed by periods of lack when Ukrainian resources were severely depleted. Troops on the ground were forced to wait while Western nations—primarily NATO members—debated further resupply. The resulting undulation of resources created a corresponding undulation in the effectiveness of Ukrainian troops in the field.

Jim Marsh had watched this pattern with interest, wondering why more hadn't been done to enhance the delivery of supplies to Ukraine. In doing that, he remembered earlier conversations with people at the Pentagon about doing that very thing. Some of their ideas were a bit quirky but some of them were quite good, particularly the one about modifying commercial drones for military use. He wondered if anything had been done to implement the idea. A quick check of Agency databases suggested it had not, so he decided to begin a conversation about it with the intention of implementing a program himself.

As an official at the CIA, Marsh had considerable latitude in developing programs that furthered the Agency's mission to assist in attaining the US government's broader goals regarding foreign policy. More specifically, as an officer on the covert side of the Agency, he already had the authority to expand on the Agency's existing missions without the need for approval of each new operation. The president and Congress had already decided to aid Ukraine in resisting and expelling Russian troops from their country. It was only a short step from that to an understanding of Marsh's authority as permitting him to initiate a drone program for the CIA in Ukraine with capabilities along the lines previously discussed.

After considering the matter for a day or two, Marsh contacted Bryan Fowler at the agency's Directorate of Science and Technology—the part of the Agency that dealt with the creation of one-off items necessary for effective covert operations. The kind of device one often saw depicted on a *YouTube* channel. Converting civilian off-the-shelf drones into tools of war seemed like a perfect project for them.

✦ ✦ ✦

Bryan Fowler was trained as an engineer at Texas A&M. He came to the Agency from Bell Labs shortly before Bell Labs was acquired by Nokia. At the Agency, he rose quickly through the ranks and was now in charge of an engineering section that worked on adaptation of readily available products. Marsh knew him first by reputation and then through their wives, who became friends. Marsh called him and arranged to meet for a drink that evening after work.

Their initial conversation didn't take long. Fowler had been thinking much the same as Marsh. "They sell drones that can conduct surveillance every day at big box retailers," Fowler said. "All we would need to do is modify the communications so we could send encrypted signals back and forth. That would transform a retail drone into a surveillance drone in just a short time."

"What do you need to get started?"

Fowler thought for a moment, then said, "I have a little slack in my budget. I can get to work on it now." He looked over at Marsh. "As long as you're providing administrative cover."

"Authorization."

"Yeah," Fowler said. "Authorization."

With Marsh providing administrative approval, commercially available drones were acquired at a store in Killeen, Texas, and modified at nearby Fort Cavazos. Once changes were finalized, the drones were tested for viability in an open field in a remote corner of the fort's reservation. When the modifications passed a brief test, the drones were sent to the NATO base at Lask, Poland, where a team of US advisors assigned them to Ukrainian units for use in gathering information about Russian troop movements in the field.

When the observation drone idea proved successful, Marsh suggested they should expand the program to include bigger, heavier delivery drones. "The kind retailers use to transport heavier items."

Fowler knew them well. "I think someone in Ukraine is already doing that," he said. "I saw a video the other day of a drone dropping a grenade on a Russian truck."

"Was it a success?"

Fowler grinned. "Destroyed the truck."

"Good. Get busy," Marsh said. "We need to help them expand on their idea."

"Okay," Fowler replied. "But there's a problem."

"What's that?"

"Who's gonna pay for it?"

Marsh's shoulders sagged. "It always comes down to money."

"I know," Fowler sympathized. "But that's how it works. Money moves power from one place to another."

Marsh liked that idea. "Okay," he said. "You apply your power to figure out the best way to modify the drones. I'll apply mine to figure out how to put them to use. And how to pay for them."

Within a month, modified delivery drones were on their way to Poland for distribution to Agency operatives working inside Ukraine. They were flown there by CIA aircraft from the Air

Branch, a division of the Special Operations Division. No one on Capitol Hill knew a thing about it.

+ + +

At Sloviansk, a little east of Bakhmut, Taras' platoon from the 112th Territorial Defense Brigade was bogged down in a fight with a Russian unit holding a position about a mile away. For the past five days, both sides had used patrols to test the strength of each other's position. They also had lobbed mortars and rocket-propelled grenades at each other from a safe distance. But neither side had sent troops in a serious effort to dislodge the other's hold on their position.

Based on the erratic places the Russian mortars and rockets struck, Taras was certain they didn't know what they were shooting at. He wondered if their own mortars and rockets were doing any better.

About noon one day, Taras was hunkered down behind a thick concrete wall that had been part of the entrance to an underground parking garage for an apartment complex. A few yards away, Seargent Lomachenko was crouched behind a dirt pile that had been formed the day before when another unit had attempted to dig a fighting trench with a backhoe. They hadn't gone far when the backhoe took a direct hit from a Russian missile. Now the machine lay on its side twenty yards away, where it had landed as a twisted hunk of metal after the missile exploded.

Just then, a mortar round whistled overhead and struck the open ground between Taras and Lomachenko. Neither was harmed but Taras wondered if it had been a randomly placed round or if it had been directed by a spotter. Or perhaps a drone. He looked to the sky and saw a tiny dark speck high above, too high to be noticed under normal circumstances but clearly discernible as it loitered in place against the background of a white cloud. Taras caught Lomachenko's attention and pointed up to it.

Lomachenko glanced up but didn't seem to notice anything at first, then a frown creased his forehead and Taras heard him grumbling obscenities. Something about the cowardly Russians being too scared to challenge us in a hand-to-hand contest. Taras thought Lomachenko's opinion was rather ironic. They would be doing the same thing if they had a drone, but before he could say anything more, he saw Lomachenko lift his rifle to his shoulder and squeeze off a round in the direction of the drone. It was futile, as Lomachenko must have known, the drone was too high to hit with a rifle but trying seemed to give him a sense of relief, so he squeezed off one more round.

A moment later, a rocket struck the far end of the wall that Taras was hiding behind. Shards of concrete flew through the air. One narrowly missed Taras' ear. Another nicked his cheek. Blood trickled down his jaw and drizzled onto his neck before blotting against the fabric of his shirt. His ears rang from the sound of the blast, drowning out all other noise.

For an instant, Taras feared he would never hear again but before long, he heard the familiar Pop! Pop! Pop! of gunfire. Muffled, at first, as if his head were covered by a pillow, but gunfire just the same, and it gradually became louder and louder. He had never been so glad to hear that sound. A moment later, though, everything began to spin around. Waves of nausea swept over him, and he thought he might vomit, then he sagged against the wall, slid to the ground, and faded from consciousness.

Sometime later—Taras wasn't sure how long it had been—there was the sound of a vehicle approaching. He waited nervously, one hand on the forestock of his rifle, the other holding the pistol grip with his finger against the trigger, wondering if he should run for a better hiding place or stay right there and fight it out with whoever was approaching. He glanced toward Lomachenko and saw him pressed against the dirt pile, craning to see the approaching vehicle. Lomachenko looked concerned, but not distressed.

In a minute or two, a Bradley Fighting Vehicle appeared on the road and Taras could see it bore the colors of the Ukrainian army. According to the markings, it was from a mechanized unit, but Taras didn't recognize which one.

When the vehicle was abreast of Taras' position, it turned towards him, rumbled through the debris that had been left from days of battle, and ground to stop a few yards away. The rear door clanked open, and a man appeared. He was dressed in combat fatigue pants but wore a gray sweatshirt with a durable work coat over it. At the sight of Taras, the man grinned but said nothing.

"An American," Taras whispered.

The man carried a duffel bag with one arm through the straps and the bag slung over his shoulder. He walked straight toward Taras, as if he'd come solely for the purpose of meeting him. His free hand grasped a rifle that he carried loosely at his side, but there was no sidearm at his waist and nothing visible beneath his jacket. Taras thought he must be either incredibly brave, or unbelievably stupid coming there in the open like that.

When the man was only a few feet away, he smiled even bigger and said, "Are you Taras Irvanets?" His accent confirmed Taras' earlier determination that he was, indeed, an American.

"Yes," Taras replied.

"Good. I have something for you." He dropped the duffel bag at his feet, then turned to the Bradley and gestured with a wave of his arm. Two men came from the vehicle carrying similar duffel bags, one in each hand. When they reached the wall where Taras was waiting, the first man took a phone from the front pocket of his trousers and placed a call. Someone answered and he gave them his coordinates, then unzipped the duffel that sat at his feet.

Before the new arrivals could explain why they were there, Taras heard a buzzing noise from above and looked up to see a drone approaching. He raised his rifle, intending to shoot at it to bring it down in the same way Lomachenko had before. But unlike the one Lomachenko shot at this one was close enough to hit. Before he could get off a round, the American grabbed his arm. "Hold your fire," he commanded. "They're with us." That's when Irvanets saw multiple drones coming toward them.

The first drone landed near the Bradley, followed by two more that landed close by. The other men went over to where the machines sat and switched them off. Then the first man, the American, turned to Taras. "My name is Tom," he said. "We were sent to show you how to fly the drones." He gestured to them over his shoulder. "Ever use one before?"

"Sure," Taras replied. "But what are we supposed to do with them out here?" He walked toward the closest drone while he talked.

Tom pointed. "Two of them are for observation. Find the enemy, take a picture of them, note their coordinates, relay that information to our central control unit. The others are for dropping explosives on enemy positions."

Taras was standing beside the drones by then. He glanced over at Tom. "Whose idea was this?" he asked.

"I don't know," Tom replied. "They sent them to me and told me to distribute them to the units fighting here. I asked who could fly them. Someone said the men in your platoon could do it. They gave me your name as the point of contact and told our driver how to find you."

Taras continued to stare at the drones. "I've never flown one that big," he said. His eyes were wide with wonder, but inside he felt bewildered.

The machines were black and had no wings, only a light frame shaped like a large H with motors and propellers on the four corners. A cluster of processors was attached to one of the crosspieces and something that looked like a small camera was mounted near the center.

"Don't worry," Tom said. "We can show you."

Lomachenko appeared at Taras' side. "What's this about?" he demanded.

"It's okay," Taras said. "They've come to help us."

✦ ✦ ✦

At Taras' suggestion, Lomachenko rounded up Vitali, and for the remainder of the day, they practiced operating the drones. As they became proficient with them, four others from the platoon were assigned to begin training and to help with reloading and refueling.

All the drones were originally designed for package delivery. Two of them had been reconfigured for observation. They were equipped with multiple cameras, a modified guidance system, and a secure link to a satellite with access to the communications hub that had been established earlier in Poland and a second inside Ukraine. The other two drones were modified to carry anti-tank grenades and anti-tank missiles. The release device that was designed to relax its grip on packages at the delivery point had been changed to one that would fit the grenades and missiles. A button on the handheld controller that operated the drone released them. Concussion fuses detonated them on impact.

Under typical conditions, inflight control came from target coordinates uploaded from one of the information hubs. Operating the drone didn't require much interaction from Taras other than to begin the flight and turn off the engines when the drone returned. Their principal duty was to make sure each drone's components functioned properly and to override the programmed flight system only in case of immediate danger.

"After you've worked with them a while," Tom said, "we'll let you fly them on your own."

Taras and his friends readily took to the drones and used them to locate the Russian troop positions that had been targeting them with rockets and mortars. The drones with cameras pinpointed their location. The ones that were armed for combat dropped mortars and rockets from as high as five hundred feet up. With the drones helping, the platoon eliminated the Russian threat in their area in a day or two. Once they were gone, Taras' platoon advanced from their position near the apartment building and took control of the intervening space.

In the days that followed, that became the process. The drone crew dropped explosives on Russian troops and guided Ukrainian units to their location. Ukrainian troops flushed the Russians from hiding and killed as many as possible. Once the area was cleared, the Ukrainians advanced farther. It was a slow, methodical process—sometimes advancing less than half a quarter of a mile at a time—but it worked.

For Taras and Vitali—the ones who flew the killer drones—combat devolved into a competition much like the video games they played at home. As they had done when playing games in the past, they kept score. The drones had cameras and with them they could focus on a target, loiter over the position until the best moment, then release an explosive device. While it dropped toward the ground, they often "called the shot," as in "wide right" or "wide left." They laughed at each other's misses and laughed at soldiers writhing in agony from a direct hit, especially from the phosphorous devices they used to kill Russians hiding in their foxholes. It was a game. A deadly game. An awful game. The laughter numbed them to the reality of what they were doing. Soon, Taras became so absorbed in the game of it that he forgot about everything and everyone else. Including his girlfriend, Mila Korot.

CHAPTER FIFTEEN

kraine's military success against Russian troops brought welcome relief to many, particularly those who lived in the western half of the country. Artillery, drone, and missiles still struck, but the threat of imminent occupation by Russian troops was no longer a source of daily gloom or worry. Ukrainian civilians who initially fled the fighting were now eager to return to their former residences. Some already had made the trek back home. Many more were preparing to do the same.

Members of Zelensky's government were elated. Ukrainian troops had cleared Russian soldiers from most of the country, confining them to a strip along the eastern border. Earlier, when the invasion first began, some were predicting the Ukraine army would be destroyed in a rapid bloodbath. Others were sure the army would collapse and the war would be over in a matter of days.

Now, Ukraine was on the verge of reclaiming all but the eastern-most region of the country.

Zelensky was proud of their achievements but careful to temper his enthusiasm. The area in the east where the Russian troops were gathered was traditionally a separatist stronghold with a long history of deeply entrenched Russian support. Confining Russian troops to that small portion of the country served only to intensify their capability. The war, Zelensky knew, was not over. Indeed, the ultimate goal of driving the Russians completely out was still very much in the balance.

With the Russian army confined but with resistance intensifying, the notion emerged that perhaps Ukraine had done enough. Perhaps it was time to reach a negotiated end to the war. After all, civilians in the occupied area seemed to welcome Russian control. At the same time, the destruction already inflicted on Ukraine seemed to suggest that a diplomatic resolution to the conflict might be in everyone's best interest. Even some within the Zelensky administration supported the idea. Zelensky, however, had rejected a negotiated settlement from the beginning and remained committed to achieving a complete military victory.

Nevertheless, the topic of how to end the war came up for discussion at the weekly Ukrainian ministers meeting. Those who spoke on the topic seemed to assume the end was at hand. Zelensky took the opposite view. "This war is not over," he said. "Our success has pushed Russian troops into a corner. Putin can see that our victory is very much a possibility. That is something he could not have imagined before and I fear it makes him more dangerous than ever."

Liubov Kurkov, the Minister of Finance, dismissed the remark with a backhanded flip of his wrist. "They're done," he said. "One last push and Putin's army will stumble back to Russia where they belong, never to bother us again."

"All he has to do is keep moving his forces eastward," another added.

"Soon they will be out of Ukraine completely," still another crowed. "There's no need for him to announce a retreat or surrender. Just reposition his troops across the border on Russian soil and the war will be over." Everyone laughed.

Ivan Laiuk, an undersecretary from the Ministry of Justice, spoke up. "That's part of the problem we face," he said. "Putin thinks the land they occupy now *is* Russian soil." Everyone laughed again, but Laiuk did not. "I think that's the point the president is trying to make. The Russians aren't going to leave on their own. If we want them gone, we'll have to make them go. Putin will never admit defeat, tacitly or otherwise."

"He will have no other option," someone responded. "Once we reduce his army to rubble, he will *have* to admit defeat."

Yet another chimed in jovially. "Putin thought they could win by depleting our resources, but we are winning by depleting theirs."

"Listen to me," Zelensky snapped. "This is becoming a war of attrition and if that's true, I'm not sure we can win."

The room quieted. Murmurs were heard. "Why not?" someone asked finally.

"Our success thus far has depended on the help of others," Zelensky explained. "We aren't firing artillery shells that were made in Ukraine. Or launching missiles that were made here. Or even firing

Ukrainian bullets for the arms our soldiers carry. Everything we use comes from somewhere else. This means we can only win if our friends in the West continue to give us the means to do so. And, if Russia's friends are prevented from assisting them."

"There's not much we can do to stop China from sending help," someone noted. "Or anyone else for that matter."

"Exactly," Zelensky said. "Our hope for a free and independent future lies in convincing the US and its NATO allies to continue supplying us with weapons. And I'm not sure how long that support will last. Many officials in the US Congress are already asking how long they can continue to support us."

"You need to visit the US," someone suggested. "Talk with them face-to-face."

"Visit the leaders of *all* the members of NATO," another added.

"We intend to do that," Zelensky replied. "But first, I want to tour our soldiers on the battlefield. The Americans may be supplying the arms, the missiles, and the drones, but our soldiers are the ones risking their lives to use them. They need to know that we personally support them, not merely as government officials." This was the first any of the ministers had heard of such a trip, but they were wholeheartedly supportive.

✦ ✦ ✦

Fomichev was in the room that day and heard Zelensky's remarks. Aleksi Smolov, Zelensky's chief of staff, was there also. When the meeting ended, Smolov gathered several presidential assistants for a meeting in a room down the hall. One of the people he called aside was Arsen Golovin.

Since the new administration had come to power, Golovin and Fomichev had worked together on several projects. As Golovin was entering the room to meet with Smolov, he caught sight of Fomichev in the hall and gestured for him to join them. Fomichev was delighted to be included.

During their meeting, Smolov repeated the broad outline of what Zelensky wanted to do—visit Ukrainian soldiers serving in every current or former battle zone across the country; then take a trip to Europe and meet with NATO leaders; and finish with a visit to the United States. Everyone was excited.

Those attending the meeting were divided into three groups and given the task of coordinating a portion of the trip. Fomichev was placed with the group advancing the trip across Ukraine. He had hoped to work on the trip to the United States—he'd never been there before and the group advancing that trip would surely be included in the American entourage—but he was glad for the opportunity to at least be in the room, working on presidential business rather than stuck in his office working on nothing of any value.

The working group for the Ukraine portion of the trip was chaired by Viktor Kuleba. Like many in the administration, he had come to the campaign from Zelensky's television production company. Fomichev knew Kuleba only in passing. They had never worked together. Under Kuleba's direction, the group put together a tentative schedule for the trip, then divided themselves into areas of interest to work out the details—transportation, events and participants, video and news coverage, remarks and speeches, and security coordination. Fomichev was assigned to events and participants.

"Your job," Kuleba explained, "is to figure out where the president appears in public at each of the stops on the schedule. Determine who is to be there to see him when he arrives—soldiers, babies, officials, whatever—and make sure they are there. Figure out how much time he can spend at each location and see that he gets it, but no more. Someone else will take care of getting him there. Someone else will work out the specifics of what he says. Your job is to pick the sites at each location, make sure the proper officials are present, and, above all, make sure we have a crowd there to greet him. We don't want him standing in an empty parking lot, talking to himself. You're the advance man. Take care of whatever needs taking care of."

An advance man. Fomichev had never worked an event in that capacity. The thought of being in the lead, handling details for the president, seemed almost overwhelming. Such an honor like that *had* to put him on the inside now. A member of the group. The *president's* group. His man for this part of the tour and perhaps a growing role in the government once the tour ended.

When Fomichev returned to his office he dove into the task with enthusiasm. As a first step, he identified and located the commanding officers for each military unit on the schedule, then located their contact information and called to find a person who could handle event details for each unit.

Because the events were arranged to occur successively at the rate of three or four per day, and because someone was needed on the ground for each one, Fomichev designated a person from his own office as his deputy and created a schedule for them. Fomichev would take the first event, then travel to the third event, while his deputy took the second, then went to the fourth. Together, they would leapfrog their way across the country with one or the other onsite for each event.

Over the next three days, Fomichev worked the phones calling back and forth to each of the site coordinators, addressing the necessary details. When he'd obtained enough clarity about who was doing what and when, he compiled a separàte briefing book for each event, then a master briefing book for himself that covered *all* of the events. He was determined that nothing should go wrong.

On his fourth day working with the coordinating group, Fomichev met with Myroslav Reznikov, chairman of a group that was arranging video crews for the entire tour. Globally, not just in Ukraine. Like many of the others in Zelensky's administration, Reznikov had come from the television show where he'd developed a reputation for being difficult to work with. True to form, Fomichev found him arrogant, abrasive, and rude.

In the midst of their conversation, Reznikov turned toward his office door, which had remained open, and shouted to no one in particular, "Could someone tell me why I am talking to this outsider who knows nothing about what we are trying to do?" An assistant came from down the hall and attempted to intervene, but her efforts proved futile and finally, Fomichev gave up. He left the office feeling deeply humiliated. On the way back to his office, he resolved that one day he would take revenge on Reznikov for his behavior.

The following day, Fomichev received an email from Viktor Kuleba, who was chairman of the Ukraine working group congratulating him on his diligent work. Attached to the email was the tentative itinerary Fomichev had prepared earlier, along with Kuleba's comments and suggested revisions. A list of email addresses appeared in the header, indicating the people to whom the message had been sent. One of those people was Myroslav Reznikov.

That afternoon, Fomichev received a second message from Kuleba telling him that he had been removed from the tour coordination project altogether. "Please forward your files to me and make sure you collect all of those briefing books you prepared."

Shortly after that, another message appeared. This one from Arsen Golovin, the man who first brought Fomichev into the tour coordination project. "Sorry to hear the news," Golovin said. "Really wanted to work with you on this. They should have never sent you to see Reznikov on your own." Fomichev was crushed.

How could they do this to him? He had so much to offer. So much they needed. So much he needed to give them. This was his moment. His chance to finally be on the inside, where the real decisions were made. Why did they offer the position to him, then snatch it away? Why would Reznikov treat him that way, and why would the others let him do it?

Tears formed in Fomichev's eyes, but he wiped them away and took a deep breath, determined not to cry. Rather than spend another moment at his desk that day, Fomichev left work and walked toward the bus stop. On the way, he received a text from a number he recognized as one of Yuriy Poroshenko's burners.

"Tonight," the message read. "Outside the café. Nine PM."

✦ ✦ ✦

As before, Poroshenko's driver picked up Fomichev in front of the café. This time, instead of taking him to the warehouse, they drove to a side street where the driver parked the car at the curb and switched off the engine. "Wait here," he said. Then he got out of the car, closed the door, and walked away.

It was a cold night. Fomichev felt the chill seep past the seal around the door and through the glass of the window. He pulled his jacket tighter around his chest and wrapped his arms over it. The night was dark and foreboding. No one on the street. No lights in the buildings around him. Fomichev began to wonder if he had offended Poroshenko, and whether this would be the moment he'd take his revenge. His mind scanned back through all he had done, searching for anything that might have offended Poroshenko. Any mistake he might have made. Any secret he might have disclosed that he shouldn't even have known. But he found none.

Then he thought of Reznikov. Maybe he was a friend of Poroshenko. Or of his driver. Did they know each other? Did Reznikov have connections to set up this supposed meeting? Was Reznikov trying to scare him off? What if they—

Just then, Fomichev heard someone outside the car. Then a remote chirped, and the door opened. Poroshenko leaned down to look inside, then slid onto the seat beside Fomichev. He had a wide grin. "I hear you're working for the top now."

"Not anymore," Fomichev replied.

Poroshenko frowned. "What happened?"

"They pushed me out."

"Out of what?"

"Zelensky wants to tour the troops," Fomichev explained. "A friend got me on the coordination group for the trip. I did exactly what I was supposed to do. Everything was going fine until I met with Myroslav Reznikov."

"Ahh," Poroshenko groaned.

"You know him?"

"Everyone knows Reznikov. The most conceited, self-absorbed man on the entire continent."

"Something I said upset him," Fomichev continued. "He got me put off the group."

"More likely, he found out you hadn't come over from the entertainment business like all the rest of those Zelensky worshippers."

"I hate that guy," Fomichev seethed.

Poroshenko patted him on the shoulder. "Cheer up. There's a lot of us in that line with you."

"It was a good setup," Fomichev lamented. "I had it all worked out, too. Now, they're going to take my work, put their names on it, and claim it was theirs all along."

"You wrote the schedule for the trip?"

"The part that's in Ukraine," Fomichev said with a nod. "A briefing book. A minute-by-minute schedule for the things Zelensky's supposed to do at each stop. Where he's supposed to be. Who's supposed to be with him. People he's supposed to talk to. Topics he's supposed to talk about. Names, addresses, and telephone numbers of everyone involved. Organized to the minute." He pounded the seat cushion with his fist. "Why did they do that to me?"

Poroshenko looked curious. "Do you still have the briefing book?"

"Yeah," Fomichev replied. "Most of that stuff is boxed up and sitting in my office. They told me to box it up and turn it in."

"Do you have a copy?"

Fomichev nodded. "I kept an extra one for myself. Just so I could prove I actually did all the work for it."

"Bring it to me."

"The briefing book?"

"Yeah. Bring it to me."

Fomichev frowned. "Why?"

"I'm curious," Poroshenko said. "I'd like to see what goes on inside the administration."

Fomichev grimaced. "I'm not supposed to let anyone see it."

"And you're probably not supposed to be associating with me, either." Poroshenko chuckled. "Zelensky campaigned on getting rid of people like me and the folks I run with." He patted Fomichev on the thigh. "Get me a copy of that book." He opened the door and stepped out of the car. "Bring it to me tomorrow," he added as he closed the door.

As Poroshenko walked away, the driver appeared outside the front door and got in behind the wheel. He didn't say a word but started the car and drove toward the apartment building where Fomichev lived. Fomichev wondered how he knew where to take him.

✦ ✦ ✦

The next day, Fomichev came to work with a leather satchel. In it was a copy of the day's newspaper folded in half. Between the fold of the paper was a sandwich wrapped in white deli paper that he brought for lunch. He occasionally did that and the guards made fun of him for it. Fomichev always laughed with them, but he didn't like it. When the guard at the building entrance saw the sandwich that morning he laughed as usual and waved Fomichev past the security checkpoint.

When Fomichev reached his desk, he found an extra copy of the tour briefing book in one of the boxes he'd begun packing the day before. He moved the copy to the bottom drawer of his desk and hid it beneath a stack of government reports and miscellaneous documents.

For the remainder of the morning, Fomichev searched the office for files, reports, and notes he had accumulated from his work on Zelensky's Ukraine tour, added them to the contents of the box, and sealed it up. When he was finished, he called for a courier.

At noon, Fomichev remained at his desk and ate the sandwich he'd brought from the deli that morning. It tasted good—he liked the deli that made it, one of the few that stayed in business through the war. As he ate, his mind wandered from lunch to fantasies of all the ways to publicly humiliate Reznikov for the way he'd treated him.

When daydreams of revenge against Reznikov grew stale, Fomichev began to imagine doing the same to Zelensky. A lone sniper in a tall building squeezing off rounds at a presidential motorcade. The chaos of war in the outlying areas of the country where the tour was going seemed like a perfect location, except that there were no tall buildings. But there were places where exploding Russian artillery shells and drone strikes would provide lots of distractions. He could get off a few shots and slip away without being detected. It couldn't be that difficult. Many people in other places had done that sort of thing against their leaders. He could do it in Ukraine. Shoot and run away to the eastern end of the country. Disappear among the dissidents. And if Zelensky survived the first attempt, there was always a next opportunity, the guy couldn't resist the public eye.

Before he knew it, Fomichev had finished the sandwich and was sitting with his hands resting on the desktop, his eyes staring blankly ahead. There was a knock at the office door, then it opened, and a courier appeared. "They said you had some boxes?"

"Yes," Fomichev said, pointing to the stack near the door. He handed the courier a form with an inventory and the address where they were to be taken.

When the courier was gone, Fomichev removed the extra copy of the briefing book from the drawer and placed it inside the briefcase with the morning newspaper on top. Late that afternoon, he sent a text to Poroshenko's burner and arranged to meet him that night.

✦ ✦ ✦

As he had before, the driver picked up Fomichev outside the café and took him to the warehouse. Poroshenko was in the office, seated behind his desk. Fomichev handed him the book with the schedules for Zelensky's tour. "There you go," he said.

Poroshenko flipped through the book. "Very impressive," he noted. "You do good work."

"Apparently not good enough."

"One can measure one's successes in two ways," Poroshenko

said. "By the objective quality of one's product, and by the kind of people who hate him for it. You have accomplished it by both measures."

"It doesn't feel like an accomplishment."

"That is the thing about success." Poroshenko laid the briefing book aside. "Whether it feels good at the moment is irrelevant. It is still success."

Fomichev pointed to the briefing book. "What are you going to do with that?"

"Don't worry," Poroshenko said with a dismissive gesture. "It is of no concern to you."

Fomichev felt a sinking sensation in his stomach, as if he'd crossed a line and betrayed Zelensky by giving the book to Poroshenko. But what had Zelensky or any of the others done for him? Yes. He had a job. But it was a job of menial tasks in an office removed from the actual work of governing. He was stuck in a government building, toiling all day with details—the kind of detailed work necessary to make anything work correctly—while Zelensky's friends were in the *real* offices on the *real* corridors where *real* decisions were made. They lived the life. A life they enjoyed because of *his* effort. His work. His creativity. A life that was meant for *him*. He had worked as hard as anyone on the campaign. Much harder than many of the people who came over from the entertainment business. Way harder than Reznikov. And he had continued to work hard once the administration was in office. But what good did it do? The campaign had been about ending corruption, purging the government of crony favoritism, and rewarding those who invested themselves in honest work to form an honest government. And look what they did to him. Pushed him aside because Reznikov didn't like him.

Fomichev knew he shouldn't feel that way. Knew he shouldn't wallow in self-pity. But he did, and the more he thought about it the deeper it burned in his soul. People weren't supposed to treat each other that way. Poroshenko didn't. His driver didn't. Why did Zelensky's people?

CHAPTER SIXTEEN

Ten days after Fomichev had been fired from the planning group, Zelensky's tour began as scheduled. Television crews covered every moment—Zelensky leaving the office, boarding the helicopter, the helicopter rising into the air. In the building where Fomichev worked, a television sat atop a filing cabinet in the common area beyond the door to his office. Others who worked on the same floor gathered there to watch. Some pausing for a moment. Some lingering while they sipped from a cup of coffee. Fomichev remained at his desk, watching through the doorway while he tried to work.

The first stop was in Lutsk, a city in western Ukraine where an infantry unit was camped on the north side of the city. Many of the soldiers in the unit were men who had rotated from the frontlines for a few days of rest, away from the intense fighting. They didn't get many opportunities away from the war, and it wasn't actually rest. Soldiers who arrived at Lutsk from the front were assigned to help coordinate assistance for the thousands of civilian refugees who had fled there, hoping to escape the constant artillery shelling and destruction that took place at the eastern end of the country.

When Zelensky's helicopter touched down at the edge of town, a crowd ran out to greet him. He waved to them as he came down the steps from the fuselage, then worked his way through clusters of soldiers and civilians, shaking hands with as many as he could reach, posing for photos with the troops, and offering words of encouragement to everyone.

From the initial landing site, he went to a headquarters tent at the army camp and met with the commanding officers. They talked mostly about troop morale and the need for more arms, ammunition, and supplies. Then he went to the center of town where he stood on the steps of city hall and gave a rousing speech that was broadcast to the crowd through loudspeakers, carried live on internet media channels, and on major European television networks. A video crew followed Zelensky and his entourage, capturing every moment, then went with him back to the helicopter for his flight to the next stop. The entire event on the ground took less than two hours.

✦ ✦ ✦

The second stop was at Rivne. As he had done at the first stop, Zelensky was scheduled to make his initial appearance before a crowd at the site where the helicopter landed, spend a few moments greeting throngs of supporters, then continue to the center of the city. When camera crews had milked those appearances for poignant images, he was to move to yet another military encampment on the edge of town. Fomichev knew all of this from the schedules he had prepared.

As the helicopter touched down at Rivne, Fomichev came from his desk and walked out to the area beyond his office door. By then, staff members from the adjoining offices who had been in the room earlier had drifted away to return to their work. Fomichev had the room mostly to himself.

Despite the bitter disappointment of being forced out of his original role in planning the trip, Fomichev found himself unable to resist noticing every detail as it occurred on the screen. As the arrival in Rivne unfolded and people on the ground approached Zelensky outside the helicopter, he counted them. It had all been laid out in the briefing book. "Ten, eleven, twelve," Fomichev whispered aloud as people shook Zelensky's hand. That was all the briefing book allowed. "Time to step in and move on," he said.

As if on cue, a handler on the ground did just that, moving to Zelensky's side, ready to take him by the elbow. When the twelfth greeter moved away, the handler steered Zelensky toward a car that would take him to the next moment on the schedule—a speech in the center of town.

Fomichev glanced around the room and saw an empty chair near a desk in the corner. He made his way to it and took a seat, then crossed his legs. There was a piece of lint on the thigh of his trousers, and he brushed it gently away, then checked his watch. Events unfolding on the television screen were almost exactly on time. Unheard of among politicians doing political events. That's what this tour was, Fomichev realized. A political event. The first event in Zelensky's campaign for a second term as president.

When Zelensky arrived at the center of town, the process repeated with crowds pressing toward him, followed by more handshakes, everyone laughing and smiling, a handler moving in to urge him forward. Zelensky stepped past the well-wishers with practiced ease and made his way toward a makeshift platform to deliver his remarks.

From his seat in the corner of the room, Fomichev studied the images on screen and scanned the crowd that was gathered at the platform, that's when he noticed someone was missing. "He's not there," Fomichev said to no one in particular. "Where's General Marchuk?"

General Marchuk was supposed to be present, standing with Zelensky to create an image of solidarity and support for the cameras, but Marchuk was nowhere to be seen. "This isn't good," Fomichev muttered. "This isn't good. They should have—"

Suddenly there was the Pop! Pop! Pop! of gunfire. The crowd around Zelensky screamed. Everyone ducked. More shots rang out. Then a hail of bullets pinged off everything. Dust in the air. Shattered glass. A civilian was struck and fell to the ground. Two soldiers were hit. Splinters of wood flew through the air as bullets raked across the podium. More people were hit. A mist of blood filled the air. Bodies tumbled in every direction.

People from offices up on Fomichev's floor came rushing back and stood before the television, hands over their mouths, gasping in horror. As they watched, there was more gunfire and the muffled sound of an explosion that occurred out of the view of the television cameras. Smoke from it drifted over the scene.

Members of Zelensky's security detail reacted as expected, shielding him with their bodies. Guns appeared from beneath their jackets. Others took Zelensky by his arms and hustled him toward a Humvee that was parked a few yards away, exactly where Fomichev's briefing book had said it should be.

A soldier who was standing beside the Humvee opened a door in anticipation of Zelensky getting inside but before the president got that far, the vehicle exploded. Everyone watched in horror as the soldier's body flew through the air and landed atop two women who were standing with the crowd to the right. There were more panicked screams, and people ran in every direction. A second Humvee exploded.

The security team pushed Zelensky behind a tank that had been parked nearby as a prop for photo opportunities. Within minutes, images of the president crouched behind the tank—eyes wide, looking obviously shaken—appeared on screens and monitors around the world.

Fomichev sat on the edge of his seat, frozen in place, his eyes fixed on the television screen. Until the gunfire had started, everything at Rivne had gone exactly as he had described in the briefing book. The helicopter had landed where it was supposed to. The crowd had assembled and were waiting to cheer as Zelensky emerged and came down the steps. A bank of microphones was ready and waiting on a makeshift platform where he was to speak. Camera crews were positioned in the correct spot to catch the angle of the midmorning sunlight. It all had happened according to plan.

And then the shooting started, turning a perfect campaign moment into a mass shooting.

To Fomichev, it seemed as if someone had used the briefing book to plan an assassination. As if someone had designed the event to place Zelensky in the perfect spot for a hit. The weight of the moment fell hard on Fomichev with the realization that the briefing book documenting all of his careful, meticulous planning might easily serve as an indictment against him. Evidence of a plot—his plot—to kill the president. That wasn't his intention, but it certainly was *someone's* intention.

The broadcast on television continued, but in Fomichev's mind, the sounds and images receded into the background. Inside his head, he heard only his own thoughts, as clear and sharp as if they were words spoken by a voice as distinct and articulate as any he'd ever heard. "On schedule. His schedule. On time. His time. Exactly as planned. His plan. In the book. His book. The briefing book." The same briefing book he had delivered to Poroshenko after he was fired from the planning group.

Fomichev's heart sank even deeper, and a feeling of dread swept over him. Poroshenko had used the briefing book to plan Zelensky's murder. He must have. It was all right there on the screen, portrayed exactly as described in the book.

"No," he argued with himself. It couldn't be. Poroshenko wasn't that kind of guy, was he? He wasn't above having someone killed, but not Zelensky. Not the president. Surely not the president.

Even if Poroshenko wanted to kill someone, he would never get his hands dirty doing the actual work himself. He wasn't that kind of guy. If he wanted it done, he would give it to someone else to do. Let them take the risk. But who would he give a job like this to? Not his regular guys. Not anyone from Ukraine, even. He'd use someone else from somewhere else. A contact of a contact. A lone assassin flown in for a single task.

But a shooting like the one they'd all witnessed on the television couldn't have been done by a single person. There had been multiple shooters involved. Who could coordinate such a thing? All the moving pieces. The logistics. The timing. All of it done in a way that no single person involved in the event knew the details of anyone else. It would take someone with experience to put that together. Someone with an eye for detail to make it work. The schedules. The timing. The precision.

Fomichev knew several people who could do it. He could do it. Oh, no! He *had* done it! Not actually, not intentionally, but that's how it would look to anyone who read the briefing book and knew that he had written it.

Another wave of anxiety swept over Fomichev, and the air seemed to rush from his lungs. There was a tightness in his chest and a tingle down his arm. He was the one. The unwitting planner *and* the scapegoat all in one. "They mean to pin this on me," he said.

But would Poroshenko really do that to him? They were friends, or so he thought, not mere acquaintances. Would Poroshenko really try to kill Zelensky and set him up to take the blame? He had to find out. He had to talk to Poroshenko. Look him in the eye and ask him.

Without making a show of it, Fomichev crossed the room to his office. He resisted the urge to collapse in the chair behind his and, instead, retrieved the leather satchel from its place in the corner. Satchel in hand, he came from the office and made his way to through the crowd still watching the TV and headed down the corridor to the elevator.

+ + +

When the elevator reached the lobby, Fomichev made his way to the door and stepped outside. A light breeze tousled his hair. The freshness of it felt good and seemed to cleanse the heaviness of the moment from his mind. His breathing returned to normal and the pain in his chest subsided. He paused for a moment and looked up at the sky. Pale blue with thin clouds drifting by. The sound of the bus caught his attention and he continued on his way.

At the corner, he paused long enough to send a text to Poroshenko, a cryptic message that said only, "We should talk." A moment later, Poroshenko responded, and they arranged for his car to bring Fomichev to a building in an industrial area along the Dnipro River. The bus passed. Fomichev took a seat on a bench and waited for the next one.

The building where he was to meet Poroshenko was too far away to reach on foot, so Fomichev checked the bus schedule and caught one that took him in that direction. He got off a block or two from the location and walked the remainder of the way but found the building was deserted. Then he saw Poroshenko's car parked behind a stack of cargo containers that shielded it from view to casual visitors. Fomichev made his way to it, opened the passenger door, and took a seat inside.

"Did you do it?" Fomichev asked as he closed the door.

Poroshenko looked confused. "Did I do what?"

"Did you arrange the attempt on Zelensky today?"

Poroshenko was taken aback by the abruptness of the question. "You're asking me a direct question?"

"I saw the attack on television," Fomichev replied. "Everything that happened went exactly by the schedule in the briefing book that I gave you."

"And you think I did it?"

"Did you?"

Poroshenko looked angry. "You're asking *me* about that before you question the Russians?"

"I wrote the book," Fomichev retorted. "I give you a copy. If they investigate, they'll ask me about it. If I tell them I gave you a copy, they'll ask *you* about it. I want to know your answer before they do that."

Poroshenko shook his head. "They won't ask me about it."

"How do you know?"

Poroshenko fixed his gaze on Fomichev. "Because if they ask you about it, you will lie."

"There's no avoiding it," Fomichev said. "They know I prepared schedules for those events. They know I wrote that book. They know I had that event laid out to the exact minute. And when they look at it, they will think I was involved in the attack. Everything that happened today followed the schedule that I prepared. They will think the whole thing was a setup and that I'm the one who did it."

"You *were* the one who it," Poroshenko said. "You're the one who scheduled it."

Fomichev glared at him. "I had nothing to do with that shooting and you know it. I gave you that book only as friend and only because you were interested."

"And because you were angry and wanted someone to know that you had created the schedules and coordinated the details of Zelensky's tour."

"Yes."

Poroshenko paused and seemed to relax. "Have you considered there might be people in your own government who want him out?"

"No," Fomichev said curtly. "Why would they? He's their meal ticket."

Poroshenko scoffed. "Zelensky is a television star. An actor playing the role of a president. He knows nothing of the history of our issues or how this country developed. How we took this country from the Soviets. The compromises that were made to gain our independence. The people to whom debts for it are owed. He knows nothing of that."

"He's a lawyer. He's not dumb."

"In terms of education from books, yes." Poroshenko nodded. "Zelensky is quite smart. But he, like many others, believes politicians are elected by the vote of the people. As an expression of some philosophic *will of the people.*"

Fomichev's eyes opened wider. "Isn't that the way it works?"

Poroshenko shook his head. "You know better than that. Politicians are elected by a vote of people like me." He pointed to himself.

"The oligarchs."

"Yes. The oligarchs. We say who goes and who comes. Not *just* in politics but in politics especially. We vote first, and we vote last,"

Poroshenko said. "No one comes to office without our approval. And they remain in office only until we change our minds about them."

"And you're saying your mind has changed."

"I'm saying we are businessmen, not idealogues," Poroshenko responded. "The only thing that matters to us is the bottom line. As long as business prospers, the politicians prosper. When business goes bad, they go away, and we find someone to replace them. Someone who will protect our interests and allow us to thrive."

"How does an attack on Zelensky help your business?"

"It doesn't," Poroshenko said. "That's what I'm saying. If we wanted him out, he would be out. Either at the next election or otherwise. We would not make some amateurish grandstand of it. Or botch an attempt on television for millions to see. He would simply be gone."

"Well, whoever did it," Fomichev said, "they set me up to take the blame for it. My name is all over that trip."

"Which is why you should consider looking at people on the inside. People in Zelensky's administration."

Fomichev sighed. "I don't know how to do that."

"Start with the man who fired you," Poroshenko suggested. "Work your way out in every direction from him."

✦ ✦ ✦

Reports of the shooting at Rivne spread quickly, and for the remainder of his Ukrainian tour, Zelensky was met by crowds that were increasingly larger and more enthusiastic. As if they could protect him with their presence and erase the attack from the minds of the public through their overwhelming emotion. And it seemed to work.

In location after location, citizens formed human shields to protect Zelensky with their bodies in unprecedented acts of selfless patriotism. News outlets carried much of it live, shifting their comments from rehashing details of the shooting to effusive praise for the public response. Millions watched online with much the same reaction. The world was swept up in the moment.

Western leaders were quick to respond, at first denouncing the attack and promising to aid an investigation, then with continual admiration for the Ukrainian people who filled the streets in a massive display of unity and determination to maintain their freedom.

For their part, Russian leaders denied any connection with the incident, insisting the attack was nothing more than a *false flag* attempt to widen the war by drawing the West into active military participation. Western leaders responded to the allegation by suggesting Putin and others were attempting to dodge the obvious by blaming the victims. Ukrainian officials dismissed the Russian allegations, calling the comments "yet one more example of Putin hiding behind his own coattails."

In public, Zelensky appeared upbeat and presented the image of a leader determined to press ahead, confident he was leading his country to victory. But behind the scenes, out of the view of the cameras that seemed to follow him constantly, he was visibly shaken. At every moment, he was in touch with his security team for the latest reports on what had been uncovered from the site in Rivne or calling home to check on his wife.

Alone with his closest advisors, Zelensky wondered aloud whether he was putting his family in danger by continuing the tour. Perhaps the whole thing—the presidency, resisting Putin before the invasion, fighting after it began—had been a mistake. But when they were back in Kiev and he'd had a day of rest with his wife and children, he insisted on continuing with the tour as planned. "Ukraine needs the world's help," he said. "And the world needs the benefit of helping us."

✦ ✦ ✦

A week after the attempt on his life, Zelensky and a small group of advisors departed on the next leg of their previously arranged schedule, taking the campaign for support to Central and Western Europe. Their first stop was in Paris.

Zelensky and his aides arrived to find a crowd that filled the street to greet them as they drove from the airport to the presidential residence. They spent the remainder of the day with French leaders and the following morning, he inspected a nearby military installation. After reviewing the troops stationed there, he examined several examples of French missiles and armored equipment, noting his country's need for both.

After two days in France, Zelensky traveled to Poland, stopping in Lask at the NATO base where he talked privately with NATO and US officials. Zelensky reminded them of the need to coordinate NATO capabilities with the efforts of Ukrainian military units. NATO officials were sympathetic to that need, but reiterated their official rules of engagement and the need to keep Ukrainian operations officially separate from Ukraine's own. Their discussions were frustrating but private. Images of Zelensky posing with NATO generals among tanks and artillery pieces appeared cordial and were broadcast around the world. The message they delivered was one of solidarity and determination, despite the limitations that circumstances imposed.

From Poland, Zelensky continued through Europe, stopping to visit each of the leaders of the remaining NATO countries, before finishing later in the week in London. He spent an hour with the king at Buckingham Palace and two hours with the prime minister at his residence on Downing Street, before departing for a long flight to America and the final leg of the tour.

That weekend, Zelensky and his advisors arrived in New York to a hero's welcome, including a parade down Broadway in Manhattan. Reporters from all of the major US media networks covered his presence. Newscasters talked nonstop about his heroics in visiting Ukrainian troops, despite an attempt on his life, and about his dogged determination to keep Western support flowing to the Ukrainian cause. When he appeared before a session of the UN general assembly, he received a standing ovation.

In Washington, Zelensky was greeted like a rock star. Crowds lined the streets from the airport to the Capital where he gave a rousing speech to a joint session of Congress. Politicians fell over themselves to praise his leadership and announce their commitment to providing additional support for the Ukrainian effort.

From the capital, he went down the street to the White House for a meeting with President Jackson. When they finished, Jackson announced a new package of military aid and submitted it to Congress that day. Prominent politicians promised swift approval.

✦ ✦ ✦

Zelensky's trip across Ukraine, then Europe, and finally to America had been a rousing success. People the world over—celebrities, politicians, and civilians alike—responded with expressions of admiration and support. Individual NATO countries announced their own military aid packages to shore up Ukraine's effort to defend itself. Even non-aligned nations in South America joined the effort. Yet despite the response, Zelensky could not get past the brazen attack against him in Rivne. On the plane as he traveled home to Kyiv, he gathered with his advisors to discuss the matter. "They tried to kill me," he said. "Someone tried to kill me."

"Yes, Mr. President," Aleksi Smolov, Zelensky's chief of staff, replied. "We've been wondering how long it would take them to try."

"I specifically ordered our people to avoid attempts on Putin," Zelensky continued. "The Americans insisted I do that, and I did it, but for what? To sit and wait while the Russians try to kill me? I am the President of Ukraine. We are a sovereign nation. We can't let this go without a response."

"We should respond with an attempt on Putin," someone said.

"An attempt to execute him at the Kremlin," another added.

"We can't do that," Smolov responded.

"Why not?"

"They started it. We can finish it."

"If we go after Putin," Smolov explained, "the Americans will be forced to defend him, at least rhetorically. European leaders will denounce us. NATO will view it as unnecessarily provocative. And besides, we don't know for certain it was the Russians who did it."

"What?" someone cried. "Who else could it be?"

"Surely not one of our own."

"We can't do anything," Smolov said, "until we know for certain. We certainly can't take a shot at Putin on a guess or a hunch."

Oleh Kostenko, one of the speechwriters who'd accompanied them, spoke up. "The optics wouldn't be good for us," he said. "The US does not want even the appearance of an all-out war with Russia, which is what an attempt on Putin would provoke. We have no choice but to honor the US wish and keep silent."

"So, what are you saying?" Zelensky asked. "We should do nothing?"

Smolov replied, "If you go after Putin, you will risk everything."

"Nonsense."

Smolov refused to back down. "You've talked to Jackson. You know what he has said. You know what he's like. If you do this, you'll risk everything. NATO, the US, the EU. You'll risk losing all of their support."

Zelensky was frustrated. "But if we do nothing, what does it say about Putin's attempts on me? What does it say about his violation of our sovereignty?"

"As I said, we don't know that the shots came from Russian operatives. We don't know *who* did it."

Zelensky glared at him. "You don't really mean that."

"Everyone has their assumptions," Smolov said. "But no one has any evidence yet regarding who was behind the attack."

"Then get some evidence!" Zelensky shouted. "I want to know who's trying to kill me!"

CHAPTER SEVENTEEN

When the attempt on Zelensky's life occurred in Rivne, informants on the ground had alerted Sergei Naryshkin, head of Russia's Foreign Intelligence Service. He, in turn, briefed Putin and provided regular updates on the situation. Putin had expressed interest in the incident at the time but since then had made no mention of it to his staff or advisors. Not even to discuss a response with Naryshkin, but then, he didn't need to discuss it with Naryshkin. Naryshkin knew what had to be done without being told. That's how the relationship worked between them. They were like opposite sides of the same mind. Naryshkin covered for Putin, Putin covered for Naryshkin in a kind of symbiotic relationship that left others shaking their heads.

From his office in Moscow, Naryshkin summoned Ratmir Bruskin, one of the Service's best utilitymen, the kind of operative commonly known in the West as a *fixer*. A specialist at solving problems and cleaning up messes caused by the mistakes of others. Naryshkin and Bruskin met in a carpark across town.

"You heard about the attempt on Zelensky?" Naryshkin asked.

"Yes," Bruskin replied. "Of course."

"Who did it?"

Bruskin shrugged. "No one knows. No one wants to know."

"I want to know."

"Men in our line of work find it is always better to avoid knowing too much about these things."

"I want to know about these things," Naryshkin insisted.

"I think we should leave this one alone," Bruskin replied.

"This kind of thing is exactly the kind of thing we need to know about." Bruskin looked him in the eye. "Find out who did it and take care of it."

"We aren't glad that someone shot at him?"

"Last year, we might have been glad. This year, we're concerned it will derail everything."

"But I thought—"

"Ratmir," Naryshkin snapped. "Take care of it."

✦ ✦ ✦

The following day, Bruskin left Moscow and traveled through Belarus to the border with Ukraine. He bribed a guard at the crossing near Stolin and entered Ukraine on a fake passport using a false name. From the crossing, it was a short distance to Rivne where the attempt on Zelensky's life occurred.

At Rivne, Bruskin secured a room in a cheap hotel, then went out to the street. In order to find the people involved in the shooting, he needed to find a starting point and for that he needed information. Truth, lies, gossip, something to give him a place to begin. Coffee shops and cafés were great places to hear gossip. A sign at the corner advertised a café. He turned in that direction and started toward it.

Inside the café, Bruskin took a seat at a table in the corner, ordered a cup of coffee, and listened. After an hour at the table, he had heard nothing of interest, so he moved to a different shop. Then another. Despite the passage of almost two weeks, he had expected the attempt on Zelensky still to be a topic of interest but three cafes later, he had heard nothing helpful about the shooting.

At the end of the day, he returned to the hotel and lay on the bed staring up at the ceiling reviewing his first attempts at finding out what really happened. He had spent all day drinking coffee and listening to conversations but had come up dry. Not a single conversation addressed the topic. He considered moving to a different town, perhaps to Kyiv where the conversation might be better, or where he might meet someone helpful through another approach, but Kyiv was a large city and there was no way to listen his way around a city of that size even if he confined himself to the shops and stores nearest the government offices. Maybe he should give Rivne one more try.

The following day, Bruskin returned to the cafés near the hotel, but the process remained frustratingly tedious, and to make matters worse most of the places served poor coffee and even poorer food. However, late in the afternoon, as Bruskin was once again considering a different approach, he heard two men talking at a table next to him. They spoke in hushed tones but even so, Bruskin heard one of them mention Myroslav Reznikov by name.

Reznikov was known in Moscow as someone with great contacts but an ego that made him impossible to deal with. The two men at the table beside Bruskin seemed to share that assessment. Apparently, they felt compelled to put up with him because he was friends with Zelensky, despite his self-centered attitude. Bruskin strained to hear more of what the two men said, but the clatter of dinnerware and the voices of patrons at a nearby table drowned out most of what the two men said.

Half an hour later, the men left the café. Bruskin quickly paid his tab and followed them down the street. A few blocks later, they parted company. The man who had mentioned Reznikov turned left. The other one kept going straight. Bruskin followed the man to the left.

In the next block, the man he was following came to a car that was parked at the curb. He opened the driver's door and got inside. Bruskin rushed around to the passenger door and opened it. "Great to see you," he said, hopping in as if they were old friends.

"Who are you?" the man protested. "Get out of my car!"

Bruskin opened his jacket to reveal an automatic pistol in the waistband of his trousers. "Just drive," he said. "And don't do anything stupid."

The man steered the car from the curb and started up the street. At the next corner, Bruskin pointed. "Turn here," he said. They turned right and a few blocks later came to a bomb-damaged building. Only the walls remained with debris from the roof strewn about the neighboring property. "Here," Bruskin said, pointing again. "Turn in here."

The man did as he was told and brought the car to a stop behind the damaged building. He took the car out of gear and looked over at Bruskin. "What do you want from me? I don't have any money."

"At the café," Bruskin said, ignoring the question. "You were talking about someone named Myroslav Reznikov."

The man frowned. "I don't know anyone named—"

"Back there," Bruskin said, cutting him off. "In the café. I heard you. You and your friend were talking about Reznikov. What was that about?"

The man looked away. "It was nothing," he said, as if he would rather not say more.

Bruskin drew the pistol from its holster and nudged him with the muzzle. "Tell me, before I lose my patience."

"That guy I was with. He—"

"What's his name? The man you were with. What's his name?"

"Melen. Andriy Melen."

"What does he do?" Bruskin asked.

"He works for the city. The city of Rivne."

"What were you talking about with him? Why did you mention Reznikov?"

"Melen knows a lot of people. And he knows about things that go on around here. So, I was telling him I had heard people talking about how the attack on Zelensky was instigated by Reznikov."

"You know Reznikov?"

"Everyone knows Reznikov. He was in that show. On television. The one Zelensky was in."

"Who told you Reznikov was involved in the attack?"

"I don't know who said it first. Several of us were talking. It was just a thing that came up. Someone said, 'I heard it was this. I heard it was that.' That sort of thing. I thought Melen might know if it was true, so I asked him."

"What did he tell you?"

"He didn't want to talk about it. Said it was better if I didn't mention it anymore."

"He threatened you?"

"No," the man said. "It wasn't like that. He and I are friends. He was just telling me it was a thing I shouldn't mention."

Bruskin gestured with the gun. "Take me to Melen."

"Please," the man protested. "I don't want to get involved in whatever this is. And I certainly don't want to get hurt by that pistol." He pointed to the gun.

Bruskin returned the pistol to the holster. "Nobody will get hurt if you do as I say." He pointed. "Take me to your friend Melen."

✦ ✦ ✦

Melen was outside his house, tending to plants that grew near the front door, when Bruskin and the guy with the car arrived. He was surprised to see them but seemed to recognize Bruskin from the shop when the guy with the car introduced them. Melen led them to a small garden inside a fenced area behind the house. Bruskin asked him about Reznikov.

"Yeah," Melen said. "I know Reznikov from my work on the city planning board."

"What kind of work?"

"The city has been trying to get a fifth generator for the nuclear power plant. Reznikov has been helping us with that."

"You were there when Zelensky arrived?"

"Yes," Melen answered. "But I wasn't out there where the shooting took place."

"Why not?"

"I'd rather not say."

"I'd rather you did."

"Who are you?"

"You don't want to know who I am," Bruskin replied. "Why weren't you out there in the crowd when the shooting started."

"Who are you?" Melen asked again.

The man with the car spoke up. "Just tell him what you know Andriy. He's not interested in us. He wants to know about Reznikov."

Melen glanced down at the tops of his shoes, as if thinking. After a moment he said, "I had a message from Reznikov telling me not to go to the arrival. That I should go to the second place."

"Zelensky was to appear at another site?"

"Yeah." Melen looked up to focus on Bruskin. "They wanted a crowd out there where the helicopter landed, and then another crowd at the place where the soldiers were camped. Reznikov told me to go out there."

"Why did he want you out there?"

"I don't know." Melen shrugged. "At the time I thought maybe he wanted to make sure there was a big enough crowd, but it bothered me."

"Why?"

"It seemed like he knew something was going to take place, but when I got out there, General Marchuk was there, too, so I didn't feel bad about it then. He originally was supposed to be at the place where the helicopter landed. Same as me. When I saw him with the troops at the other place, I thought maybe the plan had changed."

That didn't make much sense to Bruskin. According to the details in the planning book, Marchuk was supposed to be on hand to greet Zelensky as he came from the helicopter. Why did they deviate from the plan? What really happened?

And, as to make sure the crowd was large enough at the site where the soldiers were camped, the place already was full of soldiers. Some on a wartime break, others waiting to be shipped to the front. There were plenty of people at the site and whether Melen was there or not wouldn't have made any difference. It surely wouldn't have affected the size of the crowd.

Nevertheless, Bruskin didn't want to get sidetracked by that issue, so he pushed it aside and said, "Were you involved in Zelensky's campaign?"

"No." Melen shook his head. "I didn't even vote for him."

"Have you talked to Reznikov since the incident?"

"Just about the power plant."

"Did he tell you anything about Zelensky's visit, other than to send you from the helicopter landing site to the place where the soldiers were staying?"

"No."

"He didn't warn you about anything. Or maybe ask you to do something?"

Melen looked away. "No. Not really."

Bruskin heard the tone in his voice and raised an eyebrow. "What did he want you to do?"

Melen sighed. "After the event was over," he began, "there was a box—"

"Event? Which event?"

"Zelensky's visit. After it was over, there was a box of Reznikov's stuff at the office. Reznikov had brought it with him that day but left without getting it. He wanted me to find it and hold onto it until he came back."

"Did you get it for him?"

"Yes."

"Do you still have it?"

Melen gestured over his shoulder. "It's in the house."

"Can I see it?"

Melen focused on him again, as if sizing him up. "Who do you work for?"

"The government." Bruskin flashed an ID card from a nonexistent agency.

Melen seemed satisfied. "Come on," he said. "I'll show you."

They followed Melen into the house and took a seat at a table in kitchen while he retrieved the box. A moment later, Melen returned and set the box on the table. Bruskin began looking through the contents.

At the bottom of the box, Bruskin found a copy of the briefing book that Fomichev had prepared for Zelensky's tour. He flipped through the pages and was about to put it down when he noticed something scrawled on the last page. He turned to it again and saw the name, "Kuleba" followed by a telephone number. Bruskin recognized the name immediately.

✦ ✦ ✦

Early the next day, Bruskin traveled to Kyiv where he met with Poroshenko. The two had known each other a long time. Bruskin asked him about the incident at Rivne.

"That was a bold move," Poroshenko said.

"Who was in charge?"

"That was Kuleba's deal," Poroshenko said. "They had someone else putting it together at first, but Kuleba moved him out."

"Why did he do that?"

"You know," Poroshenko shrugged. "Typical Kuleba."

"Everyone thinks it was Reznikov."

"That's because we wanted them to think that."

"No one seems to doubt Reznikov might have orchestrated the whole thing. I've asked around. No one defended him when his name came up."

"That's because Reznikov is a *mu-dak*," Poroshenko growled. "No one likes him. That's why we picked him to take the blame."

"But someone is trying to place the blame on the man who wrote the briefing book for the event."

"Fomichev?"

"Yeah," Bruskin said. "Why are they trying to put this on him?"

"He's an outsider. They all think he's a nobody."

"Whose idea was it to blame him?"

"Do you really have to ask?"

Bruskin thought for a moment, then chuckled. "That was Kuleba, too."

Poroshenko smiled. "You know what to do about both of them, don't you?"

"Yeah," Bruskin said wearily. "I know what to do with them. But there's one more thing."

"What's that?"

"Marchuk was supposed to be there, but he never showed."

"Leave him to me," Poroshenko said.

✦ ✦ ✦

Unlike Bruskin, who only worked for Putin, Poroshenko lived in the middle ground, with an organization below him, which consisted of his own people, and the oligarchs above who gave him protection from high-ranking officials. The oligarchs allowed him to operate free of interference from the national government. The organization below him existed solely for the purpose of generating cash. Revenue. Money. A cut of that revenue went up to the oligarchs, and a cut went down to those who did the work. The rest went into Poroshenko's pocket.

Poroshenko's organization centered on Kyiv and was heavily dependent on contacts within the Ukrainian government—officials who kept government contracts flowing in his direction. Lucrative military supply contracts for everything from paper to food to fuel. To keep things working smoothly, Poroshenko kicked back a portion of the proceeds to the officials involved, paid his guys who handled the business, and funded his payments to the oligarchs. The balance of the income covered the cost of fulfilling the contracts and gave him money to fund a string of nightclubs and brothels. Keeping those businesses going required payments to the police, building and health inspectors, and the flesh brokers who supplied the women necessary to satisfy the customers. On top of all that, Poroshenko had a constant stream of money from hundreds of scams that siphoned money from other government agencies, some of which were controlled by his own people.

Men like Kuleba and Reznikov were insiders among government officials, but in Poroshenko's world they were at the bottom of the revenue stream. Helpful, certainly, but small pieces of an enormous enterprise. Dispensing with them would cause Poroshenko no difficulty at all and even if it did, there were people above him who could make those problems go away. General Marchuk, however, was a different matter, which was why Poroshenko wanted to deal with him alone.

Marchuk had come to the army at a time when payments of the right amount, made to the correct person, could open the door to a fabulous military career. Those payments, however, came with strings—lots of strings. Marchuk's strings were held by Oleksy Zhevago, an enormously wealthy Russian businessman who had built a fortune dealing in oil and grain. A word from Zhevago and commodities flowed freely from the port at Odesa. With a different word, that flow stopped entirely, regardless of what Zelensky or anyone else in the government said.

Poroshenko had little doubt Marchuk had coordinated the attempt on Zelensky's life that day in Rivne, but that attempt wasn't merely an attack on the country's president. It was an attack on the business of his mentors—the oligarchs with whom Poroshenko worked. Zhevago wanted the entire line, upstream and down. Marchuk was his instrument for obtaining it.

Under normal conditions, Poroshenko might have asked for permission before resolving the problem posed by Marchuk, but these were no ordinary times, and the threat was no ordinary threat. Which is why he decided to deal with Marchuk himself, but however he chose to resolve that issue, it had to look like it was done by someone else. Completely, entirely, undeniably someone else. In this case, given Marchuk's career as an army general, that resolution needed to look like the Russians took him out. Poroshenko knew of only one person who could help with that, an American known to the Kyiv underworld only as Tom.

CHAPTER EIGHTEEN

At Bakhmut, Taras' platoon had advanced from the outskirts to a position near the center of the city. Taras and the drone operation moved forward with them and now operated from a parking lot at Bakhmut Medical College. It was a risky location, being much closer than before to Russian artillery positions, but was better for shorter drone flights. Shorter flights meant the drones could make more trips and drop more bombs on Russian targets.

About noon that day, a Humvee turned into the parking lot and came to a stop near where Taras was loading a drone with anti-tank hand grenades for yet one more mission. He had been flying missions constantly since before sunrise, loading and refueling the drone by himself. He was tired, irritable, and paid little attention to the Humvee until he noticed Tom, the American, step from it.

They hadn't seen each other since the day Tom had come to train them with the drones. It seemed like a long time ago.

"I hope you didn't come to collect your drones," Taras said. "We've grown rather dependent on them."

"No," Tom replied. "I didn't come to collect the drones. I came to collect *you*."

"What for?"

"We have some special work that needs your expertise."

"Did you clear it with Seargent Lomachenko?" This wasn't the first time Taras had received a special assignment, but he knew better than to accept it without checking.

Tom pointed across the way. "I think that's him coming now."

Taras glanced over his shoulder and saw Lomachenko coming from the groundskeeper's shack at the edge of the parking lot. They had been using the shack as an operations center and makeshift barracks.

When Lomachenko was a few paces away, he caught Taras's eye. "Irvanets," he said, "I need you to go with these men."

"Where to?"

"They'll tell you on the way."

"What about the drone?"

"I'll take care of it," Lomachenko replied. "I don't think you'll be gone too long."

Taras collected his things from the groundskeepers' shack and returned to the Humvee, then he got inside with Tom and a driver steered the vehicle toward the street.

✦ ✦ ✦

Before long they were back at the edge of town near the apartment building where Taras and the platoon had been when Tom delivered the drones in the first place. The buildings looked much the same as the day they pulled out and moved forward, but the people were gone, and the neighborhood seemed eerily silent.

"What are we doing here?" Taras asked.

"We have a special mission we want you to fly," Tom said.

"Why back here?"

"It needs to be a little more secretive than what you're doing up there on the parking lot."

The Humvee came to a stop near the spot Taras and the others had used as their first base of operations, and they got out. Taras paused and glanced up at the sky. Directly above him the sky was pale blue broken only by the thin white clouds that drifted eastward. For a moment, focusing only on that spot, it seemed the day was peaceful and calm, but just then there was the boom of artillery in the distance and Taras felt the ground tremble beneath his feet a shell exploded not far away.

A delivery truck was parked nearby and as they came from the Humvee the driver of the truck opened the back doors. Inside were pieces of a drone that appeared to be much larger than any of the ones Taras had previously operated. With the driver's help they removed the parts from the truck and set them on the ground, then began connecting them together.

Like the drone Tara already was flying, this one was a modified delivery drone configured in the shape of a hashtag with two pieces down each side and two across the middle. Engines were mounted at each of the four corners allowing it to takeoff vertically.

By rotating them, the drone could move forward, backward, and side-to-side.

The drone had been made in a modular fashion. Disassembled for transportation, it consisted of four primary pieces. Assembling the drone for use was only a matter of plugging the pieces back together. In less than two hours, the drone from the truck was assembled, fueled, and ready to fly.

"Okay," Taras said when they were done. "There it is." He gestured to the assembled aircraft. "What are we doing with it?"

The driver from the Humvee brought a rocket from the truck. Taras recognized it as an *Igla*, a Russian surface-to-air missile. He frowned. "What are we going to do with that?"

"We are attaching it to the drone," Tom replied.

"We're going to launch it?"

"Yes."

"How?" The missile was designed to work with its own launcher that normally rested on an operator's shoulder. When used in the field, the operator sighted the missile on its target, then squeezed a trigger to release it. That seemed impossible to do with it attached to the drone.

"You'll fire it with the controller," Tom said.

"The one we use to fly the drone?"

"Yes. You'll press the same button you use when you release grenades."

While Taras watched, Tom and the driver secured the missile to the drone with its launcher still attached, using mounting brackets that had been bolted onto the drone's frame. When it was in place, they connected a wire from the drone to a port near the trigger housing of the launcher. When that was done, Tom smiled triumphantly. "It's ready to go."

Taras seemed unconvinced. "If you say so."

"I do."

"Where do you want it delivered?"

Tom handed him a piece of paper with the coordinates. "Put it right on this location," he said, pointing to the numbers on the page.

"Is the location already in the guidance system?"

"No," Tom said. "You'll have to enter the target information yourself."

The inflight controller for the drone was a handheld device much like the controller for a video game. It was connected to a digital processor that processed commands from the controller and relayed them to the onboard system. A monitor on the ground displayed real-time images from the drone's onboard cameras. A second monitor showed flight data—height, speed, direction, coordinates, and the like.

Taras entered the target coordinates into the system, checked one last time to make sure the setup was correct, then paused. "It'll be uneven," he said after a moment.

"What do you mean?"

"We need something on the other side to counterbalance the weight of the missile."

"Oh. Right," Tom said. "Normally we send it up with two missiles."

Taras turned to a box that was sitting nearby and took two anti-tank grenades from it. He clipped them in place on the opposite side of the frame from the missile, then added two more.

The truck driver spoke up. "How will the system know if it's releasing grenades or the missile?"

"The controller will figure it out when I press this," Taras said, pointing to small red button on the side.

They made a final check, then Taras pressed a button on the controller to start the drone's engines. He let the engines warm up a moment, made one last check of the displays, then pushed the controller's joysticks forward. The drone lifted a few feet into the air, and he let it hover there before moving it from side to side to get the feel of it. After a moment, he pushed the joysticks forward and the drone rose into the air.

Twenty minutes later, the system indicated the drone was over the target. Taras adjusted an onboard camera for a clear view of the ground and saw the image of a house in rural Ukraine on the monitor. The house had a thatched roof with masonry walls that had recently been whitewashed. There was a patch of grass in front with a garden a little farther out. A path led up from a road where a pickup truck was parked in a space alongside a four-rail fence. There were no humans in sight, only a dog that lay peacefully by the front door.

Taras called over to Tom. "Looks like we're there," he said pointing to the screen. "Is that what you were expecting?"

Tom came closer and checked the image. "That looks about right," he said. "Are we on the coordinates?"

Taras pointed to the second monitor. "The system indicates we are right on top of it."

Tom stepped over to the truck and took a satellite phone from a compartment by the front seat, then used it to place a call. The call lasted only a moment and when he was done, he returned to Taras' side. "Deliver the package," he said.

Taras pressed a button on the controller. Everyone stared at the screen and watched as the missile came into view, followed by its wispy white contrail. Seconds later, it disappeared through the thatched roof of the house and exploded in an enormous ball of fire. Debris flew in every direction.

Through the smoke and flame, a man could be seen wearing what appeared to be a tattered and torn military uniform. His clothes were on fire, and he flayed the air with both hands trying to put out the flames. There was a large gap in the front wall of the house where the door had been and he staggered toward it, then fell face down. A beam from atop the doorway fell on him, then the wall collapsed atop him, too.

Tom and the others watched in silence as the scene played out on the monitor. Taras watched, too, until the man on the ground was obscured by debris and smoke. Then he pressed a button on the controller and the drone veered away from its position above the house.

With the missile no longer attached, the drone was unstable and listed to one side. Taras circled back to the house and release two of the grenades. They exploded near where the man had fallen.

Release of the weight of the grenades made the drone more stable, so Taras dropped the other two on the truck that was parked by the road. They scored a direct hit and ignited the truck's gas tank. Everyone wanted to see the effects of the secondary explosion, but Taras knew they had to leave. He pressed the *return to home* button on the controller and the camera's image went dark. "It'll be back here in about twenty minutes," Taras said.

The driver of the truck that had brought the drone appeared with a small cooler in hand. He flipped off the top to reveal it was filled with bottles of beer. Tom took one and offered it to Taras.

Taras shook his head. "Never developed a taste for it," he said.

"Maybe now's the time to get started," the driver suggested with a laugh.

Taras declined. "I prefer coffee."

✦ ✦ ✦

Jim Marsh was seated at his desk when an assistant appeared in the doorway of his office. "The Director wants you in the Intelligence Command Center."

"Now?"

"Immediately."

Marsh came from his office and walked down the hall to the Command Center. The room was arranged much like a conference room with a long table down the middle and comfortable chairs positioned on either side, except this one was created to manage secure intelligence during times of global crisis. Each position at the table was equipped with a microphone and a bank of telephones. A large video screen covered the wall at one end. Cameras at the opposite end recorded the room's proceedings.

Director Donovan was standing at the screen as Marsh entered. "We received this today," he said, pointing to the screen. There was a look in his eyes that seemed to indicate he knew that Marsh knew exactly what he was about to discuss.

Video began to play on the screen showing images of a thatched house. As they watched, a missile struck the house, and it exploded in a ball of fire. A man staggered from the ruins, his body engulfed in flames, and fell to the ground, face down.

"This video," Donovan explained, "was taken near Lisove, a rural village in Ukraine. We received it less than an hour ago. Initial reports indicate the man in the image is Ukrainian General Marchuk. The house was apparently his home."

"Who did it?" Marsh asked. "Was it a mistake?" Marsh knew full well it wasn't a mistake.

"Our people have been going through additional images from other sources," Donovan continued, "and it turns out the missile may have been delivered by one of our assets."

The video disappeared from the screen and was replaced by the photo of a man. "This is someone known to most in the Agency as Tom. That's the name he goes by in the field. His work name is Tom Bissell. His real name is Eric Sebold. We think he arranged for procurement of the ordinance and for its delivery."

"What did they use?" Marsh asked. Once again, he already knew the answer.

"A Russian *Igla* surface-to-air missile."

"How was it delivered to that site?"

"It appears to have been attached to a drone."

"One of ours?"

"That's the question I need you to answer."

"It might take a little while."

Donovan shook his head. "I don't think so."

Marsh frowned. "What do you mean?"

"That missile killed a Ukrainian general," Donovan said. "The National Reconnaissance Office saw it when it happened." He pointed over his shoulder to the screen. "That's how we have those images we just saw. One of our own satellites picked it up, too. The NATO center in Poland tracked the drone that delivered it from the place where it took off in Bakhmut to the house where the missile exploded. We know it came from a Ukrainian-controlled site in the city, but no one knows why. Zelensky is asking why. The President is asking why. I'm due to be at the White House in half an hour and he's expecting me to give him the answer. Which is why you and I are standing in this room. I need to know what happened."

"And you think I can tell you that?"

"Using drones for weapons delivery was one of your ideas. The people over at Science and Technology say you asked them about it. Bryan Fowler, who is one of their best guys with product modification, liked the idea, too."

"I didn't—"

"I know you authorized payment for it."

Marsh looked away. "It was all above board."

"I understand," Donovan replied. "And I think you had a reason for conducting this operation against Marchuk. I just want to know what it is so I can figure out how to handle it with the President." He glanced at his watch. "And I don't have much time. So, start talking."

Marsh admitted authorizing a program in Ukraine using modified commercial delivery drones to deliver explosives. He convinced the NATO site in Poland to let him use space at their site and recruited Tom to provide operational management.

"It worked better than any of us imagined."

"What about Marchuk? Dropping a missile through his roof doesn't look very good."

"Marchuk was connected to the Russian mob."

"Half of Russia is connected to the Russian mob."

"Yeah, but Marchuk was involved in the attack on Zelensky at Rivne."

Donovan looked surprised. "You can prove this?"

"Yes."

Donovan took a seat at the table and gestured for Marsh to do the same. "Tell me about it," he said.

For the next thirty minutes, Marsh walked Donovan through everything he had learned about the attack. Kuleba, Reznikov, Marchuk, Poroshenko, Naryshkin, and Andrey Bruskin, the fixer who was sent in to clean it all up.

Donovan was stunned. "Kuleba and Reznikov have been with Zelensky a long time."

"Yes, they have."

"And they wanted him out?"

"Money," Marsh said. "They appear to be obsessed with money."

Donovan thought for a moment before asking, "Can I tell the President about this?"

The question struck Marsh as an odd one, the Director of the CIA asking a deputy director's permission about what to tell the President, but Marsh understood what he meant. He wasn't asking for permission, but rather, to know if telling the president *now* would compromise ongoing operations. "How good is he at lying?"

Donovan laughed. "He knows how things work."

"Is this going to be a problem?"

"Zelensky is upset, as you might imagine. He has the president's ear."

"I don't think he knows the full story with his government."

"Probably not."

"Marchuk was in Putin's pocket."

"Which might explain the way things have gone on the ground," Donovan said. He glanced at his watch again and stood. "I'm late," he said. "Listen for your phone. I may need to call you to join me." Then he hurried toward the door.

CHAPTER NINETEEN

aving been turned down earlier by China with a request for drones and artillery shells, Putin looked to Iran for more assistance. To make the request as appealing as possible, he invited the Iranian president, Ali Akbar Bizhani, to Moscow. They met in Putin's residence where he carefully laid out the situation. "Our forces are superior to those of Ukraine, but American and European interference has complicated our plans. Arms supplied by the West have compensated for Ukraine's inefficiencies, upon which our plans had been calculated. This has forced us to use far more ammunition than we had planned. Ukraine units have been able to attack our troops with virtually unlimited supplies of artillery shells, drones, and missiles. While our people at home have endured severe supply limitations due to Western sanctions."

Bizhani listened attentively and agreed to supply the requested support. However, as everyone expected, he asked in turn for direct support from Russia for Iran's nuclear program. "Specifically," he said, "we need key pieces of technology necessary to miniaturize components of a nuclear warhead that allow it to fit atop one of our existing missiles."

The exchange was simple, direct, and forthright. Putin struggled to find a plausible reason to delay his response before finally saying, "If we are in agreement in principle, I will consult with my advisors and determine a process for us to move forward in assisting each other."

Bizhani smiled. "We are in agreement."

✦ ✦ ✦

After Bizhani was on his way back to Iraq, Putin convened a meeting of his closest advisors. When they were assembled, he explained the situation to them and ended by saying, "I am hesitant to pursue further arrangements with Bizhani," he said.

Military officials in the room insisted the army needed the munitions. "Mr. President, we are out of options. There are no other sources for the weapons we need."

Putin shook his head. "If we give the Iranians what they're asking for, the Middle East will become a nuclear nightmare. The Iranians have done well to get this far with their weapons programs on their own, but they are religious fanatics. Pagan fanatics. We have no way to control them, and they have no means of controlling themselves. If we allow them to develop the ability to create a nuclear arsenal for themselves, they will use that arsenal to settle every dispute, even disputes they might have with us."

"Perhaps we could use this overture to pressure Wei Xing," someone suggested. "As a way of getting him to sell us Chinese weapons instead. Tell him what Iran wants from us and how desperate we are to avoid that outcome, but also how determined we are to win this war."

Someone else spoke up. "If we tell Wei Xing what the Iranians want, he might offer to sell it to them himself. Or exchange it for oil. Then we'd be in an even worse position. Iran with nuclear weapons and China as their primary ally."

Before responding to Iran's demands, Putin called Wei Xing and made the same appeal he had made to Bizhani. After a lengthy conversation, Wei Xing agreed to take up the matter with his senior advisors.

✦ ✦ ✦

When the call ended, Wei Xing convened a meeting of the Committee of Advisors, a permanent group of leaders from critical departments of the government. They gathered in a conference room near Wei Xing's office where he briefed them on details of his discussion with Putin, outlining Putin's request for assistance. "This is a delicate situation for us," Wei Xing said. "If we supply Russia with munitions, we will risk incurring US sanctions. If we deny Russia's request, we risk precipitating Russian humiliation."

"By the Americans," Zhao Guofeng added. "And their puppet state, Ukraine. Which would further strengthen America's position among the nations of the world."

"There is also a risk to us in our own region," Guo Zhongbo noted.

Wei Xing frowned. "What risk could there be to us?"

"If we supply Russia with weapons," Zhongbo replied, "the US might react by strengthening Taiwan's arms."

Some shook their heads in disgust. "They wouldn't dare. Not in the present climate."

"They have in the past," Zhongbo noted.

"Things are different now. The US is already engaged in a proxy war with Russia through Ukraine. Supplying Taiwan would open a second proxy war with us. The US doesn't have that kind of strength now. Not after all the arms and equipment they have shipped to Ukraine."

"A proxy war with US and Taiwan against us would be as it was in the past," Li Xudong noted.

"So too, the US and Western Europe against Russia and the Arab countries."

"A world war of proxy wars."

The discussion continued around the room until everyone had expressed their opinion. When they seemed to have nothing more to offer, Wei said, "Couldn't we deny the request publicly, but send the artillery shells and drones to Russia privately, by another means? Perhaps through something other than direct shipment?"

"A third party."

"Yes."

"That would require an arrangement between us and the Russians," Zhao said. "News of it would get out quickly and we would be in a worse position."

"Then we could apologize and stop, but at least something would get through."

"It wouldn't necessarily require a formal agreement," Wei Xing said.

"What do you mean?"

"For instance, we could tell the Kazaks we are sending them missiles and other items," Wei Xing explained. It seemed to him the obvious solution and it also allowed them to solidify the cooperative relationship they had built earlier when negotiating on behalf of diplomatic relations between Iran and Saudi Arabia. "At the same time, Russian officials could be alerted to this and ask the Kazaks to sell the missiles to them. We transfer to Kazakhstan, Russia buys from them, and the Kazaks pay us. The deal gets done with no documents to show that anything occurred."

Ba Renfu agreed. "Like in the old days," he said. "Business on a promise and nothing more. Not even shipping manifests."

Hu Yong noted, "We and Russia share a border with Kazakhstan. The transfers could be accomplished overland."

No one else spoke further to defend the plan and the conversation moved on. "We could send missiles to North Korea," someone suggested. "They could send them to Iran and Iran could forward them to Russia."

"That would make matters worse."

"Much worse."

"Adding North Korea to the Ukraine situation would only antagonize the Americans further."

"And the Europeans."

"The US and NATO might actively join the war with troops on the ground."

Ba Renfu spoke up again. "I favor the indirect approach mentioned earlier. We have supplied the Kazaks with artillery shells many times before. There would be nothing unusual about us doing so now. This seems like the way to transfer them."

Wei looked down the table to Dong Jingwei. "Can we get a message to Putin without alerting the world?"

"Yes," Jingwei said. "Absolutely."

"Then that is what we shall do."

The meeting was about to adjourn when Zhao Guofeng spoke up. "Paramount Leader, I don't think we should let the Americans chase us away from the decision that is best for us."

Wei seemed perturbed by the interruption. "You think we have made an incorrect decision?"

"I think the best decision for us would be to ignore the Russians and the Americans and invade Taiwan Island. Avenge our past and take it back now, while the others are in no position to oppose us."

Wei shook his head. "That would only provoke the Americans into war against us."

"The Americans are preoccupied with Ukraine and Russia," Zhao argued. "American leaders have steadily poured more and more resources into Ukraine, dangerously diminishing the resources they have for doing anything else."

Jingwei spoke up. "But reclaiming Taiwan Island would lead us into World War III."

"Nations of the world are already engaged in World War III," Zhao said. "Nations on every continent are choosing sides. The reason we're discussing what to do in this meeting is because we're trying to decide which side we're going to take. America? Russia? Ukraine? Europe? I say we should take the side of China." Nods and murmurs of support came from around the table. Zhao continued. "We should decide what's best for China and let the others worry about what's best for them. Why do we have to saddle ourselves with America's priorities? Why do we have to surrender our resources for Russia to use? We should decide based on *our* priorities. Based on what is best for us."

As Zhao spoke, the look on Wei Xing's face hardened. "And what of the world's priorities? The issues we have been discussing are an attempt to wrestle with global priorities."

"But the trouble is not global," Zhao responded. "The trouble is European trouble. The trouble in Ukraine is Ukraine's trouble. It's not Asia's trouble. And it certainly isn't *our* trouble. Putin is asking us to set aside our priorities and take up his. That is wrong."

Everyone in the room seemed to recoil from Zhao's statement. Direct opposition to the paramount leader, even in private meetings, was rarely voiced.

Wei Xing stood and looked around the room with a defiant glare. "I am Paramount Leader of the People's Republic of China," he said sternly. "I have heard your discussion and I have received your comments. Now, I must decide. The manner in which we respond to Russia's request for help is my decision to make and mine alone. We will provide armaments to Russia in the manner we have discussed, transporting through Kazakhstan." He looked over at Dong Jingwei. "You will work out the details and see that it happens."

Dong Jingwei stood. "Yes, Paramount Leader." And before he returned to his chair, Wei Xing left the room.

✦ ✦ ✦

That evening, Zhao invited Guo Zhongbo and several others to join him for dinner at Donglaishun, a popular restaurant in Beijing. They ate in a private room and discussed the meeting. "Wei is weak. He will never assert the true nature of our country unless the Americans give him permission."

"This is an opportune time to retake Taiwan as long as the Americans object."

"We need a strong leader who isn't afraid to take strong action."

"We need one who is true to China. One who understands the Dao of the moment rather than one who thinks like an American."

"Most think he is not up to the task, but they won't say it to anyone."

"Perhaps he should consider retirement."

"Shh," someone cautioned. "They might be listening."

"Let them listen. Wei was never suited for this job, even in times of peace. Now that there is trouble, he is more than a liability."

✦ ✦ ✦

Two weeks later, trucks began carrying drones and artillery shells from army depots in central China to military facilities in Kazakhstan. As with the drone attack that killed General Marchuk in Ukraine, US satellites detected the trucks. Analysts regarded their activity as suspicious and began pinpointing the places where the trucks began their journey in China and where they ended in

Kazakhstan. Based on that and tips from contractors working at the various sites, analysts concluded the trucks were transferring weapons—probably artillery shells and drones—to the Kazak army.

Agents and informants on the ground confirmed the contents of the trucks were, indeed, artillery shells and drones. The result of their work was summarized in a memo that was forwarded to Donovan at CIA headquarters, along with supporting images.

After reviewing the memo and images, Donovan met with Marsh. "What do you make of this traffic between China and Kazakhstan?"

"There's no doubt the Chinese have transferred artillery shells and drones to the Kazaks. The question is whether that activity is related to something bigger in the region, or merely an extension of their existing relationship."

Donovan gestured with the memo. "This is a lot," he said, tapping the document with his finger for emphasis. "We can track all of these shipments to the locations mentioned in the memo?"

"Yes."

"I saw something not too long ago about activity in Kazakhstan," Donovan said. "What was that about?" He knew precisely what it was about, but after the questions that had been raised about the action against General Marchuk, he had decided a more cautious approach might be warranted, even in the office, when discussing ongoing operations.

"While attempting to resolve diplomatic relations between China, Iran, and Saudi Arabia, representatives from those countries met several times in Kazakhstan."

"Right," Donovan said, nodding. "Does this recent activity with China have anything to do with that?"

"I don't think so," Marsh replied.

Donovan thought for a moment before asking, "Have you discussed this current situation with your contact at the State Department?"

"No. Do you think I should?"

"Perhaps."

"Find out what she knows about it. We need to take this to the president, but we need to know what we're talking about before we do."

✦ ✦ ✦

Later that day, Marsh contacted Janice Miller at the State Department and arranged to meet her that afternoon. "We have a situation," he said.

"China and Kazakhstan?" she asked.

"Yes," Marsh replied as he handed her the memo. "This summarizes where we are on the issue."

While she glanced over the memo, Marsh spread satellite images on her desk. "What's this?" she asked, gesturing to the photos.

"Images of the sites in China where the trucks loaded," he said pointing to one set of images. "And the site where they unloaded in Kazakhstan." He pointed to a different one.

Miller picked up one of the photos for a closer look. "This is Balkhash," she said. "The Russians used to have a radar station there. In fact, they've had several there. The last one was removed a few years ago, but they have some very useful buildings. What happened to the contents of the trucks?"

"They were unloaded at Balkhash and placed in a warehouse for a short time, then loaded onto Russian trucks and delivered to a facility in Streletsk."

"That's quite a trip. That part alone is almost sixteen hundred miles."

"What do you know about all of this?" Marsh gestured to the image array.

"Our people in China are telling us that Wei Xing and the People's Liberation Army made a deal to sell missiles and drones to Kazakhstan."

"That's all?"

"That's all the Chinese are saying."

"What's the rest of the story?"

"Other sources say that right before Chinese trucks started crossing the border into Kazakhstan, the Kazakhs were approached by the Russians about selling them this very same stuff. Artillery shells and military drones."

"Truckloads of weapons changing hands on nothing more than a handshake?"

"Definitely adds an element of deniability to the transaction," Miller said. "I doubt we'll find any documentation for it."

"This war is sucking up everyone's excess inventory."

"Isn't that a good thing?"

"Looking to the future, yes, but we have to get through the present first."

✦ ✦ ✦

When his conversation with Miller ended, Marsh went to Donovan and reported what he had learned. Based on that, he and Donovan concluded that Wei Xing had devised a scheme for selling artillery shells and drones to the Russians, despite his public remarks indicating China would avoid doing that.

"Isn't this a violation of our sanctions?" Marsh asked.

"Yes," Donovan replied. "It certainly is, but I'm not sure Jackson has the fortitude to do anything about it except deliver a speech." He stood and slipped on his jacket. "But I have to inform him, just the same." He flashed a fake smile at Marsh. "That's my job."

"How did he react to the details about General Marchuk?"

"He was upset at first," Donovan said.

"And Zelensky?"

"He was irate."

"I bet he gave Jackson an earful?"

"Every day, until we gave him the full story. Once he had the facts about the general, he seemed to understand."

"Has Jackson spoken with Zelensky about it?"

"Yes. Jackson called him the day I briefed him."

"You were in the room for it?"

"No," Donovan said. "They talked right after I left."

Marsh frowned. "He didn't want you in the room for the call?"

Donovan shook his head. "I didn't want to be there."

✦ ✦ ✦

An hour later, Donovan met with President Jackson at the Oval Office. He handed Jackson the memo about activity between China, Kazakhstan, and Russia. While Jackson read, Donovan spread the images that accompanied it across the president's desk—the same images Marsh had shown Miller earlier.

When Jackson finished reading, he picked up one of the photos, studied it for a moment, then pointed to it. "This is the warehouse where the drones were unloaded in Kazakhstan?"

"Yes, Mr. President. Missiles and drones."

"And what about the Russian trucks? Where are they?"

Donovan handed him a different photo. "That's the Russian trucks crossing the border," he said, pointing to a spot on the photograph. "They delivered their cargo to a facility in Streletsk." Donovan pointed to yet another picture.

Jackson had a curious expression. "So, China sends missiles and drones to Kazakhstan. Russia gets them from the Kazaks and transfers them to Russian troops in or around Ukraine," he summarized. "Is that about it?"

"Yes, Mr. President. Drones and artillery shells. From China, through Kazakhstan, to Russia, and into Ukraine."

"How did this come about?" Jackson asked. "Someone always approaches someone to do a deal like this. Who approached whom?"

"Russia initially approached the Chinese about buying their drones and artillery shells. Sergei Naryshkin, head of the Foreign Intelligence Service, made the ask during his trip to Beijing."

"But China said no."

"Right," Donovan said with a nod. "After the Chinese turned them down, the Russians approached the Iranians about obtaining these same items," Donovan explained. "Apparently, the Iranians were willing to sell them the arms, but in addition to payment they also wanted help with their nuclear program."

"Iran wanted help from the Russians?"

"Yes, sir."

"What kind of help?"

"As you know, Iran has refined enough uranium to build at least one bomb. And they have missiles that could reach the entire Middle East. The only thing they lack is a nuclear warhead small enough to fit atop their existing missiles."

"And you think that's what this is about?"

"That's what it was about when the Russians approached the Iranians," Donovan replied.

Jackson nodded thoughtfully. "So, you think the Russians didn't want to give Iran the technology to complete their nuclear program."

"Correct."

"So why am I looking at these photos of trucks coming from China to Kazakhstan, and from Kazakhstan to Russia?"

"Sources in all three countries have confirmed that after China said no the first time, Putin went back to them, and China figured out a way to transfer the weapons to them without officially doing it."

"Don't sell them straight to Russia. Sell them to Kazakhstan first."

"Correct," Donovan acknowledged. "And then Kazakhstan sold them to Russia."

"Sounds like the Iran-Contra deal from the Reagan Era."

"Yes, sir."

"I guess the Chinese were paying attention to us back then after all."

"Apparently so," Donovan said.

Jackson focused on him. "And you have no doubt the trucks in these pictures contained artillery shells and drones?"

"No doubt at all, Mr. President."

✦ ✦ ✦

Based on the information provided by Donovan and the CIA, President Jackson summoned the Chinese ambassador to the White House. Donovan was in the Oval Office when the ambassador arrived. Jackson came from behind his desk to greet the ambassador and the two men sat across from each other on facing sofas near the center of the office. A coffee table was all that separated them.

"Our sources tell us that Wei Xing has reached a deal with Kazakhstan to sell them artillery shells and military drones," Jackson began.

The ambassador showed no emotion. "Whatever arrangement we have made with Kazakhstan," he said, "is our own internal business, Mr. President."

Jackson shook his head. "Not if those artillery shells and drones end up in the hands of Russian soldiers who use them against Ukrainian soldiers."

"What interest does the United States have with a country like Ukraine?"

"Those artillery shells and drones will be used to further

Russia's illegal invasion of Ukraine," Jackson said. "That's a violation of the UN charter. We have pledged to support Ukraine in its effort to resist that invasion and stop Russia's incursion into its territory. And we have an obligation to uphold the integrity of the UN, as does China."

The ambassador's expression changed from emotionless to aloof arrogance. "It is always this way with you people."

"And it is the same with you, too," Jackson countered. "Anytime someone calls your hand, you give a 'what about' argument to avoid the obvious. We complain about the way you treat the Uyghurs today; you say what about the slaves we brought from Africa three hundred years ago? We complain about your treatment of Muslims in general; you say what about your treatment of Native Americans?"

"You deny doing those things?"

"Both of our countries have made mistakes in the past," Jackson said. "But I'm not talking about the past. I'm talking about the present." He gestured to Donovan who came from across the room and spread the photographs on the coffee table. "China is selling weapons to Russia." He tapped one of the photos with his index finger. "China brings them to this warehouse. Russian trucks take them out." He looked the ambassador in the eye. "Why are you doing this?"

"Why do you object to Russia asserting its rightful claim over Ukraine? The Kuomintang, a terrorist group, invaded and seized Formosa and the surrounding islands, all of which are rightfully ours. Yet America supports them in their illegal occupation. We have been forced to endure their illegal presence on our sovereign property for many decades. Will the United States now offer us its support for an invasion to reclaim it?"

Jackson was resolute. "We will never abandon our allies."

"And neither shall we," the ambassador said. "If you have chosen to support a side in the conflict between Russia and Ukraine, how could you oppose others who choose differently? Are nations not free to choose differently from the United States?"

The discussion continued in a forceful confrontation with Jackson returning again and again to the photographs as evidence of his accusations. The ambassador deflected each one with an assertion of China's independence and freedom to form its foreign policy without approval from any other leader, US or otherwise.

That evening, Jackson confronted the ambassador of Kazakhstan and received a similar response. "Kazakhstan is a member nation of the UN. As are China and Russia. The manner of our association with nations who wish to associate with us is our choice. A matter of our own internal domestic affairs, which the United Nations charter guarantees. The United States and its officials should stay out of our business."

Having been stymied on the diplomatic front, Jackson contacted China's premier, Wei Xing, by means of a secure video link. Wei Xing responded in a similar manner—the arrangement between China, Kazakhstan, and Russia was a private affair. The United States had no right to interfere.

CHAPTER TWENTY

When attempts at finding a diplomatic resolution to the trouble posed by arms transfers between China, Kazakhstan, and Russia failed, President Jackson once again gathered key members of his national security team in the Oval Office to consider how the US could force them to stop. And barring that, what steps the US could take to oppose the weapons sales?

It was late when the participants arrived. Most of the White House staff had long since gone home, but one of the porters from the kitchen had remained. He delivered coffee and cakes to the Oval Office. When he finished serving the group, they all took a seat on the sofas in the center of the room and sat facing each other. Clinton Kase, Secretary of State; Bruce Ford, Secretary of Defense; and

Stuart Meckstroth, Secretary of the Treasury were among those present, as was Donovan from the CIA.

President Jackson sat in a chair at the end nearest his desk. He pointed to the memo from Donovan and the photos that lay on the coffee table. "I'm sure all of you have seen the report and the photographs from Donovan." Everyone nodded in response. Jackson continued. "It seems clear that China has colluded with Kazakhstan to sell missiles and artillery shells to Russia. The question we face is, what are we going to do about it?"

Clinton Kase spoke up. "We can't do anything meaningful without being drawn into a war."

"Are you kidding?" Stuart Meckstroth blurted. "We can do a lot of things without getting into a war."

"Such as?" Kase asked coldly.

"We can seize their accounts at US financial institutions."

"You mean, seize Chinese accounts? We've already imposed restrictions on Russian accounts."

"All of them," Meckstroth said. "China, Kazakhstan, Russia."

"Does Russia have anything left in the US?"

"They have a few accounts remaining," Meckstroth replied. "And they have many other assets, including acres and acres of real estate."

"But will seizure actually work with the Chinese?"

"Sure it will," Meckstroth replied. "I mean, I don't know if it will produce the desired policy result, but we can do it. We know the identity of most of the corporations the Chinese government deals with here in the US. We can seize Chinese payments being made to and from those US businesses. We can impound the accounts of

Chinese companies and their related billionaires. Once we start, it won't be difficult to figure out where they're involved."

Jackson spoke up. "What banks are we talking about? Just off the top of your head."

"I know for a fact the Chinese government and its state-controlled corporations have accounts at Manhattan Bank and Trust, Lexington National, Union National, and Capital Bank and Trust. Those are the ones I can remember right now. There are dozens more. We maintain a list of them."

Someone spoke up, "And when you say *they*, who exactly are you talking about?"

"The Chinese government. The Chinese communist party. The People's Liberation Army. And a host of government-controlled corporations."

President Jackson nodded. "Get me a list of those entities, the account details, and any negatives that might influence how we handle them."

Clinton Kase spoke up. "Mr. President, I don't think we should start seizing assets and accounts just yet."

"Why not?"

"Hundreds, if not thousands, of US corporations conduct business in China. If we start seizing Chinese corporate assets, they'll start seizing assets of US corporations. The situation will escalate rapidly."

"What do you suggest instead?"

"Usually, we prefer to start slow. Expel diplomats. Close a consulate. Something like that."

"And what's the point of doing that?"

"It registers our opinion without emptying the toolbox of options."

The expression on Jackson's face registered his disapproval. He turned to Bruce Ford. "What about military options? What can we do with that, Bruce?"

"I assume you mean options short of war."

"Yes," Jackson replied. "For now."

Everyone chuckled except Ford. "Short of war, we have several good options, but we have one major issue that we should consider first."

"What is that?"

"Since World War II," Ford explained, "our national defense policy has focused on our ability to fight a two-front war. Right now, we don't have the ability to do that."

"Why not?"

"Our munitions stockpiles have been seriously depleted by the shipments we've made to Ukraine."

"Seriously depleted? How depleted is that?"

"We are rapidly approaching the point where force readiness will be degraded below acceptable levels by lack of expendables— bullets, rockets, RPGs—and by a lack of air defense missiles."

"What about conventional bombs?"

"Our inventory of bombs remains strong because we haven't shipped very many to Ukraine. They have relied more heavily on drones, artillery, and infantry weapons. But using bombs requires us to fly aircraft over the combat zone. They are the least acceptable option, these days."

"How are we on drones?"

"We're in good shape with drones."

"So, we're low on the kinds of things ground troops typically use."

"Yes, sir. Right now, if we had to put troops in Taiwan, we would be forced to decide between Taiwan and Ukraine. We can't fight in both places at the same time."

Jackson gestured with both hands. "Slow down a minute, Bruce. We aren't talking about a shooting war with China. We're talking about delivering a message, that's all."

Ford was determined to make his point. "Mr. President, what would the message be if there wasn't the assurance that we could and would follow through on our threat or demand? If we tell the Chinese, 'Don't invade Taiwan,' and they attempt to invade anyway, we will be facing a situation with Taiwan like the one we face with Ukraine. Do we send troops and fight or send ammunition and let Taiwan do the fighting? And I'm saying, our stockpiles are so low from supporting Ukraine that we can't do both at the same time."

"I see your point, but what are our options?"

"In the past," Ford began, "we have started slowly by moving part of the Pacific Fleet into the area around Taiwan."

"That's it? Just move some ships closer?"

"Sending any part of the US Navy into any part of the China Sea is a big deal to the Chinese. They assert control over the region. The same as if a dozen Russian ships pulled up off the coast of Texas or Louisiana."

Jackson nodded by way of acknowledging the situation. "Is there any reason not to send our ships there now?"

"The risk," Ford replied.

"The risk?"

"Given the present situation there and globally," Ford explained, "China would almost certainly view a move like that as an one aimed at their claims of sovereignty over Taiwan Island and the China Sea. They would see it as a threat."

"That's what we want them to see it as."

"And that gets back to my earlier question. If we aren't able to back up the threat, and they go ahead against Taiwan, what else are we going to do? Where would we see this going? How will it end? Are we going to go nuclear on the Chinese navy to protect Taiwan, which would most certainly be wiped out in a counterstrike?"

"We'll get to those questions," Jackson said, "but tell me, how long does it take to reposition a large enough naval force to make a statement?"

"We would need at least a carrier strike group," Ford explained. "Depending on where our strike groups are at the moment and on the nature of their current tours, we could get one of them headed that way today."

"Where are they right now?"

"I would have to consult Fleet Command for the exact information. I know the *Nimitz* left California last week on its way to Japan. It could be diverted to the South China Sea and arrive on station within six to seven days. I'm not sure what ships we have that are any closer right now."

Jackson seemed displeased. "Would a single strike group make much of a statement?"

"A single carrier strike group makes quite a show," Ford said.

"A carrier with its airplanes. Two guided missile cruisers. Two or three destroyers. A supply and fuel ship. Usually a submarine."

Jackson appeared to think better of the idea. "Okay. Let's do this. Turn the *Nimitz* toward the South China Sea and start planning for two more strike groups to join it."

Ford looked surprised. "Mr. President, we only need to—"

"Move the *Nimitz* closer. Send it to the South China Sea, not Japan," Jackson said, cutting him off. "And start preparing to send two more groups to join it. Don't reposition the other two until I give the order but find them and start planning to move them. We need to make a definitive statement." He turned to Meckstroth once more. "What else can we do with sanctions?"

"In addition to asset seizures," Meckstroth said, "we can limit China's access to the US financial and securities trading system. Block them from trading on US commodity exchanges. Halt grain purchases. That sort of thing."

Someone spoke up. "If we limit their access to commodities, a lot of Chinese civilians will go hungry. They don't grow enough in China to feed the entire nation."

"And it will noticeably affect trading volumes on those exchanges," someone added.

"We can't worry about that right now," Jackson said as he turned to Kase. "What are the usuals steps from State?"

"We usually limit the number of diplomats a country can have in the US. Force them to recall a noticeable number to attract press attention. We could recall our own ambassador from Beijing, but that wouldn't be a good move right now."

"Why not?"

"With situations like this, we need our people to remain over there in order to help us understand and manage the situation."

"But we could remove dependents and non-essential staff," Jackson noted.

"Yes, Mr. President," Kase replied. "We could remove staff dependents."

"I think you should get ready for that," Jackson said. "Do as much as you can without making a public announcement and without actually flying people home."

"Yes, sir."

"I'm sure you have Embassy employees in the United States right now who came here for various purposes but intended to return to China."

"Yes, sir."

"Perhaps you should hold them here and not allow them to go back."

Kase nodded. "We typically have twenty or so who have traveled over from China."

"Keep them here for the time being."

"Most of them have families over there."

"I understand," Jackson said. "But I think they should remain here for now. Don't publish that information. Just find a way to keep them here for the moment."

Jackson scribbled a note on his legal pad, then stood. "Okay," he said. "That's enough for now. Let's get to work on this immediately." He moved over to his desk and took a seat, then called to those in the room as they started toward the door. "Get me a list of options for measures against China and Kazakhstan within the next two hours. And think of additional options we can take against Russia. We need to make a definitive statement against widening the war in Ukraine. Work up some policy options that have real teeth with China. They need to know we mean it when we object to arms trading with Russia."

✦ ✦ ✦

Three days later, President Jackson called a press conference and released information to the public about the transfer of weapons from China, through Kazakhstan, to Russia. Included with that release were recordings of conversations between the parties, satellite images of trucks en route from China to Kazakhstan, then from Kazakhstan to Russia. His remarks concluded with an announcement of severe sanctions against all parties.

After seeing a live transmission of Jackson's press conference, Wei Xing convened another meeting of the Committee of Advisors. "I told you this would happen," he said. "But you said we had to be strong. I told you if we supplied munitions to Russia, we risked incurring US sanctions and that is precisely what has happened."

"It is the price we pay for being independent," Zhao Guofeng replied.

"And I told you that if we supplied Russia with weapons," Zhongbo replied, "the US might react by strengthening its position with Taiwan."

"Are they?"

"They have turned the *Nimitz* away from its previous course toward Japan. It is now steaming toward us."

"All the more reason to make our own definitive statement," Zhongbo argued.

"And what would that be?"

"Invade Taiwan."

"Are you for real? Invade Taiwan and enter the proxy war we discussed earlier?"

"We would be putting the US in a two-front proxy war. One front in Ukraine, the other in Asia. They cannot possibly sustain both," Li Xudong noted.

"But they are heavily invested in both."

"And, unlike Ukraine, Taiwan has a long history of association with the US."

"The US has a long history of defending them, too."

"What are you saying?"

"I am saying, Taiwan has the capacity to do a better job of defending itself than Ukraine."

The discussion continued around the room until everyone had expressed their opinion. When they seemed to have nothing more to offer, Ba Renfu spoke up. "Perhaps we should consider terminating our transfers to Russia."

Zhao Guofeng spoke up. "Paramount Leader, as I said before, I don't think we should let the Americans chase us away from the decision that is best for us."

Wei Xing seemed perturbed. "You think we should follow through with supplying Russia the arms it needs for its war in Ukraine, while also dealing with Taiwan?"

"Yes."

"And place our country in a two-front war also? One front far away in Europe, the other in the South China Sea."

"Yes."

Wei Xing shook his head in disgust. "Are you not thinking?" Others in the room seemed to recoil at the comment. Wei Xing ignored their response. "Right now," he explained, "we have the advantage over the US. They are supporting a war in Europe, thousands of miles away from their mainland. While at the same time, threatening to offer support for resistance to any advance on Taiwan, which is also thousands of miles away from the US homeland. They cannot sustain both measures. They will have to choose between one or the other. If they choose Ukraine, we can achieve our goals for Taiwan Island with little resistance. If they choose Taiwan, our Russian allies can achieve their goals in Ukraine. If that happens, and we have continued to supply the Russians with arms, we will emerge from the situation as Russia's strongest ally. If we drop them to take Taiwan, and are successful, both Russia and America will be our enemies."

"So, you favor doing nothing?"

"As I have said many times, the only way to prevail in the current environment is to sit quietly and watch while Russia, the US, and NATO deplete their strength on each other, then we can pick up the pieces."

Zhao Guofeng grumbled, "You are a coward."

Wei Xing came from his place at the head of the table and walked calmly toward Zhao Guofeng. "Only a shallow man would suggest that waiting for a strategic advantage is an act of cowardice. You prefer to slaughter millions of people—ours and theirs—in a pointless attempt to feed your weakness. But never ever speak to the Paramount Leader as you have today."

Zhao Guofeng was standing by them as the two men faced each other, nose to nose, but before Guofeng could respond, Wei Xing landed a backhanded blow against his jaw. Guofeng staggered backward and fell into his chair.

Wei Xing stood over him. "'The Americans are preoccupied with Ukraine and Russia,'" he shouted in a mocking voice. "Isn't that what you said before?"

Guofeng didn't dare respond.

"'American leaders have dangerously diminished their resources,'" Wei Xing continued. "Isn't that what you said?"

Again, Guofeng was silent but shifted positions uncomfortably in his chair.

Wei Xing continued. "And yet, the Americans are coming toward us right now. A carrier with all of its accompaniments. And I am told they have two more they can send if they wish." He pointed toward the south. "Soon, the China Sea will be filled with American warships. And you are telling me they are too weak to respond?"

Wei Xing paused for a moment to catch his breath. "'We should decide based on what is right for us,'" he continued. "Didn't you say that, too?" He scanned the room, letting everyone see the intensity in his eyes. "This plan of supporting Russia was *your* idea and I, regrettably, suggested we attempt to follow your lead on it. But it has made European trouble *our* trouble. Yet, instead of taking responsibility for that trouble, you accuse me of being a coward."

The room remained silent as Wei Xing returned to his place

at the head of the table but did not take a seat. While he remained standing by his chair, Zhongbo asked, "What do you propose we do?"

"We must maintain a position of dignity that benefits and affirms our historic sovereign right to further our best interests, while at the same time, we must find a diplomatic means of unwinding this situation. One that incrementally moves us back from armed conflict with the US. The day will come when we can seize Taiwan Island at will, but that day has not yet arrived." Then Wei Xing left the room.

Less than an hour after meeting with the Committee of Advisors, Wei Xing issued a written statement that said, "The People's Republic of China asserts its right as a free and sovereign nation of the world to support its ally, Russia, with military assistance necessary for its defense, just as the US and European nations have done in supporting Ukraine. Our decisions in this regard arise from internal policy matters. We have taken no aggressive action against any other nation but will respond strongly to any outside interference in matters of China's national interest."

✦ ✦ ✦

Bruce Ford was in his office at the Pentagon when he received a copy of Wei Xing's statement along with an analysis of it that was prepared by the Defense Intelligence Agency staff. The short memo suggested Wei Xing was attempting to protect the integrity of China's status as an independent nation while staving off a conservative element within the Chinese government and attempting to step back from the developing situation.

After re-reading the statement and memo, Ford telephoned the White House Situation Room and asked for an assessment of Wei Xing's statement. The duty staff had nothing new to add to the memo Ford's own staff had provided, so Ford called the President's secretary and asked for a few minutes with the President. Ford and Jackson met in the Oval Office.

"What does this statement mean?" Jackson asked.

"I think it means they know we're upset, and they must defend their actions, but they don't want any trouble. China and Russia are large countries that share a long border. They—"

"And they have a common ideology," Jackson said, interrupting.

"Their ideology isn't as common as it once was," Ford noted, "but China is adamant about its position with regard to Taiwan. They will not tolerate any other country asserting control over it, nor will they tolerate anyone encouraging Taiwan towards independence. They have been unwaveringly consistent on that topic."

"Do they see this as a good time to take control of Taiwan?"

"Some do. Some think our support of Ukraine has weakened our ability to support another military encounter."

"They don't think we can handle two at the same time."

"Right. And some in our own government agree with that position. But I think Wei Xing is signaling an interest in stepping back from whatever brink a standoff like this pushes us toward."

"Well Bruce, I've got people in this building telling me I should send the other two carrier groups we discussed earlier into the South China Sea."

"I wouldn't do that, Mr. President."

"Why not?"

"If Wei Xing is signaling a desire to pull back from confrontation with us, stepping up the intensity of our response would cut his legs out from under him. He would be unable to do anything but ramp up China's position to match ours."

"My people say he means to take Taiwan."

"Some of your people don't think very well."

Jackson laughed. "That's what I tell them, but they don't listen to me."

CHAPTER TWENTY-ONE

One week later, a carrier group led by the *USS Nimitz* entered the South China Sea and loitered off the coast of Taiwan. At news of its arrival, Wei Xing met with the Committee of Advisors. As might have been expected, Zhao Guofeng was incensed. "This is an act of war," he shouted. "First, they impose sanctions against us. Now they are preparing to blockade Taiwan Island. We must invade Taiwan immediately." He pounded the table with his fist. "It is our sovereign territory, and it is only one hundred twenty miles away. Our ships and troops can be ready by tomorrow. We can be there in five hours. We should go now, before the entire US fleet arrives."

Zhongbo, who had been silent through many of the previous debates, said quietly, "I agree. We must respond. But not with ships. And not with men. And not with airplanes."

Guofeng glared at him. "Then by what means should we respond?"

"We must respond with a nuclear attack on the United States. Our missiles can reach Los Angeles in less than half an hour. Perhaps then they will realize we mean what we say."

Wei Xing argued for restraint. "We are in this position because we agreed to enter the conflict between Russia and Ukraine. We did this to ourselves. We owe it to the world to find a way out."

"We owe it to the world to rid the world of the American menace," Guofeng retorted.

"This is a fight between European countries and their American cousins," someone said. "We should have refused to get involved."

"If they want to destroy each other, we should let them. If we intervene against the US over Taiwan, it will be seen as if we are siding against America and with Russia."

"We already took sides by selling Russia arms and munitions."

"Which is why we must stop the transfers and move ourselves away from the conflict."

"If we return to a status of neutrality, we can wait for them to destroy each other. Then we can pick up as much of the world as we want when the fighting ends."

The argument continued back and forth around the room with tempers rising at every turn until Wei Xing ended the session. "We will return after tempers have cooled," he said.

✦ ✦ ✦

Late that evening, Zhao Guofeng contacted Lei Haifeng, a billionaire with numerous business interests and one of Guofeng's staunchest supporters. They arranged to meet that evening at Haifeng's home.

Haifeng's wealth was built on a vast network of businesses, most of which he accumulated with the assistance of prominent government officials. Along the way to building a fortune, Haifeng had made numerous friends and even more enemies. To keep those relationships in balance, he cultivated extensive associations with members of the Black Society, the most heavily entrenched wing of the Triad, China's oldest organized crime group. The Black Society provided the muscle that kept Haifeng's business interests secure.

As they sat in Haifeng's study that evening, the conversation turned to the government's recent decision to supply Russia with drones and artillery shells. Haifeng seemed to disapprove. "Why are we interested in helping Russia?" he asked. "Other than having thousands of nuclear weapons, they are a second-rate economy. They used to be a large player in the oil market, and still are in Europe, but they have done nothing with their profits except enrich a group of Putin's friends."

"Precisely my point," Guofeng said. "This war with Ukraine has weakened Russia and it will weaken us if we get involved."

Haifeng laughed. "We'll be running around the world like Putin begging others for weapons to keep fighting. 'Oh, please. Oh, please. Let me kill some more Ukrainians.'" His countenance turned serious. "And for what? What can we accomplish by joining in Russia's war?"

Guofeng shook his head in a disapproving gesture. "I've tried to tell them the same thing, but Wei Xing and his supporters will not listen."

"We should be using this time to broaden our reach by solving the Taiwan problem while no one is in a position to stop us."

"Apparently the US Navy would disagree with you."

"Arg," Haifeng scoffed. "It is an insult to have them in the South China Sea."

"And it proves no purpose other than to make a statement."

"And what statement? They can sail over here and make a big show of their arrival, but they can't last. They are thousands of miles away from their supply lines. All we need to do is prevent them from resupplying their ships once, and they will be trapped."

"Isn't the carrier nuclear powered?"

"Yes, but the aircraft are not. They require fuel. And the crew require food. All of which have to be restocked eventually."

Guofeng nodded. "Our sources say their support of Ukraine has diminished their own military stockpiles lower than their officers want. Perhaps not as low as Russia's, but low enough that they can't fight in two places at once."

Haifeng raised an eyebrow. "Then we should confront them. Right now. Drive them off our coast."

Guofeng agreed. "I have been telling everyone that, too."

Haifeng's eyebrows narrowed. "Wei Xing does not agree that the US is in a vulnerable position?"

"Wei Xing says we should let America and Europe fight it out in Ukraine and pick up the pieces that are left once they have worn themselves out."

"Wei Xing is old school."

"Very much."

"Is he up to the task of leading us?"

"No." Guofeng shook his head. "He is not."

"And what strategy do you favor?"

"I think we should attack now," Guofeng said. "No one can stop us taking full control of the South China Sea."

"Why aren't we?"

"Because Wei Xing is still alive."

They stared at each other, neither one speaking, until Haifeng said, "You think that is what it would take?"

"Yes," Guofeng said softly. "For the good of the country."

✦ ✦ ✦

The following evening, just before sunset, Wei Xing came from his residence and strolled along a path through a garden in Zhongnanhai, a compound adjacent to the Forbidden City. He was deep in thought and paid no attention to his surroundings as he came to the opposite end of the compound and turned to make his way back toward the entrance. When he'd gone only a few paces in that direction there was the sound of a gunshot, like the crack of a limb breaking from a tree at a far distance. It was followed quickly by two more.

The first bullet struck Wei Xing from behind at the top of his spine near the base of his skull. The force of the bullet caused his head to snap backward, then flop forward. He was still standing when the second and third bullets struck him. One hit his skull at the rear lobe near the apex of its outward arc and continued straight through his head, exiting at the bridge of his nose. The third shot struck from the side, clipping the top portion of his ear before entering his skull. It continued straight across, exiting above the ear on the opposite side. Blood, bone, and brain matter spewed onto the flowers by the path as Wei Xing finally collapsed to the ground.

So little of Wei Xing's head remained intact that attendants could only identify him by the shape of his hands. A DNA match from his sister was required to make an official identification of his body.

✦ ✦ ✦

At the same time Wei Xing was killed, a car arrived outside the home of Dong Jingwei, head of China's Ministry of State. His participation in the government was one of the key elements behind its efficient operation. He also was one of Wei Xing's closest supporters and used his authority to keep dissenting members of the government in line.

The driver came from the front and opened the rear door for Jingwei. He stooped to enter and as he crawled onto the seat, he noticed the driver was different from the man who normally picked him up, but he said nothing as they drove from the compound. He watched out the window as they continued up the street as usual, then made a left turn at the next corner. They normally went to the right.

"Where is my regular driver?" Jingwei asked.

"His wife has the flu," the driver replied.

"Hmm." Jingwei's groan betrayed his suspicions.

"They didn't want you to be exposed to it," the driver quickly added.

"I suppose not."

A few minutes later the car turned into an old neighborhood with traditional wooden houses and treelined streets. Ahead of them, a breeze scattered leaves across the pavement and Dong Jingwei let his eyes follow them as they swirled against the curb, then rose in the air before dropping onto the sidewalk on the opposite side. That's when he noticed the lights were out in all of the houses. Children who normally played outside until sunset were nowhere to be seen.

Jingwei turned toward the driver to ask about the children and saw the driver's arm come over the top of the front seat. In his hand was an automatic pistol with a silencer fitted into the end of the barrel. The gun was pointed straight at him.

An instant later, the driver's finger squeezed the trigger. Flame and smoke erupted from the silencer and for a moment Dong Jingwei was certain he saw the point of a bullet coming toward him. Before he could react, an awful pain pierced his skull near his left eyebrow. Intense pressure built inside his skull, then spewed out the back in a sudden release that rushed through a hole in his skull made by the bullet. Blood and brain coated the leather upholstery where he sat. Pieces of his skull clattered against the glass of the rear window. His head flopped forward. His body went limp, slid from the seat, and crumpled onto the floor of the car.

✦ ✦ ✦

Wei Xing's body was found within the hour by a servant who went looking for him when he did not return as expected from his walk. Someone was sent to notify Dong Jingwei, but he was not at his residence and his body had not yet been found. Security officials were notified but with Wei Xing no longer alive, and with the moment already tense of the presence of US warships so near to China's coastline, it seemed urgent to install a new leader who could maintain stability in the government and in China's relationship to world powers.

Li Yang, now the ranking member of the Central Committee of the Communist Party, appointed a nominating group and convened a meeting that evening. With little discussion and no objection, the group nominated Zhao Guofeng as head of state. At midnight that same evening, the Central Committee executive group approved Guofeng's nomination and conferred on him the office of head of state and of government, giving him the power to do as he pleased.

Shortly after his appointment was announced, Guofeng issued an order closing China's border and placing its military on full alert. Then, secretly, he directed China's military leadership to prepare for an invasion of Taiwan.

"We'll go on our own time," he said when issuing the order, "but make no mistake, we are going."

✦ ✦ ✦

It was midmorning when news of events in China reached Washington, DC. President Jackson was in a meeting with a select group of senators about pending legislation when aids called him away. He arrived at the Oval Office to find Bruce Ford, General Halstead, Clinton Kase, Stuart Meckstroth, and Bob Donovan waiting for him.

"Well," Jackson said, "I see we have a full house this morning. There must be trouble somewhere in the world." He glanced over at the Secretary of State. "Bruce, why don't you tell me about it, then we'll take comments from everyone else."

"Mr. President," Ford began, "a few hours ago, Wei Xing, the Chinese premier, and Dong Jingwei, China's second highest ranking official were shot dead in Beijing."

Jackson frowned. "They were murdered?"

Ford nodded. "Both men were shot in the head at point-blank range," he said.

"How did it happen? Were they killed at the same location?"

"No, sir. They were killed in separate incidents."

"So, this was a coup?"

"It looks that way," Ford replied. "But we're still analyzing the intelligence."

Jackson turned to Bob Donovan. "Bob, what does the CIA know about this?"

"Our analysts are certain it is a coup, Mr. President," Donovan said flatly. "Zhao Guofeng has been planning this for a long time."

"He's in charge now?"

"An interim leader, but with full powers of head of state and of government. We expect him to be confirmed as soon as members of the Central Committee can get to Beijing."

Jackson turned to General Halstead. "Have they made any changes in the status of their military?"

"They're on full alert, Mr. President."

"As might be expected."

"Yes, sir," Halstead said. "But it's also a good opportunity for them to position their troops for a move against Taiwan."

"Good point," Jackson said. "Have they?"

"Not that we can tell."

Clinton Kase spoke up. "Mr. President, in that regard, I think we ought to remember that whatever decisions we make here today, we have a carrier strike force sitting in the South China Sea. We might want to consider moving it out of the way."

A murmur was heard around the room. Jackson looked over at Kase. "Wouldn't that send the wrong signal? Trouble's coming, we're ducking out now boys?"

"It might," Kase said. "But if China really intends to mobilize and if that mobilization means deploying elements of their navy to the South China Sea, our ships will be sitting in a location that will be primed and loaded for a catastrophe."

"I see your point," Jackson said. "But isn't that the reason we sent them there? To get in the way?"

Kase could only shrug in response. Jackson turned to the room. "Is there any way of getting a message to Guofeng?"

"Saying what?" Donovan asked.

"That we understand the difficulty of the moment for them and stand ready to join them in defending their territory."

A shout in unison went up from the room. "No!"

Jackson appeared startled. "What's wrong with that? They offered us support after 9-11."

"The situation was a *little* different then, Mr. President," Kase suggested. "If we make that offer, their response will be, 'The assassination squad came from Taiwan. Help us find them and put them down.' And then we'll be accompanying the People's Liberation Army as it invades Taiwan."

"Well," Jackson said. "It seems like this coup offers us a good way to turn back the clock on the situation."

"No, Mr. President," Halstead responded. "It traps us right where we are. We can't insert anymore forces in that location."

"And we can't take any out either," someone added.

"So, we have to sit tight?" Jackson asked.

"Yes, sir," Halstead replied. "And hope they don't do anything stupid."

"So, what do you all think we should do, other than sitting tight? Issue a statement of condolence?"

Ford spoke up. "Mr. President, you should place our military on alert."

"What kind of alert?"

"We need to go to DEFCON TWO."

"Which means?"

"Air Force ready to mobilize immediately. Everyone else ready to deploy and engage in less than six hours. It's the highest level short of nuclear war."

Jackson nodded. "Holds on retirement, leave, promotions? Strict clearance at the gate? That sort of thing?"

"No, Mr. President," Ford said, correcting. "Army and Marines assembled, armed, in full battle gear, waiting for the order to board a plane or transport. Fighter jets on the runways, pilots in the cockpits, engines on and ready. Ships deployed. Crews at battle stations."

"Safety's off on the nuclear arms?" Jackson asked.

"No, sir," Ford said. "There's one more step before we get to that."

Jackson thought for a moment, then asked, "What's DEFCON THREE?"

"Sir—"

"We need time," Jackson said curtly. "We need time. If they escalate and we respond by escalating, then they will do the same, and we'll do the same, and we will walk ourselves into a nuclear war of our own making." He took a breath. "What is DEFCON THREE?"

"Heightened readiness but no one ready to deploy immediately."

"No planes on the runways?"

"No, sir. Planes ready to fly within fifteen minutes of the order."

"Very well," Jackson said. "Issue the order. Place us at DEFCON THREE."

Ford used a phone at a desk near the door to notify the duty officer in the Situation Room.

✦ ✦ ✦

Despite the change of leadership in China and the disruption to its government, shipments of artillery shells and drones for distribution to Russian troops on the battlefield in Ukraine continued unabated. With those supplies on hand, Russia increased the pace and ferocity of its attacks, methodically destroying Ukrainian towns and cities. Inching forward from their positions near the border. Bombarding the next location, then moving their troops forward. It was a brutal campaign, but typically Russian—level the houses and buildings, drive out opposing armies and civilians, occupy the void—in the way their ancestors had suppressed domestic minorities and foreign governments for centuries.

As it had done each time before, the US and NATO, along with many other Western countries, responded by increasing their aid to Ukraine, supplying larger artillery pieces, more artillery shells, and advanced versions of military drones. They also provided a wider array of battlefield intelligence which yielded improvements in pinpointing Russian troop movements and coordinated Ukrainian attacks on their positions.

Armed with updated weaponry from the West, Ukraine's army was more than a match for the Russian army, which proved unable to withstand Ukraine's improved accuracy and increased firepower. The Russian surge that seemed so overwhelming at first, now slowly ground to a halt, then began to collapse. At the same time, Russian casualties increased, and the old, familiar logistical problems returned.

Once again, reports of impending catastrophe on the frontlines sent Putin into a fit of rage. Given to dark and brooding moods, he became convinced that the increased US military aid was a direct attempt to humiliate the Russian army and the Russian people and began to talk about increased Western aid in terms of an invasion. "Troops from NATO member nations and from America's army are trespassing on Russian soil," he fumed. "They are fomenting revolution among Ukrainian citizens against the Empire." Aids cringed at the mention of empire—many had lost ancestors in that era—but Putin seemed convinced the events in Ukraine were a repeat of history.

"The Americans aren't helping Ukraine win. They are helping Ukraine bleed us dry! We cannot allow that to happen. The time has come when we must use nuclear weapons. I see no other option for us."

"But how will we prevent the West from launching a counter-strike."

"The West?" Putin shouted. "Would they sit quietly and watch their troops march, wave after wave, to their death and *our* hands?"

"But nuclear? Surely the use of those weapons requires a provocation of unprecedented proportion."

"And surely this is provocation enough," Putin retorted. "Surely the world will understand our predicament."

Everyone who was present at the meeting was horrified by the suggestion they escalate the conflict to nuclear war, but most remained silent. Especially the younger ones. Putin had a reputation for eliminating his opposition in much the same way he now proposed to eliminate Ukraine—totally and completely.

Several of those at the meeting who were Putin's age were less intimidated. One of them, Valery Gerasimov, spoke up. "We have approached Iran twice about helping us and they have agreed to do so, but we have been unable to reach an agreement with them because of the condition they imposed. Perhaps now would be the time to revisit that situation. Surely they could provide drones and artillery shells and if we are assessing the possibility of using nuclear arms, why shouldn't we first move forward with an exploration of their conditions for conventional arms?"

"It would give us an opportunity to press for larger quantities," someone added.

"Even if we had to supply them with the expertise they need for building a warhead, and if they succeeded in doing that, we would be in a better position than if we dropped nuclear bombs on Ukraine."

Putin frowned. "How so?"

Gerasimov responded, "If we launch a nuclear attack on Ukraine, we will be issuing an open invitation for NATO and the US to do the same against us in an effort to stop us. Whatever we hoped to gain by occupying Ukraine would be lost to contamination and the ire of the world."

"And if we send our technicians to help Iran," someone suggested, "we could also send enough extra people to monitor and control how far they go with it."

"We could even send troops to Iran under the guise of providing extra security for our scientists."

Encouraged by their remarks several more joined in and finally, Putin relented. "Okay," he said. "Perhaps we should send someone to Tehran one more time to discuss the matter."

That evening arrangements were made for one of Putin's trusted advisors to approach the Iranians in Tehran. This time, however, he sent Sergei Shoigu, Russia's Minister of Defense, instead of Naryshkin.

✦ ✦ ✦

Two days later, Shoigu traveled to Tehran and met with Ali Akbar Bizhani, the president of Iran. After an initial greeting, they came quickly to the reason for Shoigu's visit. "We would like to revisit the question of obtaining weaponry from you."

"As you know, we talked about this when I was in Moscow and I understood we had that all worked out but, at the last minute, President Putin was unable to meet our conditions. Those remain our conditions today."

"And they would be?" Shoigu wanted to be certain.

"We need better centrifuges," Bizhani said. "Ones with higher capacity and that work more quickly."

"There are limitations to what we can deliver," Shoigu replied. "As you are aware, we both are under sanctions from the West and the Americans have ways of discovering whatever we do."

"We also need advice and equipment for miniaturizing a warhead to fit atop one of our existing missiles."

"As we have said before, we—"

"We need it immediately. Israel already has nuclear weapons, though they deny it. Saudi Arabia is attempting to obtain nuclear capability from China. Neither of them denies that. When the Saudis become a nuclear power, the regional balances will shift dramatically. We have no intention of being at their mercy."

For three hours, Shoigu and Bizhani thrashed their way through multiple issues—regional stability, reliability of early warning detection systems, issues with distinguishing targets to avoid erroneous indications of impending attacks, and safeguards to protect against accidental or hasty use. By the time that conversation reached an end, they had talked through the framework of an arrangement that included not merely the supply of technical expertise but the creation of a reliable armament system that might increase regional stability by confining to clearly defined usages.

As Bizhani was about to leave the room, Shoigu asked to talk with someone familiar with the program at an operational level. His stated reason was to inspect for himself the kind of equipment Iran was using in its nuclear program. His unstated reason was to evaluate Iranian personnel to determine if they seemed capable of doing the kind of complex work necessary to miniaturize the element of a warhead. His first conversation was with Mostafa Qorbani, Iran's Minister of Defense. Afterward, he was introduced to Mehdi Kalhor, director of the Organization of Defensive Innovation.

After a lengthy discussion with Kalhor, Shoigu traveled with Kalhor to Natanz where they followed Majid Roshan through the underground uranium enrichment facility. Roshan, being a nuclear scientist by training, was able to explain the operation in detail.

✦ ✦ ✦

After spending a week in Iran, Shoigu returned to Moscow and reported to Putin. "Iran will supply artillery shells and drones in exchange for help with their nuclear program. They want the parts and technology necessary to create a warhead that will fit on one of their existing missiles. And they want it quickly."

"Can they do it?"

"Yes," Shoigu replied. "If we help them."

"You've seen their facilities?"

"Yes."

"And their personnel?"

"Yes," Shoigu said. "The man who runs the program is Majid Roshan. I have met him before. He is quite capable. Far more than the Iranians realize. If we survive to the end of the year, we should consider bringing him into our program."

Putin was amused by the comment but the truth of it was not lost on him. "Do you think we will survive?"

"If we get drones and artillery shells from Iran, there's a good chance. If not, and we go nuclear, there won't be much left for anyone anywhere."

The following day, Putin discussed the Iranian proposal with the same group of advisors he'd been consulting since the war in Ukraine began. "They're offering us the same deal as before," he said. "Artillery and drone support in exchange for nuclear assistance. I see no option but to take it."

The group seemed divided. One side saw the proposal as escalating the situation in the Middle East without producing any real change in Ukraine. "The key to our situation is reducing Western support. If we get more weapons from Iran, the West will supply more to Ukraine. Every time. Back and forth. Until one of us is unable to continue with the corresponding increase. At which point we will lose."

"We have no choice but to accept their offer. Besides, changes in the Middle East are not our immediate concern. We cannot win a conventional war of attrition against Ukraine and all of the West by ourselves."

"We can't win a nuclear war, either. No one can."

The discussion continued into the night but ended in a stalemate. Afterward, Putin told Naryshkin, "Notify the Iranians that we will agree to their terms. Artillery and drones in exchange for nuclear assistance. Meet with Shoigu. Get the details from him of what they discussed during his visit. But make the deal."

CHAPTER TWENTY-TWO

Preparing the garage in Ottawa to receive the suitcase bombs from the warehouse took longer, and required more sheets of plywood, than Abbadi expected. Pirzad contacted Kalhor who readily agreed to cover the costs. Money to finance the project came by way of several transactions to an account in Andorra, then through a consulting firm in London before arriving at an attorney's office in Toronto. Pirzad collected it as a check and deposited it into his account. A few days later, he withdrew it in cash and brought it to Abbadi.

When Abbadi and Pirzad completed work on the garage, they returned to the warehouse to get the duffel bags. Abbadi was nervous on the drive over, wondering if the bags would still be there.

"Relax," Pirzad said. "I'm sure they'll be there."

"But what if they aren't?" Abbadi said. "And what if they're just duffel bags full of old clothes?" He sighed. "I'll look like an idiot."

"If Kalhor said they are bombs, they'll be bombs."

"He never saw them," Abbadi groaned. "He was told the bombs existed, but he never saw them."

"He saw some of them."

"Yeah," Abbadi said. "He did."

They parked the truck behind the warehouse and entered through the same door Abbadi had used before. When they reached the office structure in front, it appeared to have been untouched since Abbadi was there the first time. He opened the door and Pirzad shined a flashlight into the space. He gasped at the sight of ten duffel bags, obviously filled to capacity, stacked in the center of the room. "If they leak like you said," he said, "why wasn't there a spontaneous explosion?"

Abbadi frowned. "What do you mean?"

"A pile of radioactive material like this would be more than enough to form a critical mass."

Abbadi's heart sank. Pirzad had raised an issue he hadn't considered, but one that seemed to suggest the suitcase bomb stories had been fake all along. If the bags leaked, and Abbadi was certain they did, the radioactive material inside the bags would emit neutrons that would collide with the nuclear material inside the other bags. With all the bags stacked together, neutrons from the bags would bombard each other, releasing many more neutrons in an exchanged that would quickly become so intense the stack would spontaneously chain react, all on its own. That should have happened the day the bags were brought to the warehouse. The fact that it obviously didn't sent waves of panic over Abbadi. "We should get out of here," he said. "Forget the whole idea. And hope whatever is in those bags doesn't cause us a problem."

Pirzad seemed surprised. "And just abandon the whole thing? After all we've done?"

Abbadi pointed. "They can't be nuclear bombs."

"Why not?"

"They would have detonated already," Abbadi said.

Pirzad seemed to understand what he meant. "Well," he said, "we've come this far, let's see what's in there." He stepped toward the pile and took hold of a duffel bag.

Abbadi's eyes were wide. "What are you doing?"

"I'm gonna unzip it and see what's in there," Pirzad said as he set the bag at his feet.

"You can't just open it up."

"How else are we gonna know what's inside?"

"We can get a radiation detector at one of those building supply stores we went to. I saw them on a shelf." They had been to several to prevent anyone from being suspicious about what they were doing. "We can get one of those and check the bags, before you tear into one of them."

Pirzad shook his head. "Those detectors are used in construction projects. They detect background radiation, mostly. They aren't very accurate for this kind of thing." He unzipped the bag and froze, his eyes fixed on the contents.

Abbadi saw the look on his face. "What is it?"

When Pirzad didn't respond, Abbadi came closer and glanced over Pirzad's shoulder. Inside the bag was a square metal container that appeared to be completely sealed. On the top there was a panel with a button and small display screen barely wider than Abbadi's thumb. Writing on the face of the panel was in Russian which Abbadi read. "That's how you set it," he said, pointing. "You push that button. The screen tells you the amount of time until it explodes."

"How do you know that?"

Abbadi pointed. "That notice right there above the screen tells you."

Pirzad pulled the fabric of the bag away from the container. "I don't see a remote detonator."

"There isn't one," Abbadi said. "I think it's preset on the time. You press that red button to activate the device and whatever time they set when they created it is all the time you have."

"You really can read this stuff?" Pirzad asked, pointing to the writing on the panel.

"Well enough," Abbadi replied.

Pirzad turned to look in his direction. "We probably should have a more accurate translation than that," he said.

"Okay," Abbadi said with a chuckle. "Do not push the red one until ready to activate."

"That's what it says?"

"Yes."

Pirzad zipped the bag closed and stood. "So why haven't they produced a chain reaction before now?"

"The bomb is built into a sealed container," Abbadi said. "I'm guessing the inside is lined with lead. How heavy is it?"

Pirzad lifted the bag. "Noticeably heavy," he said.

"How much is that?"

"More than you'd want to carry all day."

Abbadi checked it himself. "Yeah," he said, holding the bag with one hand. "It has some kind of shielding inside the container. Lead, based on how heavy it is. But they have other things that work, too." He lifted it up and down a few times to check again.

"Smart," Pirzad noted. "A suitcase bomb in a sealed lead-lined container stuffed inside a duffel bag."

Abbadi smiled. "Especially for the Russians."

They loaded the bags into the truck and took them to Pirzad's garage. Abbadi still was suspicious of how stable they were and placed them as far apart as space allowed. It wasn't much but it gave him a sense of relief that he had done as much as possible, given their circumstances. The lack of a remote detonation device bothered him, too, and he returned to the topic with Pirzad, who agreed to ask Kalhor.

✦ ✦ ✦

A few days later, Kalhor sent a message to Pirzad that confirmed what Abbadi already had sensed. The bombs came with a preset detonation time that was activated by using the red button next to the display screen, but he hadn't known all there was to the process. "Press the red button next to the screen," Kalhor's message read. "When it blinks twice, press it again. The device will be armed, and a countdown will begin."

"How long is it between pressing the button and detonation?"

"Twelve hours," Pirzad said.

"Can you stop it once it starts?"

"He didn't say."

"So that means we can't."

"I suppose."

"How will we distribute them?" Abbadi asked.

"Kalhor has friends. We can use them to help us."

"Friends in Canada?"

Pirzad nodded. "Canada. The United States. Mexico. One of them drives a bomb to Boston. One of them heads to Vancouver. Another to Detroit. Across the border into Texas and California."

Abbadi scowled. "How would we get the bags to Mexico?"

Pirzad seemed to realize the problem of transporting the bags that far and the risk associated with crossing the border more than once. "That might be a problem," he conceded. "But Kalhor also has friends in other places."

"How many friends does he have?"

"Vancouver, Chicago, Detroit, Toronto." He ticked them off with his fingers. "That's four," he said. "And there's you and me. That makes six. I think there are others, but I never counted them all."

"What will we do with the rest of the bags?"

Pirzad thought for a moment. "Maybe we could send them to random people in other places."

Abbadi had a pained expression. "You mean ship them?"

"Yeah." Pirzad nodded. "We could send them by bus. They used to take packages as freight. I assume they still do."

Transporting packages by bus was common in Iran, but Abbadi had never considered people in the US might do the same. "How would that work?"

"We take the bags to the bus station. Ship them to various

people in the US using names and addresses we find online. The bags get to the bus stations near the destinations. Attendants at those stations put the bags in a holding room and notify the person to come and get it. They get them. The bags blow up at the appointed time."

Abbadi looked doubtful "Or the bus takes too long, and the bags blow up on the way."

Pirzad shrugged "Here or there, it doesn't matter. Wherever they blow up, it will have the same effect."

Abbadi still was skeptical. "We can send an item by bus without having a passenger to go with it?"

"Yes."

"Does the bus company inspect the baggage before putting it on the bus?"

"I don't think so," Pirzad said. "I really think the bus might be the best way to send the extra ones. Unless we get specific instructions otherwise."

"We'll have to put the duffels in something," Abbadi said. "We can't send them as a duffel bag alone. Not the way they are." The bags were old and looked it. "Someone will notice them and try to check the contents."

Pirzad thought for a moment. "We'll use a box," he said.

Abbadi frowned. "If we remove them from the duffels and put them in cardboard boxes, someone might see what they look like with the button and screen. That would be a problem."

Pirzad hadn't thought of that. "What about sending them by train?" he asked. "Can we do that?"

"I guess," Abbadi said. "You're the expert."

"I think it might work."

"We have to get these things out of here quickly," Abbadi said. "I don't like them being in the garage."

"I know."

"Did Kalhor give you a timeline for when we are to use them?"

"No," Pirzad replied. "Did he tell *you*?"

"No," Abbadi replied. "He just said to find them."

"I think he wants to keep them here for now."

"I'm not sure we can do that indefinitely," Abbadi said.

"Perhaps."

"And whichever way we use them, it has to work the first time. We won't get a chance to repeat."

✦ ✦ ✦

The following week, Rusty Johnson, the man who loaned Pirzad and Abbadi the pickup truck they'd been driving, received a visit from an Ottawa police officer. After determining Johnson was the owner of the truck, the officer began asking questions about where the truck had been. Johnson tried to dodge the question but finally said, "I loaned the truck to a friend. Has something happened?"

"Does this friend have a name?"

"Jalal Pirzad."

A hint of interest registered in the officer's eyes. "Do you know where we can find Mr. Pirzad?"

Johnson gave him the address but failed to mention that Abbadi was the real beneficiary of the loaned vehicle. The officer continued, "Your truck was seen in the vicinity of a warehouse in Greenboro.

That's a neighborhood on the east side of the city. The truck was being driven by two men who appeared to be of Middle Eastern descent. Do you know anyone who fits that description?"

"No, other than Pirzad."

"Any reason why someone like that would have been using your truck in that area?"

"I haven't a clue," Johnson said.

"Regardless of the physical description, the person who called in the report said there were two men in the truck. Was one of them you?"

Johnson slowly shook his head. "I haven't seen Jalal Pirzad in over a month. Maybe longer." He gestured to himself. "And, as you can see, I'm not of Middle Eastern descent."

"So, you weren't in the truck last Thursday?"

"No. What time was it?"

"A little after sunset."

Johnson had a knowing look. "Thursday evening, I was at my mother's house for dinner." It sounded cliché but he really was at his mother's house for dinner.

"Any idea what time that was?"

"I'm sure I was there by five. She likes to eat early."

After a few more questions the officer seemed satisfied and returned to his patrol car. As he drove away, Johnson took his phone from his pocket call Abbadi to warn him. The call went straight to voicemail.

✦ ✦ ✦

Once the bombs were safely in the garage behind Pirzad's

house, Abbadi purchased one of the radiation detectors that he had seen at a building supply store. He used it to scan the duffel bags and confirmed radiation was not leaking from them and that only background radiation was present in the garage. Freed of concern about contamination or spontaneously starting a chain reaction, he stacked the bags to one side where they were hidden from view by lawn and garden equipment. Pirzad even went back to parking his SUV in the garage.

Other than occasionally wondering if the duffel bags contained anything at all or had been created by the Russians as decoys, Abbadi relaxed and concentrated his attention on obtaining an extension of his visa. He even considered changing his visa to one that allowed him to work, but Pirzad convinced him not to. "If you do that," he argued, "they will send someone around to investigate us. We don't want to risk attracting any undue attention to ourselves," he said.

Ultimately, Abbadi agreed with Pirzad about the visa and contented himself with planning the details of how to distribute the duffel bags once Kalhor gave the order. It was a peaceful existence, reading about potential locations and planning a trip across the continent, going all the way to Vancouver. But after only three weeks, that peace and tranquility came to an abrupt end.

Not long after the police visited Rusty Johnson about the truck, a knock on the door jarred Abbadi from an afternoon nap he'd been enjoying on the couch in Pirzad's living room. He rolled on his side to see through a window in the top half of the front door. A policeman peered at him through the glass. Abbadi rolled off the couch and opened the door.

"We've been talking to Rusty Johnson," the officer said. "Mr. Johnson told us he loaned a pickup truck to someone at this address."

Fear shuddered through Abbadi at the mention of Johnson's name. He was Pirzad's friend. The man from whom they had borrowed the pickup truck that Abbadi had been driving. Abbadi didn't want to get either of them into trouble, and he thought about running, but he didn't want to make a bad situation worse by overreacting. "Yes," he replied. "I believe you're talking about Jalal Pirzad, the man who owns this house."

"Yes," the officer replied. "Is Mr. Pirzad home?"

"No." Abbadi glanced at his wristwatch. "He's still at the university. He teaches there and took the truck with him today. He'll be home a little after five."

The officer asked a few more questions but nothing troublesome. He departed, suggesting someone would be around that evening to follow up with Pirzad later.

As the officer left the house, Abbadi slipped his hand in his pocket and felt his cell phone. He hadn't checked it since falling asleep. When he looked at it, he saw he had a voicemail. It was from Rusty Johnson. "The cops were asking about that truck."

Rather than calling Rusty to find out why they were interested in the truck, Abbadi went to the garage and began loading the duffel bags into Pirzad's SUV. He found two lawn chairs and lay them on top of the duffel bags, along with a canvas bag of baseball equipment, to hide the duffel bags from obvious view. With that done, he ran inside the house and stuffed some clothes into an overnight bag, grabbed his wallet and a stash of extra cash, then returned to the garage. Moments later, he was on the highway headed out of town.

Relaxed and thinking again, Abbadi called Pirzad at his office and told him the officers were looking for him. "Keep going," Pirzad said. "I'll call you later tonight."

CHAPTER TWENTY-THREE

s the sun set late in the afternoon, a Mossad operative working for a delivery service based in Moscow arrived at a production facility in Sarov, a closed city located to the east, known as the center of Russian nuclear research. The driver was Mordvin, an ethnic people group native to an area near the Ural Mountains. He had been recruited by the owner of the delivery service who was, himself, a Mossad operative.

While waiting for workmen to unload his truck, the driver caught a glimpse of Russian technicians inside the building. They appeared to be packing items that were designed for a highly specialized application—among other things, stainless steel tubes, and an actuator of some kind. One by one, technicians wrapped the items in protective material and placed them on a worktable. To the right he saw wooden shipping crates and it appeared they had been dividing the items between the crates as they wrapped them, placing some in one crate and others in another. He counted four crates.

When the truck had been unloaded, the driver climbed into the cab and started the engine to leave. Before he left, he glanced out the window to the side mirror and saw the items still sitting in the warehouse near the shipping crates. Using his phone, he captured several images of them from their reflection in the mirror. No one seemed to notice. He put the truck in gear and drove away.

The next day, a second operative positioned near the warehouse observed workmen using a forklift to bring the crates from the warehouse to the loading dock. He identified the crates as the same ones seen the day before by the numbers stenciled on the side. The crates were loaded into the back of a freight truck and the doors were sealed shut. A few minutes later, the truck came from the warehouse facility accompanied by heavily armed Russian security guards traveling in Tigr SUVs.

✦ ✦ ✦

Mossad operatives, working in teams, followed the convoy south until it reached the docks at Makhachkala, a port city in Dagestan, Russia, that lay along the Caspian Sea. There, the crates were transferred to the *Molana Safi*, a light cargo vessel, for transport down the sea to Iran.

While the ship waited at the dock to cast off, a Mossad operative boarded it and located the crates. Working quickly, he drilled a small hole in the side of the largest crate and inserted an inspection camera through the hole for a look inside. He videoed the contents, noted the name of the ship, and sent the information to a Mossad contact. When he was done, he covered the drill whole with an official-looking label that contained an imbedded RFID chip. The pressure of his hand against the label to seal it in place activated the chip which began emitting a signal. Mossad agents picked up the signal and began tracking it as the ship set sail.

✦ ✦ ✦

In Tel Aviv, Israeli analysts working for Mossad examined the images taken inside the crate onboard the *Molana Safi*, and determined the items were precision parts, most likely destined for use in Iran's nuclear program. Using an account created by the USB flash drive Shiraz Parsi planted at the uranium enrichment facility in Natanz, they located records for the *Molana Safi* and retrieved the manifest for the crates. According to the manifest, the crates were destined for Bandar Anzali, a Caspian Sea port in Iran. When reports about the crates reached the office of Yossi Oron, the director of Mossad, he phoned the prime minister's office and made an appointment to brief him.

Like most in the Israeli government, Eichler had spent the required years of military service. Unlike many, however, he enjoyed it and considered making it a career. An encounter with an American professor from Harvard turned Eichler in the direction of politics, but Eichler never forgot the military perspective he acquired from the army. He knew at once what the images and reports meant. A serious threat against Israel was gathering. A threat not just against its independence, but against its very survival and posed an obvious question—should the ship be allowed to reach Iran, or should it be sunk immediately?

The ministers gathered in a conference room that adjoined Eichler's office. Almost immediately they were divided into two equal groups, each with strong opinions. Half favored sinking the ship as it crossed the Caspian Sea—and doing so within the hour. The other half thought they should let it pass. "If we sink it now," they argued, "we will be injecting ourselves into Russian affairs."

"And," someone suggested, "we will be telling the Iranians that we have access to their system."

"That we've been *living* inside their system," another added.

"Deep inside."

"But if we let it go, Iran will use the contents of those crates to build a nuclear bomb and they will drop that bomb on *us*."

"We don't know that for certain. Let's let it play out a little more."

"We don't need to know for certain they're building a bomb or that they're threatening us with it. That has never been our criteria for defending ourselves."

Eichler let the discussion continue a while longer. When he finally spoke, he began by noting the current situation was different than those Israel faced in the past. "They are not sending weapons," he said, "only items needed to make weapons. They have not changed the status of their forces. And they have not shifted any portion of their army toward any front that would be favorable to them in a war against us. I think we should wait a little longer before acting."

When the meeting concluded, Eichler retreated to his private office, out of the hearing of anyone else. Yossi Oron was with him.

After they were alone and the door was closed, Eichler said, "I want you to share our information with the CIA."

"Certainly," Oron replied. "I can set up a call with Bob Donovan right now."

"No," Eichler said, shaking his head. "Tell him in person. Find out what they know about this and what they think should be done about it. We don't want to get too far ahead of them, if possible."

"Okay," Oron replied. "When would you like me to do that?"

"Leave as soon as you can. Get it done and be back here tomorrow night. The day after at the latest."

Oron frowned. "You're worried?"

Eichler nodded. "I'm concerned."

"Me, too," Oron said.

✦ ✦ ✦

Less than two hours later, Oron once again boarded a jet at Ben Guion Airport in Tel Aviv for a flight to Washington, DC. Twelve hours later, the plane landed at Dulles International Airport. A car was waiting and took him to CIA Headquarters in Langley, Virginia. Bob Donovan and Jim Marsh were waiting in Donovan's office when he arrived.

After a moment to greet each other, Donovan, Marsh, and Oron went to work. "We received new information on the situation in Iran yesterday," Oron said. "I came as quickly as I could to review it with you in person." He handed Donovan a flash drive. Donovan plugged it into the terminal on his desk. Images of the crates in a warehouse appeared, followed by images of the crates being loaded onto a ship. He scrolled through others and then continued to a screen with a memo prepared by Mossad that provided details of the crates, their contents, and their movement. "We feel certain," he added, "that the items in those crates are bound for use in Iran's nuclear program."

"And the ship?" Donovan asked. "Where is it headed?"

"It appears to be sailing for the port in Bandar Anzali."

"That's not far from Rasht," Marsh noted.

"Correct," Oron said. "Which may be the reason they chose that port, but the primary location for their nuclear program is in Isfahan, about nine or ten hours south from Bandar Anzali."

"And your analysts have reviewed all of this?"

Oron nodded. "They're convinced the crates contain parts for Iran's nuclear program."

Donovan had a knowing expression. "You didn't come all this way merely to share this information. What does the Prime Minister want to do about the situation?"

"He would like to wait before doing *anything.*"

"And the ministers?"

"Most of the ministers want to sink the ship now, before it arrives in Iran."

"That would be an act of war against Russia," Marsh said.

"Yes," Oron acknowledged. "Which is why he wanted me to meet with you. In person. So that there is no mistake about our discussion. He thinks the parts alone are not enough to warrant military action. But he remembers our experiences in the past with matters like this. Waiting to see how events will unfold has not proved very successful for us."

"And I'm sure he wants to avoid war with Russia," Donovan said.

"Yes," Oron responded. "Very much. We can handle our neighbors, militarily. But we cannot handle the Russians on our own, though our army would fight to the death to defend Israel."

Donovan leaned back in his chair. "Are you here to ask for our help?"

"I am here to inform you of what we have learned," Oron responded, "and to learn what the US position is on this matter. Regardless of their various opinions about what to do, the Prime Minister and his council do not want to act in any regard on this situation without a clear understanding of America's position on the matter."

Donovan glanced over at Marsh. "Do our analysts have this?"

"They do now," Marsh replied.

"Have they provided a report of their analysis on it?"

"Not yet," Marsh said. "They've only had it about as long as we have."

Donovan turned to Oron. "We'll have to take you to see President Jackson. He's the only one who can give you a definitive statement on this."

"I understand."

"I know you've had a long trip already, but are you okay with going to see him now?"

"Certainly," Oron replied. "That is why I came."

✦ ✦ ✦

Donovan, Marsh, and Oron rode to the White House together

to inform President Jackson of the situation Israel faced. By then, CIA analysts had vetted the information Mossad had gathered and they had prepared an initial report on their findings. That report confirmed what everyone already knew—the crates contained parts and equipment that were essential to creating a nuclear warhead, as well as parts to begin upgrading Iran's centrifuge farms to speed up their enrichment program.

"However," the report continued, "based on the configuration of the trucks used to transport the items at various points along the way, and based on the manner in which those items are packaged, we are of the opinion that nothing in those crates is radioactive."

President Jackson was seated at his desk when Donovan, Marsh, and Oron entered the Oval Office. The report lay before him on the desk. From notes scribbled in the margins, it appeared Jackson had read the report already. Before they'd had time to shake hands, they were joined by Kase, Ford, and Halstead.

After a thorough discussion of the situation, Jackson concluded that the US could not participate in sinking the ship carrying the crates. "The technology that ship is carrying is a problem, but we can't sink it without provoking open conflict with Russia. Right now, with all that's going on everywhere else, we're doing our best to avoid open conflict with them."

Oron nodded. "I understand your situation, Mr. President. And I think it is probably wiser to let the ship continue to its destination. That is also the position of the Prime Minister."

"We'll keep an eye on Iran," Jackson said. "But for now, it does not appear to be a critical issue." He noted the look in Oron's eye and quickly added, "For us. I understand it's rather ominous for you anytime the words *nuclear* and *Iran* are mentioned in the same sentence."

"I'm sure that is the view from this side of the Atlantic," Oron replied.

"You have a different view?"

"Our enemies are not tens of thousands of miles away," Oron said. "Our enemies are next door. Missiles from Iran can reach Israel in a matter of minutes."

General Halstead spoke up. "Are you suggesting you intend to attack Iran?"

"I am suggesting the Prime Minister wanted me to give you the courtesy of prior notice on this situation and to discuss with you possible alternatives for action. But Israel reserves the right to make its own decisions as to what is in its best interest."

"No one is asking anything more from you," Jackson answered. "Tell the Prime Minister that we stand with Israel, but we do not defer to Israel. There are many moving parts to the current situation. This issue with Iran and Russia is just one of them."

Ford looked over at Oron. "Do you need anything from us? Missiles, aircraft, that sort of thing."

"I appreciate the offer," Oron said. "But if we accept additional arms from you right now, we will tip the Iranians that we know they are up to something."

"We don't want to do that," Jackson said as he stood. "Make sure you stay in touch with Bob. The CIA will share whatever we have on the situation."

When the meeting ended, Donovan accompanied Oron on the

ride to the airport for his flight back to Israel. Oron had been surprised by the lack of interest in Iran's conduct displayed by Jackson and the others when they were in the Oval Office. Like the others, Oron did not think immediate US involvement was warranted but he had hoped they could outline several defensive scenarios as a framework for developing tactical plans. That they had not left him unsettled and occupied his mind as he and Donovan made their way through traffic.

Finally, with the airport in sight, Oron glanced over at Donovan. "Does President Jackson understand the gravity of the situation?"

"Your situation or the world's?" Donovan responded.

"Both."

"Yes," Donovan said. "He understands the situation and he understands that it is a problem, especially for Israel."

"But he does not wish to get involved in another Middle Eastern conflict."

"Russia's presence makes him hesitant."

"He is scared?"

"He is President of the United States," Donovan replied. "He must *never* say that."

Oron nodded. "Our prime minister has that problem, too."

✦ ✦ ✦

The *Molana Safi* arrived at Bandar Anzali with the crates onboard. Mossad operatives were present to observe them as they were unloaded and placed on separate trucks. Operatives followed the trucks at a safe distance as they drove from the port facility and headed south. Two hours later, one of the trucks turned off the main road onto a highway that led to Rasht.

The second truck continued south and reached Isfahan nine hours later. It was cleared through the security checkpoint at the entrance to Iran's nuclear development facility, then disappeared inside a secure building.

On the same day that the *Molana Safi* arrived at Bandar Anzali, Russian operatives began arriving at the airport in Tehran. They appeared to be traveling in three groups, with some travelling to facilities in Natanz and Isfahan, while others went to Rasht. That Russians would visit Natanz and Isfahan seemed obvious, but a group visiting Rasht left Mossad operatives troubled. There were no nuclear enrichment facilities there, only manufacturing facilities for drones, missiles, and artillery shells. When a report of the activity reached Mossad analysts in Tel Aviv, they were troubled, too.

"But Rasht *is* a site for weapons systems development and construction," someone suggested. "And it is the location where many of their best weapons systems have been built."

Still, the situation was perplexing and Mossad supervisors wanted more details, so they sent a Kurdish operative to investigate the site.

✦ ✦ ✦

At Natanz, Russian technicians began preparing the site for new equipment upgrades. They brought Russian security experts with them and, with the help of Iranian technicians, swept the facility's computer system for spyware. They also checked the current operating system on Iran's computers for technical compatibility with Russian programs necessary to operate the proposed upgrades for the system. New equipment that recently arrived by ship was supposed to be controlled through that same central system, but before that could be done, it had to be checked for compatibility.

In the course of completing those sweeps and checks, technicians discovered the user account created by Shiraz Parsi for Mossad when he inserted the USB flash drive in a computer at the enrichment center. Not long after that, they discovered the program that had been uploaded to give Mossad access to the system. And then they found the flash drive itself, still inserted in the USB drive of a laptop at one of the Natanz workstations.

✦ ✦ ✦

A month later, and with the Israeli government increasingly apprehensive about events in Iran, a team of Iraqi Kurds working as operatives for Mossad tapped phone lines at the Iranian president's office and other key government offices in Tehran. Information from those lines was fed across town by piggybacking on a news service microwave link to a device installed in a utility box near Faraja Officers University. That device retransmitted the information through a secure encrypted link to a Canadian satellite. With a secure satellite link, Mossad operatives transmitted data from the Iranian telephone system, in near real-time, to Mossad headquarters in Tel Aviv. Analysts working day and night examined the stream of data thoroughly.

In addition to landline taps, cellphone micro-towers were placed in strategic locations around Tehran. These were used to pick up transmissions from cell phone numbers that had been previously identified as belonging to key Iranian officials.

Mossad staff examining the transmissions from these sources learned that Iran's leadership planned to authorize a strike against Israel as soon as the scientists and technicians prepared a workable nuclear warhead. Based on information obtained through the system at the enrichment facility in Natanz, many Mossad analysts thought Iran could have a warhead ready for service in a month. Others thought it would take a little longer, perhaps two. No one thought warhead development would take more than three.

In accordance with Oron's discussion with President Jackson and others in the Oval Office, Mossad's information was conveyed through appropriate channels to Donovan and Marsh at the CIA. After a discussion with Donovan, Marsh forwarded the information to a team of CIA analysts who reviewed it, including Mossad's supporting telephone intercept transcripts and accompanying satellite images, and prepared a report. Their opinion remained much as it had been earlier—the information supported an ominous scenario that threatened Israel's existence, but the timeline was not consistent with Mossad's estimates.

"Production of workable warheads for use with Iran's current inventory of missiles could be accomplished within the proposed timeline only by adapting an existing Russian warhead for that purpose. Re-engineering a Russian concept and creating an entirely new Iranian warhead would require at least a year's worth of designing and testing and would likely push functional completion into a second year."

Regardless of differences about exactly when Iran could have a warhead ready, there was unanimous agreement among Israeli and CIA experts that Iran's first target would be Tel Aviv. No matter what Russian politicians said to the contrary, and no matter the Russian status in their war with Ukraine, the mantra was universal among Iranians of every class and every station throughout the Iranian government. "Strike Israel, the little Satan, and the Big Satan, the United States, will be forced to retaliate and when they do, the resulting disaster on earth will usher in the Madhi from heaven to save us."

✦ ✦ ✦

With Mossad's analysts convinced Iran was on the verge of having a functional atomic weapon ready, Yossi Oron briefed Yehuda Eichler at the prime minister's office. After reviewing Mossad's report and the evidence that supported it, Eichler reached the same conclusion many Israel leaders had been forced to accept. "We can't wait for them to go first."

"No," Oron agreed in a somber voice. "If we hope to survive, we must go first."

Eichler glanced across the room to a portrait of David Ben-Gurion that hung on the wall. "Do you think he ever considered it would come to something like this?"

"I don't know," Oron replied. "But if he did, I think he was praying Israel would have a prime minister like you when that day arrived."

They were silent for a moment, then Eichler said, "Are you ready to brief the cabinet?"

"Yes, Mr. Prime Minister."

"I'll call a meeting."

CHAPTER TWENTY-FOUR

espite protests from the US and NATO, shipments of drones and artillery shells continued to reach Ukraine from China. With them, Russian forces succeeded in driving the Ukrainian army out of Bakhmut and threatened to drive them even farther toward the west in a thoroughgoing rout.

Facing a crisis in the war, Donovan came to Marsh. "The administration intends to interdict Russia's supply lines into Ukraine in a major way."

"Is that wise?" Marsh asked. "Given the situation in China?"

Donovan was dismissive. "No one is concerned about China. They always protest when we enter the Asian theater. It's just noise. But they are concerned about Ukraine."

Marsh was skeptical. "Is that *your* assessment, or someone else's?"

"Ah," Donovan said with a shrug. "These things get worked up in the bowels of government and circulated around at various levels."

Marsh arched an eyebrow. "Meaning this one originated with the State Department."

"In the end, we're all just soldiers," Donovan said. "We go where ordered and do what is needed."

"Did anyone consider the possibility that this time Chinese leadership might not be merely talking and posturing?"

"Why would this time be any different from the others?"

"Well," Marsh said, "for one thing, someone recently murdered their top two leaders. Shouldn't that make us rethink our position?"

Donovan was nonchalant. "That's not our concern."

"You mean, the president has decided this interdiction must be done."

"And you know how these things work."

"Will this be a military interdiction?" Marsh asked.

"If it was, I wouldn't be talking to you." Donovan turned toward the door. "Work something up for it," he said as he opened the door.

"Do you want to see it before we implement it?"

Donovan glanced back at Marsh with a smile, then continued on his way.

✦ ✦ ✦

The following week, Taras Irvanets was hunkered down behind the remains of a Russian troop carrier, dodging incoming mortar fire when he saw a dinted and patched Humvee approaching. It came to within a few yards of his position and the front door opened. The American he knew only as Tom stepped out. "Where's your drone?" he asked.

"The Russians destroyed it," Taras replied.

Tom grinned. "Then it's a good thing I brought my own. Get your gear and come with me."

Taras hesitated. "Shouldn't we check with Seargent Lomachenko?"

"I already did," Tom replied. "Hurry up. I don't want to get hit by one of those Russian mortars."

Taras slung his backpack over one shoulder, grabbed his rifle, and hurried after Tom. When they were seated inside the Humvee, Taras glanced over at Tom. "Where are we going this time?"

"This is a special mission," Tom replied.

"Doing what?"

"Do you care?"

"Not really," Taras said, "but where are we going?"

"We're going behind the Russians."

Taras eyes were wide. "Behind the Russians?"

"Someone has decided we need to harass their supply line."

Taras glanced around. "Where's the drone?"

"We'll catch up with it in a little while."

Taras settled into the seat, rested his hands in his lap, and closed his eyes. A few minutes later, he was sound asleep.

✦ ✦ ✦

Traveling in the Humvee, Taras and Tom drove south toward the coastline and came to Kherson, a city at the mouth of the Dnipro

River. Before the war, Kherson had been a major port of transit for goods of every kind coming in and out of Ukraine. Since the Russians occupied it, the port had been a major source of equipment and arms supporting Russian troops. Most recently, it had become a primary entry point for shipments of drones and artillery shells sent from China by way of Kazakhstan.

The city was located south and to the west of the heavy fighting along Ukraine's eastern border, which placed it in a strategic location. From Kherson, weapons and ammunition could travel behind Ukraine's defenses and reach the central portion of the country with much less risk than they would encounter by coming straight across from the border.

It was dark when Taras and Tom arrived, and their first stop was in an alley near the center of town. Tom brought the Humvee to a stop behind a delivery truck. "Take everything you brought and get in the cab of the truck."

They cleaned out the Humvee, then left it behind and drove away in the truck. "Where are we going?" Taras asked.

"You ask too many questions," Tom replied.

They rode in silence to a remote spot near the water and parked the truck behind a thick stand of trees with the rear doors facing away. Then, working together, they unloaded the drone and set it on the ground. They set two monitors on the tail of the truck, with the doors closed enough to shield the glow of their screens. When all of that was in place, Taras turned on the system.

While the electronics and guidance programs loaded, they assembled the drone, then loaded it with anti-tank grenades. Taras checked the onboard tank to make sure it was full of fuel and adjusted the onboard camera angle to the setting he'd used before.

When the drone was prepared, and the guidance system was ready, Tom took a map of the port from one of the cases and pointed to a spot on it. "The ship we want is right around there," he said, tapping the location with his finger. "I don't have an exact position for it but if you can put the drone in this spot, I think I'll recognize it from the camera's image."

Using the map as a reference, Taras determined the coordinates for the location and entered them into the drone's guidance system, then checked one of the monitors to make sure the numbers were correct. When he was certain they were right, he took the controller in hand and pressed a button to start the drone's engines. Once the engines were warm, he moved the controller handles forward and the drone rose into the air. Soon it was invisible against the dark sky.

Two minutes later, the guidance system indicated the drone was over the harbor and a moment after that a beep sounded as it reached the desired location. Taras pressed a button on the controller to turn on the drone's camera, then glanced at a monitor to check the images. Beneath the drone he saw a ship moored to a dock. Workers moved about busily unloading cargo from the ship's hold.

Taras turned to Tom. "We're there," he said. "Is that the ship you were looking for?"

Tom studied the drone's images a moment. "Yes," he replied. "That's it." He pointed to a spot on the image. "Drop one of the grenades right there," he said.

The image showed the doors of the cargo hold were open. "You want one in the hold?" Taras asked.

"Right in the middle," Tom replied.

Taras pressed a button on the controller and a grenade fell from the drone's frame. He watched the monitor as it twirled downward toward the ship, then disappeared into the cargo hold where it exploded in a sudden burst of orange flame.

The drone hovered in place and waited until smoke from the explosion cleared. Images from the camera showed the grenade did little by way of damage. Instinctively, Taras released a second grenade.

As the second grenade twirled downward, he could see everyone on the deck of the ship starring into the sky, as if searching to see where the explosion came from. None of them seemed to notice the second grenade falling directly toward them. They still were staring into the sky when the second grenade reached the cargo hold. Unlike the first one, however, this one made a direct hit on something big.

The initial explosion shot blue flames and smoke straight up from the point of impact. Workmen inside the hold were killed instantly. Then a secondary explosion gashed a hole through the side of the ship, followed by a third and fourth explosion as the ripple effects of the initial blast traveled up and down the ship, all the way to the bow on one end and the stern on the other.

Taras' mouth fell open at the sight of it. Tom was slack jawed. Both men turned from the monitors on the back of the truck to stare across the harbor at the port facility where the ship was totally engulfed in flames.

"What was that ship carrying?" Taras asked.

"Whatever it was," Tom replied, "We must have scored a direct hit on it."

They stood together watching as the ship was engulfed in flames, then finally Tom asked, "Where's the drone?"

Taras glanced at the monitor and saw only a dark image on the screen. "I'm not sure," he replied. He turned the camera as far as it would go in either direction, but saw nothing different, then he spun the drone, intending to cycle it all the way around in a circle. As it neared one-hundred-eighty degrees, he saw an image of the docks with flames from the ship. He checked the data in the system. "Looks like we're south of where we'd been before."

"The force of the explosion must have pushed it out of the way."

"What do you want to do with it?" Taras asked.

"We have two more grenades?"

"Yes."

"I suppose we could drop them on something."

"They'll be watching for that," Taras said. "If they see us, they'll follow the drone back here."

"Might they do that anyway?"

"Perhaps."

"Take it higher," Tom said.

Taras pressed the handles on the controller and the drone rose higher. When it reached a thousand feet, he held it stationary. "That's a thousand," he said.

Whatever Tom had been thinking, he seemed to have changed his mind. "Fly it back here yourself," he said. "That way, we won't emit a signal."

"We still have to communicate with it."

"Well. . .do it that way anyway."

"Where else can we hit?"

"I have a list," Tom said. "But it can wait. We'll do the next target tomorrow."

✦ ✦ ✦

Over the next three weeks, Taras and Tom struck additional sites in and around Kherson. A warehouse that held ammunition and supplies awaiting transfer to the front. Another ship at berth in the harbor. Then they found a petroleum refinery not far away. Apparently, it wasn't on Tom's list of targets but the value of it seemed too good to pass up.

The refinery was located on the west side of Kherson and was supplied by pipelines that brought unrefined oil from ships docked in the port. It also received oil from drilling rigs operating in Ukrainian oil fields north of the city.

At Taras' suggestion, they moved the truck to a location closer to the target. An abandoned industrial site, part of which had been used as an enduro track for motorcycle enthusiasts. They parked the truck on the far side of the property near a road that led out to a major highway. Tom thought it would be good to have an escape route handy. "If we can hit one or two of the refinery's storage tanks, we might get all of them to explode."

"If that happens," Taras suggested, "we won't be far enough away to be safe."

Tom laughed. "If we get the tanks to explode, no one will be safe at any distance."

"We're also close to the airport," Taras added. He pointed to the map to indicate the location.

Tom noted the spot. "I don't think it's operational right now. At least, not for commercial flights. The Russians are using it exclusively."

"If the Russians are using it, won't they be monitoring the sky constantly?"

"We can't eliminate every problem," Tom replied. "And if they hit the drone, they hit it." He shrugged. "We need to bomb the refinery."

With the truck in a good place, Taras and Tom took turns sleeping through the day. Taras went first and found a spot a good distance from the truck. Close enough to know if someone was approaching, but far enough away to be missed in an initial encounter should someone arrive to confront them. He lay on the ground in a level place, wrapped himself in his coat, and closed his eyes. His body relaxed and it felt good to rest, but his mind would not stop.

He had been enthusiastic about the war at the beginning, and initially it really had been an adventure with his friends from the university, but those days were long gone, as were many of his friends. Flying drones had offered him a way to fight without being in the middle of combat and he liked that. Now, with most of his friends dead and the war dragging on and on with no end in sight, he'd become less enthusiastic about the entire affair. Not totally disillusioned but less naïve. War was about killing people and blowing up things. Day after day. Constantly. With very little joy. And now, behind the front, in territory occupied and controlled by the Russian army, it seemed he and Tom weren't so much patriots as outlaws.

Sometime later, Taras felt someone shaking his foot. Startled by it, he sat up abruptly with a fist cocked and ready to fight. Then he saw Tom standing nearby, grinning. "It's alright," he said with both hands raised in a defensive pose. "It's your turn to stand watch."

Taras rubbed the sleep from his eyes and stood. "Did you have any trouble?"

"No," Tom replied with a shake of his head.

"No visitors?"

"None."

Tom stretched out his body on the ground where Taras had been lying, rested his hands on his chest, and closed his eyes. It seemed a practice routine that he had done many times before.

Taras stepped away and walked toward the truck, hoping to find something in the cab to eat. There wasn't much, just a candy bar and half of a sandwich. He munched on those and had a sip of water from a canteen, then sat on the ground beside the truck and propped against a rear tire. Soon, he was sound asleep and when he opened his eyes again, it was almost night.

Rather than disturbing Tom, Taras opened the rear doors of the truck and began setting up the equipment to fly the drone. A CPU to run the system's software. Two monitors—one for images from the drone's cameras, the other for telemetry—and the controller. Ordinance was stacked near the drone at the opposite end of the truck. From his place in back, he saw several boxes of grenades and containers for six anti-tank missiles. He thought missiles would be best for an attempt on the refinery. They were more powerful than—

Just then, Taras felt a hand on his shoulder. He whirled around to see Tom standing behind him. "You seem to have things almost ready."

"Almost," Taras said. "Thinking about which weapons to use."

"I was thinking we'd use a couple of those missiles," Tom said, gesturing to the containers in the truck.

Taras smiled. "That's exactly what I was thinking."

Together, they moved the drone to the ground, then spent the next thirty minutes fueling it and loading the missiles, one on each side of the drone's frame, as they had done before when they destroyed General Marchuk's house at a time that now seemed long ago. As a last-minute thought, they added a grenade on each side for extra ballast to help counteract the weight shift from using one of the missiles.

When nighttime had fully fallen, Taras started the drone's engine, checked the monitor to make sure all was in order, then manipulated the controller for takeoff. As the drone rose into the air, he switched on the camera and checked the image. Seeing all was in order, he turned the drone in the direction of the refinery and cruised toward it, flying at about fifteen-hundred feet.

The refinery wasn't difficult to locate. Like the port along the river, it was well-lit, and the storage tanks were obvious, aligned in rows and connected with pipes that snaked between them. When the drone was over the facility, Taras turned to Tom. "Which place looks best to you?"

Tom checked the monitor and shrugged. "I suppose we should have flown over it earlier to scout the best location."

"Too late to worry about that."

Tom gestured to Taras. "You make the choice. Pick a spot that looks obvious and hit it."

Taras scanned the area, then chose a tall cylindrical tower in the center of the plant, thinking an explosion there might affect other areas of the facility. He positioned the drone at the far end of the tank farm, focused the targeting device on the tower, and fired a missile in that direction. As the missile left the rack, the weight of the drone shifted to one side, and it became unsteady.

The rocket struck a distillation tower used for heating crude oil to break it into its constituents. It was full of petroleum components of varying volatility. When the rocket exploded, the tower did too, sending an enormous fireball into the air and scattering pieces like shrapnel across the entire plant. Secondary explosions ravaged adjoining sections and in less than a minute, the entire facility was on fire.

With the weight shift from loss of the rocket, Taras had to fight to keep the drone under control. Then he remembered the grenades attached to the frame for ballast. To equalize the weight, all he had to do was fire the second missile. He turned the drone towards the tank farm, chose a tank near the center, and fired the missile. Seconds later, it penetrated the side of the tank and created an enormous explosion that blew the drone in the opposite direction. Tanks on either side exploded. Followed by the ones that adjoined those. Then others erupted until the entire facility was ablaze. With the refinery in shambles, Taras steered the drone toward the truck.

Destroying a refinery with two anti-tank rockets, delivered from a retrofitted delivery drone, seemed impossible, but there it was. A fully functional oil refinery with an adjoining tank farm that minutes before held hundreds of thousands of gallons of fuel reduced to rubble. Precious reserves of fuel destroyed. Production capacity eliminated. And then Taras checked the monitor for images from the drone and saw hundreds of houses in the outlying area had been damaged by the explosions. Windows blown out. Cars and trucks on fire. Bodies of the dead lying on the ground.

Tom watched the images, too, and shook his head. "War is hell," he said with a pat on Taras' shoulder. "It's the price we pay for victory."

"It's the price *they* pay," Taras corrected. And staring at the images, the hope he'd have of winning the war seemed farther away than ever, and the price enormously high.

✦ ✦ ✦

While Taras and Tom attacked sites at Kherson, other drone squads hit other targets in other locations. Zaporizhzhia, a city farther to the north that sat astride the Dnipro River—one half in Ukraine, the other half in Russia. Mariupol, a city along the Sea of Azov at the mouth of the Kalmias River. And half a dozen more, all of them major points for shipments of supplies coming from Russia to the front and for arms coming from China. At the same time, Ukrainian jets, including F-16s supplied through NATO allies, struck a bridge linking Crimea to the mainland, effectively cutting off access to it by land and disabling Crimea as a point of resupply for the Russian army.

These attacks and the facilities they destroyed seriously crimped Russia's ability to fight. Shortages already apparent became even more pronounced and once again, as they had in earlier phases of the war, some Russian army units came to a halt, unable to fight for lack of ammunition and unable to move due to lack of fuel.

At the same time, economic sanctions imposed by Western nations continued to inflict a serious toll on Russia's domestic economy. Every region of the Russian homeland experienced crippling shortages of food and household goods. As a result, public discontentment with the war rose to unprecedented levels, boiling over into the streets in public demonstrations. A few politicians even went so far as to suggest a general strike was warranted.

From his office inside the Kremlin, Putin saw all of this as evidence that the West really had conspired against him and the Russian people to use the war as a means of destroying Russia, militarily and economically. Threatening their survival. Their dignity. Their rightful place in the world order. And as the situation in Ukraine became more desperate on the ground, his mood grew steadily darker.

Day after day, over and over in his mind, Putin remembered the day when he was installed in office as president. The Patriarch of the church in Moscow appointed him Chief Exorcist, to bring about the De-Satanification of Ukraine and, indeed, all the territory once held by the Empire. And appointed him Defender of Christianity throughout the civilized world. President, Defender of the Faith, Chief Exorcist. Since that day, the redemption of the Mother Land had been his calling. His birthright. To save the empire, the church, and the world. And he had understood in a moment, as if in a vision, how to accomplish that goal—solidify control of the government, streamline its operations, reclaim the empire's territory. Returning Ukraine to the fold was a major step toward that goal.

Yet here they were, bogged down in a never-ending war that consumed more and more of Russia's time, resources, talents, and reserves. And the Americans. . .the thought of it made him shudder. So arrogant in their confidence that *they* were God's chosen. That *they* were the ones to save the world. And for what? For democracy and capitalism? As if *they* were ordained to impose their will on everyone else. And what goal did they have? To consume Russia's resources? The world's resources? Its people? To consume them on America's profligate lifestyle of consumption and waste while everyone else starved? While everyone else lived in squalor? The more he thought about it, brooded over it, meditated on it, the angrier he became. And with each thought, each moment he descended deeper and deeper into the blackness of the vengeful hatred that had plagued him throughout his life each time he encountered the US.

Finally, Putin reached his limit. He'd had enough. Action was what he needed, what the nation needed, what the troops on the ground needed. Decisive, game-changing action. The kind of bold leadership that marked the mighty emperors of old. And to get things moving in a better direction, he called for a meeting with a select group of advisors to discuss the situation and announce his decision about the next phase of the war. As before, the gathering was held in a secure conference room at the Russian Department of Defense's main building in Moscow.

Among those in attendance were Nikolai Patrushev, Secretary of the Security Council, Sergei Naryshkin, head of the Foreign Intelligence Service, and Sergei Shoigu, Russia's Minister of Defense. Also in attendance was Valery Gerasimov, the Army Chief of Staff, and several officers overseeing operations on the ground in Ukraine.

"The time has come for decisive action," Putin began. "If this war persists any longer, our nation will collapse and that is precisely what the Americans want. We cannot give them the satisfaction of seeing that come to pass. Since this war began, the US and its allies in NATO have given Ukraine just enough to keep them going. Just enough to keep them fighting. But not enough to win. And it occurs to me that is precisely what they want, because if Ukraine continues to fight, they can keep us in the war as long as they like, draining and draining our military, our economy, and our people, until we collapse. But we must not let that happen. We must not let them win."

It was an all-too-familiar Putin rant. Most of the experienced officials in the room had heard it many times before and kept quiet, to avoid encouraging him. But Naryshkin, who had become his right-hand man, could not resist showing his support. "What do you propose we do, Mr. President?" he asked in an expectant, if not overly enthusiastic, voice.

Putin squared his shoulders, braced himself, and looked directly at those seated before him. "I propose we turn to the use of low-yield nuclear devices. And that we begin by dropping one on Kryvyi Rih, Zelensky's hometown."

Everyone, even his staunchest supporters, were stunned, and the room was deathly quiet. Finally, Nikolai Patrushev spoke. "A nuclear weapon, Mr. President?"

"A low-yield nuclear weapon," Putin corrected. "If we drop it on Kryvyi Rih, we can break the stalemate in the east and our forces can move out towards the west. And by dropping it there we will send a message that Zelensky is the real problem."

Those in the room exchanged glances of disbelief. Valery Gerasimov finally spoke. "We're already moving in that direction, Mr. President. We've destroyed Bakhmut. Our forces control most of the ports and coastline to the south. We can—"

"Apparently that is not quite so," Putin growled. "Did you not hear of the havoc Ukrainian forces have wreaked in Kherson? Ships, port facilities, warehouses, even a refinery—destroyed. And the bridge to Crimea. They are cutting off our access to supplies and weapons."

"But a nuclear weapon?" Gerasimov continued. "The world will line up against us."

"The world is already against us," Putin countered.

Sergei Shoigu, Russia's Minister of Defense, spoke up. "Mr. President, we are making good progress now with conventional weapons. Won't political repercussions of using a nuclear weapon outweigh any benefits from it?"

"You are a general in the army," Putin snapped. "Your job is to win battles. Solving political problems is my job. Leave that to me." He glanced around the room again. "Just think of it. With a nuclear weapon, the mighty Russian army can roll across Ukraine until we reach the next city stupid enough to resist. Then we will drop a bomb there and proceed to the next one, until we reach Poland."

"That would embroil us in a major nuclear war," someone shouted.

"It will never come to that," Putin replied. "Before we reached the third city, the Ukrainian people will have had enough of our bombs, and they will force Zelensky to agree to our terms. Or, perhaps, they will force him from office entirely. And if he misses the point, we will continue dropping bombs until there are *no* cities left in Ukraine."

Unlike Putin's rants in the past, this time there was no deterring him and when Naryshkin, Shoigu, and Gerasimov stood and applauded, everyone else knew there was no point in resisting.

Late that evening, members of a special Russian army unit fired an intermediate range missile from a mobile launcher in central Russia. The missile was armed with a single low-yield nuclear warhead. Fifteen minutes after launch, the missile struck the center of Kryvyi Rih with a 10-kiloton explosion, instantly leveling the center of the city and causing widespread damage over a thousand-square-mile zone. Over one million people were killed in the blast. Even among those who survived, almost no one escaped injury.

✦ ✦ ✦

Taras was still with Tom at Kherson when he felt the ground tremble beneath his feet. He glanced in Tom's direction. "Did you feel that?"

"Yeah," Tom replied. "Put the drone up and see if you can spot what happened."

Taras launched the drone and took it above two thousand feet, then spun the drone slowly in a circle allowing the camera to pan the sky in every direction. He stopped it as a familiar mushroom cloud appeared on the horizon. "Vot der 'mo!" he exclaimed.

"What is it?"

Taras pointed to the screen. "Look at this!" he shouted.

Tom hurried to his side and stared at the screen. "That's a nuclear explosion," he said in disbelief.

They both stared in silence at the image on the screen, then Tom asked, "Where is it? Can you tell?"

"I'll have to check the telemetry."

While Taras checked the details on the second monitor, Tom stepped away and made a phone call. It was risky, someone might easily use the phone's metadata to determine their locations, but he needed to confirm what had just happened.

Meanwhile, using the drone's position and telemetry, Taras hastily made a series of calculations, then compared the results to map. "By my reckoning," he said, catching Tom's eye, "they hit Kryvyi Rih."

Tom ended the phone call. "That's exactly what they did."

Just then, a horrendous gust of wind swept through their position. It stripped the leaves from branches of the trees and turned the truck on its side as the overpressure from the explosion reached them.

"If that was a nuclear explosion, were we exposed?" Taras asked.

"Most definitely," Tom replied.

Tom seemed to take it in stride, but Taras, knowing the consequences of excessive radiation exposure to the human body was overwhelmed by a sudden sense of his own mortality. He thought of his mother and of Mila, his girlfriend, back in Kyiv. The plans they had made for a life together. A future with children and laughter and friends over for all the seasonal gatherings, especially Christmas. None of which seemed possible now.

If he was going to die—and by then he was certain he would die a miserable death—he didn't want to spend his last days on the battlefield. And even if he lived another year, he didn't want to do so far from the people he loved. He gathered his belongings and stuffed them in his backpack, then slung it over his shoulder and started toward the road on foot. A Russian sniper might shoot him in the open, but at least he would die on his way to a future he had planned, rather than one that was imposed upon him.

CHAPTER TWENTY-FIVE

Within minutes of the explosion at Kryvyi Rih, experts from the United States Strategic Command determined the location of the blast and specific details regarding pressure, radiation, heat, and seismic activity generated by it. Based on that information, they concluded the explosion was, indeed, from a nuclear device. Bob Donovan and Bruce Ford briefed President Jackson at the Oval Office and reviewed the data with him.

When the briefing ended, Jackson lodged a complaint with the Russian government in Moscow and with the UN Security Council. He summoned the Russian ambassador to the White House and delivered a complaint to him in person.

Sarah Foster, the president's chief of staff, suggested they should notify the public of the explosion through a press release, perhaps in the context of a short press conference. "Just a statement," she said. "No questions."

Jackson shook his head. "We'll tell them what happened and what we've done, after we do it."

"There might not be much left when we're finished with that," she countered.

Jackson glared at her. "The people elected us to make decisions for them based on the best information available using our best judgement. We don't have time to take a vote or a poll or a survey before responding. By my calculation, we have less than two hours to get this done."

And with that, Jackson proceeded downstairs toward the Situation Room where relevant department and agency heads were gathered. But before he'd gone far, he turned back to her. "It's a stressful time," he said in a calmer voice. "Prepare a statement and I'll look at it. Just keep it brief."

✦ ✦ ✦

The room was full when Jackson arrived. Cabinet secretaries and agency heads were seated at the conference table. Aides and undersecretaries occupied chairs that lined the wall all the way around the room. When everyone was seated, Donovan and Ford presented the same information to those in the room that they had given Jackson early. After they finished, Jackson said, "The obvious response is to launch a proportional nuclear counterstrike, but I think we have to do better than that."

"Why?" someone asked. "Why do we have to be the ones who take the high road? And why do we have to restrict ourselves to a *proportional response*? Why isn't an overwhelming response appropriate?"

"I know the situation is confounding," Jackson said, "but we must respond in a way that tells the Russians we aren't going to let them get away with it, but without forcing a nuclear confrontation on the world. Despite our anger, we really don't want a nuclear war." The room became eerily silent. Jackson looked around the group. "You all represent some of the best minds of your generation. Not just in America but in the world. Now dig in. Tell me how we respond without using nuclear weapons?"

Clinton Kase from the State Department broke the silence. "Mr. President, you seem to want a discussion, but I think I speak for most people in the room when I say, 'What is there for us to discuss? What is there for us to debate?' Russian military leaders used a nuclear bomb against a Ukrainian city. For all practical purposes, that city no longer exists. Doesn't their action answer any questions that might arise from it?"

"But they didn't drop it on us," someone responded.

"I don't care where they dropped it," Kase said, in an emotional outburst. "We have to retaliate in kind. They used a nuclear bomb, we must respond with a nuclear bomb, and we must drop it on Russian forces, same as if we were the Ukrainian government."

"But we're not the Ukrainian government," Jackson responded.

"And where will a response like that end?" Donovan asked.

Kase glared at him. "Then what do *you* propose?"

"Frankly, I don't know," Donovan admitted. "I don't have a specific action to propose. But whatever we do, it should be done with conventional weapons."

"Why?" Kase demanded. "Why conventional? What's the point of having a nuclear arsenal if we don't use it?"

"We need to contain the situation," Ford interjected. His voice was calm and even. "If we use nuclear weapons now, the situation will only escalate."

Someone else spoke up. "I think a nuclear response would be a mistake, but that doesn't relieve us from issuing a massive response."

Kase scoffed at the suggestion. "We'd have to bomb every Russian troop location east of Kyiv to make it a response proportional to what they did to Kryvyi Rih. We can't let this go with a perfunctory response. It would be the same as ignoring it."

"No one is suggesting we ignore it."

Someone else spoke up. "Maybe we should empty the bin. Use all we have at once, in a single counterstrike."

"In Ukraine?"

"I was thinking of Russia."

"Hit all of our priority targets in Russia?"

"Yes."

"If we only hit land-based missile sites," someone noted, "they would still have missiles on their submarines to launch another round at us."

An undersecretary spoke up. "I suppose we should be glad Bill Clinton convinced the Ukrainians to give up their nuclear weapons."

"I'm not," Kase snapped.

"You think we would be safer if Zelensky still had them?" Donovan asked.

"If Ukraine had nuclear weapons," Kase argued, "they could respond to this attack on their own, without involving us directly, and the world could avoid a wider war."

"I think you're losing it."

"He has a point," General Halstead said. "If we respond with a nuclear attack, this war will become the US against Russia in the thermonuclear nightmare we've all wanted to avoid. But if Ukraine responded in a similar fashion, it would only be Russia against Ukraine."

"But that isn't the situation now because President Clinton gave that option away," Kase declared.

"Please," Donovan said with disgust. "Presidents solve the problems of the present—their present, the present they live in at the time the problem occurs. Not the present someone else lives two or three decades after they leave office. Clinton could only deal with the circumstances that confronted him at the time he was president."

"Perhaps," Halstead seemed to concede. "But our current situation would be far more manageable if Ukraine launched a counterstrike and not us."

"And yet, that's not where we are now," Donovan replied, his voice tense with frustration. "We can't blame someone from the past because their decisions, that solved the circumstances they faced back then, don't fit the circumstances we face now."

"Gentlemen," Ford said in an attempt to calm those at the table. "If we could deal with the present, please. We need to narrow down the options. If we use a counterstrike, should it be against military targets only, or should we hit civilian targets, too?"

"For any countermeasure to be effective," someone suggested, "it will have to be a strike against Russian troops."

Donovan leaned close to Marsh, who was seated near him. "Feels like a final meeting, doesn't it? Like the night before the end." He smiled. "Like that Last Supper in one of those books you're always reading."

"The Gospels?"

"Yeah."

Marsh didn't like the lighthearted tone Donovan used, given the seriousness of the moment, but he felt compelled to respond. "I think we've moved several books away from the Gospels. More like we're in a chapter of *Revelation*."

"The end of time?"

"Yes," Marsh said.

Donovan nodded. "Then it would definitely be a good time to pray."

"I've been doing that since long before now."

The discussion around the table continued. "If we hit their military with nuclear weapons, they will hit ours the same way."

"And where will it stop? We hit their bases, they hit ours. Will it remain merely an exchange between armies?"

"I would hope."

"But how will we prevent this from escalating to nuclear strikes on civilian targets? We hit Moscow, they hit Washington? We hit St. Petersburg, they hit New York?"

"We could launch all of our missiles now and get it over with."

"Maybe we should move to Argentina."

"Why?"

"If the nuclear exchanges remain in the Northern Hemisphere, the Southern Hemisphere will miss most of the fallout."

The discussion continued a while longer until Jackson said, "I've heard enough." He glanced over at Ford, "We'll begin by using conventional weapons against every Russian target of significance in Ukraine located east of Kyiv. Draw up a plan and have it ready for me to review in two hours. But get the missiles ready, just in case."

✦ ✦ ✦

While the world watched in horror as events unfolded in Ukraine, Mossad's attention remained steadfastly focused on Iran. Satellite images downloaded three days earlier showed Iran's medium-range missiles being loaded onto mobile launchers. The most recent images, however, showed two Simorgh rockets—the kind Iran used to place satellites into orbit—sitting on the launchpad at Semnan Space Center.

When Yossi Oron saw the missiles loaded on mobile launchers, he had counseled the prime minister to refrain from direct action. "Those missiles have conventional warheads. We don't want to provoke something bigger."

Reluctantly, the prime minister had agreed and refrained from destroying the launchers. But two Simorghs on the launchpad and ready to go was a very different scenario. Simorghs were intercontinental missiles. They could reach Jerusalem before an announcement could move civilians into shelters, and these missiles could easily be carrying nuclear warheads. No one had confirmed that Iran did, in fact, possess such a thing, but Israel could not wait to find out. Rockets of that kind, fueled and ready to launch, required immediate and decisive action.

Convinced they no longer had the option of time, Oron rushed to the prime minister's office, and barged into Eichler's office without waiting for the secretary to announce him. "They have two Simorghs that are prepared to launch."

Eichler was startled. "I thought there was no urgency," he said.

"There wasn't for the ones on the mobile launchers. But these are intercontinental missiles. They could reach us before we could get to the basement.

"They're loaded with nuclear warheads?"

"We can't confirm it," Oron said. "But we can't wait to find out."

"How long before they're ready to launch?"

"Any minute," Oron replied. "They appear to be fueled already."

"No time to convene the cabinet," Eichler sighed.

"We have no time to waste on the politicians."

"Are we ready to launch ours?"

"Waiting on your order, Mr. Prime Minister."

Eichler seemed to hesitate. Oron urged him. "It's the only way we can survive."

Eichler nodded. "Very well," he said. "It's a go."

Oron used the landline on Eichler's desk and relayed the order to the Israeli Defense Minister authorizing use of 'The Samson Option'—an overwhelming strike against preselected targets inside Iran using Israel's previously unacknowledged nuclear force. Ten minutes after the order went out, Israel's air force launched a dozen missiles toward Iran, each carrying nuclear warheads. Another ten minutes after that, the warheads detonated at facilities in Isfahan, Kashan, Rasht, the Semnan Space Center, and Tehran, eliminating Iran's known nuclear weapons facilities.

Before news outlets had time to report the launch, Tehran lay in ruins, as did most of Iran's other major cities. However, the components necessary for Mehdi Kalhor's alternative attack plan were untouched. Six cargo containers loaded with biological weapons and dirty bombs, prepositioned in friendly countries around the world and the sleeper agents he had recruited in Canada were ready and waiting, needing only to be activated.

Kalhor, too, was harmed. He had been relaxing at an Iranian resort on the Persian Gulf near the Iraqi border when the Israeli missile strikes came. The moment news of it reached him, he departed for Kuwait where an accommodative government official gave him access to a secure communications system. Within hours of the destruction of Tehran, Kalhor issued orders to his operatives commencing Operation Mahdi. It was a modified version of the grand plan he had previously envisioned, but one that, in the end, seemed far more workable than the first and at least as devastating.

At Kalhor's order, the cargo containers were loaded onto ships bound for New York City, Philadelphia, Houston, Los Angeles, San Francisco, and Seattle. Then he sent a text message to Jalal Pirzad, his cousin living in Canada, telling him to deliver the suitcase bombs to the members of his cell. When he received no response, he sent the same message to Abbadi, but was unable to reach him, either.

CHAPTER TWENTY-SIX

ll morning, Abbadi traveled through a stretch of sparsely inhabited Canada with few people and even fewer cell phone towers. Service for his phone was sketchy.

Despite Pirzad's assurances that Kalhor's sleeper agents were eagerly awaiting deliver of the duffel bags, Abbadi had little success in locating them and no success in convincing the few he found to take even one of the bags. He had knocked on so many doors and been rejected so many times, he began wondering if one of them might have called the police. He never told them he had a bomb to give them, never mentioned nuclear explosion, or any of the supposed targets, but they knew. They had to know. And if they reported him, the cops might be following him right now. He glanced in the mirror to check but the road was clear behind him, then tuned the radio, hoping to find something to listen to.

A while later, he saw a billboard advertising a convenience store on the east side of North Bay, not far from Lake Nipissing. When he came to it, he turned off the highway and brought the SUV to a stop in a parking lot beside it. He was glad to get out of the SUV, even for a short walk to the front door, but he hesitated. Should he leave the duffle bags unattended? He couldn't lug them inside. Maybe he should go on to the next exit? Perhaps it would have a fast-food restaurant and he could use the drive-through. His stomach growled. He pressed the button on the key fob to make sure the SUV's doors were locked, then started inside the store.

The store clerk and six or eight customers crowded around the counter; their eyes focused on a television that hung from a support column near the cash register. On the screen Abbadi saw images of the destruction in Iran and heard the voice of a TV announcer speculating the attack had come from Israel. "Again," the announcer said, "I must emphasize, no one has confirmed how this happened or who was behind it. We're grappling with it the same as you are. But to be clear, missiles launched from somewhere—some have suggested Israel—carrying warheads that contained nuclear devices have hit multiple sites in Iran. The devastation is widespread, and we have received unconfirmed communications indicating every major city in Iran has been hit, millions are dead, millions more are injured."

With Iran in ruins and with the sleeper agents in Canada non-functional, Abbadi realized the plan would never work. He took his phone from his pocket to call someone—Kalhor, Pirzad, anyone—and noticed the text Kalhor had sent earlier. "You're our only hope," it read. Abbadi's heart sank. Whatever they did, it was all down to him and with the reports in Iran showing there was nothing to return to there, Abbadi felt he was free to choose any response that seemed fitting to him.

Abbadi purchased a bag of chips, two sandwiches, and a large soft drink, then left the building and walked toward the SUV. On the way he saw a tractor trailer truck as it came from the highway and lurched to a stop in the parking lot. Hanging underneath the trailer was a rack to support the trailer when it was no longer connected to a cab. The rack was folded up against the bottom of the trailer to keep it out of the way. With the frame in that position the underpinning created a cavity just large enough to hold one of the duffels. Abbadi's heart skipped a beat at the thought of his first bomb.

When he reached the SUV, Abbadi took one of the bags from back and set it on the driver's seat. He unzipped it to expose the bomb itself and pressed a button near the screen. The screen blinked and then showed only zeros. He waited for the screen to blink, then pressed the button again. When the screen showed twelve followed by two zeroes, and began counting down by seconds, he zipped the bag closed, stuffed it into the support rack beneath the trailer of the truck, and returned with an unhurried gait to the SUV.

Abbadi did his best to appear calm and composed, but every part of his body trembled and his heart was racing. By the time he reached the SUV he was sweating from every pore, and he fumbled with the key fob to get the door opened. Once he did, he collapsed on the front seat and propped his head against the steering wheel. Drops of sweat splattered on the floor mat between his feet. He started the engine and turned on the air-conditioner, then adjusted the vents to blow cold air against his face.

After a few minutes, Abbadi regained his composure enough to take a drink from the bottle of soft drink and a bite or two from a bag of chips he'd bought in the store. The salt from the chips helped even more than the sugar from the drink, and he felt refreshed. Feeling under control again, he took a map from the glovebox, found his location, and checked the route. He'd hoped to skirt along the north shore of Lake Michigan and perhaps reach Regina that evening, but now, with Iran devastated and the sleeper agents nothing like the organized force Kalhor had described, making the trip all the way to Vancouver seemed a pointless risk. He needed to use the bombs he was carrying and use them quickly before someone put the pieces together and realized he had them.

"I need to go back through Ottawa, to Montreal." He traced the route on the map with his finger. "Then cross into New York at Champlain, take the highway down to Albany and over to Boston." Kalhor had told him many times that Boston must come first, though he gave no reason why it was important.

With a plan now in mind, Abbadi steered the SUV onto the highway and drove back toward Ottawa, retracing the route he'd come earlier. A few exits later, he found another truck parked outside a convenience store that he hadn't notice before. He parked the SUV near it, took a bag from the SUV, activated the time, and wedged the bag where the stand on the trailer folded up against the trailer frame. Two of the twelve duffle bags were in place. Ten remained.

In Ottawa, Abbadi left a bag in a garbage bin behind a store not far from the capitol, and one more in an abandoned warehouse in Greenboro, on the opposite side of the city where the bombs had been stored before.

Sometime after lunch, he arrived in Montreal. It was a big city with many options, but he knew little about which place would generate the most attention, so he chose the obvious sites. One near the baseball stadium. Another in a cluster of office buildings in downtown. With those in place, only four remained. He paused to check his watch. Not even two hours remained before the first bomb would detonate. *Better get across the border. They might close it when the bombs start exploding.*

From the center of the city, he drove south and crossed into the US at Champlain. No one harassed him at the border but driving that far had taken too long to permit him to reach Boston with any hope of making it to New York City. By the time he reached Albany, Abbadi had decided to forgo the plan he'd made earlier and drive straight south to New York.

It was after midnight when he reached Manhattan with four bombs remaining. He put one in the back of a garbage truck just starting to make its rounds. Hid another in a newspaper delivery truck that was being loaded for its morning route. He parked the SUV in an underground garage beneath a high-rise and left the third in it, armed and ready to explode. The fourth bomb was with him. A strap slung over his shoulder, his eyes heavy and drawn from driving the last twenty-four hours with no rest.

At the corner, he boarded a subway train still carrying the final duffel. The train followed a route that led to the World Trade Center

Park. He caught a glimpse of himself in the window beside the seat where he sat. He looked like a person who'd been sleeping rough for too long.

When the train reached the park, he stepped off and carried the bag with him up to the street. A bench was open in the center of the park, and he sat down with the duffel bag against his side, armed and ready.

Six hours later he still was seated on the park bench across from where the Twin Towers had stood. The sun was up but it was early. The city was just coming alive. An hour later, he had a hotdog from a vendor. Sipped a soft drink. Thought about the airplanes hitting the buildings when Osama bin Laden's appointees toppled them, reducing the place to a heap of metal and broken glass. Paralyzing the city. Almost paralyzing the country. The Americans were so proud of themselves for rebuilding. His people would be equally proud when they learned that he had destroyed them. One faithful Muslim, with one bomb. Surely, they would know he did it. Kalhor wasn't the kind of person who could keep a thing like that to himself. He would tell everyone he knew about what he'd done.

A moment of realization hit him. *That's exactly what Kalhor would do. He would tell them he was the one who did it and take all the credit.*

Sadness swept over him. And frustration. Leaving him with a feeling that he had been duped. Kalhor had talked of big plans to further the revolution. To bring glory to Allah. And all along he'd had nothing in mind but his own glory. And a hollow glory at that, brought about by inducing others to sacrifice everything while he sacrificed nothing. That had been the story since . . . the beginning. Those with power convinced the weak to give everything while giving nothing themselves. Leaders like that, men like Kalhor, were no better than the Americans.

Abbadi thought of leaving the duffel bag in the park and leaving. He could take a bus, or a train, and drive south. It wouldn't take long to get beyond the radius of the blast. He checked his watch. Only forty-five minutes left on the timer. Not enough to get anywhere safe. A sense of doom came over him, as if that was the wrong choice anyway. Better to do as he'd thought earlier. To sit on the bench and then it would all be over. He would have the glory. A glory far better than Kalhor's contrived, self-effacing, prideful boasts. He would have the glory of Allah. He closed his eyes and drifted off to sleep.

✦ ✦ ✦

Sometime later, Abbadi was awakened by the noise of sirens and horns blaring. He glanced around to see police cars, fire trucks, and ambulances lining the streets on either side of the park. Panic gripped him. Did they find out? Did the bomb go off and he didn't know it? The bag was still next to him. He was still there. And the bench where he'd been sitting. He hadn't heard an explosion, but something had happened. He unzipped the bag and glanced at the screen on the device. It showed a little more than nine minutes remaining before it was set to go off. But what had happened to cause such a commotion?

On the opposite side of the park, police officers entered from the sidewalk by the street and made their way in his direction, moving at an unhurried pace, looking from side to side as if they were searching for something, or someone. Abbadi sat up straight on the bench as they approached and instinctively placed a hand on the duffel bag, drawing it against his side.

The bag felt warm, which surprised him, and he wondered if the bomb was defective and leaking uranium after all. He had no qualms about dying for Allah, but he had serious reservations about a long, slow, agonizing end. "Just get it over quickly," had been his prayer, though he never said it out loud. One wasn't supposed to tell Allah what to do. Only to do what Allah said. But that was how he felt. Going up in a nuclear explosion, on the other hand, being carried aloft by a billowing mushroom cloud in an intense column of heat, rising up to the heavens with the city below, devastated in every direction as far as he could see, that was an end to which one could aspire.

A police officer came to a stop in front of him. "You need to get out of here," he said in a demanding tone."

Abbadi had no intention of leaving but he dared not cause a fight. "What's happened?" he asked.

"There was an explosion in the harbor," the officer explained.

"Was anyone injured?"

The policeman frowned. "A ship blew up. You didn't hear it?"

"No," Abbadi replied. "I guess I was asleep."

The policeman was suspicious. "What are you doing here?"

"Waiting for a friend."

The policeman seemed to know what that meant. Most likely he thought Abbadi was a drug dealer. "Well," the officer said, "this is your lucky day. Just take your bag and get out of here. We won't be busting drug dealers today." He gestured toward the street with a wave of his arm.

Abbadi remained seated. "There must be more to it than that," he said. "I don't think anything around here is damaged or on fire."

The officer sighed, as if troubled by the necessity of saying more. "Look." He leaned closer. "Our sniffers have detected high levels of radiation."

"Oh." Abbadi's eyes opened wide. "Radiation?"

"Yes." The policeman took him by the shoulder to lift him off the bench. "Now you know the full story. So, move!" he shouted.

Abbadi stumbled free of the policeman's grasp and started toward the street, but his mind was thinking only of the ship that had blown up. A ship that apparently carried contaminated cargo. That's when he thought of Kalhor and the other ideas he had for attacking the West.

One of those ideas had been to use cargo containers to carry pathogens or bombs made with dirty conventional explosives—a bomb wrapped with nuclear waste. Kalhor had thought of them on a grand scale using cargo-container quantities. Though they were the least likely to succeed of his plans, Karim Nawab had volunteered to give it a try. Now Abbadi wondered if he'd succeeded in making it happen.

As he stepped from the park onto the sidewalk by the street, Abbadi felt the bag growing warmer against his hip. At the corner, he slowed to thread his way through the crowded space between the emergency vehicles. The time must be near. Should he duck into a café? Should he enter the lobby of a high rise to maximize the destruction that was about to happen. The thought of such a thing seemed funny but he couldn't think anyway. His mind was cluttered, no longer able to focus.

Just then, he heard the bomb whining inside the duffle bag. High pitched. Soft, but noticeable. Like the flash on a camera charging up. And then his left arm ripped free from his shoulder, but he didn't mind. Heat ingulfed him. Hot and searing. He was above the street by then, looking down on the trucks below as they melted. As he passed the top floor of a building, another arm tore loose. His legs snapped free at the hips. And Abbadi could see no more.

CHAPTER TWENTY-SEVEN

nitial reports of the explosions in New York reached Marsh's office as he was preparing for a meeting in a conference room down the hall. An assistant entered his office as he was placing items in his briefcase. "Wait," she said, noticing the stack of documents he was gathering. "You can't leave yet."

"I have to," Marsh insisted. "I'm late." He was standing, with documents in one hand, holding open the briefcase with the other.

She ignored his reply and walked to a television screen that was mounted in the wall across from his desk. Using the remote-control, she turned on the screen. Images of an urban area, looking bleak and gray with smoldering damage, appeared.

"What is that?" Marsh asked.

"Ottawa," she replied.

His eyes opened wide in a surprised look. "Ottawa, Canada?"

"Yes," his assistant said.

"That looks like damage from an explosion."

"It is," she replied.

"When?"

"A few hours ago."

"Why haven't we heard about it before now?"

"Widespread damage across Canada. Confusion up and down the East Coast. This footage only reached us a few minutes ago." She switched to a different view on the same screen. Images showed similar damage at a different location.

"That doesn't look like Ottawa," he commented.

"This is Montreal," she replied, pointing to the monitor.

Marsh sagged into his chair. "What is this. . .?"

"Wait," she said. "There's more." She pressed the control again and a different city appeared, followed by another, and another.

"All of these are in Canada?"

She shook her head. "As best we can determine, there has been a string of low-level nuclear explosions extending from central Canada, all the way across to Montreal and down to. . ." She pressed the remote again and a new image appeared.

"That looks like New York City," Marsh said, leaning forward in his chair.

The screen showed a view of Central Park, with parts of Harlem and a glimpse of Yonkers visible in the background. In the foreground, though, the park was filled with people, all of them panicked, confused, and desperate.

"You're sure this is New York?" Marsh asked with a blank expression. He knew it was, but he couldn't think of anything else to say.

"Manhattan," she said, flatly "What's left of it."

He frowned. "What's left of it?"

"We have reports that everything below Gramercy Park is gone."

"Anyone have a camera down there so we can see what happened? Maybe security footage from the police. Or a traffic cam."

She looked him in the eye. "It's all gone, Jim," she said solemnly.

"Gone?"

"Obliterated." She gestured with her hands for emphasis. "Wiped out."

Marsh found her statement incomprehensible. "From what?" he asked.

"From a nuclear bomb," she replied.

Marsh leaned back in his chair and stared up at the ceiling as he struggled to understand what it all meant. After a moment he said, "Get someone from downstairs to tell us what they know."

✦ ✦ ✦

Thirty minutes later Shelly Elliott, a supervisor from the Counterintelligence Center, came to Marsh's office. She sat across from him at his desk and reviewed everything the Center knew about the bomb that exploded in Manhattan and how it might have arrived.

"Basically," she said, "we haven't a clue how a nuclear device ended up in Lower Manhattan."

"That's not possible," Marsh said. "Counterintelligence exists to know things like that."

"You know that's not true," she replied.

"But you must have *something*," he insisted.

"Our resources show no visible evidence of an external attack. Nothing on radar or from the satellites shows anything to indicate a plane, missile, or object of any kind entered US airspace. There was nothing aloft in the atmosphere or in space that threatened an attack."

"Damage like this couldn't have come from a single bomb," Marsh said. "How many devices were used?"

"Based on what we know right now—and this is a fluid situation—most of the destruction in Manhattan came from a single device that detonated in Liberty Park, across from the site where the Twin Towers used to be."

"What kind of device?"

"Nuclear," she said flatly. "This was a nuclear bomb."

"You're sure?"

"Positive."

"But you said *most* of the destruction. There were multiple detonations?"

Elliott nodded. "There was an explosion at a secondary site on the East River. We think it came from a ship at the Brooklyn Naval Yard, but we haven't confirmed that yet. Our analysts are focused on *The Dolat Abad*, a ship that was tied up at their docks."

"A ship?"

"Yes, sir. As best we can tell. We're still working on the details. As you can imagine, things are a bit chaotic in New York right now."

"And you've confirmed both of these explosions were from nuclear devices."

"The one in the park was most definitely nuclear," Elliott said with a quick nod. "There's no doubt about that. The one at the Naval

Yard might have been a dirty bomb. We're all but certain from the explosive signature that it was a conventional device wrapped in radioactive material, but we're still working to confirm that. The site is heavily contaminated."

"How contaminated?"

Elliott sighed. "We've detected lethal levels of radiation as far north as 143rd Street."

"Are any of our people on site?"

"Not yet," she said.

"How are you getting your information?"

"Most of what we know is from the locals and from NSA."

Marsh frowned again. "NSA? How'd they get there ahead of us?"

"They have a large presence there on a permanent basis. Offices all over the region."

"Get our people in there," Marsh said. "We need people who can give us information from *our* perspective, not just from a law enforcement point of view."

"They're on the way."

"Where is the president?" Marsh asked.

"The Secret Service put him in the Bunker."

The Bunker was a secure Emergency Operations Center constructed beneath the East Wing of the White House. It was rated to survive all but a direct hit from a nuclear bomb.

Marsh shook his head. "He needs to be in the mountain."

"They'll get him there, eventually," Elliott replied. "But they thought the Bunker was better for now. Apparently, the president wanted to be fully accessible."

"Who's with him?"

"All the usuals," Elliott replied.

"Is Donovan there?"

"Yes," she replied.

Just then, an assistant appeared at the door to Marsh's office. "Sir, they want you at the White House."

Marsh stood to put on his jacket and glanced over at Elliott. "Duty calls."

"Keep me informed," Elliot said.

"I think that runs the other way," he replied. "I want to know about any new developments. Preferably before the others do."

As he started toward the door, his assistant handed him a file. "This is everything we have so far." He took it from her and hurried to an elevator.

✦ ✦ ✦

A helicopter flew Marsh to the White House lawn where he was met by a presidential assistant who escorted him to the Emergency Operations Center and into the main conference room. Members from across the government were gathered around a large conference table. Among them were Bruce Ford from the Defense Department, Clinton Kase from the State Department, Albert Newman from NSA, as well as Clark Aspin from the Navy, General Halstead from the Joint Chiefs, and a roomful of others Marsh only knew in passing.

Marsh caught Donovan's eye and slid onto a chair beside him. Bruce Ford was briefing the group about other issues of the day, beyond the explosions in Canada and New York.

"Right now," Ford said, "we have no additional known threats in the US, but we *are* tracking several ships that appear suspicious."

"How many?" someone asked.

"Five at last count," Bruce replied.

"Isn't that important?"

"That's why we're monitoring them."

"Maybe we should board them and inspect them."

"We will," Bruce said, "but we need to verify our information before we do that."

"Under the circumstances," General Halstead noted, "I would think we're beyond official procedure and probable cause now."

Kase spoke up. "Where are these ships?"

"One is docked at the port of Philadelphia," Ford replied. "And we're watching additional ships in New Orleans, Houston, Los Angeles, San Francisco, and Seattle."

"Philadelphia is not far away," someone noted. "Houston is on the Gulf. The others cover the length of the West Coast. Adding the one in New York, these ships completely encircle the country." There was a note of alarm in his voice.

"We should board and inspect them now," someone demanded.

"Inspecting a ship is a complicated process," Bruce said. "We can't just—"

General Halstead spoke up. "Mr. President, we need to move these ships to sea. Now."

Aspin nodded. "Excellent idea."

A staffer sitting against the wall said, "If someone is actually planning an attack, won't that just tip them off that we know about these ships?"

"Who cares!" Halstead exclaimed. "If these ships are armed with explosive devices like the ones we've seen so far, we can do whatever we want with them."

Aspin glanced down the table. "Mr. President, towing them to sea does seem like the least confrontational option available. You should order it immediately."

Several in attendance voiced their objection to the proposal. Others shouted their approval, and the discussion quickly devolved into a heated argument. Pandemonium threatened to consume the entire group.

Jackson rapped his knuckles on the table to restore order. "Calm down," he demanded, and he glared at them until they returned to their seats. "The situation is bad enough as it is," he continued. "There's no need to make it worse by fighting among ourselves." He paused a moment before saying, "I agree with the idea of moving these ships to sea." He turned to Ford. "Bruce, order the ships to leave port immediately and remove themselves to international waters. Beyond the two-hundred-mile limit. Have the Coast Guard escort them."

"And if they refuse?" Ford asked.

"Board them, take control of them, and do it for them. But get them out of our ports within the hour."

"Mr. President," Aspin said, "several of these ships have not yet entered our ports."

"Even better," Jackson said. "Order them to return to international waters. The two-hundred-mile-limit. If they refuse or even equivocate, sink them where they sit. Immediately."

Silence filled the room. Most stared blankly ahead, stunned

by the directness of the president's words. But not Ford. He used a phone at the table to issue the necessary orders. As he finished that call, someone entered the room and handed Albert Newman a message. Newman read it quickly and stood.

"Mr. President," Newman began, "I've just learned that a large Chinese flotilla has been spotted leaving Guangzhou, sailing in the direction of Taiwan." He handed the note to the assistant who took it to Jackson.

Jackson read it and leaned back in his chair. "Can it get any worse?" he sighed. "How did they assemble such a force and we failed to notice it?"

No one answered. Someone passed the note to Kase, Ford, and the Secretary of State. He read it quickly and spoke up. "Mr. President, we've had nuclear explosions in the US and Canada, now a situation in China, and Russia is lurking in the background. This has all the indications of a coordinated attack. We should consider declaring a state of emergency."

"Until we know the contents of those ships," someone responded, "we won't be able to say *what* is in them or what kind of threat we face."

Ford glanced around the room. "Does anyone have any evidence of coordination on the explosions in Manhattan? Or anything further about the cargo on the ships in question?"

Aspin stood. "The ships are registered in various countries. Those registrations appear to be genuine, valid, and legitimate. None of the countries in question have posed any threat to us in the past. The cargo that the ships currently carry was scheduled for delivery in our ports through Qasim Logistics which is a Pakistani shipping agency in Karachi. All the cargo on those ships belongs to manufacturers with ties to Iran, according to the manifests."

"Iran," someone muttered.

"Muslims," another growled.

"I knew it."

"Not merely Muslim, but Iranian radical Muslims."

"They have wanted to destroy us since they took over from the Shah."

While the incendiary comments continued, Marsh flipped through the file he received from his assistant as he was leaving the office. The first page was an analysis of the explosion in New York City. Beneath it was an analysis from residue at one of the blasts in Ottawa. He compared the two and saw the numbers were substantially the same. He pushed the file toward Donovan and pointed to the similarities. Donovan frowned. Marsh whispered, "The plutonium in all of these bombs came from the same reactor."

"Which one?"

Marsh pointed to the top of the page where the reactor source was noted. Donovan's eyes opened wide. "Mr. President," he said. "We've been looking at the bomb signatures for the explosion in Lower Manhattan, and for one of the explosions in Ottawa. They both appear to have used plutonium from the same reactor."

"Which reactor was that?" Jackson asked.

"ADE-2 at Krasnoyarsk, Russia," Donovan replied.

Murmurs were heard from the room. Most were shocked by the news.

Jackson turned to Newman. "Albert, do your people have anything on this?"

"We have the reports," Newman said, "but when I left to come over here, our analysts were still reviewing them. They've had a lot to analyze since breakfast."

Jackson nodded. "Get an update from them so we can see if their review matches with the CIA's opinion."

Just then, Sarah Foster came to the president's side and whispered something to him. Jackson turned to the group. "I'm told I have a call from Zhao Guofeng, the new Chinese premier. Given the circumstances, I should like to take the call here, in front of you all, but I need you to remain quiet while we talk. You'll have a chance to discuss what is said, but I don't want you shouting your questions at him while we're on the phone."

Jackson nodded to an assistant who handed him the receiver. "Premier Zhao," he said, "this is President Jackson."

"Mr. President," Zhao began, "I am sorry for the trouble you have had today."

"Thank you. You have been through a lot as well."

"Such is the business of leadership."

"We've been watching your forces in the South China Sea."

"And we have been watching your carrier near Taiwan."

"It appears to our analysts that you are preparing to invade Taiwan."

"That is precisely what we intend to do," Zhao Guofeng said. "Which is why I am calling you now, to make certain there is no misunderstanding between us."

"We have an aircraft carrier in your way."

"It is directly in our path."

"What do you propose to do?"

"You cannot remove your carrier fast enough to get out of our way," Zhao noted. "If you will assure me you won't intervene, we will guarantee the ship and crew's safety if it remains in its present location."

"And the accompanying ships, too. The carrier has an escort of about six ships. Will you guarantee their safety as well?"

A conversation was heard in the background, but the translator couldn't determine what was said. Then Zhao returned to the phone. "Yes, Mr. President. We will guarantee the safety of all your ships and crewmen. But they must remain in their present location. We need your answer within one hour."

"Very well. I will get back to you before the hour is up."

As the phone call ended, Newman turned to Jackson. "Mr. President, the Chinese ships will break the *Nimitz's* defensive perimeter within the hour."

"What happens then?" Jackson asked.

Newman's response was stern and authoritative. "Admiral Rodman has standing orders to maintain a secure perimeter around his carrier and around the escorts accompanying him. If the Chinese breach that perimeter, the *Nimitz* will respond with all force necessary to prevent them from taking the ship."

"How long before the *Nimitz* can get underway?"

Aspin spoke up. "Two hours if they already have steam in the turbine. Otherwise, probably three."

Jackson pointed to Kase and Aspin. "What do either of you recommend?"

"You should call Zhao Guofeng and warn him off," Aspin said.

"You mean beg for mercy," Kase said snidely.

"We aren't begging anyone for anything," Aspin retorted. "We just need time to get our carrier out of the way."

Marsh spoke up. "We're in no position to demand anything," he offered. "Begging is all we have."

Ford was angry. "The US will *never* beg anyone for *anything*." He banged his fist on the table for emphasis.

Marsh stood his ground. "And you don't get to decide when and where we go to war."

Ford turned to Jackson. "Mr. President, if we bow to China's demands now, they will rule the South China Sea for decades."

"They already rule it," Jackson replied tersely. "Make the call. Tell Zhao we prefer to move our carrier and its accompanying ships out of the way ourselves, but to do that we need more time. Ask him for two hours." He glanced over at Aspin. "Tell the *Nimitz* to prepare to get underway."

"Mr. President, we can't just—"

"Make the call, Bruce," Jackson barked. "Tell Zhao we're moving our ships out of the way. We bear the Chinese navy no ill will, but we prefer to move our ships out of harm's way."

Ford shook his head. "What I've been trying to say is, if we prepare to get under way, the Chinese will see what we're doing, and they might take it as a hostile gesture."

"Which is why I want you to call them," Jackson retorted. "And do it now. In the room so we can hear you."

"You don't trust me?"

"It's not just me," Jackson responded. "We all need to trust you and we need to trust each other. Some of our colleagues might have doubts about who's doing what. There's a phone right there," he said, pointing. "Make the call."

Everyone sat in silence while the call was placed. Ford stood at the phone with a translator listening in on the conversation. The call went through without any trouble, but there seemed to be a complication in the discussion. Sharp words from Zhao. Insistent responses from Ford insistent. An impasse.

Ford turned to Jackson. "Zhao wants to talk to you," he said.

Reluctantly, Jackson joined the conversation. "Mr. Premier—"

"No conditions!" Zhao shouted. "No changes in our terms. The carrier must remain where it is. If you try to remove it, we will destroy the ship and its crew."

"We intend to move our carrier out of harm's way," Jackson responded. His voice was firm, but even. "Along with all of its accompanying ships."

"You must not!" Zhao shouted. "It would be an act of war."

"No, it would not," Jackson replied. "The ship is not safe where it sits, and we will not allow it to be captured by you or anyone else."

There was a moment's silence. Voices were heard in the background. Then the line went dead. Jackson turned to Aspin. "Tell them to get underway with all haste."

Aspin delivered the order.

Minutes later, an aide came to Aspin with a sense of urgency and handed him a paper. Aspin whispered a question. The aide responded, then Aspin stood. "Mr. President, we have learned that Admiral Rodman powered up the *Nimitz's* turbines several hours ago. He is getting underway now."

Jackson looked troubled. "Did the Chinese know this when I talked to Zhao the first time?"

"That's difficult to say," Bruce responded. "Under similar circumstances, we would have noticed it if the scenario were reversed."

"What happens next?" Jackson asked.

"They have set a course due east," Aspin replied.

"From where?"

"The *Nimitz* is sailing east from the southern end of Taiwan."

"Where does that course take them?"

"If they simply traveled east from their last position, they would come to Hawaii in a few days."

"Good," Jackson said.

"But they're not there yet," someone cautioned.

"I understand," Jackson replied. "But we're making progress." He seemed satisfied with himself. "Now," he continued, "where are we with Russia?" When no one responded immediately, Jackson chided them, "Come on. We destroyed most of their army in Ukraine a few days ago. Surely you remember Putin. The Russian army? The war in Ukraine?"

After all that had happened, trouble with Russia and the war in Ukraine seemed like a topic from another era. They stared at him a moment, then, as if on cue, those seated at the table reached in their briefcases for a new set of files. Aides and assistants reshuffled their papers. Someone asked for a cup of coffee. Another stepped out to find a restroom.

At last, Donovan spoke up. "After we bombed Russian positions in eastern Ukraine with conventional weapons, there appears to have been a dispute among Moscow leadership about what to do next. Our failure to respond with nuclear weapons apparently placed them on their back foot. Which might explain why nothing else has happened so far."

Jackson seemed pleased again. "They were expecting a nuclear strike from us?"

"That would have been the standard response," Donovan noted.

"But they didn't get it."

"Correct."

"And now," Jackson continued, "if they retaliate with nuclear arms, they will be seen as the aggressor. They will be the ones who turn the war in Ukraine into a nuclear conflict. Am I correct?"

"They already did that with the attack on Kryvyi Rih, Zelensky's hometown," Ford said.

"I know," Jackson acknowledged with a gesture. "But work with me on this."

Donovan nodded. "For the most part, Mr. President, that would be correct. If they responded to our *conventional* bombing with *nuclear* weapons, they would confirm their intention to raise the war generally to the level of a nuclear confrontation."

"So," Jackson tapped the tabletop with his index finger. "Is there any hope they won't do that anyway? Any hope they won't take the war in Ukraine toward a nuclear confrontation?"

Donovan seemed to consider the question before saying, "Some of their leaders are still clinging to the hope that the conflict can be contained to a conventional war, and that we can all walk each other back from the brink, but they are losing the majority in the Russian discussion."

"More of their leadership do not favor going nuclear?"

"Yes."

Jackson thought for a moment as he considered the issue. "I'm getting the sense, Bob, that you don't think we're going to be able to back away from *the brink*."

"I have my doubts," Donovan replied.

"That's what makes you good at your job." Jackson turned to Halstead. "General, do you have a reliable casualty estimate for a Russian missile strike?" The room turned noticeably silent.

Halstead looked uncomfortable. "A nuclear strike?"

"Yes. Of course. That's the topic of discussion today."

"From Russia against Ukraine? Or from Russia against the US?"

"I mean, if we're weighing our options, and nuclear weapons are on the table, we ought to know how many people will die if we use them."

Halstead cleared his throat. "Mr. President, we've worked this scenario up several ways and our people are convinced that, in a nuclear war, with both sides using a roughly equal number of warheads, the losses would be about a third across the board."

"A third?"

"Yes."

"A third of what?" Jackson asked. "Of soldiers? Of equipment?"

"Of everything," Halstead replied.

"The losses would break down in thirds."

"As a rough estimate."

"A third of people," Jackson said. "A third of animals. That sort of thing?"

"Yes. And a third of the potable water," Halstead added.

Jackson seemed surprised. "You calculated the loss of potable water?"

"Mankind can't survive without drinkable water. It's more important than food."

"So, what would be the ultimate result of all that?"

"If we're talking about a global nuclear war between two super-powers, the result would be global collapse in every sense of the word. Physically, economically. In every way."

"Loss of a third of the people would produce a corresponding decline in economic activity," Jackson posited.

"Yes, Mr. President. Something like that."

"Let's hope it doesn't come to that."

While they talked, Marsh used his phone to find the verses from the *Book of Revelation* he and Donovan discussed in an earlier conversation. When he located them, he turned his phone for Donovan to see. "If that's the case," Donovan whispered, "nothing we can do will make any difference."

"Except repentance," Marsh replied.

Donovan frowned. "What are you talking about?"

"Throughout scripture, repentance always makes a difference."

Jackson noticed their discussion. "What's that, Mr. Marsh? You have something to share with the group? We certainly could benefit from some fresh input."

"We were reviewing a quote from the book of *Revelation*, Mr. President."

"Ahh." Jackson arched his brows. "A word from the *Bible*."

"Yes, sir."

"What does it say, Mr. Marsh? Might be good to have a few

lines of scripture for the moment. Read it to us."

Marsh stood and read,

> *And I saw the seven angels who stand before God,*
> *and seven trumpets were given to them.*
>
> *Another angel, who had a golden censer, came*
> *and stood at the altar. He was given much incense to*
> *offer, with the prayers of all God's people, on the golden*
> *altar in front of the throne. The smoke of the incense,*
> *together with the prayers of God's people, went up*
> *before God from the angel's hand. Then the angel took*
> *the censer, filled it with fire from the altar, and hurled*
> *it on the earth; and there came peals of thunder, rum-*
> *blings, flashes of lightning and an earthquake.*
>
> *Then the seven angels who had the seven trum-*
> *pets prepared to sound them.*
>
> *The first angel sounded his trumpet, and there*
> *came hail and fire mixed with blood, and it was hurled*
> *down on the earth. A third of the earth was burned up,*
> *a third of the trees were burned up, and all the green*
> *grass was burned up.*
>
> *The second angel sounded his trumpet, and some-*
> *thing like a huge mountain, all ablaze, was thrown into*
> *the sea. A third of the sea turned into blood, a third of*
> *the living creatures in the sea died, and a third of the*
> *ships were destroyed.*
>
> *The third angel sounded his trumpet, and a great*
> *star, blazing like a torch, fell from the sky on a third of*

the rivers and on the springs of water—the name of the
star is Wormwood. A third of the waters turned bitter,
and many people died from the waters that had become
bitter.

The fourth angel sounded his trumpet, and a third
of the sun was struck, a third of the moon, and a third of
the stars, so that a third of them turned dark. A third of
the day was without light, and also a third of the night.

As I watched, I heard an eagle that was flying in
midair call out in a loud voice: "Woe! Woe! Woe to the
inhabitants of the earth, because of the trumpet blasts
about to be sounded by the other three angels!"

"So, according to that," Jackson said. "No one will win."

"Not exactly," Marsh replied.

"Oh? What you just read sounded rather final."

"Christian theology teaches that mankind has neither the authority nor the ability to destroy the earth."

"So, there's always hope."

"Sort of."

"What do you mean?"

"A third are destroyed, but two-thirds survive."

"It doesn't say that."

"No, but that's how the math works out," Marsh said. "But though the destruction might not be complete in a total sense, the survivors of a nuclear catastrophe such as we are contemplating here today *would* have to endure a long and terrifying nuclear winter."

"A nuclear winter?" Jackson frowned. "What would that be like?"

"There would be a prolonged period of cooling temperatures caused by the large amount of soot and other particles thrown into the atmosphere from the fire and destruction produced by hundreds of nuclear bombs erupting in a relatively short time."

"And how long would this *nuclear winter* last?"

"No one knows for certain," Marsh replied. "The answer would depend on the size and number of warheads that were used and how widespread the destruction is. But it would affect the entire globe and greatly reduce crop production. Some have suggested it would take as long as ten years before things return to current climate cycles."

"Climate," Ford chortled. "You guys never miss a chance to beat that drum, do you?"

Marsh ignored the comment. "Regardless of our differences on the climate," he continued, addressing his remarks to Jackson. "We're all in agreement that a third of the vegetation, a third of the sea life, and a third of the potable water would be eliminated as a result of a thermonuclear war."

Jackson nodded thoughtfully. "So, you're saying—" His assistant entered the room again and caught his attention. He waved her to his side. She leaned close and told him something that turned his face white. He opened his mouth to speak, but before he could say anything, phones around the room began to ding and vibrate. Everyone checked for a call or a message.

Marsh checked his, too, and leaned down to Donovan. "The Chinese hit *The Nimitz*."

Donovan was startled. "Hit it?" he whispered. "With what?"

"An anti-ship missile armed with a nuclear warhead."

Donovan seemed befuddled. "How. . .how much damage did it do?"

"The *Nimitz* is gone."

CHAPTER TWENTY-EIGHT

atellite images of the *Nimitz*'s demise showed a bright flash in the South China Sea. Video of it appeared on a screen in the Emergency Operations Center where President Jackson was gathered with his advisors. They stared at the screen in horror and disbelief.

After the explosion replayed several times on a loop, Bruce Ford, the Secretary of Defense, said, "We also have video from the *USS Cameron Winslow*, a guided-missile destroyer in the *Nimitz* strike group. One of its cameras was transmitting on a live feed at the time of the explosion."

The video appeared on the screen, showing the *Nimitz* as it steamed east. One of its escort ships could be seen in the background. Suddenly, there was a bright flash, and for an instant, debris could be seen flying through the air. Then a giant wave collided with the *Winslow,* and the screen went black.

"What about the *Winslow*? Was it destroyed?"

"It survived and is loitering in the region," Ford replied. "As are two other guided-missile destroyers from the strike force."

"And wasn't a submarine with them?"

Ford nodded. "It's fine."

Someone else spoke up. "Mr. President, we have no choice but to respond."

"Absolutely," another agreed. "A full attack against all their nuclear facilities."

"On the mainland?" Jackson asked.

"Yes, sir."

"They sank our carrier," Jackson replied with a hint of disdain. "They didn't destroy Los Angeles."

"Who's to say that won't be next?"

"Why are you so afraid of responding?"

Jackson bristled at the comment. "I'm not afraid. I'm just very much aware of the consequences, which I don't think you are."

"Mr. President, regardless of the consequences, we have no choice."

Jackson glanced at Ford. "Have they shown any evidence of preparing a wider strike against us?"

"No," Ford said. "But the lead ships in their flotilla have now arrived off the coast of Taiwan. It appears their troops are preparing to disembark."

"They're on the verge of invading?"

"Yes."

"How long will that take?"

"They can be fully ashore with a first wave in fifteen minutes if they're only establishing a beachhead."

Jackson nodded. "Get the first troops ashore, then expand as others arrive?"

"Yes."

The president's chief of staff appeared, interrupting the discussion. "Senator Redwood is on the phone for you," she said. Her voice had a note of urgency.

"What does he want?"

"He has heard reports that the Chinese are preparing to invade Taiwan and wants to know what you're doing about it."

"He's upset?"

"Yes, sir."

"Redwood is always upset about something," Jackson said. "Tell him to watch the news."

"I think he is, sir."

"Good. He'll know what we're doing just as soon as everyone else does." Jackson turned his attention to Ford. "This missile that struck the *Nimitz*, it was a tactical nuclear device?"

"Yes, sir."

"And we have similar weapons of our own deployed in the area as well, don't we?"

"Yes.

"Why can't we use them against the Chinese fleet? Take out their ships instead of bombing Beijing and killing a few million innocent civilians."

"We can, but we'll need to reposition some of our Pacific Fleet to do it."

"How long will that take?"

"Approximately six hours," Ford replied.

"Get the ships started towards the area," Jackson said, "and return here in two hours with a plan to cripple the Chinese fleet."

✦ ✦ ✦

Two hours later, Ford returned with a plan for attacking the Chinese fleet, and with very little discussion, President Jackson authorized Ford to go forward with a counterattack against the Chinese flotilla. One that would destroy their ability to support their invasion of Taiwan and serve as the US response to the attack on the *Nimitz*.

Late in the afternoon—early in the morning in Beijing—elements of the US Pacific Fleet launched an attack on the Chinese Navy's ships in the South China Sea. Using bombs delivered by aircraft and missiles of several types, the US destroyed or disabled almost every ship in the Chinese flotilla that lay off the coast of Taiwan. Troops that had already gone ashore as part of China's effort to reclaim the island were left stranded, pleading only to Taiwan's military for mercy and a means of escape.

✦ ✦ ✦

In Moscow, Putin, still furious over the US attack on Russian forces in Ukraine, watched in helpless rage as the US made quick work of the Chinese navy. "This is more of the US conspiracy against its former enemies. More of its conspiracy against the world. First against us. And now against the Chinese," he shouted in a rant that had continued, on and off, for days. At every meeting, he was always the same. "America is trying to humiliate us. The West knows nothing but what the Americans tell them to think."

Most of his advisors urged him to exercise restraint. To be patient. That events would turn in Moscow's favor. "The world will come to our defense," they said. "We don't want to be seen as the aggressor."

For the most part, they had succeeded in avoiding an escalation of events on the ground, but when China destroyed the *Nimitz*, and the US responded by eliminating the heart of China's navy, Putin's rants went to a new level.

"The Americans are vulnerable," he said with glee. "I have seen it. The Chinese have seen it. If we strike at the heart of the American homeland, the Chinese will join us, and together we will destroy the US and NATO. Once and for all, we will be rid of their pesky meddling and their thousands of insults."

Most in the room were confused. "Germany?" they murmured. "Has he lost his mind?" Many were certain he had. "Surely he only misspoke," another offered.

"We should wait," someone suggested. "Surely, the US will respond with more than they've shown so far."

"And after they deplete all their missiles, China will wipe them out in a counterstrike against the US mainland. Then only Russia and China will remain. We can divide the world between ourselves."

"But if China leads with a first strike, they will claim credit for obliterating the Americans, and then they will claim *they* are the world's leader."

"They can claim anything they like," someone responded. "But after expending all of their nuclear arms on destroying America, they will have nothing left to use against us. They will be unable to oppose us as we roll over Europe and into the Middle East. We can take control of as much of the world as we like."

"We will become the Russian Empire the men of old could never have imagined."

Putin, caught up in the moment, continued to rant. "The Russian Empire does not need others to fight its fights. We can do that for ourselves." He turned to General Gerasimov. "I want a nuclear strike against all key targets in the US."

Glances were exchanged around the room. Gerasimov sat with his hands resting on the tabletop, his eyes focused on his fingers. No one else moved or spoke.

After what seemed like a long moment, someone asked. "Are you sure about that?"

Putin appeared taken aback that someone would question his opinions, but as he was about to respond, Gerasimov spoke up. "US satellites will see our preparations. Even if we can launch our missiles, the Americans will know what we're doing. Before our missiles have cleared Russian airspace, US missiles will be on their way toward us in a counterstrike."

"If we go first," Putin shouted, "ours will reach their targets first."

"Yes, but we will be obliterated by US missiles even as they are obliterated by ours. No one can survive such an exchange."

"We have no reason to do this," Sergei Shoigu argued. "The Americans are focused on China right now. They will take no action against us. And certainly not a first strike."

"All the more reason we should go first," Putin insisted.

Through the afternoon, the argument continued round and round the table. And the longer they talked, the more their frustration grew. After an hour or two, the discussion became heated. Then a fight broke out. A gun appeared. There was a struggle, with men grappling each other across the table. During the confusion, the gun went off. The sound of it was deafening, and everyone shrank back to see General Gerasimov lying on the floor, surrounded by a pool of blood.

✦ ✦ ✦

In the US, officials at NORAD's Cheyenne Mountain facility detected Russia's preparation to launch what appeared to be an overwhelming missile strike. Intercepted telemetry indicated the missiles were targeted at North America. The watch commander phoned the White House situation room. "We need a response from the President," the commander said. "Nothing can happen without his order."

"Stand by. The president will be available shortly."

Five minutes later, President Jackson was on the phone with NORAD. Unlike the ponderous way he preferred to handle emergencies, a pending launch of Russian missiles required immediate action. Missiles stationed in Russia could be ready to launch in fifteen minutes. Once in the air, they could reach targets in the US in as little as thirty minutes. If he waited to assemble his cabinet leaders, the crisis would be over, and America would be devastated.

"Either we respond," the Situation Room said, "and we maintain the status quo in our relationship with Russia, or we wait and are forced to live in a world where Russia and China are the sole superpowers, and the United States is a third-world country."

"Very well," Jackson said. He'd delayed the inevitable as long as he could. "Launch our strike against Russia."

Jackson ended the call and rolled out of bed to get dressed. Before he was out of his pajamas, Secret Service agents burst into the residence and escorted him to the basement beneath the West Wing. From there, they guided him toward a tunnel that led beneath the Washington Monument to an exit at the corner of K Street and Independence Avenue. A car was parked at the curb. As the president appeared, the rear door opened, and the Agents shoved Jackson onto the seat. The door slammed closed, and the car started forward.

✦ ✦ ✦

Across the city, key US officials were removed from their homes and offices by the Secret Service and taken quickly to secure locations inside the District of Columbia. Others, who had been designated as essential under continuity of government plans, were taken to a secret bunker in the Appalachian Mountains of Virginia. Undersecretary Janice Miller was among those rushed from the State Department building. She arrived at the bunker and was taken immediately to an underground situation room where she was seated with officials from across the government. Moments after their arrival, they were connected by video with the White House situation room to review and assess the global situation.

✦ ✦ ✦

Marsh, who'd gone home for a nap and a change of clothes, was alerted by a knock on the front door of his house in Langley, Virginia. He glanced out the window and saw the caller was Bob Donovan. Marsh opened the door.

"Where's your wife?" Donovan asked without waiting for a greeting.

"She went to visit her sister," Marsh replied. "What's going on?"

"Russia launched an attack against us."

Donovan pushed his way inside. Marsh closed the door behind him. "I suppose that means everyone is rushing to get out of town." He sounded almost unconcerned.

"Not everyone," Donovan said with a knowing look.

"Just those on the list," Marsh noted. It was a statement, not a question.

"Yes."

"No announcement to the public. No warning to *duck and cover*. Nothing for the hapless citizens." There was a hint of sarcasm in Marsh's tone.

"Would only make the situation worse," Donovan said, continuing the trope. "And why deprive them of the peace of their final moments." It was a well-worn, well-practiced justification for keeping critical information to themselves.

"So why should we run?" Marsh asked. He knew Donovan had come to take him away from the city.

"I've been asking myself that all the way over here," Donovan said.

Their eyes met. Donovan seemed deeply worried, but Marsh was unconvinced it had anything to do with the crisis they faced. Donovan seemed to be gathering his courage and after a moment said, "Tell me again what you said before, about repentance you mentioned the other day."

Marsh turned aside and gestured for Donovan to follow. "Come on," he said. "We can talk about it in the kitchen. There's probably time for a cup of coffee and a prayer before the missiles arrive."